Disaster in Transport

A Kash and Calynn Adventure

Preface

Wow, are these guys fun to write. This one took off like a rocket... I had to hold on for dear life. Corrupt bureaucracies are so much fun, aren't they? (*Insert eye roll here.*) Well... they make a great bad guy anyway.

We pick up where *Poncia Problems* ends, and much to my mom's dismay... they aren't going after any crystals to fix the Slip. *Shucks.*

Hi, Mom!

Yes, yes... I can feel the sarcasm flow. It is the source of your power and the pathway to the—oh look, a cookie. But anyway...

I hope everyone enjoys this chapter of Kash and Calynn's adventures as much as I enjoyed writing it. It truly was a rollercoaster ride into the unknown and took so many turns along the way.

To my wife: thanks for still putting up with me.

To my daughter: thanks for being a sounding board, yet again.

To my best friend Mike and his amazing wife, Ruth-Ann: we love you both and hope that Ruth-Ann gets better soon. We miss you.

A special thank you to Franki Wilson for her amazing work on the cover art, April for your help, and Leslie—for all that you do. You're a rock star.

And thank you *(insert name here)* for that thing that you did or whatever because... reasons. Hey, nice hat. Enjoy the veal, and don't forget to tip the wait staff.

Enjoy.

ISBNs:

Hardcover: 979-8-9916795-3-4

Paperback: 979-8-9916795-4-1

eBook: 979-8-9916795-5-8

Kash and Calynn's Adventures

A Favor

"Mmm… that feels good," Kash mumbled.

"What feels good?" Calynn asked over comms. "You two better not be fucking while I'm working."

"Relax… she's only sucking my balls a little…"

"No, I'm not," Triana interrupted, swatting him on the arm. "I'm just rubbing his back… he's got a hell of a knot near his shoulder blades."

"You're no fun."

"I beg to differ," Triana laughed.

"Remind him he said that later when he's trying to get you naked," Calynn chuckled.

"Just once I want one of you on my side, so we can pick on someone NOT me," Kash laughed as well.

"Aww," Triana said as she wrapped her arms around him. "Is the poor little man getting picked on by the big mean girls?"

Kash shook his head while Calynn and Triana had a laugh at his expense. Triana was caressing his chest while they were giggling, so Kash spun his chair around to face her. She straddled him as soon as he was facing her and hugged him tight. Kash had his hands up the back of her shirt so he could feel her soft skin.

"I have movement," Calynn interrupted suddenly.

Kash spun his chair back toward the helm and checked his monitors. Triana leaned to the side so he could see around her. He zoomed in on the motion Calynn detected and waited to identify it.

"I wish our sensors actually worked here," Kash complained. "These magnetic fields fucking them up does actually sucks balls."

Kash watched the monitors and waited. Eventually, the critter revealed itself.

"It's just one of those damn trash-eating rodents," Kash announced.

"Damn it," Calynn complained. "I guess I'm not enticing enough for them to attack me."

"I can go put on my costume and take a turn," Triana offered.

"That would be super," Calynn confessed. "I need to go demagnetize myself. The magnetic fields fuck with my body."

Triana and Calynn took turns dressing as homeless women for the rest of the night while Kash stayed out of sight. The criminals they were trying to lure out never took the bait. They knew the bandits operated near this scrap yard, but the attacks were sporadic at best.

"Let's call it a night," Kash conceded. "We'll try again tomorrow night."

"Good," Triana replied over comms. "I'm freezing out here."

The trio showered, got something to eat, then all climbed into bed. Kash's bed wasn't really big enough for three people, but they made do. Kash had his back to the wall with Triana pressed up against him to warm herself, and Calynn was in front of her. Kash still wasn't interested in anything sexual. He tried once at the start of their journey, but even Triana could tell he wasn't into it.

When Kash woke up he had rolled onto his stomach, half on top of Triana. Calynn had turned to face them and had her leg laced over Triana's leg. The girls were so close, they were touching foreheads. Kash didn't want to squash poor Triana, so he started to roll off of her.

"Mmm no, come back," Triana mumbled, reaching for Kash's arm.

"I didn't want to smoosh you."

"But it's so warm and cozy," Triana complained. "And I don't want to get up yet."

"What if I suffocate you?" Kash asked as he rolled back onto Triana.

"Still warm and cozy," Triana's reply was muffled by the pillow.

"I agree," Calynn added as she pulled herself closer.

Kash found Calynn's hand and laced his fingers through hers. He gently caressed the back of her hand with his thumb. The two shared a glance and a warm smile as Triana shifted around under them.

"She's awful wiggly," Calynn noted with a big grin.

Kash let go of Calynn's hand, shifted to the side, and swatted Triana on the ass.

"Hey," Triana squealed.

Kash chuckled as he whipped off the covers and jumped up.

"Dibs on the shower," Kash exclaimed as he rushed to the bathroom.

"Dibs on Calynn," Triana giggled.

Kash stopped and turned around. Triana was hugging Calynn and rolling on top of her. Kash turned back around and continued into the bathroom. He took a quick shower, got dressed, and went out to the helm to check the news. Eventually he heard the shower cycle run as the girls finally got out of bed.

"You two wanna go out for breakfast slash lunch?" Kash hollered from the cockpit.

"But it's cold outside," Triana complained.

"Wear some clothes," Kash rebutted.

"Ha ha smart ass."

"I don't want to hang out in a scrap yard all fucking day," Kash stated. "So let me rephrase that... I'm going out for breakfast... are you coming?"

"Fine," Triana conceded. "But I'm wearing one of your sweatshirts."

The trio got dressed for the winter temperatures and headed into the local city. Maie was a small city with a population around two-million. The city was well run and kept relatively clean. The enormous fuel refinery along with other industries provided the tax base needed to provide its citizens with a substantial social safety net. Unfortunately, that safety net was soon being strained by an influx of vagrants and the homeless from cities all over the planet. The city did its best to manage the needs of the less fortunate, but the needs always seemed to be outpacing the supply. The homeless population was drawn to the scrap yard because of makeshift shelters that were readily available. They didn't have to build anything, just open the door of an old space freighter and viola... your very own place to live. The city owned the scrap yard, so they allowed the squatting until they figured out a better option.

"Can we go shopping after breakfast?" Calynn asked as they walked. "They have some..."

"Cute little shops," Kash interrupted. "I know... I know."

"Or Triana can keep wearing your clothes," Calynn bantered.

"Let me rephrase that," Triana added, wrapping an arm around Calynn's waist. "We're going shopping... are you coming?"

"You're not allowed to use my own sayings against me," Kash chuckled. "There's rules against that."

The three friends spent the afternoon shopping and taking in the sights that Maie had to offer. They watched a couple shows at the tiny casino. The magician was surprisingly good and had a few tricks that Kash had never seen before. The girls made him go watch the acrobats perform also. They had dinner and drinks at an expensive restaurant before grabbing their packages and heading back to their ship for the night.

"Who's going out first?" Kash asked the girls.

"Damn, Kash, can we have a minute to warm up before you throw us out into the cold again?" Triana complained.

"I'll go first so you can warm up," Calynn offered.

"I'll go get the drones airborne and the cameras rolling," Kash said as he headed toward the helm.

Kash stopped in the kitchen and made himself a mug of hot tea before continuing to the cockpit. He could hear the girls chatting while putting their clothes away in the cargo bay. It only took a few keystrokes to activate the cameras and send the drones to their assigned spots. Kash was sipping at his tea when Triana joined him at the helm. She sat on his lap and draped a blanket over the two of them.

"Is this for me?" Triana asked, stealing his tea.

"No," Kash complained but let her take his mug.

"I'm not built for this cold."

"Petite woman such as yourself never are," Kash agreed.

"Mmm... this is good. What is it?"

"Black tea sweetened with honey."

"Like from Earth?"

"Well, I got that from a merchant on one of the deep-space substations," Kash recalled. "It was kinda funny... the universal translator said it was royal tree leaves and bug wax."

"Bug wax?"

"Bug wax."

"I can believe it," Triana added. "That stupid translator had me agreeing to do things at the brothel that I never wanted to do. That damn thing has gotten me... violated."

Triana shuttered when she finished speaking and leaned back into Kash. He wasn't sure if she was seeking warmth or comfort from her memories. Kash tried to lighten her mood.

"You say violated like it's a bad thing," Kash said flirtatiously. "I'm pretty sure I have violated every inch of you with no complaints."

"You have," Triana agreed, laying her head against his. "But you did so gently. If I told you it hurt to do something, would you stop doing that or fuck me harder to make me cry?"

"Aww... You better be hugging her or I'm coming up there," Calynn said over the comms.

"I got her," Kash replied, wrapping his arms around Triana.

"Here," Triana said, pulling on her shirt. "Put your big warm hands on my soft sweet-smelling skin. Did I mention that's like the best compliment ever?"

"Once or twice," Kash chuckled.

Kash complied and placed his hand on her bare belly. Triana pulled her shirt down over his hand and pulled the blanket up to her chest.

"That's better," Triana said happily.

"I'm heading out," Calynn stated. "Watch my back."

"We got you, Baby Girl," Kash replied.

The night passed slowly. Triana reluctantly took her turn as bait, but she couldn't stay outside as long as Calynn could. The bitter cold got the better of her. Triana couldn't get out of her costume and onto Kash's lap fast enough. Her whole body was shaking, and her teeth were chattering when she curled up in his lap.

"Poor thing," Kash said softly. "You're a Popsicle."

"Hands... skin," Triana stuttered.

Kash wrapped his arms around Triana's midsection as she covered them with a blanket. He tried to help warm her by also rubbing her legs vigorously.

"I've got movement," Calynn suddenly stated.

Triana shifted to the side so Kash could check the monitors. He immediately saw the men they were chasing.

"It's them," Kash announced, lifting Triana off of his lap. "Watch the monitors. I'm going to go help Calynn."

"On it, Boss," Triana affirmed.

Kash hurried back to the cargo hold and grabbed some weapons. He pulled on his snow pants and jacket and darted out the door toward Calynn's position.

"Damn, it is a little cold," Kash stated as the frozen air hit his face.

"I told you," Triana replied. "You're gonna freeze out there."

"It's okay. I can take the cold. I'm like thirty percent Viking," Kash replied as he ran. "What do you have on the monitors?"

"It looks like six men, no wait... seven men."

"They're making grunting and hooting sounds," Calynn added. "Should I pretend to be frightened?"

"You gotta draw them in."

"They are moving to surround you, Calynn," Triana announced.

"Oh, look at me... I'm running in circles because I'm scared and don't know what to do," Calynn said comically. "Oh, no... I have fallen... whatever will I do?"

Kash slowed his pace as he approached Calynn's position. He scanned the area to see if he could see any of the men, but they remained hidden for the moment. Kash squatted and ducked behind a pile of scrap metal to stay hidden himself.

"They haven't made their move yet," Calynn announced. "What are they waiting for?"

"An eighth man," Triana replied. "He just showed up and he's giving some kind of hand signals to the others... I think they're about to attack."

"Here they come," Calynn confirmed.

Kash stood and started moving toward Calynn's position again. When he turned the corner, he could see the group of men closing in on her. They were coming from all sides. Calynn was cowering in the middle of the path like she was trying to hide in her coat. The coat was tattered, dirty, and far too big for her. Her matted blonde wig was blowing in the breeze, and a pair of oversized pants completed her disguise.

When the men reached Calynn, they started thrusting their hands at her... they were all carrying something. Kash didn't have to wonder what it was for very long. Calynn had very little skin showing, but what he could see... started to light up along the grid in her flesh.

"Tasers... really?" Calynn asked sarcastically. "Can I fight back yet?"

"Absolutely," Kash replied as he approached.

"Thank the Gods."

Calynn was quickly back to her feet. She grabbed one of the men and threw him in Kash's direction. Kash timed his roundhouse kick perfectly as he kicked the flying assailant in the face. The man fell to the ground landing awkwardly on his head.

"I've got him," Calynn stated.

Kash looked and saw Calynn holding the smallest man by the arm. The man was desperately trying to pull away as Calynn fought off his friends with one hand. She shoved the biggest man backward as Kash arrived to help. Kash used a leg sweep to knock the big man down, then stomped on the man's throat to incapacitate him. Kash lunged at another attacker and punched the man so hard he nearly did a flip in the air. Kash and Calynn had each taken down three of her attackers, and she still had a firm grip on the seventh man.

"Fuck this," the last man hollered, running away.

"I'll get him," Triana said calmly. "I just need to swoop this one down... and..."

Kash watched as one of the drones smashed into the man's back as he ran. He tumbled into the hull of an old ship and lay motionless on the ground.

"Let go of me you freak," the man Calynn was holding barked.

"Hi, Kittelli," Kash said to the man. "Your daddy says it's time to come home."

"My Dad?" Kittelli asked angrily. "Fuck him! ...and fuck you..."

Kash punched Kittelli in the face stopping his protest and knocking the man unconscious.

"I hope it's just his clothes that smell so bad," Calynn protested. "Whoa, mama, that's ripe."

"Let's drag him back. We can strip him and sanitize him before bringing him aboard," Kash said, grabbing Kittelli's other arm.

Calynn and Kash dragged their captive back to their ship. They removed Kittelli's crusty clothes, dumped sanitizing gel on him, and bound his hands and feet. Kash pulled a handle on the wall of the cargo bay revealing a set of prison bars. The bars extended from the floor up to the catwalk above and enclosed the area behind the ladder. Kash locked the bars in position and placed Kittelli inside the holding cell.

"The drones retrieved the extra cameras, and everything is stowed away, Boss," Triana stated from the catwalk.

"I'll get out of these rags and get us under way," Calynn added.

"And I'll be in your quarters waiting for some body heat," Triana continued. "I'm still a Popsicle."

Triana disappeared from view, and Kash turned to Calynn. Calynn shrugged her shoulders and continued to remove her costume. Kash removed his heavy jacket and pants and put them away. Calynn had changed into jeans and a light peach T-shirt. He followed her up the ladder. Calynn proceeded to the cockpit and Kash went to his quarters. Triana was already in bed with the covers pulled up to her nose.

"Get in here. I'm cold," Triana complained.

Kash stripped down to his boxers and joined her in bed without saying a word. Triana backed into him and hugged his arm to her chest. Her skin still felt cool to the touch and her body occasionally shuddered. She shifted her body so she was on her belly, and he was half on top of her.

"That's better," Triana cooed.

"You like being smooshed?"

"It's warm and cozy."

"If you insist," Kash conceded.

Kash hugged the girl tight and wrapped his leg around hers. They lay like that for a few minutes until Kash heard the HLD spinning up.

"I have to email Aja to let her know we are on the way back… sooner than later."

"Ten more minutes," Triana said, wiggling into him. "Please."

"I can increase the cabin air temperature, Boss," Calynn said from the doorway.

"That would be fantastic," Triana said gleefully.

"Boss?" Calynn asked.

"Fine, but only two degrees," Kash ordered. "I'll be sweating my ass off if you make it warmer than that."

The three-day journey back to the Ooga system was relatively uneventful. Kash emailed Aja all the details surrounding her cousin. Aja said she would inform her uncle and make all the necessary preparations. Kittelli would occasionally cause a ruckus and would need to be subdued and sedated. They even had to contact Meesha when Kittelli started convulsing. She told them which medications to give him for withdrawal from whatever drugs he was addicted to. Kash kept the man sedated for the last eighteen hourns of their flight so they could have some peace and quiet.

The Ooga system planets all had Ooga in their names along with part of the Royal Family's name. Aja's planet, Ooga Khoama, was the largest planet in the system. They were heading to the neighboring planet, Ooga Belli, where her Uncle Lavelli ruled.

"Being a mining oligarch must pay well," Triana blurted out as they came in for a landing. "That palace is huge."

"Don't mention that," Calynn stated. "In fact, don't mention anything related to size."

"Not this again," Kash sighed.

"And try not to look as big as you are," Calynn added.

"Are you serious?" Kash exclaimed. "I can't fucking shrink."

"Maybe slouch a little," Calynn explained meekly. "And I can do all the talking… if you want."

"I hate this system already," Kash sighed again and buried his face in his hands.

"I like it," Triana added. "I feel tall here."

Calynn glared at Triana and Kash had to laugh.

"It's not funny," Calynn argued. "They're very sensitive about their stature."

"It's kinda funny," Triana giggled.

Calynn glared at her again and shook her head. Calynn then shot a look at Kash.

"Don't look at me," Kash chuckled. "I don't care if I'm offensive."

"You two are impossible," Calynn complained.

"I'm going to go get our prisoner ready," Kash said, heading out of the cockpit. "Come on, you bully."

Kash and Triana retrieved Kittelli from the holding cell and gave him a shot to help keep him compliant. Kittelli was barely taller than Triana, but she probably outweighed the man. He had a very slight frame like Aja. Kash heard Calynn communicating with the palace as they directed her where to land. The Cat banked gently before settling onto the ground. Calynn joined them in the cargo hold shortly after.

"Wait," Kash said, opening the weapons locker.

He retrieved a small black case from the upper shelf. Inside the box was a black, metallic button and a black glove. Kash put the glove on his right hand and affixed the black button to the back of Kittelli's neck. He held down a button on the side of the glove until a little blue light appeared on the device on Kittelli's neck.

"What's that?" Triana asked.

"Insurance," Kash replied. "To make sure we get paid for our hard work."

"Ooo-kay," Triana added slowly.

"You should probably stay put," Kash said softly to Triana. "If something goes sideways... I don't want you to get hurt."

"Is that a possibility?" Triana asked. "The sideways thing?"

"There's always a slight chance..."

"Sometimes rich people don't want to pay their tabs," Calynn interrupted. "Especially to those they deem beneath them."

"So, we take precautions," Kash added.

"And go into every interaction with our eyes wide open," Calynn continued.

"And finish each other's sentences," Kash smirked.

"I could have kept going," Calynn bantered. "Why did you stop?"

"Because I want to get this done so we can be on our way."

"Do we have somewhere else to go?" Triana asked.

"Anywhere but here," Kash said a little more forcefully than he intended.

Kash sighed and calmed himself before continuing.

"I despise being in royal palaces," Kash admitted. "They're always so... creepy. It's like... it's like I can hear the whispers of the secrets that nobody dares speak. Murder, rape, incest... royals are always hiding more blood and torment than they let on."

"Then go," Triana said, placing her hand on Kash's chest. "Finish the deal so we can be on our way."

Kash smiled at Triana, and the woman smiled back.

"Kiss her and let's go," Calynn said, impatiently.

"Ruin moods much?" Kash asked sarcastically.

"Sometimes."

"Are you going to open the door?"

"Are you ready?"

"I'm always ready."

"Oh, geez." Calynn sighed and turned to open the door.

The opened and Kash looked out onto the crowd of soldiers. The soldiers were all in tan uniforms except for one man. His uniform was tan trimmed with blue, and he had a lot of insignias on his chest. Kash pulled Kittelli over in front of the door and waited to see the man's reaction, and was relieved to see the man's demeanor soften.

"Kittelli?" the man asked. "Is it really you?"

"It's really him," Kash replied to the man. "Take me to his dad so I can get paid."

Kash pushed Kittelli out the door and down the steps. He was careful to not let the man fall, but overall he wasn't too concerned about Kittelli's wellbeing.

"Get the medics," the man barked at his subordinates. "Let's get the prince to the hospital and..."

"He goes nowhere until I get paid!" Kash demanded, pulling Kittelli back from the approaching soldiers.

"There's a substantial bounty for his safe return, and we wish to secure our reward before he is removed from our custody," Calynn added, diplomatically.

"I assure you both..." the leader started to say.

"No, I assure you that I have been ripped off by more than enough royals to know NOT to trust them," Kash interrupted. "The medics can have him AFTER we receive our payment and not a moment sooner."

Kash held his position at the bottom of the steps and scanned the faces of the soldiers. If they were given orders to betray Kash, he hoped one of their faces would convey that truth to him. Calynn moved in front of Kittelli and grabbed his restraints. The duo was ready to whisk Kittelli away if they tried to take him by force. Kash waited a few more tense seconds before he pulled Kittelli back toward his ship.

"Tell your Lord to contact me when he actually wants his son back," Kash growled.

"Wait," the leader replied reluctantly. "Follow us."

The man sent most of the soldiers away with a wave of his hand. Four soldiers stayed with their leader as the rest dispersed.

"This way," the man in charge said, motioning them into the palace.

Kash and Calynn shared a quick glance and Calynn nodded. He trusted her judgment implicitly, and she thought it was safe to proceed.

"Lead on," Calynn said to their hosts, taking position in front of Kash and Kittelli.

The soldiers led them up a short flight of steps and through the grand entrance of the palace. Kash took a moment to admire the craftsmanship of the palace doors. The doors were carved from vein stone, each five meters tall, three meters wide, and twenty-five centimeters thick. The green glow of the gemstone complimented the ornate tree design that was carved into the massive doors. The beauty of the doors was only matched by the feat of engineering it must have taken to mount them. This planet truly had some exceptional craftsmen. Kash was impressed.

The group walked through a long hall with portraits of all the previous Lords of this planet. At the far side of the great hall were a few more steps, and portraits of the Royal Family of Ooga. Kash smiled at the portrait of Aja. She was only a teenager in the painting, but it was definitely her. At the top of the stairs was another set of vein stone doors. This set had blue gemstone, and swords and shield carved into their face.

The throne room was next and was as Kash expected. Gray stone tile floors with vein stone accents. The masonry continued up the walls and was adorned with red tapestry with what Kash assumed was the family crest. Kash found himself admiring the craftsmen of Ooga yet again when he looked at the ceiling. Ornate wooden beams spanned the width of the room and appeared to be supporting vein stone slabs that comprised the ceiling itself. Intricate crystal chandeliers and more tapestries hung from the beams as well.

"Mr. Kash," a voice called.

"Just admiring the skill of the artisans who built this palace," Kash replied, still looking at the ceiling. "It would be a shame to not appreciate their time and efforts."

"This palace is nearly a thousand years old," the voice replied.

"Making it all the more impressive," Kash continued, finally addressing the man speaking.

"I'm a busy man Mr. Kash," Lavelli stated curtly.

"Great. Transfer my credits so I can release your son and be on my way."

"The time spent is not deserving of that many credits," Lavelli explained with a haughty tone. "If you think you've earned two billion credits then you've gone mad."

"Oh, so you don't value the speed at which I conduct business?" Kash asked sarcastically. "I can let him rot in a jail cell with his friends for a while and bring him back later if that suits you better."

"No son of mine will rot in a jail cell!" Lavelli bellowed. "Our great name will not be soiled!"

"Then pay me the bounty. The entire bounty YOU offered," Kash insisted. "You are not paying me for my time. You're paying for my experience and efficiency. I won't apologize for being the very best at what I do, nor for the speed at which I do it."

"So instead, you wish to take advantage of my generosity?" Lavelli asked rhetorically, keeping the same arrogant tone. "I was expecting this job to take longer and incur more expense. I only offered such a hefty bounty as a measure of my benevolence, not to be extorted by… such rabble."

"Why does everyone try to punish me for being so fucking good?" Kash asked sarcastically. "Sorry if my efficiency offends you. I don't come wrapped in a bow or with a royal decree attached."

"What my captain means to say is that our experience and skill allow us to complete the job much faster than anyone else," Calynn interjected diplomatically. "If your chefs spent an extra day preparing your next meal would that make the food more valuable since you would be hungrier? Or do you value the prompt serving of your meals before you're famished?"

"My meals do not cost two billion credits," Lavelli continued to argue.

"Your son does," Calynn replied sharply.

"Or we can take him back where we found him," Kash added. "He might live a few more months… a year at best."

"I'm not paying you the two billion…"

"Fine!" Kash barked, turning to leave. "Then you don't get your kid!"

"What makes you think I would allow you to leave with him?" Lavelli asked forcefully, banging his fist on the arm of his throne.

The five soldiers that led them to the throne room moved to block the exit as their Lord shouted. Kash closed his eyes and shook his head. This is why he hated dealing with royals. They always resort to violence when they don't get their way. Two can play that game.

"Because if you don't, the explosive device on the back of Kittelli's neck removes his head," Kash stated, his voice eerily calm. "You can pay me, or watch him turn into a bloodstain on the floor. Your choice."

Lavelli's lips pressed into a thin line and his nostrils flared.

"I should have you killed for saying such nonsense!" he growled, his fist slamming against the arm of his throne again. "I am a Lord of Ooga, and you will respect me!"

"Respect is earned," Kash shot back, his tone sharp as a blade. "And if you try to kill me, I will end your entire family line."

He took a deliberate step forward, his eyes boring into Lavelli.

"You have no idea what I'm capable of," Kash continued. "I suggest not testing me."

Lavelli stiffened, his eyes darting to the guards. A flick of his fingers sent them advancing a step, rifles at the ready. Kash smiled… a thin, dangerous curve of his lips.

"Careful, Lavelli. Your guards look nervous. Do you think they'll act fast enough before my thumb finds this little button?" Kash raised his gloved hand just enough to draw the Lord's attention to it. "Or before Calynn here throws your son back to the gutter where we found him?"

The tension in the room grew thick enough to choke on. For a long moment Lavelli held Kash's gaze, his nostrils flaring, growing more flushed by the second. The guards hesitated, clearly uncertain about who they should be more afraid of… their Lord or the madman threatening the Prince.

"Uncle Lavelli!" Aja's voice rang out, sharp and clear, breaking the impasse. "Stand down."

"Princess Aja," Lavelli said, surprised. "Why are you here?"

"Preventing you from making a mistake, Uncle," Aja replied as she approached Kash. "How did you find him so fast? All of my Consortium agents couldn't find a trace of him."

"You were on the right track. We started in the Allio system, like you suggested," Kash replied. "He was there but had since moved on."

"I ran a background on Kittelli while Kash interviewed a few of his associates," Calynn added, smiling at Aja. "Hi, beautiful."

"Based on his previous and current drug dependency, his tendencies to harm pets and the palace staff, and his overall demeanor, we established a profile for Kittelli," Kash continued.

"The profile matched that of a sadist," Calynn stated. "A sadist that seeks validation for his actions to be more precise."

"We knew he had to be working with a group of like-minded individuals," Kash continued. "So, we searched the cyber-web for news articles and such that matched our description."

"Which eventually led us to reports coming out of Maie on the planet Soddoue," Calynn said in turn. "Reports of cruelty inflicted on those less fortunate. It fit our profile."

"We watched from low orbit until we knew if Kittelli was part of the crew torturing and killing homeless women," Kash added. "Once his identity was confirmed, we laid a trap to capture him. We let them attack Calynn, overpowered them, grabbed Kittelli, and here we are."

"What happened when they attacked you?" Aja asked Calynn.

"They tried to use tasers to subdue me," Calynn answered. "It didn't work out too well for them. We were prepared for that."

"I see," Aja replied somberly.

Kash and Calynn exchanged a glance as Aja approached, her shoulders squared but her steps hesitant. She looked different from the confident Princess who had hired them. The situation weighed heavy on her delicate frame, and she was wilting under the pressure.

"Aja, are you all right?" Calynn asked softly, taking a step toward her.

Aja didn't answer at first. Her eyes lingered on Kittelli, full of emotion. She clenched her hands into fists at her sides, her jaw tight. Kash was suddenly worried he might have to stop the Princess from assaulting his captive.

"What happened after we left?" Calynn pressed, sensing Aja's turmoil.

Aja shook her head, as if trying to clear it.

"The catacombs were worse than we feared," she admitted, her voice barely above a whisper. "They… they tortured those girls. Some of them were just kids… and there were so many…"

A tremor ran down her spine, cutting off her own words. What she saw there was the eating at her very soul.

"Lies!" Lavelli barked.

"Hush, Uncle!" Aja barked back, snapping out of her sorrow. "Or shall we tell everyone why his sister lives in my palace and not yours? You've failed both of your children!"

The weight of her words settled over the room like a shroud. She pressed the heel of her hand to her temple, as though physically holding herself together. Kash closed the distance between them in two strides, his hand lightly gripping her elbow. When Aja finally looked at him, her eyes glistened with unshed tears.

"They didn't have to die like that," she whispered.

Kash wrapped his arms around her without a word, and she sank against him, her composure crumbling. Calynn joined them, resting a hand on Aja's shoulder as she wept softly.

"I can't do this now," Aja said suddenly, pulling away from their embrace. "Sorry, but I can't. We have to deal with this."

Aja wiped the tears from her cheeks and tapped the comm in her right ear. She straightened her uniform and tried to pull herself together.

"What's going on, my Princess?" Lavelli bellowed with some disgust in his voice.

Kash looked up from Aja to see four Consortium agents entering the throne room. When he looked back at Aja, she was standing as tall as she could clenching her jaw.

"I'm not here as your Princess," Aja replied determinedly. "I'm here as Detective Aman, an agent of the Consortium Constabulary… and we are taking Kittelli into custody."

"Why?" Lavelli asked.

"Because he's a sick man, Uncle."

"We can get him help here… at home…"

"No… you've tried that before," Aja said somberly. "He needs actual help, not to be coddled. You enable him and that's not what he needs right now."

"But they might… and the allegations against him," Lavelli stammered. "Who will keep him safe?"

"My friend Kash and I have taken care of that," Aja replied, staring into Kash's eyes. "Thanks to him, I have all the leverage we need to make sure Kittelli is treated according to my wishes."

"You be careful with that video," Kash stated. "Just because Festo is dead doesn't mean…"

"I know," Detective Aman interrupted. "One of them has already been in contact with me. I did as you instructed… we should be safe."

"I don't understand," Lavelli stated, shaking his head.

"Allow me to explain," Aja said angrily, moving around Kash to address her uncle. "Kash and Calynn grabbed Kittelli before calling in the Constabulary so he wouldn't go to jail with the rest of those monsters. Believe me when I say he would have been tried, convicted, and executed before we knew he was there. Then he offered to give me the biggest piece of blackmail I have ever seen, so I could use it as leverage to keep Kittelli safe while he is in the system."

Aja took a few quick strides towards her uncle placing herself between the Lord and Kash.

"He saved your son from killing himself on those drugs he was taking," Aja continued, pointing at Kash. "And he saved him from being arrested by the wrong Consortium Agents. And he saved him from future prosecution while he gets the help he needs. Kash put himself at risk doing what I asked of him and warned me that it would put me at risk also. Perhaps you should show him the respect he deserves."

Lavelli's mouth opened as if to respond, but no words came. His usual air of authority wavered, his gaze darting toward Kittelli, then to the Consortium agents, and finally to Kash. For a moment, he sat on his throne, frozen, chest rising and falling with shallow breaths. His arrogance softened, and his shoulders sagged as if he finally realized the weight of his failure. It broke him.

"Am I worth the two billion now?" Kash asked sarcastically.

The look on Lavelli's face was priceless.

An Unexpected Job

"No peeking," Calynn said, holding her hand over Kash's eyes.

"I'm not peeking," Kash replied. "Especially from way down here."

"Oh wait," Triana exclaimed. "I want to see his face when he sees it."

Kash heard Triana scamper past him and up to the catwalk, leaving him and Calynn alone in the cargo hold.

"You're both being silly," Kash told Calynn. "I wanted to rework my quarters. We needed a place for your clothes, and I wanted you to help since it's our quarters now instead of just mine. I'm not sure how it turned into all this…"

"We wanted to surprise to you," Calynn interrupted.

"It better not be too girly and frilly."

"It's not… but we did add some color."

"Color isn't bad… can I just see it?"

"Okay… I hope you like it," Calynn said nervously. "Eyes closed until I say… okay?"

"Fine."

Calynn led Kash up the ship's ladder to the catwalk and stopped him in front of their quarters. She then removed her hand from covering his eyes and grabbed Kash's hand. She laced her fingers through his and hugged his arm to her body.

"Why do you feel nervous?" Kash asked Calynn, squeezing her hand.

"Because I am… a little," Calynn replied. "Open your eyes."

Kash opened his eyes and the first thing he saw was Triana smiling at him. His eyes then darted around the room. The next thing he noticed was the red rug along the side of the bed. He thought about how nice it would be to not have to walk on the cold hard floor barefoot when going to the bathroom. Next, he looked at his bed. It sat higher than before, on three rows of drawers, and appeared to be longer and wider than his old bed. The girls covered the steel walls with taupe wallpaper and the ceiling was covered with wooden slats.

"Look," Triana exclaimed, pushing a button on the wall. "This is so cool."

A clothes rack rolled down from the ceiling holding some of Calynn's dresses. Another button revealed a different rack with Kash's suits. Triana was bouncing up and down with glee and Kash couldn't help but smile at her.

"There's almost no room to walk now," Kash said, entering the room. "That bed is huge. Is that new too?"

Kash noticed that his desk was now wooden instead of a simple steel frame and he had a new monitor as well.

"There's still enough room for us to get dressed," Calynn stated nervously. "And yeah... I wanted the desk to match everything else... I put a full-length mirror in this corner too, but that's more for me than you."

Kash turned to his left and saw the mirror mounted to the wall at the foot of his new bed. He had to admit it was nice that he could see his entire body in the reflection. He smiled at himself in the mirror and then turned to Calynn.

"Do you like it?" Calynn asked.

"It has more frills than I would prefer since I am all about practicality," Kash replied. "But it does feel more like a home. You did good, Baby Girl."

"Thanks, Boss," Calynn said, smiling. "Try the bed... it's really nice."

Kash smiled at Calynn and pulled off his T-shirt. Kash heard the overhead clothes racks returning to their stored position, so he turned to watch them, but the sight of Triana distracted him. Triana was already topless and was pulling off her shorts. She threw the covers back and climbed into the new bed.

"It's like your floating," Triana cooed, laying on the bed.

Kash paused to stare at Triana, and he actually had some carnal thoughts. He felt a little guilty about having those thoughts, but for the first time in months he actually had the desire back. He didn't just want to smell Triana's soft skin, he wanted to taste it... all of it. Kash pulled off his jeans with haste and climbed into his new bed.

"Maybe I should hold you down, so you don't float away," Kash said seductively.

He lay on top of Triana and started sucking on her neck. Triana must have felt his growing erection, so she wrapped her legs around him and tilted her pelvis up into him. She had one hand clawing at his back and the other darted down his boxers.

"Gods, do I miss this," Triana purred, stroking his manhood. "Fuck me… fuck me hard."

Triana shifted her hips and pushed on Kash's left shoulder. Kash obliged her request and rolled off of her and onto his back. Trie mounted Kash and started grinding herself into his erection and kissing his chest.

DO DO DING DO DING

Kash heard the noise but barely recognized it. His hands were getting reacquainted with every inch of Triana's skin.

DO DO DING DO DING

The sound barely registered at first, a distant annoyance in the haze of heated breaths and Triana's soft skin. For the first time in months, Kash let himself forget the world outside. He focused his energies on the gorgeous woman before him… but the chime was relentless.

DO DO DING DO DING

"Oh, shit," Kash exclaimed, realizing what the sound was. "Let me up… fuck!"

"What's wrong," Triana asked, sliding herself off of Kash.

"Boss, I don't have access to that," Calynn said, pointing at his monitor.

DO DO DING DO DING

"It's a government channel," Kash explained, grabbing his shirt from the floor and pulling it on. "Both of you stay out of sight."

Triana scurried down the bed and stood next to Calynn in the doorway. Kash mussed his hair and then answered the incoming comm.

"Mmm… hello," Kash said with a scratchy voice, like he had just awoken.

"Captain Smith," the voice replied. "I was beginning to think you weren't going to answer."

"I was asleep," Kash replied. "You're lucky I heard it."

"Code in," the voice ordered.

"Dude, I just woke up," Kash fake yawned. "Give me a minute."

"Code in," the voice repeated.

"Umm… it's Zebra Alpha X-ray zero zero seven zero… I think."

"I see you changed your last name."

"Yes. I did so to honor a foster parent that passed away."

"And Smith isn't your birth name?"

"Nobody knows my birth name. I was dropped off in front of a police station when I was a few days old. You would need to somehow find my birth parents and ask them, which is impossible. Believe me, I tried," Kash replied, annoyed by the question. "So, I was given the name Smith, just like all the other kids in that particular orphanage. The rest of my name was computer generated. All of which is in my military file so what's with all the damn questions?"

"And you use the alias, Kash?" the voice asked, ignoring Kash's question.

"Affirmative," Kash replied in a more annoyed tone. "I started going by Kash after my tour of duty, have so for years."

"And you work alone?"

"Not anymore," Kash responded, smiling at Calynn and Triana. "I hired a pilot, and our last bounty required the aid of an additional operative."

"Do they have any clearances?"

"Negative."

"This task requires Class M clearance. The pilot and operative must exit the ship."

"Negative. Depending on the task, the operative may or may not be needed, but the pilot stays," Kash stated, still looking at the girls. "That is non-negotiable."

A silence hung on the line for several seconds. Kash figured the bureaucrats were probably trying to decide how to proceed. Kash hated dealing with bureaucrats. They were always so hard to negotiate with and had pompous attitudes at best. They expected everyone to bow to their every whim, but Kash wasn't built like that. Knowing some politician or corporate executive who could appoint you to an internal position in the Consortium didn't grant you real authority… or the respect that came with it. Yet, they always insisted on asserting their perceived authority regardless.

"Give us the pilot's name," the voice continued.

"Negative," Kash replied. "I can file the paperwork through the proper channels to ensure proper record keeping. I'm sure you can expedite the process if needed."

"Unsatisfactory. We need the pilot's name now," the voice ordered.

"Job refusal," Kash replied with authority. "Per section K paragraph seventy-four of my charter."

"On what grounds?" the voice barked.

"The pilot's safety!" Kash barked back. "I will not allow her to be swallowed up in your bureaucracy and become some politician's sex toy! We will submit her information through the proper channels to create all the appropriate paper trails needed to ensure her safety, or we refuse the job!"

"Refusal of this job will result in you being removed from the public sector registry!"

"Good!" Kash shouted. "Your jobs typically suck fucking balls anyway! Nobody likes doing them."

"And a monetary penalty!"

"Where do I send the credits?" Kash hollered. "I'll transfer them right now!"

"And a warrant for your arrest!"

"Good fucking luck finding me!" Kash boasted sarcastically, then chuckled. "Who are you trying to kid? You'd probably need to hire me to find me, you fucking idiot."

The government agents were again silent. They were trying to force him to do this job, and Kash was more than a little curious as to why. What job could be so important that they would threaten him like this? He wanted to know more, but was hellbent on making sure they didn't have the upper hand. If he did this job for them, he would do it on his terms, not theirs.

"Can we start over, Kash?" a different voice asked.

"Sure, but if the other guy speaks again my rates are tripled."

"Fuck him," Kash heard the distant voice of the first man say. "Tell that prick to…"

The man's voice fell off like he was being removed from the room, and he wasn't too happy about it.

"Sounds like triple to me," Kash said sarcastically. "You probably should have waited to get him out of the room first."

"When I tell you about the job, triple might not be enough," the second man said.

"Is that so?" Kash asked.

"Oh, yeah," the man continued. "For certain."

Kash paused for a moment just for theatrical effect.

"Go on... you have me intrigued."

"The job is of a... sensitive nature," the man explained. "Too sensitive to disclose over open comms. Can we meet?"

"I might be convinced to do a meeting... maybe... for the right price, of course."

"That can be arranged... look, Kash... can I be frank with you?"

"I certainly wish you would."

"We need a fast ship... rumor has it, yours is among the fastest."

"My new pilot can certainly push it to its limits."

"This will be one of the more... unorthodox jobs... you'll ever be asked to do," the man explained. "And it's also fairly time sensitive... so can we meet?"

Kash glanced at Calynn, his brow furrowing slightly as he cocked his head to the side. The unspoken question lingered in the air between them. Calynn paused and glanced around the room like she was searching for the answer in the shadows. But then her lips curled into a smirk, her eyes sparkling with a mix of mischief and assurance. Without a word, she gave a small, deliberate nod. In that silent exchange they communicated more than words ever could. She understood the dangers, but was willing to face whatever challenges lie ahead.

"I suppose we can meet."

"Great," the man replied. "We will send an encrypted email with the location. Please, Kash... make haste. Oh, and remit the paperwork for your pilot. However... we would prefer a limited staff for this job to limit our exposure. I'm sure you can under..."

"So, you want me to drop off my other operative first," Kash interrupted, staring at Triana.

"It would be a requirement of the job... do you accept?"

"That will delay us some. I refuse to drop her off in some random location," Kash explained. "What's your timetable?"

"As soon as possible," the agent replied.

"Then pick one," Kash said firmly. "Either I have a crew of three, or you wait until I can take her home."

"We could send a local transport…"

"Oh, hell no!" Kash barked, interrupting the man. "I've seen what you fucks do with pretty girls and that will not be her fate. She stays with me, or I make sure she is home safe. Those are your only two options. Pick one."

"I'm not sure we can wait that long."

"Then find someone else to do the job," Kash explained.

"Kash, please…"

"I'm not the only privateer out here. Call someone else."

"But we really need you on this…"

"Why me?" Kash interrupted again. "Why does it have to be me? And be precise."

"We need your expertise."

"To deliver a load?" Kash asked rhetorically. "Any idiot can deliver a load. My specialties lie elsewhere. Have you even checked my file?"

"You have the clearances…"

"So do many other privateers."

"But not as trustworthy as you."

"The trustworthiness of your other privateers sounds like a you problem, not a me problem."

"Your government needs you."

"I already did my tour of service."

"So, you understand the importance of…"

"What part of be fucking precise are you failing to comprehend?" Kash interrupted, forcefully. "I'm growing tired of your bullshit! Tell me exactly why it has to be me… exactly!"

"Listen, Kash… we really need you on this one."

"Job refusal," Kash barked. "Kash out!"

Kash ended the comm and walked away from his desk. He started pacing back and forth angrily, scowling at the floor.

"Fucking assholes," Kash growled. "Trying to force me to do some bullshit job, and you know it's probably illegal too... that way they can try to arrest me later for doing the thing that they asked me to fucking do. Damn, I hate bureaucrats."

"What if they come after us?" Calynn asked, concerned.

"They'll never find us... never."

"What if they find me?" Triana asked timidly. "Or our friends on Poncia?"

"They'll wish they never did," Kash growled.

DO DO DING DO DING

Kash marched over to his desk and answered the incoming comm.

"Job refusal!" Kash barked and ended the comm.

"Boss..."

Kash held up one finger to shush Calynn, his gaze fixed on his monitor like it had personally insulted him. The trio stood in tense silence, the hum of the ship's idle systems were the only things audible. Kash's shoulders were stiff, and his jaw clenched so tight that Calynn could probably hear him grinding his teeth.

The government bureaucrat didn't keep them waiting.

DO DO DING DO DING.

Kash didn't move. He looked at the girls and pushed out his arm with the finger still raised, urging them to remain still and quiet. Kash was going to make the government's man wait or maybe ignore the call all together.

DO DO DING DO DING

Triana started to look a little worried when the alert chimed again. Kash answered the comm, said nothing, and ended the comm immediately. Calynn and Triana both gasped.

Beep Beep

An encrypted email popped up on Kash's monitor. Kash slid into his chair and opened it immediately.

"Is that your contact?" Calynn asked.

"Yep."

"What's it say?"

Kash skimmed the message quickly and sighed heavily. When he turned to Calynn and Triana they both looked worried. Kash hung his head, sighed again, then shook his head.

"What is it?" Calynn pleaded softly.

"Kash, you must do this job," Kash read the message from his friend in the Constabulary. "The video Aja used to gain leverage has made her a target. Luckily, she was smart enough to let them know that she had backup. This mission is a ruse to look into you, but if you do not do it, they will move against Aja."

"The government would attack one of their own?" Triana queried. "She's a constable."

"They wouldn't hesitate," Kash said, his voice grim. "Aja, her family, anyone who's a liability… they'd make them disappear. I've seen it happen before… and they'll come for us too, if they think we're worth the trouble."

"Oh no," Triana whispered.

"What do we do?" Calynn echoed Triana's concern. "I want to help Aja, but if it's just a ruse just to look into us… keeping me away from the Consortium was your biggest rule… what if they look into us and look at me too hard… what if they figure out what I am?"

DO DO DING DO DING

Kash buried his face in his hands as he thought. If he did the job, he would put Calynn at risk and break one of his own rules. If he didn't do the job, there's no telling what kind of hell would be in store for Aja. There was no right answer. He pushed back from his desk, stood, and started pacing again.

"If it's up to me," Kash said through his hands. "I'm going to be selfish and choose me and my ship."

"The ship that I control, so you would choose me," Calynn replied, but there was no rejoicing in her tone. "But what does that mean for Aja? What about her?"

"Months if not years of mental and physical torture at the hands of some pretty sick bastards," Kash sighed.

"That's sounds awful," Triana stated.

"But if they figure out what I am?" Calynn asked.

"You'll either get plugged into a floating city to run it or they dissect your brain in a lab somewhere, so you'd be gone, and I'd be stuck with the impossible task of replacing you."

"That sounds worse," Triana added.

"So, our choice is either to have Aja in a dungeon or me cease to exist?" Calynn asked rhetorically.

"Pretty much."

"Do the job," Calynn said softly, her voice steady.

"What?"

"Do the job," Calynn repeated, meeting his gaze. "You know it's the right thing to do."

"And what happens if something goes wrong, huh? If they figure out what you are?" His voice dropped. "I can't lose you, Calynn. Not you."

Her expression softened for a moment, and she reached for his hand.

"You won't lose me," Calynn continued softly, reaching for his hand. "But if we don't help Aja, then who are we? We have to do something."

"We can't save everyone!" Kash barked, turning away from her. "We couldn't even save…"

Kash lost control of his emotions as the words fell off. His memories betrayed him as pictures of his precious Omia popped into his head. He saw the gash in her head and the wounds on her belly and chest. There was so much red… so much blood. Kash was so lost in his memories that he didn't even notice that he was now embracing Triana. Once he realized she was in his arms, Kash hugged her tighter for a moment. He wanted to get lost in her embrace, but his anger came rushing back.

"No, fuck that," Kash said suddenly, pushing Triana away. "This is what happens when you help people. It's why we should never get involved."

"What's that supposed to mean?" Calynn growled. "Helping people is what we do."

"And for our troubles we are stuck in a situation that we know we should walk away from but can't." Kash argued back. "We should have just killed Aja's cousin and been done with it."

"So, murder is the answer."

"It's better than this shit."

"Murder is better than helping…"

"You're damn right it is!"

"Both of you stop it!" Triana hollered, jumping up and down. "Arguing about this won't make it go away. Helping people shouldn't be a liability but here we are... stuck, just like you said. It would be more productive to figure what to do about it rather than obsessing over how we got here."

Before Kash could reply, Triana approached and put her finger on his lips. He almost lashed out at her until he looked into her eyes. She was scared and worried. Her eyes were filling with tears that threatened to fall. It gave him pause.

"Am I just a liability also?" Triana asked softly. "Or am I more than that?"

Kash sighed and softened his stance. Triana read his body language and stepped in for a hug. She wrapped her arms around his waist and his were around her shoulders. He laid his head on hers and sighed again.

"I know you are both still hurting, but please don't take it out on each other," Triana continued. "Please."

"I'm sorry, Boss," Calynn said softly. "I didn't mean to yell."

"Come here," Kash said, moving away from Triana towards Calynn.

The two hugged tightly. Kash felt Calynn's fists clenching the back of his shirt. He was holding her with equal purpose and affection. Nothing else mattered but this hug... right here, right now.

"Now that we love each other again," Calynn murmured into his chest. "What are we going to do?"

DO DO DING DO DING

Kash looked at his computer and then back to Calynn. He smiled at the girl and then moved to answer the comm.

"This is the way it's going to be. First, you either tell me EXACTLY why it has to be me right now or I am charging you an exorbitant amount of credits," Kash announced with authority. "Second, on top of the mountain of credits that you are going to prepay me... yes, I said prepay... we also have a list of demands. And lastly, depending on how much of an asshole you continue to be, we reserve the right to end this negotiation at any moment."

Kash was staring into Calynn's eyes as he waited for the bureaucrats to reply.

"Go on," the voice replied after several seconds.

"You will transfer command control of your base over to my nerve center to monitor the meeting," Kash stated. "This shit feels like a fucking trap, and I won't be snared in your net. The only way I set foot on that base is if we have complete control."

"That's not possible, but..." the voice stated, then paused. "But I could get you the security feeds and full control of the docks."

"I could maybe make do with that... for a higher fee."

"What are the rest of your demands?"

"Zero scanners," Kash demanded. "If you scan either of us or my ship, the deal is off and I'm probably going to have to destroy your entire base."

"The scanners are for our safety," the voice replied. "I don't think I can comply with that request."

"Then we're back to it being a job refusal," Kash stated smugly.

"But if you have weapons..."

"Let me save you the trouble," Kash interrupted. "I'm going to have weapons. In fact, I guarantee I will have weapons on my person during this meeting."

"Why would..."

"Because I really... really don't trust you," Kash interrupted. "Because this feels like a trap, and you still have yet to even remotely explain why it has to be me doing this job."

"I'm not sure you will be allowed..."

The voice fell off and it sounded like the comm was being grabbed by somebody. The comm got noisy, then muffled, then noisy again and finally settled.

"Fifty million credits," a third voice stated.

"Just to show up?" Kash asked.

"Correct."

"And my demands?"

"Will be accommodated within reason."

"Within reason, he says," Kash chuckled. "How about followed to the letter or..."

"Seventy-five and we negotiate terms," the voice interrupted.

"Ninety," Kash countered, looking at Triana. "Plus, you pay the operative that doesn't get to come along."

"Fine!"

Kash looked at Calynn. She shrugged her shoulders. Her brow was raised and her eyes full of worry.

"Ninety million credits plus another twenty for the operative, paid in full right now," Kash reiterated. "And that's just for the initial meet. If there's anything I don't like…"

"Transferring now," the voice interrupted.

Kash waited and watched Calynn. She had her eyes closed and her head was making small movements like she was looking back and forth between screens. When she opened her eyes, she nodded.

"Very well," Kash conceded. "We accept."

"Very good," the second man stated. "The location has been sent. Until then… good day."

The comm ended and Kash looked at Triana. She was standing beside Calynn staring at the floor, her shoulders sagging. Kash could see the sadness written on her face.

"I guess that means I have to go home," Triana mumbled.

"It sounds like it," Kash conceded.

"Home is two days away," Calynn explained. "You have some time."

"And she's already almost naked," Kash added, smirking.

"Two whole days?" Triana asked, a smile returning to her face.

"Two days and six hourns to be precise," Calynn replied.

"I might be able to get my fill of her by then," Kash said, smiling at Triana.

"Don't stain my new sheets," Calynn said as she headed to the helm.

"You're not joining us?" Triana asked, disappointed.

"No," Calynn replied. "I'm not… I'm not ready for that yet… but you two have fun."

Triana turned to Kash with a worried look on her face.

"We're both still… you know… I'm sure she will get there eventually," Kash explained, pulling his shirt off. "Now get that ass over here before I change my mind too."

Kash and Triana were both insatiable for the next two days. They spent every waking moment together getting reacquainted with each other's bodies. The two were almost never not touching each other. They even ate some meals while having sex. Kash was exhausted by the time they finally dropped the pixie off on Poncia.

"It's not fair," Triana cried. "Why can't I stay with you?"

"Because we have work to do, and one of the conditions of said work is that you can't come along," Kash explained.

"It's still not fair," Triana whined.

"Boss, we gotta go," Calynn said as she approached. "Trie, we love you, but we gotta go."

Calynn wrapped Triana in a hug before she could protest. The women embraced each other for a moment before Calynn pulled back. She caressed Triana's face, kissed her on the lips, and gave her a warm smile. Triana's face wrinkled as Calynn walked away. She was definitely going to start crying again.

"What if my reward for a job well done… is you?" Kash asked Triana, smiling. "You let us go, we do the job, we come back here…"

"And you'll be with me again?" Triana interrupted.

"Every last bit of you," Kash said, kissing her head. "But we have to leave… now."

"You better hurry back," Triana said stepping back, her voice quivering. "If you make me wait too long, I might just find someone else to keep me warm."

Kash gave Triana one last smile and a kind wave as the cargo doors closed. Calynn had them airborne moments later. Kash joined her in the cockpit.

"I need some ice," Kash joked as he approached Calynn. "That girl fucked me so much I think my dick is raw."

"It was nice seeing you get back in the saddle though," Calynn stated.

"Doc Uva is going to be upset with me."

"Why? Was that love or just lust?"

"Lust… but I do really like her."

"She is a sweetheart."

"And really good in the sack."

"I think I hear a but coming."

"But... I don't know," Kash sighed. "Maybe I'm just not ready for more."

"I think Doctor Uva would be pleased to hear you say that," Calynn said, smiling. "Displaying some emotional maturity..."

"Yeah, yeah," Kash interrupted. "Where are we at on your paperwork?"

"Changing the subject to avoid talking about it," Calynn smirked. "That's so you."

"Paperwork?"

"Submitted."

"And what will they find when they look for you?"

"An orphan from the same orphanage as you."

"That's good. It explains our bond and effectively hides your true origins."

"I planted a trail for them to follow," Calynn explained, brushing her hair behind her ear. "It's messy enough to pass a scan. It looks like I tried staying off the grid with little slip-ups here and there, nothing that'll ping as fake. The constables who could poke holes in it are long gone, either dead or retired. And I routed everything through their system to keep it clean, thanks to your contact."

"That's some damn good work, Miss Smith."

"Thank you, Captain Smith."

"Anything else I need to know?"

"My middle name is Olivia," Calynn added. "In case they ask."

"I doubt that will come up, but... Calynn Olivia kinda rolls off the tongue," Kash smiled. "I like it."

"Me too," Calynn smiled back.

"What's our ETA to our secret rendezvous?"

"We're three days out," Calynn replied. "You napping?"

"I'm napping."

Kash returned to his quarters, striped down to his boxers, and lay in bed. The new bed was amazingly comfortable. Kash felt weightless in the sheets, it also had a cooling property that helped maintain sleep quality. It didn't take long for Kash to fall into a sound sleep.

Kash slept peacefully at first. He only awoke for a short time when Calynn lay down with him. It was nice to curl up with only her again. Calynn hugged his arm and placed her cheek in his hand. Kash caressed her face and fell asleep once again.

Occasionally, his dreams still tormented him and Omia still haunted him. In his dream Omia would always say it wasn't his fault, but he still felt guilty for not being able to save her. He never wanted to forget her face, or her figure, or her laugh… he still missed her.

Kash awoke with a start when the ship shook.

"What the hell?" Kash asked, sitting up.

"It's just a gravitational anomaly," Calynn explained, reaching for him. "Come back."

"That's a hell of a way to wake up," Kash explained. "Scared the hell out of me for a second."

"Sorry… now can I have your arm back?"

"Maybe," Kash teased.

Calynn rolled over and pulled Kash back down onto the bed. She threw a leg over his, wrapped her arm around him, and laid her head on his chest. Kash hugged the young woman and kissed the top of her head. He was just getting comfortable when he heard his stomach growl.

"It's lying," Calynn murmured. "You are not hungry."

"I gotta piss too,"

"Ugh," Calynn groaned, rolling off of him. "Fine… go."

"Have you eaten?" Kash asked, climbing over Calynn to get out of bed.

"No, but I should."

"Compote?"

"Mmm… that sounds good."

"Are you doing okay?" Kash asked from the bathroom. "Been a bit since you were needy."

"Mostly," Calynn replied from the bed. "It is nice having you all to myself again. It's so… restful."

"Because I'm such a simpleton that you can turn off most of your brain?" Kash teased, reentering the bedroom.

"No, you ass," Calynn protested, throwing a pillow at him. "You just... You're my anchor. I rest more when I have you to myself."

"That sounds selfish, Miss Smith." Kash continued teasing her.

"No... just needy," Calynn smirked. "Now go make me a Nutra-shake."

The rest of the trip was uneventful. The duo talked about current events in the news, their current mission, their friends, and of course... Omia. Talking to Calynn about Omia proved to be very calming for Kash. Calynn also missed Omia, so they didn't have to dwell on those parts and could chat about the happier times. Kash felt rested and at ease when they were on approach to the Consortium Star Base.

"Are you ready for this?" Kash asked Calynn.

"Breaking the rule about keeping me away from the Consortium?" Calynn asked sarcastically.

"Ha ha, smart ass."

"Yes, I am," Calynn grinned. "I'll avoid getting separated from you, and make sure I am not scanned, and do whatever else you say to make sure I don't end up dissected."

"If things go sideways, you do whatever it takes to get back to The Cat and get gone," Kash explained. "Even if that means leaving me behind."

The Pick Up

The star base was shaped similarly to an hourglass with a bunch of large hoops around its axis. The first thing Kash noticed was the multitude of large caliber guns. The base had enormous cannons at the skinniest point in the center, and on either end.

"That thing is huge! And crazy looking," Calynn blurted out. "What's with the hoops?"

"The hoops are defense rings," Kash explained. "They are able to slide along the axis to crush any would be assailants or missiles between the rings, and they also house dozens of gunner pods. The cannons on the top, bottom, and middle can decimate planets."

"They can destroy whole planets?" Calynn asked, surprised.

"Not destroy exactly, but definitely end all life upon said planet."

"I just did a quick search on them," Calynn stated somberly. "The dust clouds choke out the sun, and those craters are... by the Gods... I can't believe they use those against people."

"I've seen them used once when I was a legionnaire," Kash explained. "That... horror... shouldn't be witnessed by anyone... ever."

"Are we sure we want to work with these people?"

"They're the government, Baby Girl," Kash told her. "We kinda don't have a choice."

"Approaching Starship, approaching starship, state your business," a man's voice came over the comms.

"Here we go," Kash said to Calynn and then keyed the comm. "This is The Alley Cat Savant. We are here at the request of your C.O."

"Transmit your clearances," the voice ordered.

"Transmitting," Kash replied.

Calynn tapped a few keys as he spoke.

"And now we wait," Kash sighed. "Hold your position here until they tell us to approach."

"Will do, Captain."

Calynn brought them to a stop as they waited for clearance to approach. She was fidgety and tapping her fingers on the control wheel. Kash moved so he was standing behind her and placed his hands on her shoulders. He felt her physically relax a little bit when he did so.

"You're nervous," Kash observed.

"That I am."

"Care to elaborate?"

"Locked in a government box reasons."

"Say no more," Kash said, leaning down to kiss her head.

The duo stood in silence as they waited for the word to approach from the star base. Kash was caressing Calynn's shoulders to help keep them both calm. After several minutes, Calynn started to get impatient. She leaned back in her chair and looked up at Kash.

"What's taking so long?" Calynn asked, exasperated.

"Government red tape," Kash replied with a kind smile. "They probably have to fill out a bunch of forms and get them signed in order to request the forms they need to request the form for us to approach."

"That's a ridiculous number of forms."

"I'm only half joking… they literally have forms to request forms."

Calynn scrunched her face and scowled at him like she thought he was lying to her.

"I'm serious," Kash continued. "To get a license to be a privateer, you have to fill out a form requesting the forms you need to become a privateer. As a former legionnaire, I had two EXTRA forms that I had to fill out."

"That's dumb," Calynn stated.

"That's the government."

"Alley Cat Savant," the man on the comms said. "You are cleared to enter dock four. Follow the guidance drone and do not deviate from its course."

As the man was speaking, a small guidance drone approached. The drone had a cylindrical body with two large screens mounted on either end. The screens lit up when the drone was close enough. Each screen had a green arrow pointing towards the star base.

"Match the speed of the drone to keep our distance the same," Kash informed his friend. "If it gets too far away from us it gets confused."

"Follow the dumb robot," Calynn replied. "Got it."

Calynn did as Kash suggested and maintained the distance to the drone. Kash's nerves were on edge as they approached the defense rings. He had seen what happens to vessels when they are struck by the massive rings. The memory made him shutter.

"You okay, Boss?" Calynn asked.

"I'll be better when we're out of range of those rings."

"I'm following the drone like you said," Calynn whined. "I won't..."

"It's not you that I'm worried about, Baby Girl," Kash interrupted. "I've seen a ring move randomly so it accidentally hit a barge. I do not want us to be involved in an accident like that."

"Who knew gyroscopically stable rings could be so deadly?" Calynn asked rhetorically.

"I was told they weigh in excess of fifty-thousand kilos per linear meter," Kash added. "Which honestly sounds low considering their size and the materials used."

"Is that Corlium Pyrite?" Calynn asked, surprised. "That shit is super dense."

"I've seen them hit with some enormous missiles and it didn't even leave a scratch."

"Hey Boss, what's that?" Calynn asked, pointing out the windshield.

Kash looked out at what Calynn was pointing toward. He could barely see the drone that was hiding around the back of one of the defense rings. Kash grabbed Calynn's hand on the control wheel and turned them slightly so he could get a better look.

"Scanner drone," Calynn announced.

"Pull up," Kash ordered. "Mother fuckers, we told them no scans."

Calynn yanked back on the controls and pushed the throttle. They circled up and out of range of the defense rings.

"Alley Cat Savant," the man's voice came over comms. "You are off course."

"You're damn right we are," Kash barked into the comm. "You were fucking told not to scan us!"

Kash heard a voice in the background before the man replied.

"We didn't scan..."

"We saw the fucking drone. I warned you not to fuck with me," Kash interrupted. "We're out of here."

Kash ended the comm as Calynn sped away from the star base. Calynn fired up the HLD and a bubble of light surrounded the ship. They needed some distance between them and the big guns. Calynn seemed to have the exact same thought as Kash. She dropped them out of faster-than-light travel a fraction of a second later, then ducked them into a small asteroid field.

"We should be safe here. We're just out of sensor range," Calynn said, looking up at Kash. "What do we do now?"

"Cloak us... now," Kash ordered. "I guarantee we're being followed."

DO DO DING DO DING

"WHAT?" Kash barked into the comm.

"Kash, where did you..."

"We left because you broke the fucking rules!"

"But Kash..."

"But nothing... I knew I shouldn't have trusted you."

"Kash, please reconsider," the voice pleaded. "What can we do to make it right?"

"A quarter of a billion credits for this new attempt, AND FULL COMMAND CONTROL OR NO FUCKING DEAL!" Kash shouted.

"I can't authorize that."

The Cat suddenly went dark as Calynn cut the main power. Kash was confused about what had just happened for a moment until he looked at Calynn. She was staring out into space very intently. Kash looked out the windshield also. He scanned the area quickly but didn't see anything.

"What's wrong?" Kash asked.

"Fighters... three of them," Calynn replied softly. "Cloaked."

"Plot a course in case hiding doesn't work."

"I already did th..."

Calynn's words dropped off as she cocked her head. She closed her eyes for half a second and they were glowing when she opened them again.

"What is it?" Kash asked.

"Those are long-range fighters, their nerve centers are weak and not well guarded," Calynn replied. "If all three get close enough, I can hack them. I don't want to do it one at a time… they'd be able to warn each other."

"I didn't know that was possible."

"It's probably not supposed to be, but I can see cracks," Calynn explained, smiling. "And… I got them."

"Why are we out here?" a voice said from the comms.

"Juhn is probably being a weasel again," a second voice replied.

"He gives me the creeps," a female voice added.

"Is that the pilots?" Kash asked Calynn quickly.

Calynn smiled and nodded.

"Shit, Dolly, he gives me the creeps too," the second man replied.

"Does he accidentally touch your ass on purpose too?" the woman asked playfully.

The pilots all shared a laugh, and it made Kash smile. This was the only part of military life that Kash missed… the camaraderie.

"Can you isolate their comms so I can talk to them and only them?"

Calynn cocked her head for a second and then looked at Kash.

"Done."

"You're fucking amazing," Kash gushed.

"I know," Calynn replied confidently.

"Want some help with Juhn?" Kash asked the pilots on comms. "We'd love to help."

"Who is this?" the first man asked. "Identify yourself."

"This is Kash. I am the captain of The Alley Cat Savant," Kash replied. "You know… the ship you are currently hunting."

"How did you hack our comms?" the woman asked.

"Actually, we hacked your whole ship," Kash replied. "Let's talk… face to face."

Kash released the comm mic and turned to Calynn.

"Bring them to us so the base can't see what's happening," Kash told Calynn.

The pretty blonde didn't respond. She restored power to the ship as her eyes glowed bright white. Kash watched as the three fighters slowly approached.

"What the... my controls aren't responding," the woman stated.

"Sorry, that's us," Kash replied. "I know you have no reason to trust me, but we mean you no harm. I was hoping we..."

"Radio silence," the first man ordered forcefully. "That's an order!"

Kash thought about pressing on, but if the pilots were loyal to their leader they wouldn't speak further. Having a conversation with the pilots was probably futile at this point, but he decided to try anyway.

"I know you guys will follow that order, because I would do the same when I was a legionnaire," Kash explained. "But I will explain myself anyway. We were invited here to discuss delivering some cargo somewhere that you guys shouldn't be seen. Contracts like that always make me nervous, so we made some very specific terms for our meeting. Those terms were broken. The scanning drone could have been a simple mistake, but sending three cloaked fighters... look, why would I casually approach your top-secret base unless I was given your location and was invited to be here."

DO DO DING DO DING

Kash paused and looked at the incoming comm. Instead of answering, he continued to address the pilots.

"You were already airborne when I got here. I know that because there's no way you were scrambled that fast," Kash continued. "And I would like to apologize for what happens next... the three of you just became my leverage. We will let you listen in though. Compare what you are about to hear with your orders. I guarantee they contradict each other. Patch us in, Baby Girl."

DO DO DING DO DING

Kash answered the comm.

"Now what?"

"Kash, what happened?" the man asked.

"Oh, sorry," Kash said sarcastically. "We had to cut power to evade the three cloaked fighters you sent to kill us. That's one hell of a fucking welcome wagon."

"But we didn't send any fighters."

"You fucking liar."

"We didn't send them... they must be rogue."

"Is that your play?" Kash chuckled. "Throwing the pilots to the wolves? If I ask them about their orders, would they agree with you? Glad to see you pricks still treat us pilots like we're disposable."

"They aren't our pilots."

"The fuck they aren't!"

"Kash, please... we can talk this through."

"Oh, we're definitely going to talk," Kash snapped. "And we're going to talk face to fucking face! I'm going to head back now, and I'm gonna use your pilots as human shields. We captured your people, so you're gonna have to kill three of your own to get a shot at me. And if you do try to attack me... know this... I will get on that base and when I do... we are going to have a conversation that you can fucking feel! Recompense for trying to kill me, you motherfucker! Kash out!"

Calynn already had them moving by the time Kash ended the comm. She moved the three fighters directly in front of their ship and accelerated back toward the base. If the star base fired on them the fighters would offer them some protection. Enough for them to get away, anyway.

"Make sure their shields are up," Kash told Calynn.

"I already did," Calynn replied.

"I can't believe I'm about to say this, but..." Kash paused and sighed. "If the base fires on us, give the pilots control of their fighters."

"Oh, I was hoping you were going to say that," Calynn said with some relief. "I didn't think I could make them all evade an assault."

"Pilots... look, I know you won't reply, but... but if they shoot at us break left and we'll break right," Kash explained. "We will try to draw their fire before we jump away so you three get home safe. You're caught up in this shit the same as us."

"Boss, can you take the helm so I can concentrate?" Calynn asked. "In case I need Goddess mode again."

"As you wish, Your Grace," Kash replied smiling.

The two switched seats and Kash prepared himself in case they had to fight their way out. He squinted at the star base to try and see it better than he actually could, then checked the position of the fighters.

"Raise the center fighter seven meters and lower the one on the right two meters," Kash said calmly. "That way when they break, they have more room to maneuver."

Calynn did as he asked without saying a word. She was just as focused as he was, and he was thankful for it. Kash's eyes darted back and forth as he scanned the space in front of them. He was looking for anything that could remotely be a trap. The closer they got to the base, the more nervous and vigilant Kash became.

"Shit!" Kash complained.

"What's wrong, Boss?"

"The position of the defense rings," Kash replied. "They intend to fire. Pilots, hands on your controls and get ready to use your countermeasures… and remember… we fly fierce, strike fast, BREAK BREAK BREAK!"

Kash jerked the wheel to the right as soon as he saw the guns of the star base spring to life. He accelerated hard and rolled the ship over so he could still see the base. He banked hard again to avoid a volley of bullets and then rolled the other direction to evade more. He tried to keep them positioned so he could see the base as they fled. It gave him an extra half second to try to avoid the bullets.

"Missile inbound!" Calynn shouted.

"Spin up the…"

"I'm on it, Sir," the female pilot interrupted.

Her fighter suddenly appeared just above The Cat, and she was already firing at the incoming missile. The ace quickly destroyed the inbound ordinance and then moved to flank Kash and Calynn.

"Popping flares!" she continued. "Pull up."

Kash did as the pilot said and settled into a trailing position. He couldn't turn as tight as the fighter could, so he kept the formation loose. It only took a moment for Kash to tell that she was an exceptional pilot. It was something about the way she pitched and rolled her fighter while evading a hail of bullets. It was effortless for her.

"Dolly to base. Dolly to base," Dolly said over an open comm channel. "Why the hell are you firing on me and the vessel I am escorting?"

"Dolly?" a man's voice replied. "Why are you there?"

"Saveen?" Dolly replied.

"Dolly, return to formation," one of the other pilots barked.

"Fuck that, Commander," Dolly barked back. "We were clearly lied to, and I won't be party to killing innocents. Fuck Juhn and his secret orders!"

"Dolly!" the commander yelled.

"He didn't have to let us go!" Dolly argued. "His choices were let us die or let us live at the risk of us attacking him. He chose to let us live, so I'm choosing to let him live also."

"Why the hell aren't you firing?" a man said distantly.

"Sir, that's Dolly," Saveen replied.

"I don't care," the man barked. "Fire!"

That time the man was close enough to the mic for Kash to recognize his voice. It was the first bureaucrat that he argued with a few days ago.

"Dolly, is that Juhn?" Kash asked.

"Sir, yes, sir," Dolly replied. "And his insubordination will not go unpunished... I can promise you that."

"If you get me on that base, I promise that pervert will never be able to touch your ass again," Kash replied.

"STAND DOWN!" a raspy voice bellowed over the comm.

"NO!" Juhn shouted. "We're under attack! Keep firing!"

"All hands, Stand Down!" the unknown voice shouted again. "That's an order!"

The base guns were dormant once more and Kash sighed with relief. When the realization hit him, he snapped his gaze to Calynn.

"Is that you?" Kash asked Calynn suddenly. "The voice?"

"No... it's not."

"Dolly?" the raspy voice asked.

"Yes, Admiral," Dolly replied.

"Do you have our guests in tow?"

"Yes, ma'am," Dolly answered.

"Would you be so kind as to escort them to dock four, please?" the Admiral asked politely.

"It would be my pleasure, Ma'am."

"Shoot down any drone that approaches," the Admiral continued.

"Ma'am?"

"We are not to scan them or their ship. Our base will honor your terms, Captain Smith," the Admiral stated. "Even if the suits will not."

"Thank you, Admiral," Kash replied. "I am very grateful."

"However… I am reluctant to transfer full command control of my base," the Admiral continued. "Would full control of the defense rings suffice?"

"That's a reasonable compromise," Kash replied. "I can agree to that."

"Transmitting the codes now."

Kash turned to Calynn and waited for her to acknowledge the codes. Calynn smiled softly and nodded.

"Codes received," Kash replied. "Thanks again, Admiral."

"Dolly, you are on protection detail. Do not leave their side until I personally relieve you, understood?" the Admiral continued.

"Yes, ma'am."

"Admiral out."

"Follow me, Captain Smith," Dolly stated. "Standard formation."

The other two fighters joined the formation with Dolly in front followed by Kash and one of the other fighters, and the last fighter trailing them. The four spacecraft made a diamond shape as they approached the base. Calynn had moved the defense rings to the far end of the base which made Kash feel more at ease.

"Captain Smith, can I ask you a question?" Dolly asked on a private channel.

"Sure, Dolly."

"Were you really a legionnaire?"

"I was."

"What was your call sign? If you don't mind me asking?"

"My call sign was Dagger," Kash replied. "Let me guess why you're asking… they still don't let girls fly with them."

"No, Sir, they do not," Dolly's disappointment was evident in her voice.

"I would have flown with you, Dolly," Kash replied. "You're one hell of a pilot."

"Thank you, Sir," Dolly replied. "That means a lot."

"Dolly to dock four control. Dolly to dock four control," Dolly continued over the open channel. "We're on final approach… Captain Smith, stay in your ship…"

"Nose out and ready to bolt," Kash interrupted. "I'm well aware of protection detail protocols, Dolly."

The blast doors for the dock opened as the other two fighters broke formation.

"Where are they going?" Calynn asked.

"They pull back to make sure that we aren't being stalked," Kash responded. "Only the lead ship and the escorted ship enter the landing zone. It's to protect us at our most vulnerable."

"Match speed and set your stabilizers to max power," Dolly stated. "Prepare for gravitational transition."

"Copy that, Dolly."

"I've never done this before," Calynn stated, grinning. "Part of the ship with gravity and the rest without."

"It's a little bumpy, so hold on," Kash told her.

The Alley Cat shook a little as they entered the dock through the two atmospheric fields. Once the cockpit was through the second field, Kash could finally see around the dock. A large metal crate sat alone in the center of the dock and a small group of people were waiting for them at the far side near the receiving office. Kash spun the ship around and landed so they could make a quick getaway if needed.

"Now we wait for Dolly," Kash told Calynn. "She has to secure the area before we exit the ship… it feels kinda weird being on this side of the protection detail."

"Does that make us V.I.P's?" Calynn giggled.

"Don't let it go to your head," Kash chuckled.

They didn't have to wait long.

"Do you remember Barbie Dolls, Boss?" Calynn asked, standing up to look out the window.

"The children's toy?"

"Yes."

"Kinda… why?"

"I think I know where Dolly got her call sign."

Kash looked out the window at the female pilot. She had long brown hair, pale red skin, and a big, beautiful smile. It was her figure that had caught Calynn's attention. Dolly had a huge bust, tiny waist, and medium hips. Her flight suit could barely contain her voluptuous curves when she waved to them.

"The fucking body on her," Kash said under his breath.

"Let's go meet her," Calynn purred.

"Let's," Kash agreed.

The duo walked to the back of the ship where the cargo door was already on its way down. Dolly was waiting at the bottom of the ramp when they got there.

"Captain Smith," Dolly said, offering a handshake. "I'm Captain Barbella. It's a pleasure to meet you."

"Please," Kash stated, shaking her hand. "Call me Kash."

"It's been a long time, Kash," the raspy voiced Admiral said loudly. "How are you?"

Kash looked at the Admiral and couldn't believe his eyes. The Admiral was one of his first clients. He hadn't seen her in twenty years. She had more gray hair and gained some weight, but she still had that motherly smile. Kash smiled at the Admiral and nearly forgot about Captain Barbella.

"Excuse me," Kash told Dolly and started to jog towards the Admiral "I'm so sorry… I didn't recognize your voice."

"That's a long story involving my ex-husband and a chef's knife," the Admiral stated, lifting her chin to expose a massive scar. "I should have let you put him in the ground instead of a jail cell."

Kash slowed as he approached the woman. She smiled softly and moved to greet him. Kash was expecting her to just shake his hand in front of the others, but her hands went up around his shoulders and she gave him a warm hug. Kash hugged her back and smiled fondly. The Admiral was the like the mother he never had. Kash had the utmost respect for her.

"It's so good to see you," the Admiral stated, still hugging Kash. "You haven't aged a day."

"My aches and pains disagree with that assessment," Kash chuckled, and finally released his embrace. "It's good to see you also."

"Who's the blonde?"

"Sorry, where are my manners," Kash said, motioning toward Calynn. "This is my pilot, Calynn Smith... Calynn this is Admiral..."

"Just Admiral," the Admiral interrupted. "You are the only one aboard this base that knows my real name, Kash. And I mean to keep it that way."

"Sorry, ma'am," Kash apologized.

"Mrs. Smith you are so beautiful," the Admiral said to Calynn as she approached. "And so young."

"Thank you, ma'am, but it's just Miss Smith," Calynn said with a soft smile, shaking the Admirals hand.

"Miss Smith?" the Admiral questioned.

"We grew up in the same orphanage as children," Calynn explained. "Twenty-five years apart, but the same one, nonetheless. They gave us the same surname."

"We formed an immediate bond because of it," Kash added. "She's family now."

"Good," the Admiral said fondly. "You need someone to look after you. I bet she can tell me lots of stories about you."

"I'd love the chance to do that," Calynn giggled. "We could go get some drinks."

"Where's the officers lounge? I'm buying," Kash added. "It would be wonderful to catch up with you."

"But he's here on official business," a man said from behind the Admiral. "And there's a job to do."

"Duty always calls," the Admiral smiled reluctantly.

"Unfortunately," Kash complained.

"And what business brings you to my base?" the Admiral asked.

"A delivery that apparently only I can do," Kash replied sarcastically.

"I thought you did acquisitions not deliveries?"

"Me too."

Kash and the Admiral both looked at the man who had spoken. He looked nervous under their gaze and adjusted his tie. His light blue suit was tailored perfectly and looked far too expensive. The man fidgeted with his suit jacket and avoided Kash's gaze. He took two steps to his right and motioned that way before he replied.

"It's just here," he said nervously. "In that crate."

Kash looked at where the man had motioned to the large metal crate painted drab green. The crate was easily six meters tall, eight meters wide, and thirty meters long.

"That won't fit in my ship," Kash stated. "It's too long."

"And I know what's in that crate," the Admiral stated, stepping in front of Kash. "That's not going in my Kash's ship."

"But it must," the bureaucrat argued. "That's why he's here."

"Nooooo… I'm here on a retainer," Kash corrected the man. "A non-refundable retainer to meet and discuss the job offer. I haven't actually accepted the job yet."

"And it's a job that I won't let him do," the Admiral added. "Pay him the retainer and let him leave."

"Admiral, we need him for this," the suit argued.

"The only way that thing fits in his ship is if you split it in half," the Admiral stated. "Which means leaving the containment system power supply behind. And that means the system could achieve critical flux."

"You want me to carry a BLASTR System?" Kash blurted out. "Are you fucking kidding me?"

"No, I don't want you to carry it," the bureaucrat replied. "But I'm told that several groups of space pirates intend to stop any freighter that leaves here. They somehow know the weapon is here and that we're about to ship it. According to my informant, our only shot at getting it out is on a smaller ship. That's why we needed Kash… because of his speed."

"So, your solution is to have him race between star bases before that monstrosity has a meltdown?" the Admiral asked sarcastically.

"The Cat doesn't produce enough energy to keep it stable," Kash added. "And the hospitality of your bases is well documented. So if I'm detained on approach…"

"We would still be getting shot at if the Admiral had not intervened," Dolly interrupted. "I think you're asking the impossible."

"Especially with all of our red tape," the Admiral added. "There needs to be protocols in place to expedite his arrival at each base."

"We can't broadcast our plans across the verse," the suit argued. "That would put the mission at more risk."

"So, you have a mole?" Kash asked.

"No, we don't," the bureaucrat replied almost too quickly.

"We clearly do," the Admiral countered.

"No, we don't!" the bureaucrat repeated angrily.

"Job refusal," Kash said calmly. "Pay the retainer and I'm gone."

"But you have to do this," the bureaucrat complained.

"Give me one good fucking reason why," Kash said firmly.

"Because the miners are getting killed!" the bureaucrat shouted.

Kash stopped and stared at the man. The bureaucrat was showing some actual emotion, and maybe even some empathy towards the plight of the common working man. Kash was pleasantly surprised by the man.

"They're just trying to do their jobs," the suit added. "They don't deserve to die."

"So, send a battalion," Kash replied. "Unless you can't, because..."

Kash paused as he got an uneasy feeling in his stomach. There was something about this job that just screamed for him to walk away.

"Because of politics," Dolly finished his thought for him. "You're sending this weapon for its shock factor."

"It's meant to be a deterrent," the bureaucrat argued. "To keep the savages at bay."

"Savages?" Kash questioned sarcastically. "I bet I don't have to guess who was on that land first, do I? This is why nobody likes you fucks. You move in to take what you want and kill the people who live there if they get in your way. When are you going to learn that you don't fucking own EVERYTHING?"

Kash was losing his temper, frustration boiling over as he lashed out at the bureaucrat. He had to turn and walk away from the man before he hit him just for existing. Dolly and Calynn followed him as he gained space. When he stopped, the two women were standing right there with him. They both looked a little worried.

"I can't believe I'm saying this, but I think you should do it," Dolly said softly. "The miners are only there doing their jobs. The suits are to blame, not the workers. They just do what they're told. The other thing to consider is that they are sending something to be a deterrent and not just bombarding the planet from a star base."

"It still feels wrong," Calynn added.

"I know, Baby Girl," Kash sighed. "But it might be the lesser of two evils."

"If you do it make sure there's a dumping clause," Dolly added. "They only get so many minutes to get you into the dock or you jettison the payload. That way they can't fuck with you too much."

"That's smart," Calynn replied.

"Juhn is gone," the Admiral reported as she approached. "He took a shuttle and scurried away."

"He was definitely the mole," Kash replied. "This whole thing was a setup from the start."

"He was trying to kill us," Calynn added. "I wonder why?"

"It might have been something I said," Kash chuckled.

"You were rather rude to him," Calynn giggled.

"This is no time to jest," the Admiral scolded. "If this mission is a trap, then it is over… now."

"Unfortunately, we have a friend that is also snared in the trap," Calynn explained. "If we back out, the axe falls on her neck."

"So, you have to do it?" Dolly asked.

"As much as I don't want to," Kash sighed. "Yes, we do."

"That's a dangerous game, my friend," the Admiral said, solemnly. "Intentionally walking into a trap is ill advised at best."

"Which is why I'm going to need some help," Kash explained. "I'm gonna need every piece of literature you have on that weapon system. I need schematics, service manuals… whatever you can find."

"I can get that from engineering," Dolly replied and trotted off.

"Get everything," Kash hollered to Dolly before turning to the Admiral. "And I need any help you can give me. Some security codes or whatever to make sure the other bases can't slow me down. Maybe if I can run ahead of schedule they won't have time to set the trap properly."

"I have something that can help with that," the Admiral replied. "It may take some time… I'll see what I can do."

"You… bureaucrat," Kash hollered to the man in the suit. "You have a big fucking transfer to initiate."

Over the next few hourns, the bureaucrat's men loaded the BLASTR into the cargo hold. Kash oversaw the work from the catwalk while flipping through the manuals that Dolly had brought him. He studied the circuit diagrams while taking swigs of bourbon straight from the bottle.

"I'm surprised you can still read," Calynn said, grabbing his bottle from his hand.

"Yeah, well," Kash slurred. "I'm trying to forget that thing is here."

"And if I need you to be sober to help me figure something out?"

"You're the god, not me."

"Seriously?"

"Can I have that bottle back now?"

Stop #1

"Sssnnnrrk," Kash awoke with a start.

Kash rubbed his eyes and then wiped the drool from his mouth. His head was pounding and his stomach felt sour. He definitely had too much to drink.

"Are you going to wipe the drool off of me too?" Calynn asked with a snarky tone.

Kash slowly became aware of his surroundings. He was in bed with Calynn. That wasn't an unusual thing, but he seemed to be much lower than her. His head was on her stomach... her lower stomach. His arm was wrapped around her leg, and his hand was on her ass... her bare ass.

"Why are we naked?" Kash asked, looking up at Calynn.

"Because you were horny and wanted to fuck," Calynn grumbled.

"Oh, no... did we?"

"No," Calynn complained. "You wound me up and then passed the fuck out."

"Good," Kash said, relieved.

"No, not good," Calynn argued. "I'm still wound up and need some relief. I have needs too."

Calynn started rocking her pelvis beneath him. The movement soured Kash's stomach further. A burp burned the back of his throat, so Kash hurriedly crawled out of bed to go to the bathroom. He nearly fell because he forgot how much taller the new bed was than the old one.

"Hey," Calynn whined. "Where are you going?"

Kash didn't reply. He was too focused on getting to the bathroom before the contents of his stomach expelled themselves. The room was tilted, or he was so drunk it seemed tilted anyway. He had to reach out and brace himself on the wall. He barely made it through the bathroom door when he lost the battle with his stomach. Kash vomited the contents of his stomach into the sink.

"Oh my… Kash."

Kash closed the door before Calynn could get to him. He didn't want her to see him like this. His stomach retched again, and he spewed out some more brown liquid. It was probably undigested bourbon, and his body was getting rid of it before he suffered alcohol poisoning. His body tensed up and he heaved again and again until nothing came out.

Kash laid his head against the cold sink and tried to settle himself. The room was still spinning and tilting so he lay down on the nice cold floor. He soon fell asleep.

He heard Calynn's voice and felt her fingers running through his hair, but didn't know what she said.

"Come on, Kash," Calynn repeated softly. "Let's get you to bed."

Kash didn't answer. He let Calynn help him to his feet. He wrapped his arm around her shoulders, so she could help support his weight. He was thankful to see she was wearing a bra and panties now. Calynn helped him to the bed, and he crawled onto it. Calynn crawled into bed with him and laid on her back. She had a wet towel in her hand that she folded and placed on her stomach.

"Here, this should stay cool," Calynn offered, gently pulling him towards her. "Lay down."

Kash laid his head on the cool, wet towel on Calynn's belly. It felt surprisingly good. He snuggled into her belly and wrapped his arms around her.

"Get some rest," Calynn said softly. "We have some time before the first stop."

Kash passed out again quickly.

He was alone when he awoke. The cool wet rag on his forehead was probably Calynn's doing. His head was pounding but he no longer felt sick.

"We need to get some electrolytes in you," Calynn said, smiling as she entered the room. "Without you vomiting it out again."

"In the pantry there is…"

"Virellium Root and a chunk of mineral salt," Calynn interrupted. "It's already in this."

She pulled a Nutra-shake out from behind her body and handed it to him. She sat on the edge of the bed and beamed her beautiful smile at him. Kash took a sip of the offered beverage and swallowed hesitantly. He was worried his stomach was still too sour but was pleasantly surprised when the liquid seemed to settle his stomach. It was better than the alternative. When he looked back at Calynn, she was still grinning ear to ear.

"Why are you so happy?" Kash asked.

"You were talking in your sleep."

Kash sighed and covered his face with his hand.

"It was nothing bad," Calynn continued. "You must have had the dream where I am a goddess again. You said such sweet things."

Calynn swooned and placed her hands over her heart. She was rotating her torso left and right ever so slightly, and she was glowing she was so happy.

"Uh, oh," Kash sighed. "What did I say?"

"Your punishment for having sex with me should be having more sex with me," Calynn giggled. "Your Goddess commands it."

"Oh, no."

"Look, I know I got a little sex crazed when I got my body…"

"A little?" Kash interrupted.

"But," Calynn said assertively, ignoring his interruption. "I have that under control now and would like to explore an arrangement where we just take care of each other's needs from time to time."

"Friends with benefits?"

"Exactly," Calynn smiled. "I wasn't sure if you knew that term."

"Baby Girl…"

"Before you argue," Calynn interrupted, but was still smiling her brilliant smile. "I know we both care about each other a lot, and neither of us want to be hurt again. If we keep that between ourselves then we don't have anyone that can… I want to protect us from another… so we don't end up brokenhearted again."

Calynn's smile faded as she finished speaking. Her shoulders slumped forward, and her head fell so her chin was in her chest. She must have noticed her mood swing and quickly righted her posture. She tried to smile again but it didn't reach her eyes.

"Sorry for the roller coaster of emotions," Calynn apologized.

"It's okay," Kash smiled back. "You have way more control than before and you recognize when you're doing it now."

"I'm trying."

"How far out are we?"

"Epic subject changes as per usual," Calynn mumbled, running her hands through her hair.

"Because if we have time," Kash raised his voice a bit to get her attention. "I wouldn't mind a nap... with you."

"Just a nap?" Calynn asked with another genuine smile.

"I'm too hungover for benefits."

"How about you drink your shake first," Calynn said, standing up. "We need you to be on point in six hourns. In the meantime, I'm going to go analyze the weapon some more."

"Ugh... my eyes still hurt from staring at those technical drawings for hourns," Kash replied, sitting up on the bed. "But we need to find a way to keep that fucking thing stable."

"From what I can see, the containment field keeps the plasma core from expanding or something."

"The plasma reacts with several common radiations," Kash explained. "Like some of the parts of light or some shit."

"So, we just need to keep the containment field charged?" Calynn asked excitedly and sat back on the edge of the bed. "Let's just plug it into the Cat's batteries."

"It's not that easy," Kash replied. "The corporate idiots that built it thought it was a good idea to make the charging system proprietary."

"What's that mean?"

"If you don't charge it with their charging station it goes boom."

"Boom?"

"Boom."

"Damn."

"Yep."

The duo sat in an awkward silence for a moment. Calynn wore her worry on her face and began picking at her fingers. She was more nervous than he was about having the weapon on board. He could see it in her body language.

"So, what do we do?" Calynn asked softly.

"I think we can trickle charge it," Kash explained. "If we match the Hertz and Amplitude of the containment field, I think we can add enough power to slow the degradation of the containment field… as long as we add the energy slowly enough."

"I'll make sure to analyze that thoroughly to make sure we do that correctly," Calynn said, standing up again.

Kash reached out quickly and grabbed her arm before she could leave. She paused and looked back at him with caring eyes.

"I'm not used to having… this," Kash explained, motioning back and forth between them. "I change the subject when I don't know what to say."

"I know," Calynn replied, aglow. "Omia told me."

"I told you she could see through my bullshit."

"Drink your shake and get some rest. I'm going to go analyze the big dumb laser."

"Throw me that spec manual on your way out," Kash said, pointing to the thick book on his desk.

Calynn picked up the manual, held it with both hands at her thighs, and bounced it off each leg as she walked. Her tongue was sticking out of the corner of her mouth, and she had a devious look in her eye as she approached. Kash wasn't sure what she was doing. He was about to ask her when she suddenly lunged forward and plopped the book down beside him. She kissed the top of his head and giggled.

"I love your giggle," Kash blurted out.

"I know," Calynn responded, touching her forehead to his. "Now drink."

Calynn turned and marched out of their quarters and headed to the cargo hold.

"Yes, dear," Kash hollered after her. "Anything for you dear."

Kash opened the manual and turned to the section with the wiring diagrams. He studied each page, tracing the wire routes with his finger for hourns. He had to find a weakness in the design… something the engineers missed while they designed it. He must have nodded off when he was studying, because the next thing he knew Calynn was standing over him.

"Hey, sleepy head," Calynn said with a soft smile.

"Oh, shit," Kash exclaimed. "How long was I out?"

"Not too long," Calynn replied. "You still have time to shower before we get to the first stop."

"Did you learn anything more about that monstrosity in our cargo hold?" Kash asked as he climbed out of bed.

"Not really... you?"

"Not yet," Kash replied as he entered the bathroom. "There's still a lot of schematics to go over. I'll find something."

Kash stripped down and climbed into the shower.

"Did you get the frequency of the containment field?" Kash asked from the shower.

"I did," Calynn replied. "It's actually a repeating series of frequencies and amplitudes. It's rather complex."

"Can we mimic it?"

"It will take some time, but I think so."

"Good," Kash said, exiting the shower. "Can I have my towel?"

"Can I stare at you a bit first?" Calynn asked, sitting on the edge of the sink, smirking at him.

"Is that part of your benefits package?"

"I'd love to benefit from your package."

"Seriously?" Kash chuckled. "That was a horrible pun. You should work on..."

"Oh, shit," Calynn exclaimed, dropped Kash's towel, and ran out of the bathroom.

Kash nearly lost his balance when the ship suddenly decelerated. He retrieved his towel and hastily dried himself. He was pulling on his jeans when he joined Calynn in the cockpit.

"What's going on?" Kash asked, looking out the windshield.

"Well, they weren't lying about the pirates," Calynn answered. "They have an EMP trap set up."

"By the Gods."

"Is it weird that I could feel it?"

"Not weird for you, no. Can we get around it?"

"Yeah, I just had to cut the HLD so they couldn't detect our Hyper light cone. I've plotted a new course around them," Calynn explained. "And what's that supposed to mean? Not weird for me."

"You can manipulate energy, so it makes sense you could feel it."

"Oh... okay."

"What?"

"I thought you were calling me weird."

"Now why would I do that?" Kash asked sarcastically, returning to his quarters. "Weirdo."

"Ass," Calynn replied.

Kash checked the news and Trade Commission website to see what chatter there was about the uptick in pirate activity. He wasn't surprised to find nothing. The Consortium would not allow anyone to advertise their shortcomings. People might start questioning where their tax credits were being spent if they knew about their government's inability to deal with a piracy problem.

The last leg of their journey was uneventful. They soon found themselves on approach to another star base... with more big guns... and those damn defense rings.

"This one has more rings than the other one," Calynn observed.

"Yeah, there's two planets in this system that are warring with each other and resisting Consortium rule."

"Well, let's hope the codes your Admiral friend gave us work."

"Approaching starship, approaching starship," a man said over the comms. "Hold position and state your business."

"This is the diplomatic courier, the Alley Cat Savant," Kash replied. "We are the ones you are expecting for a recharge."

"Transmit your clearances and diplomat codes," the man ordered.

Calynn did as the man asked and the duo waited for the base's response. The response came much quicker than Kash expected.

"Expedited codes received. Continue on your present course until I get confirmation of which dock is set to receive you."

"Well, that was fast," Kash said to Calynn.

"And easy," Calynn added.

"Alley Cat Savant," the man's voice said over the comms. "Proceed to dock seven. Your defense protocols are in place."

"Our defense protocols?" Kash questioned.

"Boss, look," Calynn stated pointing at the base.

The defense rings moved along the axis of the base so they were far away from the docks. Kash and Calynn would have an easy approach to the base with no fear of being bumped by one of the massive rings.

"And not a drone in sight," Kash remarked as they got closer to the base. "Good job, Admiral."

"So, how did you meet her?" Calynn asked. "The Admiral."

"She hired me to prove her estranged husband had embezzled a bunch of credits that they were blaming her for taking," Kash explained. "The husband, who was a bureaucrat at the time, used her credentials to siphon billions of credits from the Consortium Defense Fund into his fake business. He was able to cover up his involvement by implicating his own wife. Anne, the Admiral, tried to handle it through proper channels, but quickly learned that it was a losing battle. Her husband even hired an assassin to kill her. If she was dead, she couldn't try to defend herself against the embezzlement allegations, but luckily she found me before the assassin found her."

"That's why she said she should have let you kill her husband," Calynn added.

"I tried to warn her that it wouldn't be over if he just went to jail... unfortunately, I was right."

"It also explains why she called the bureaucrat a suit when we were there."

"Yeah... she's not a fan of those pricks."

"Alley Cat Savant, this is Dock Seven Control," another man said over comms. "We have you on approach. Opening the blast doors now."

"Setting stabilizers to max power and preparing for gravitational transition," Calynn replied to the man at the docks.

"What... er..." the man sounded distant like he didn't actually try to reply.

"That was odd," Kash noted.

"Remain on board your ship until told otherwise," a grizzly man's voice barked. "I'm on my way."

Calynn looked up at Kash with her eyebrows raised, her mouth agape, and her head cocked to the side. She was clearly just as puzzled as he was. Kash shrugged his shoulders at Calynn and looked out at the dock. A security team rushed in through the doors onto the dock as their ship touched down.

"Boss… why are they armed?"

"I wish I knew, Baby Girl."

The duo continued to watch as the security team moved to surround their ship. Kash noticed the charging station for the BLASTR was at the far end of the dock. The team of engineers at the charger looked just as confused about what was happening as Kash and Calynn were. They had started to bring the charger over to the ship, but the soldiers were ordering them to back up. Kash knew what the soldiers were doing, and it angered him to be treated like a threat.

"Fuck this," Kash announced. "I'm going out there."

"But Boss…"

"If they are going to surround us because they think we are a threat, I am going to be a fucking threat!" Kash growled as he marched towards the cargo bay.

He grabbed his shoulder holster and two sidearms from the weapons rack and walked to the back of his ship. He used the mag gun in his right hand to push the button that lowered the cargo doors. Calynn was soon by his side holding a mag gun in each hand as the door lowered. The duo shared a determined look at each other and then turned their focus to the commotion outside.

The security team positioned themselves at the bottom of the cargo ramp and were barking orders at Kash and Calynn. Kash ignored the soldier's orders and slowly walked to the bottom of the ramp. Kash glared at the men pointing their weapons at him. The soldiers backed up a step when Calynn joined him at the bottom of the ramp.

"I told you stay aboard your ship!" the raspy voiced man yelled.

The man looked cross as he marched towards them with purpose. Kash assumed the man was a general based on all the insignias on his uniform. The man had bright red hair, but Kash had never seen someone with the General's complexion. The General's face was yellow with hints of orange. He had a pronounced lower jaw and chin, a bulbous nose, and beady yellow eyes. He waddled when he walked probably due to his large stomach and short legs… well, short by comparison to the rest of his body, anyway. As the General was just as tall as Kash.

"I am aboard my ship!" Kash barked, motioning to his feet that were still on the cargo ramp.

"You getting smart with me, boy?" the General griped.

"Could you follow along if I did?" Kash quipped.

"I'm warning you, boy," the man growled as he moved closer.

"Come get some, you fat fucking slob," Kash said snidely. "I'll show you who the boy is."

The General stopped and stared at Kash with a fierce gaze. His eyes narrowed, and his jaw clenched. The General's face was turning red as his seething anger built.

"I think I struck a nerve," Kash said to Calynn. "His head might pop."

"Fat men in glass houses shouldn't throw stones," Calynn stated coldly.

"If men have to look like him," Kash added. "Remind me to never be a man."

"Just my boy toy," Calynn giggled.

"SHUT YOUR MOUTH, WHORE!" the chubby man shrieked.

"Did he just call me..."

"What did you call her?" Kash interrupted Calynn.

"She's a WHORE!" the man yelled.

"I'd really like to see you come over here and say that," Kash growled.

"Why would he call me that?" Calynn asked.

"Only whores gallivant around in star ships!" the General continued shouting, his voice dripping with disdain. "Women should stay at home like they are supposed to."

"So, my location makes me a whore?" Calynn asked sarcastically.

"And whores definitely shouldn't speak to men like that!" the fat man continued. "You should speak only when spoken to. Know your place, whore. It's ridiculous that you think you belong out here in the stars. You should be at home tending to your domestic duties. It goes against your nature to be out here... unless your nature is to ride every cock in the galaxy like the WHORE YOU ARE!"

"Call her that again and I'm going to dump this fucking laser on your dock and let it go critical," Kash muttered through gritted teeth. "What gives you the right to say some stupid shit like that to her?"

"It's not stupid to tell a woman to stay home where she belongs!" the General barked.

"This is our home!" Kash shouted. "So technically, SHE IS HOME!"

The General didn't respond this time. He just stared at Kash, and Kash stared back.

"I guess it never occurred to you that she might be my daughter, huh?" Kash hissed. "Or maybe my wife? What if… what if we sold our home to see the stars together… as a family? In either case you just called someone precious to me a whore, and that… oh, that doesn't sit well with me… so this is what's going to happen. I'm going to destroy this whole motherfucking star base if you are rude to her just one more time. So, choose you words carefully."

The General stared at Kash, sizing him up. Kash adjusted his grip on his pistols. The General noticed the movement of his fingers, and his look changed. He was unwilling to test Kash's resolve physically, but something in his eyes told Kash this standoff wasn't over yet.

"There are no wh…" the General paused and looked back and forth between Kash and Calynn before continuing. "There are no women allowed aboard this star base!"

The man raised his chin in the air and looked down his nose at Kash, as if doing so gave his edict more validity. The General stood there smugly, nearly smirking. Kash squinted his eyes at the man debating beating the sexist pig senseless.

"This one is," Kash proclaimed. "And it's not up for debate."

Kash holstered both of his weapons and nodded at Calynn to do the same. She wasn't wearing a holster, so she tucked the firearms into the front of her pants.

"There's no way this happens without her," Kash continued. "And the sooner you come to grips with that, the better."

Calynn moved closer to Kash, gently grabbed his arm, and popped up on her toes.

"Thanks for defending my honor, Mr. Smith," Calynn said softly and gave him a soft kiss on the cheek.

"Anything for you, Mrs. Smith," Kash replied still staring at the General.

"She is a distraction to the men," the General announced. "She needs to go."

"She's also the brains of the operation and will be the one that attaches the charger to the big piece of shit in our hold," Kash replied firmly.

"Then she needs to cover her body more appropriately," the General rebutted.

"I'm wearing jeans and a T-shirt," Calynn complained. "How much more covered do I need to be?"

Calynn raised her arms and looked down at her own body, examining herself. She patted her belly and lifted her breasts like she was looking for where she was exposed. She even turned to try and look at her own butt, before looking at Kash with a puzzled look and shrugging her shoulders.

"Maybe your curves are giving them… a hard time," Kash suggested.

Calynn looked at Kash, cocked her head, looked at the men before them for a moment, and then looked back at him with her mouth hanging open. Calynn covered her mouth with her fingers and giggled, whimsically. The motion of several men adjusting themselves caught Kash's attention, and he couldn't help but shake his head.

"She needs to remove herself from our presence, IMMEDIATELY!" the General shouted as he approached.

"No, she doesn't," Kash replied calmly. "She stays here, regardless of your ridiculous rules."

"My rules keep my men safe," The General argued.

"Your rules keep your men lonely," Kash rebutted.

"I could take command of this base by just removing my top," Calynn said comically.

"Which is why women do not belong here!" the General scolded. "Remove yourself."

"Remove my top?" Calynn jested. "Okay."

Calynn grabbed the bottom of her shirt like she was going to pull it off. Six of the soldiers were grasping at Calynn before she could get her shirt above her belly button. Calynn jumped back before the men could actually touch her. One of the men rushed at her and received a kick in the chest for his trouble that stopped him in his tracks. Calynn then grabbed the man by the arm, rotated swiftly, and threw the man twenty meters across the room.

The other men were in shock at her display of strength and backed off. Calynn approached the rest of the men demonstratively. The men wisely backed down. Even the General looked scared.

"Grrrrrrr," Calynn actually growled at the men. "Who wants some?"

CRACK

One of the soldiers fired a single mag round at Calynn, spinning the blonde beauty around so she was kneeling on the ramp. Some of the men were mumbling to each other after the shot, but Kash wasn't paying attention to them. He was more concerned about what Calynn would do next.

"Who fired that shot?" The General asked. "Who…

The General's words fell off when Calynn suddenly stood up. She turned around and smiled at the men. She was shaking something in her hand, tossed it into the air, and caught it again.

"It's a good thing I got those new implants," Calynn said, still tossing the bullet. "Which of you morons thought it was a good idea to fire a bullet at a ballistic laser system, hmm?"

"That's impossible," one of the men let slip.

"Not if you have a magnetic trap in your hand," Calynn replied.

She held out her hand and the bullet hovered about ten centimeters above her hand.

"If I hadn't activated it," Calynn continued. "And this round cracked the containment field…"

"We would all be dead," the General finished her sentence.

"Ding, ding, ding," Calynn announced, pointing at the man. "Give the sexist pig a prize."

"You will not talk to me like that," the General grumbled.

"Talk to you like… do you want to never talk to me again? Get that fucking charger over here, so we can charge this stupid fucking laser and be on our way," Calynn said coldly. "Preferably, before another one of your morons tries to kill us all."

 The General turned and scowled at Kash. The man was furious. He clenched his jaw, and a deep crease formed between his eyebrows. Kash almost chuckled at how often the man was flaring his nostrils but managed to control himself. Laughing at the man when he was seething angry would have escalated things too much. He did decide to poke a little fun at the man.

"Hey, don't look at me," Kash remarked, pointing to Calynn. "She's the one in charge."

"Whores…" the General paused, struggling to correct himself.

The General's eyes darted back and forth between Kash and Calynn. His face was turning redder by the second.

"Women… cannot… be… in charge," the General muttered through his clenched teeth. "They are meant to submit, not lead."

"Well, she is in charge, sooo…" Kash replied snidely.

"Hey, pig," Calynn asserted as she approached. "Do you want me off your base or not?"

"Yes!" the General barked.

"Then tell the minions with the guns to go away," Calynn said, motioning with her hand like she was brushing them away.

"Have those minions over there," Calynn continued, pointing at the engineers. "Bring the big charger over here, so we can charge the piece of shit in there."

Calynn finished her rant by pointing into the cargo hold at the ballistic laser system they were carrying. She wasn't scowling at the General when she spoke, but she was being firm.

"Every minute you delay is another minute she's here," Kash added. "If her presence bothers you as much as you claim…"

"Stand down!" the General barked at his men. "Get that unit over here… don't just stand there, go help them move it!"

The men started to scurry about as the General barked orders at them. Calynn walked over and stood in front of Kash. She laced her fingers through his, and wrapped his arms around her midsection as they watched the men work.

"The charging will take four hourns," the General commented. "Could you take your distraction elsewhere?"

"Is that me?" Calynn asked, looking up at Kash. "Am I the distraction?"

"You are very distracting, beloved," Kash swooned, rubbing Calynn's belly. "But maybe it would be best to just distract me. Come on."

Kash wrapped his arm around Calynn's waist and gently lifted her off the ground. He spun them around and set her down facing into the cargo hold. Calynn was giggling and grinning ear to ear. Kash gave her a playful swat on her butt.

"Eeek," Calynn squealed playfully. "Thank you, sir. May I have another?"

"Get your ass up there before these guys start masturbating on you," Kash chuckled.

"Eww," Calynn complained. "Not that circle jerk thing again."

Stop #2

Kash was in the cargo hold examining the ballistic laser when he heard the HLD engaging. He noticed the change in color of the containment field. Fully charged the field had a light blue hue, but as its energy depleted it became a darker blue.

"I still say you should have fucked me with the bedroom door open," Calynn announced, entering the cargo hold.

"And I said I'm not an exhibitionist and didn't want to further enrage the man," Kash replied, glancing at Calynn. "What are you eating?"

"A spoonful of the berry compote."

"Straight?"

"I wanted to know how it tasted when it isn't in a shake."

"You're crazy."

"Why is that crazy?"

"It's basically concentrated berries, silly girl."

"It's really good," Calynn said, taking another lick of her spoon. "A little strong, but good."

"Well, don't eat all of it."

"I won't."

"We are weeks away from the farmer's market that makes it."

"I thought you made it?"

"No, I mean... I guess I could. I know how to make it. I just really don't want to spend all that time doing it, so I paid a nice lady at the market to make it for me," Kash explained. "She makes the compote and then reduces it down to concentrate it, so it doesn't take up as much room. Which is why... you only need a little bit."

"So, we'll get you some berries to make more."

Kash stopped and stared at Calynn for a moment. She was staring back at him, expressionless, like she didn't realize what she had just said. Kash slowly raised his left arm to point at the laser they were transporting.

"I'm not sure we have the time," Kash said, sarcastically. "This thing does go boom if we don't keep it charged."

"Oh, not like right now," Calynn explained. "Later."

"Or, and just hear me out, we wait... and go see the nice lady again," Kash added sarcastically. "So... maybe stop eating it right out of the jar so it lasts... okay?"

"Whatever," Calynn replied nonchalantly.

Kash shook his head and tried to focus on the ballistic laser again. All of the circuitry for the charging system had redundancies built in to prevent charging the laser without the proprietary charger. Kash couldn't see a way to bypass the self-destruct sequence that was built into the machine. He was looking for an impossibility. Maybe this machine didn't have a flaw to exploit, but he had to keep trying.

"I know that look," Calynn uttered as she approached. "You get that look when you think something is hopeless,"

She laid her hand on his chest and smiled softly. She was trying to be encouraging, but her furrowed brow told him a different story.

"You'll figure it out," Calynn continued. "I believe in you."

"Ahhhhh," Kash sighed loudly. "Maybe... maybe I just need a break... or a drink... the stronger the better."

"Go lay down and I'll make you that drink," Calynn told him. "And then give you a back rub to help you relax. We have twenty-seven hourns until the next stop and you need some rest."

"That's the best idea I've heard all week," Kash smiled.

When Kash awoke from his nap he was alone in his quarters. Calynn had the manuals for the laser sitting on his desk along with a mug. Kash got out of bed, pulled on his jeans, and sat at his desk. The mug was hot tea with honey that Kash happily sipped. Before digging into the manuals, Kash checked his email. There was one from Admiral Anne that he read briefly.

"Hey, you," Calynn said, entering the room. "How'd you sleep?"

Calynn walked up behind him and placed her hands on his shoulders.

"Wonderfully," Kash replied, looking up at her. "Thanks to those gifted hands of yours."

"You carry so much tension in your back, it's ridiculous. You're all knots."

"Yeah, well… I keep putting us in stressful situations, so it's kinda self-inflicted."

"I'll be sure to give you daily massages from now on."

"You just want to rub me with warming oils," Kash chuckled.

"Now why would I want to do that?" Calynn asked rhetorically.

Her hands moved down his chest and then she wrapped him in a hug.

"It's not like you have all these sexy muscles or anything," Calynn continued comically.

"Sure… it has nothing do with that," Kash said, matching her tone. "Not even a little bit… but I guess I can't blame you. I was voted sexiest man on board seven years running."

"Ass," Calynn giggled, standing up and smacking him gently on the arm. "Maybe I'll start walking around here topless and see how you like it."

"Fine," Kash feigned annoyance. "I'll put a shirt on, so my perfect physique doesn't bother you."

"Or… you can just not complain about me touching you."

Calynn put her hands back on his chest and rubbed around quickly. She was being silly, not sensual. When Kash looked up at her again, she was grinning ear to ear with her tongue hanging out the corner of her mouth. The smile definitely reached her eyes, and Kash was once again in awe of the body that was built for her. Calynn's synthetic body was nearly indistinguishable from an organic body, but her attitude was even more incredible than her body. She lived a life of extraordinary trauma, and she somehow came through that mess and ugliness… beautiful.

Kash smiled, grabbed Calynn's hand and led her around to sit on his lap. He wrapped his arm around her so his hand was on her belly and kissed her shoulder. She leaned back into him, laced her fingers through his, and pressed his hand firmly to her midsection. Kash was rubbing her thigh with his other hand and turned his attention back to his computer.

"Oh, it's from the Admiral," Calynn said, reading his screen.

"Yep, I asked her about that sexist general," Kash explained. "Turns out, he was the base commander."

"He was such an asshole," Calynn replied, laying her head against his.

"Read this part," Kash said, pointing to the paragraph on the screen. "Apparently, his whole planet is like that."

"It's their religion and their political beliefs?" Calynn asked rhetorically. "A whole planet of suppressed women that aren't allowed to do anything or go anywhere by themselves. That sounds horrible."

"Aww, what's wrong?" Kash joked. "You wouldn't want to be a kept woman?"

"Just lay here in bed and wait for you to come fuck me?" Calynn remarked with an edgy tone. "No, thank you. I rather like being able to go shopping and wearing the clothes I buy. I like going out to see shows or going to restaurants with you... And not having to ask permission to do everything or expressing my free will."

"And most importantly, not being in a damn box."

"I really like not being in a box," Calynn purred, snuggling into Kash. "That's my favorite thing ever. I never want to be in another box."

"I know, Baby Girl," Kash replied, hugging her tight. "I know... and I promise not to point out how square this room is or how much it resem..."

Calynn turned and punched him in the chest to interrupt him. She didn't hit him too hard, but it wasn't a light tap either. She tried to get off his lap, but he was laughing and holding her down. Eventually, Calynn joined in his laughter and finally relaxed. She grabbed his hand, lifted her shirt, and placed his hand on her bare stomach. She held it there with both hands like that was his punishment for his comment.

"You're so mean to me," Calynn whined.

"I just like to pick on you."

"I normally don't mind, but sometimes box jokes make me sad."

"I'm sorry I made you sad," Kash apologized.

Kash pulled Calynn's leg over the arm of the chair so she was now sideways on his lap. She nuzzled into the side of his neck and kissed him softly. She pushed her right arm around his back and had her other hand on his chest. It was the first time in a while that she did something that Omia used to do, and it made him tense up ever so slightly. Calynn must have sensed what he was feeling somehow, because she lifted her head to look at him.

"What?" Kash asked.

"Something changed just now," Calynn replied. "What was it?"

"Oh... you, uh..."

"What?"

"It was the first time in a long time that you did an Omia-ism," Kash blurted out.

"Huh... oh, the neck kisses," Calynn replied. "I forgot she did that. I'm sorry."

"It's okay," Kash smiled softly. "You do it so rarely now, but I guess it still gets to me sometimes."

"Me too," Calynn moped.

"Let's forget about doing more research on that stupid laser for a bit and take a nap together," Kash said, trying to uplift their moods. "Just me and you spooning like we used to do... warm skin and warm kisses... holding hands and long hugs. What do you think?"

"That sounds wonderful," Calynn smiled.

The rest of their journey to the next star base was uneventful and they soon found themselves on approach. Their diplomatic status ensured they docked quickly, and the defense rings were positioned far from the dock once again.

The base commander was an energetic young man that greeted them personally. The man was all smiles and a pleasure to be around. His men cheerfully followed his orders and seemed to feed off his energy. He insisted that Kash and Calynn just call him Lee, and also invited them to have lunch. The base was clean and well maintained. Every crew member they passed smiled at them, and the Commander knew them all by name. Kash could tell immediately that this was a very well-run base which put him at ease.

"This base is so much better than the last one," Calynn announced, grinning from ear to ear.

"Oh yeah

," Lee replied. "Why is that?"

"We weren't allowed off the ship for starters," Calynn stated matter-of-factly.

"Seriously... Why?" the Commander asked.

"Because I'm a girl," Calynn giggled.

"You're kidding?"

"I wish we were," Kash answered. "You are way more hospitable than they were."

"And we could really use a good hot meal," Calynn added.

"I'd offer you a cot too, if you were staying longer," Lee offered. "I find that happy people work harder and make better decisions, and way out here… that's kind of important."

"You got that right," Kash agreed. "You definitely don't want a mutiny on your hands out here."

"Excuse me, Commander," a soldier addressed the man as she approached. "You're needed in the Con."

"I'll be right there, Neeria," Lee replied and then turned to Kash and Calynn. "I guess this is where we part ways for now. The galley is just at the end of this hall on the left. I'll meet you there as soon as I can."

The Commander followed Neeria and left Kash and Calynn to find their own way to the galley. Everyone they passed in the hallway smiled and said hi as they walked. It was almost surreal how everyone aboard the base was so happy. When they entered the galley, two officers stood up to greet them.

"You must be Kash and Calynn," the woman said as she approached. "I'm Captain Gura, but you can call me Kadee, and this is Captain Thorkel."

"Levi is fine," Captain Thorkel told them, extending his hand. "A pleasure to meet you both."

"Are you hungry?" Kadee asked, motioning into the galley.

"Famished," Calynn replied, smiling.

Kash and Calynn ate their fill while chatting and laughing with the crew. When the combat pilots showed up, the stories were getting exciting. Kash told stories from his time in the Legionnaires and devoured every tale the other pilots told. He was having so much fun, he almost forgot why they were there.

Calynn's face was practically glowing from her smile. She was having just as much fun as Kash listening to the pilot's tales. Some of the pilots were telling the stories directly to her. Kash figured they were trying to impress the gorgeous blonde. Calynn must have figured that out also, because she moved a little closer to Kash and made sure she was touching him or he was touching her at all times… when she wasn't getting more food, of course.

Calynn was on her third piece of pie when the base suddenly shook. The galley got quiet instantly as everyone looked around trying to figure out what was going on. The silence seemed to hang on forever until red lights started flashing and an alarm broke the silence.

"Battle stations. Battle stations," a robotic voice echoed through the base. "All hands, battle stations."

Kash grabbed Calynn by the hand and raced out of the galley. He turned the corner into the hallway and they both sprinted back towards the docks. The hallway quickly became crowded as the crew scurried to their stations. Kash felt the base shake again and slowed his pace for a moment so he didn't lose his balance. Once the shaking subsided, he accelerated again.

"What could make the whole base shake?" Calynn asked as they ran.

"I don't know, but it can't be good."

When they got to the docks, Kash tried to jerk the door open, but it was locked.

"Fuck!" Kash yelled and tried the handle again.

"What do we do now?" Calynn asked, she had a little fear in her voice.

Kash looked down both sides of the long hallway at the back of the dock. He wondered if they could get to their ship another way.

"Let's try down here," Kash said as he started to run down the hall.

When they got to the next door of their dock, Kash jerked the handle but the door didn't budge. Kash jerked on the handle in frustration a few times and growled. He needed to get to his ship and get off this base to keep Calynn safe. He calmed himself before turning to Calynn.

"Let's keep going," Kash told Calynn.

The duo ran further down the hallway until they got to a T. Kash looked right then left. He saw combat pilots to the left, so he turned that way and jogged after them. He hoped that if he followed them, he would find an officer barking orders. An officer that could hopefully get them to their ship.

Kash and Calynn followed the pilots through a door that was marked 'pilots only'. Kash recognized it as a ready room. The pilots that were on standby would be here and ready to launch at a moment's notice. And then Kash heard what he was hoping to hear.

"This isn't a drill people! Get your heads in the game!" a man barked as he ushered pilots to their fighters. "Now move, move, move!"

The man barking orders was dressed in overalls that were folded down with the sleeves tied around his waist, and his military-issued drab gray undershirt. He appeared to be in his mid-to-late thirties with his hair and beard trimmed to the same length. Kash did notice the man was just as muscular as he was, just shorter. As soon as Kash saw the man's rank on his shirt he approached with a purpose.

"Chief, I can't get to my bird!" Kash said, sharper than he intended, but there wasn't time to hold back.

"Are you the one with that monstrosity on board?" the Chief barked.

"Indeed I am."

"That dock is on lock down!" the Chief continued. "Damn pirates are bombarding us with everything they got to get at that thing."

"How do they know it's here?" Kash queried.

"I was about to ask you the same thing," the Chief replied.

"We think there's a mole," Calynn added. "There's no way they tracked my flight path. I used a variation on a Clothoid Curve wrapped helically around a parabolic axis."

"That was a whole lot of words to say you didn't fly straight, young lady," the Chief remarked.

"We think a bureaucrat is working against us," Kash added.

"That would explain how they know which dock to attack," the Chief replied. "They're coming in under the rings and hitting that dock directly."

"They can do that?" Calynn asked.

"The defense rings have one weakness," Chief explained. "If you can squeeze in at the far ends of the base…"

The base shook again from the attack, interrupting the Chief. Everyone except Calynn lost their balance and nearly fell to the ground. The pretty blonde only needed to take a half step to widen her base and she was able to remain standing with ease. Kash and the Chief fell to one knee but quickly righted themselves. The chief gave Calynn a look of disbelief as he got back to his feet. He stared at her with raised eyebrows and his mouth hung open as he tried to understand how the beauty was still standing.

"I have exceptional balance," Calynn answered his question before he asked it.

Kash wanted to get the Chief back on point quickly. Firstly, to get back on The Cat, and secondly, so he didn't ask too many questions about Calynn.

"Chief, if we're gone, they won't have a reason to continue their assault," Kash said, adamantly. "Get me to my ship and we'll go."

"You won't stand a chance..."

"I'm a combat pilot, Chief," Kash interrupted.

"Then suit up and get into a fighter!" the Chief barked.

"I'm better in my bird," Kash explained.

"And I can do tiny hyper-light jumps that make it impossible to attack us," Calynn added.

"Trust me, Chief," Kash continued. "It's better for everyone if we're aboard The Alley Cat Savant."

The Chief paused and looked back and forth at Kash and Calynn. His brow was still furrowed but Kash couldn't tell if it was concern for them or disbelief. He had no reason to trust them, but every reason to get rid of them. His posture and eyes changed when the Chief made his decision. His brow relaxed and he stood tall to address the duo.

"Follow me," the Chief ordered.

The Chief jogged back down the hallway towards the dock where Kash's ship was moored. He stopped at a maintenance door and used his ID card to open the lock.

"This is the mechanical corridor between this dock and yours," Chief explained. "Follow the ramp down to the T, turn left, and go about a hundred meters until you get to the second access ladder. That will bring you up into the dock close to your bird."

"Thanks, Chief," Kash said, smiling at the man.

"I'm not done yet," the Chief continued, "I want you on comms to coordinate, and you follow fucking orders! Are we clear?"

"Yes sir, Chief," Kash replied, snapping to attention.

"We're on Theta spectrum, Wave 5332, and drop the hertz by point four four," Chief continued.

"Theta 5332 with a point four four drop, aye, Chief," Kash confirmed, offering a handshake.

"Good luck out there," the Chief stated, shaking Kash's offered hand.

"You as well, Chief."

Kash smiled and nodded at the man before jogging down the corridor with Calynn in tow. Another attack rocked the base as they got to the T, slowing their pace. Kash stumbled and had to brace himself against the walls of the narrow dimly lit passageway. They were back up to speed when the shaking subsided. They continued moving until they got to the second ladder. Kash quickly ascended the ladder, flipped open the access door, and climbed up into the dock.

Kash glanced around and saw the dock was empty except for The Cat and the charger for the ballistic laser. Kash grabbed Calynn's hand to help her up and kicked the access door closed. The duo jogged the short distance to The Cat and climbed the ramp to the cargo hold. Kash immediately noted the color of the containment field. It looked like it was mostly charged, but not as charged as it was before. The charging unit was still hooked up to the laser by a set a cables that were as big around as his arm.

"We have to shut down the charger before unplugging it," Kash instructed, pointing at the cables. "There should be a big, red kill switch on the control panel."

"On it," Calynn replied and walked to the charger.

The hum of the charger soon stopped and Kash disengaged the couplers on the charging cables so Calynn could pull them out of their ship. Calynn closed the cargo doors, and they worked their way to the cockpit.

"You fly and I'll shoot?" Calynn asked.

"Sounds like a plan to me. Be ready on the HLD too."

"I'm already plotting a course."

As soon as Kash got the comms tuned to the base's channel, they were bombarded with chatter. Pilots shouted over one another, calling out targets, desperate warnings, and pleas for backup. Kash closed his eyes for a moment, letting the chaos wash over him as he tried to piece together the situation. The pirates were sending strike-fighters inside the defense rings while pounding the base from a distance with heavy artillery. The defense rings were forced to focus on shielding the base from the artillery, leaving the base's pilots outnumbered and unsupported inside the rings. One by one, they were getting picked off by the bigger and stronger strike-fighters.

Kash and Calynn looked at each other for a moment. Their new friends were dying as fast as they launched. The determination grew in Calynn's eyes and Kash felt it growing inside him also. Although they had only just met, they weren't going to let them get slaughtered.

Kash adjusted the trim on the ship and keyed up the comms.

"Dock six control, this is The Alley Cat Savant," Kash spoke concisely. "Open the doors and get me in this fight!"

"They're after your ship, Kash," Lee replied. "You should stay put."

"Fuck that! I'm ramming it right down their throats. Let me at 'em!"

The Base Commander didn't have to think long about Kash's request. The lights came on above the hanger doors to indicate they were opening. Kash's heart was hammering in his chest. He readjusted his grip on the controls as he waited for the door to slide open. For those ten or twelve seconds, he was a caged animal yearning to be set free. Kash gripped the controls tight and took a deep breath trying to control his adrenaline. He needed to be focused, not feral.

"Here we go," Kash uttered, pushing the throttle.

Kash didn't want them to be a sitting target, so they shot out of the dock at a blistering speed. As soon as they exited the dock Kash had to immediately evade one of the pirates' strike-fighters so they didn't collide. Kash spun The Cat around to give Calynn a good shot, and she delivered. The cockpit of the enemy vessel ripped open like a tin can from the pressurized air inside escaping to the vacuum of space. The nose of the ship was completely destroyed, but everything from the forward stabilizers back to the main wings and engines was intact.

Calynn was already firing on a second and third enemy ship before Kash completed his spin. Both cockpits suffered the same explosive decompression as the first, air screaming out into the void. They had barely been in the fight for five seconds and Calynn already killed three enemies. Four more strike-fighters turned to engage them, but they didn't fire their weapons. As the enemies closed the distance, Kash had to jerk the controls into a steep dive in order to dodge two magnetic tethers that were launched at them. One tether was close enough that his gauges went haywire for a split second.

"What were those?" Calynn asked, firing at the enemy ships.

"Tethers," Kash replied. "They mean to capture us. Get us out of here."

Kash heard the HLD spinning up, but then nothing happened. When he glanced at Calynn her head was cocked and her brow furrowed.

"Something is interfering with the Hyper-light cone," Calynn announced. "I can't… it won't engage."

"Shit!" Kash spat. "They must have deployed a Hyper-Lumic Shroud."

"The what now?"

"Scan for energy dispersal patterns outside of the normal Hyper-Light spectrum," Kash instructed, urgently. "The shroud uses inverse energy waves to interfere with the hyper-light cone so it can't form. The bubble is dispersed so we can't travel within it."

"Scanning," Calynn replied.

Kash was too busy evading the enemy ships to see what Calynn was doing, but he chanced another glance at her when he heard her gasp.

"What?"

"Kash, it's… it's everywhere," Calynn's voice was barely a whisper. "The whole star base is completely surrounded."

"They're trying to trap us here," Kash relented, his voice tense. "And if we can't break through, we're as good as theirs."

"So, what do we do?"

"I don't know," Kash sighed.

"Kash…"

"I Don't Know!" Kash interrupted forcefully. "Oh, shit!"

Kash jerked the controls hard to the right at the last moment to avoid another magnetic tether. He pulled up so they were skimming the surface of the star base. He hoped being that close to the base would hinder the enemy's targeting.

"Sorry," Calynn apologized. "Sometimes I forget that you can't multitask like me."

"Yeah, I have to focus on what…"

"Kash, why are you still here?" Lee's voice burst over the comms.

"They're using a Hyper-Lumic Shroud," Calynn replied.

"They can't have those," Lee replied, sounding puzzled.

"Well, they do," Calynn added. "Scan for it yourself."

Kash was glad Calynn was conversing with Lee. This let him focus on flying. Especially since he was skimming the outer surface of the base. One wrong move spelled disaster for him and the entire base, but it was keeping the enemy from firing more tethers at the moment. More importantly, it was giving them time to plan.

"You can't do your Goddess thing to get us out of here?" Kash asked.

"I can't see the energy that they are using, let alone manipulate it," Calynn replied. "I guess because it disrupts energy so well... maybe?"

"So, it takes a weapon meant to engulf entire planets built by a government think tank with an unlimited budget to actually contain you... nice."

"At least it proves that I am not a god, contrary to your dreams. WATCH OUT!"

Calynn drew his attention to a strike-fighter that was trying to flank them. Kash banked hard to avoid yet another tether and turned directly into the path of the enemy ship. The enemy fired a second tether followed closely by a third. Kash performed a barrel roll to avoid the shots and Calynn returned fire mid roll. Her aim was perfect as usual, and the ship's pilots were sucked out into the vacuum of space. Kash marveled at how it looked like if you plugged a new cockpit into the ship, it would be perfectly functional again.

"How are you doing that every time?" Kash asked her. "You're leaving ninety percent of the ship unharmed."

"Their shields are weak at the back of the cockpits," Calynn replied. "It's almost like a seam or something, but it's easy..."

"Kash, I'll send a barrage from the cannons to disrupt the shroud. You need to follow the shots through," Lee cut in urgently over the comms. "It might just work."

"Let's do it," Calynn replied, no hesitation in her voice. "If you get us out of here, they'll hopefully pull back on their assault against your base. We're clearly their target."

"Calculating firing solution," Lee responded, his voice tight.

"Oh, and make sure all pilots know the strike-fighters' shields are vulnerable right at the base of the cockpit, just before the stabilizers," Calynn added. "They'll need to aim from above."

"I'll relay it. Proceed to... here," Lee ordered. "Move now!"

A new nav-point blinked onto their screen, and Kash rolled the ship over, accelerating toward it.

"How will we know if the barrage works?" Calynn asked.

"You'll either still be under power," Lee replied hesitantly, "or completely disabled. One or the other."

"That sounds super," Calynn replied sarcastically. "And not at all terrifying."

Kash ignored Calynn's comment. He was too focused on getting through the defense rings and beyond. Kash was at full throttle when he hit the gap between two of the defense rings. He held his breath until they were clear of them and let out a sigh of relief.

"We're not out of danger yet, Boss," Calynn said. "We have two fighters tailing us and artillery at your three o'clock high."

Kash hoped that The Cat was fast enough to outrun the fighters, and his evasive maneuvers could evade any artillery strikes at this range.

"Firing the cannons... now... now... now," Lee announced.

Kash watched as the first set of rounds crossed paths at the perimeter of the shroud. He quickly figured out what the plan was as did Calynn. She already had the HLD spinning up. The second set of rounds impacted each other and exploded. The third set struck each other also and the shock wave shook The Cat. A bubble of light soon engulfed their ship.

Kash knew they were relatively safe traveling faster than light, but it took a moment for the relief to sink in. The tension slowly left his body, and he turned to look at Calynn.

"We're away," Calynn smiled. "Away and safe."

"Thank the Gods."

Stop #3

"Are you sure there nothing from the shroud on the hull?" Kash asked Calynn.

"Yes, I'm sure," Calynn replied, but she sounded unsure. "It's just..."

"Just what?"

"I don't know, but... something feels off."

"And you scanned everything and there's nothing on the sensors?"

"I did," Calynn said, exasperated. "Maybe I'm just being crazy."

"Stay away from my sweaters," Kash teased.

"Ha ha, asshole," Calynn retorted with some contempt in her voice. "Just... never mind."

"Oh, come on, Baby Girl," Kash chuckled. "I'm just trying to help."

"Then why are you grilling me like that?" Calynn whined.

"Because maybe I will ask a question that you haven't thought of yet," Kash said, soothingly.

Kash knelt down beside his beautiful companion who was seated at the helm. Her arms were crossed across her chest, and she was blankly staring into her lap like she was trying to be emotionless. He tried to reassure her by placing one hand on her lap and the other on her arm. He smiled at her softly and caressed her.

"I trust your intuition more than any other... well, maybe I trust Plekish's intuition more, but you're a very close second," Kash reassured her. "If you feel like something is off... then I believe you and want to help you figure out what it is."

Calynn finally looked up from her lap and looked him in the eye. She remained blank and emotionless at first, but Kash knew her too well to assume she would stay that way. He stood up just before her brow raised and she scrunched her face. She leaped into his arms and started sobbing.

"It's okay, Baby Girl," Kash soothed her. "Just let it out."

The duo stood there for a few minutes while Calynn cried. Kash held her tight and kissed the top of her head repeatedly. He wasn't sure why she was on this emotional roller coaster, but he would help get her through it if he could. He hoped that her feeling something was off was just some pent-up emotions from narrowly escaping from the pirates and being accosted by the other base commander for simply being a girl.

"Wait," Calynn said, suddenly stiffening and pulling back. "Do you hear that?"

Calynn held him at arm's length as she looked around the room at... nothing. Or so Kash thought.

"Son of a bitch!" Calynn hollered suddenly.

Calynn marched back down the hall towards the cargo hold and sealed the doors. As soon as the double doors closed, Kash noticed a difference in the ambient sounds coming from his ship. Calynn hurried back to the helm and pulled up the one monitor. She was using her link to run the scans, because the data on the screen was flipping impossibly fast. Kash had to wait for it to settle before he understood what she was looking for.

The screen settled showing a sound frequency. An alert popped up on the screen that was flashing pictures of death and destruction. Horrible imagery from wars and murders rapidly flashed before their eyes. Kash's emotions darkened immediately, because he knew what it was from his time with the Legionnaires.

"Those mother fuckers!" Kash growled.

"That's meant to attack nerve centers like me, isn't it?" Calynn asked, pointing at the screen.

"It's psychological warfare. It incapacitates nerve centers by overwhelming them with despair and sorrow or some twisted shit like that. I've seen it used to make ships go dark or make them collide with a sun while using the HLD," Kash said, angrily pointing back towards the cargo hold. "It's coming from that fucking laser, isn't it? They planted another device in it somewhere, didn't they?"

"They sure did," Calynn said assuredly. "And it's nasty."

"By the Gods... this has been a fucking suicide mission from the word go!"

"It got stronger when I started to cry. Like it was trying to press its advantage over me," Calynn explained. "It was only then that I could detect it."

"That's what it does. It slowly cracks into the subconscious and gives you horrible dreams. Then, when the mind is vulnerable it amps up the attack until the mind breaks," Kash said, turning to go to the cargo hold. "Send that frequency to my goggles. I'll find it and..."

"Wait, Boss," Calynn said, grabbing his hand.

Kash turned back to see Calynn smiling. He must have looked as confused as he was because she answered his question before he asked it.

"I can detect it now," Calynn explained, grinning ear to ear. "I got this."

Kash relaxed his brow as the realization hit him and he smiled back at Calynn.

"God mode?" Kash asked.

"Goddess mode, thank you very much," Calynn replied, with a snarky tone. "My tits still haven't fallen off."

"And you're still not allowed to use my own sarcasm against me," Kash chuckled. "There's rules against that."

"You can spank me later," Calynn smirked.

Kash shook his head and watched Calynn's eyes start to glow. He glanced over her shoulder to see the frequency was still up on her monitor. The wave fluttered, got more intense, fluttered again, then disappeared from the screen. Kash looked back to Calynn who was smiling and shifting her weight back and forth like she was doing a little dance.

"It tried to fight back, but they clearly don't know who they're messing with," Calynn stated confidently.

"Poor little A.I. didn't stand a chance against a walking, talking supercomputer, huh?"

"I created a feedback loop in its main power supply, so it cooked its own processors," Calynn explained. "That way they don't know that we know about it, and now I know they exist so I can scan for them."

"I'm beginning to think we should dump our cargo, go get Aja, and whisk her away somewhere safe," Kash admitted. "Before this shit gets out of hand."

"Don't I wish," Calynn agreed.

"I was expecting you to argue."

"Yeah, well, after seeing all those government weapons they used against us…" Calynn shuddered, trailing off. "Those horrible weapons that… that you knew. How did you know what they were? What exactly did you do when you were in the military?"

"I told you already. I was a combat pilot."

"But how did you know?"

"Because I fought for the side that used them!" Kash's words burst out of him. "As a Legionnaire I helped the Consortium… we murdered entire planets. They deployed the Hyper-Lumic Shroud to contain the ships… my job was to destroy anyone trying to escape! That's why I can't stand them now! And… and I hate myself for…"

Kash's words fell off, the weight of his past pressing down on him. Before he realized it, Calynn was holding him, her arms wrapped tightly around him, pulling him close. He closed his eyes and let himself sink into her embrace, feeling the grief he'd buried for so long break through. A grief that few knew he possessed.

After a moment, Kash took a deep breath, the scent of her skin grounding him. Slowly, he pulled back, meeting her gaze. Her eyes were wide, her expression soft… she was worried about him, not judging him.

"You know you don't have to worry about me, right?" Kash asked Calynn softly. "Since having you here is the cure."

Calynn didn't respond with words. She smiled softly, popped up on her toes, and gave him a warm kiss on the lips. It was a small gesture, but it was exactly what he needed.

"You still find ways to amaze me," Kash whispered, embracing her again.

Kash spent the rest of their journey to the next stop trying to apologize for his outburst, and Calynn spent that time trying to comfort him. Kash felt surprisingly relaxed when they arrived at the next star base. He joined Calynn at the helm as they made their final approach.

"Attention star base, attention star base… this is the diplomatic courier, the Alley Cat Savant," Calynn announced over the comms. "Please advise a course."

The duo waited for a reply that never came.

"Are you on the right channel?" Kash asked.

"I checked twice," Calynn replied. "Attention star base, attention star base, this is the diplomatic courier, the Alley Cat Savant. Come in."

Again, they waited for a reply.

"Hello. Hi, I'm here," a man's voice finally replied. "Who did you say you were again?"

"The Alley Cat Savant," Kash responded firmly. "We're the diplomatic courier you should be expecting."

"Oh… okay, umm," the voice replied. "I, uh… don't see, oh wait, there you are. Oh, shit. You have the thing. You need to go to dock six."

"Great… and where is dock six?" Kash asked, annoyed. "Or should I just guess?"

"Hey, Boss," Calynn whispered, pointing out the windshield. "No drones anywhere."

Kash scanned the area around the base and she was right. There were no drones of any kind anywhere to be seen. It would be one thing for the maintenance drones to be absent, but it's very unusual for there to be no guidance or patrol and surveillance drones flying around. The base nearly looked abandoned.

"Umm," the voice continued, but sounded shaky and unsure of himself. "I don't know how to, uh… can I just go down and open the blast doors? You'd be able to tell which one it is that way?"

Kash paused for a moment, dumbfounded. He couldn't believe what he just heard. When he looked at Calynn she looked just as confused as him.

"Is he serious?" Kash asked Calynn rhetorically, then keyed the comms again. "Are you serious?"

"Sorry, sir," the man answered, "but we are terribly undermanned. I'll meet you at the dock in a couple minutes."

Kash didn't know how to respond to that, so he just stood there silently… still dumbfounded.

"I guess they're just undermanned," Calynn repeated sarcastically, breaking the silence.

"You don't say?" Kash feigned curiosity.

"Yep… oh, hey… you know what happened the other day?" Calynn added with a snarky tone. "So, we were going to this big government star base, and the weirdest thing happened."

"Was it undermanned?"

"How ever did you guess that?" Calynn faked her surprise. "Weird right?"

"How about you just get us closer so we know which dock to enter… when the doors open… apparently."

"I'm guessing this never happened before?" Calynn asked, as she moved them closer to the base.

"I've never even heard of something like this happening," Kash replied, confidently. "There's normally too many people for the number of bunks and you end up having to share with someone on a different shift."

"So, this is waaay off base… pun intended."

"And a little unsettling too."

Calynn took them in, and they waited near the center of the base where the docks were. As they waited, Kash examined the surface of the star base. He noticed some of the marker lights were burned out, which violated Military Regulations. The next thing he noticed was a few of the maintenance panels were slightly ajar. Someone had done some work there, but they didn't replace the panels correctly. Sloppy craftsmanship like that wasn't tolerated on a star base for obvious reasons. Complacency, especially when maintaining the base, could lead to a catastrophic failure of vital systems… and the death of everyone aboard.

"It's too quiet," Calynn muttered. "I don't like it."

"I'm not liking it much either, Baby Girl."

"Dock six control to… uh… the diplomatic vessel," the man said. "Opening the blast doors now."

Kash and Calynn both scanned the area looking for the dock that was opening. When they didn't see anything, Calynn moved them to the next group of docks.

"There it is," Calynn announced. "Taking us in."

Kash paid particular attention to the atmospheric fields as they passed through them. The condition of them made him the most nervous, but they seemed to be in perfect working order. They buzzed as The Cat passed through them, then closed behind them making Kash feel slightly better about being there.

Three men were waiting near the charger for the ballistic laser. One of the men was waving cordially as they wheeled the charger closer. Kash found it odd that the men all had on a different colored uniform. The man waving was wearing the navy blue of the engineers and mechanics, one man was a custodian in food service, and the last man was a pilot.

"Are we supposed to wave back?" Calynn asked, tilting her head as she watched them.

"I haven't a clue," Kash replied absently.

"You sound nervous."

"That's because I am."

"What can I do to make you less nervous?"

"Tell me that this base is somehow fully functional and NOT falling apart at the seams."

"Well… I suppose I could hack it and find out," Calynn said playfully with a sly smile.

"You do know that there's more than one…"

"More than one nerve center," Calynn interrupted. "Yes, I know… but they still aren't me. I've been freed from my box and am no longer… shackled to the same limitations. I can get it done."

"You stay put and work on that hack," Kash ordered, gesturing for her to stay in the cockpit. "I'll go meet our new friends."

"On it, Boss," Calynn confirmed, her eyes glowing bright white.

Kash turned and headed to the cargo hold. Calynn had the door already lowering before he got there. The three men were waiting for it to lower so they could pull the charging cables up the ramp to charge the ballistic laser. Kash stopped at the top of the ramp and took a closer look at the men. They seemed cheerful despite looking like they hadn't showered or washed their clothes in days if not weeks.

"Welcome aboard, Captain Smith," the man in blue greeted him, smiling. "Sorry for the state of affairs here, but uh…"

"But we've been abandoned," the pilot finished his sentence.

"Abandoned?" Kash queried.

"That's a long story, Captain," the man in blue answered. "Let's get you charging first."

"Give me a hand with this, Hemsan," the man in blue said to the pilot, and then turned to the other man. "Orsil, once we have it hooked up, you can fire it up with this button."

"You got it, Chief," Orsil replied.

"Chief?" Kash asked, puzzled. "Wasn't it you that answered when we hailed?"

"It was, Captain," the Chief answered.

"Chief Volci is the base commander now," Hemsan added.

"No, I'm not," Volci explained, albeit reluctantly. "I'm just trying to keep us breathing... hopefully we get a new Commander soon."

"Forgive my bluntness, Chief, but your boat looks like it's about to sink and you're clearly an engineer," Kash snapped. "Commander or not, the fucking maintenance needs done!"

"I KNOW!" Chief Volci hollered.

The man had a fire in his eyes for a split second, but then his attitude changed to something more... defeated. He stared at the ground and shook his head.

"I'm supposed to have a team of two hundred to do the maintenance of the ships and the base itself," Volci admitted solemnly. "I only have forty-five left."

"We try to help," Orsil added, "but we have to be taught how to do everything."

"We do our best," Hemsan agreed.

Kash looked past the men at a pile of dismantled drones. It appeared like they had been pillaged for parts. Kash felt a pang of guilt as the reality of the situation became blatantly obvious. He just barked at the Chief insinuating his incompetence, but it wasn't that at all. They weren't on the brink of disaster out of laziness or that they didn't care. They were fighting a losing battle against time. Without proper support, the base would crumble around them faster than they can put it back together.

"What happened here?" Kash asked thoughtfully.

Chief Volci didn't respond. He continued to stare at the ground... defeated.

"We're probably not supposed to tell you this," Hemsan muttered, leaning closer to Kash, "but the commander, sorry... former commander... well, his dad assigned him this post. He's a big-time bureaucrat and wanted the prestige of having a son as a base commander. And now that things have gone to hell... he'd rather let us rot than admit his son was a screw-up."

"Everything was so messed up when the commander left," Volci mumbled, dejected. "All the other officers packed up and left right after he did. They didn't even want to try to fix it."

"And they took all of their families and support teams too," Hemsan added. "They took all of our biggest ships and needed pilots to fly them. So now, we don't even have a single cargo ship left."

"Wait, what?" Kash asked urgently. "No cargo ships... then how do you get supplies?"

"I built a crate," Volci replied, pointing at a makeshift crate sitting down the dock. "We tow it behind a fighter."

"Pain in the fucking ass," Hemsan murmured under his breath.

"But at least we can eat," Orsil concluded.

Kash gritted his teeth as his anger grew. These people weren't just abandoned... they were written off. Their lives were forfeit because their commander's father didn't want any bad press.

"Motherfucking bureaucrats!" Kash's temper boiled over. "Those fucking assholes just... sorry."

Kash paused his rant, closed his eyes and took a deep breath. He was yelling at the wrong people. These were the victims of the bureaucracy, not the perpetrators. After another deep breath Kash continued.

"Sorry about that. Sometimes I get... frustrated with our wonderful government," Kash explained with a hint of sarcasm.

"Trust us," Hemsan replied. "We understand."

"Frankly, I'm a little surprised that they didn't send something because of your arrival, Captain Smith," Volci stated.

"Please, call me Kash," Kash offered with a soft smile. "And why do you say that?"

"The orders for your visit came from higher up than the father," Volci explained. "I was hoping they wouldn't want you to see... this."

Volci motioned to the pile of disassembled drones.

"I figured they would want to make everything look better than it is," Volci continued. "We've been able to do so much with nothing that... we could have stretched the extra supplies so far."

Volci noticed Kash was still staring at the pile of scrap. When Kash looked back at him, he saw a hint of confidence… no… no, it was grit and determination that he saw in Volci's eyes.

"It's amazing what you can build with the right spare parts," Volci added with a sly smile.

"I'm impressed, Chief," Kash offered. "And I'm guessing by the lack of the commander's presence, they felt the base wasn't safe enough for his return?"

"We have the entire bottom half shut down and sealed off so we can use it as parts," Volci explained. "We only left ourselves access to that side's nerve center… so we still have some base defenses."

"But we've been out of food for them for months," Orsil added. "We've been grinding up what we can but…"

"I have some NeuroPaste," Kash interrupted.

"They really need it," Calynn added from behind him, with a sorrowful tone. "They're struggling so much. You're going to start losing all the systems they control soon."

"It's already started…"

Kash heard one of them speaking but his attention was on Calynn. She looked fidgety while descending the ladder. Her big eyes and raised brow told Kash everything he needed to know. She wasn't just worried about the other nerve centers, their condition had her a little scared. She rushed over to Kash and handed him two tubes of NeuroPaste. Kash held her shaking hands in his. He knew what he did next would help soothe her, so he didn't hesitate.

"How can we help?" Kash asked, spinning back to their hosts. "Can we push this big piece of shit laser out of here and go get you some supplies? There's plenty of room for food, spare parts…"

Kash turned and stared into Calynn's pretty, brown eyes before he continued.

"Lots of NeuroPaste, too," Kash added. "We wouldn't want your nerve centers to suffer in silence. They are completely at our mercy for their nourishment."

The three men didn't reply because they clearly didn't know what to say.

"It can sit here and charge while we're gone right?" Calynn asked timidly. "Chief?"

"Uh… sure," Chief Volci mumbled. "But… why?"

"Because those corporate bureaucrat assholes are fucking you every bit as hard as they're fucking us," Kash replied with an upbeat tone. "And I think it would be funny if we helped each other just to spite those fuck heads."

"You would really help us?" Hemsan asked in disbelief.

"Absolutely," Kash smiled.

"I... I don't know what to say," Volci added, mirroring Hemsan's tone.

"Say yes, silly," Calynn said gleefully. "But can someone go feed the nerve centers quick? They are pretty weak... sorry, but I scanned them."

Kash knew she was lying about the scan, but the others didn't. Calynn's information was due to her hacking the nerve centers.

The three men looked at each other, and Kash watched as their disbelief finally faded. An air of confidence returned to the Chief. He squared his shoulders and stood tall.

"We've been hanging on by a thread, but if you're serious about helping... maybe we've got a fighting chance," Volci said confidently. "But I have to ask why?"

"We would absolutely love to have this monstrosity off of our ship for a little while," Kash answered.

"What a stress relief that would be," Calynn added. "Although someone else might have to be the pilot, because I... might be able to actually take a nap with that thing gone."

"So, we relieve some of your stress for a temporary relief in ours," Kash continued. "It's win win."

Chief Volci thought for a moment, nodded, and smiled at Kash and Calynn. His relief was evident when he started barking orders to his comrades. He radioed for more people to come and assist with moving the laser out of The Cat's cargo hold. A teenaged girl came to get the NeuroPaste and scurried off quickly once she had it. The group used four hover-skids to skillfully remove the laser from his ship and then celebrated the small victory.

Word had spread throughout the base about the impending supply run and a crowd had gathered. A small committee had formed to discuss what they needed the most. Kash heard them prioritizing parts for much needed repairs over even food. The grit of these people was astounding. For many of them the base was home as they had nowhere else to go, and they were adamant about saving their home.

Kash turned to Calynn and nodded for her to join him for a private conversation. The duo moved to the far end of the cargo hold near the ladder.

"Why are you so fidgety?"

"I've been in their minds, Kash," Calynn murmured, her voice tinged with sorrow. "Trapped, used... used for what you can do, and not for who you are. Those nerve centers didn't ask to be put in those boxes, but now they're keeping an entire base alive."

"I didn't think they had... awareness?" Kash glanced at her, frowning.

"Not like me," Calynn admitted. "But they're alive, Kash. And when you're alive, whether you can scream it or not, you feel pain. And believe me when I say... those nerve centers are in pain."

"Then I hope that little girl gets to them quickly," Kash said soothingly, hugging Calynn tight.

Kash buried his face in Calynn's hair and kissed the top of her head. He was so worried about her that he didn't notice Volci approaching.

"Is she okay?" Volci asked kindly.

"She will be," Kash replied, looking up at the man. "She's worried about the health of your nerve centers."

Volci suddenly looked puzzled by Kash's comment.

"Without going into too much detail," Kash continued. "She had a family member that had the misfortune of becoming one."

"That would..." Volci paused and laid his hand on Calynn's shoulder. "I'm so sorry for your loss. I guess I never thought of them that way."

"No one ever does," Calynn murmured into Kash's chest.

Kash rested his chin on Calynn's head and squeezed her tight.

"Is there something we can do to make sure they don't suffer anymore?" Calynn asked, her face still buried in his chest.

"We have more NeuroPaste on our list as a top priority," Volci said with a slightly guilty tone. "Enough to hopefully get us through until we get..."

"Hopefully?" Calynn interrupted, pulling her head back to look at the man.

"Hey, you," Kash said, rubbing Calynn's back. "Remember, they are the victims also."

"I know… sorry."

Calynn returned her face to Kash's chest and squeezed him tight. Calynn's outburst gave Kash an idea though.

"Hey, Volci," Kash addressed the man. "What if we solved all of your supply problems?"

"I don't follow," Volci replied.

"What if I called my friend Dorn, and we scheduled regular resupplies for you?"

"In exchange for?" Volci asked suspiciously.

"Well… if you searched for me on the cyber-web, you'll find that I have a reputation in retrieval," Kash explained. "Some of those jobs are… more dangerous than others, and we could possible need the services of a resourceful group of individuals on a remote star base…"

"Whoa, whoa," Volci interrupted. "I can't trade the base for…"

"Hiding a kidnapped Queen?" Calynn interrupted this time.

"What?" Volci asked, surprised.

"We're not asking for your undying loyalty, Volci," Kash laughed. "We're just asking for some assistance when we need it, like for instance… returning a kidnapped Queen, or hiding children from their abusive parents."

"That doesn't sound so bad," Volci admitted.

"Look… some of the jobs we take could be seen as less than lawful," Kash continued, "but I never involve my friends in any of those jobs. However, if we needed help in one of those situations, I assure you we tell the truth and let you decide whether or not to help."

"And what happens to us if I say, no?"

"We still help, regardless," Calynn answered. "The health of your nerve centers is more important."

"Really?" the Chief asked.

"How about we discuss the details while we go get your supplies," Kash smiled. "The first load anyway."

The trip to the supply depot had been unexpectedly pleasant. Kash, Calynn, and Chief Volci shared laughter and camaraderie as they traveled. By the time they arrived, Volci's initial hesitation about their partnership had given way to cautious optimism.

Joining them was Milo, the head chef, who was eager to secure some food for the star base.

The depot workers quickly loaded previously placed orders while Volci searched for parts to patch critical systems. Kash's attention was drawn to a set of unusual drones, sleek pyramids with rounded edges and six articulated arms.

"What are those?" Kash asked, pointing at the machines.

"Advanced maintenance drones," the shopkeeper replied. "One of these can replace ten workers."

Volci let out a bitter laugh.

"Don't I wish," Volci added between laughter. "The Consortium will never cover something like that."

"How many do you have?" Kash asked, ignoring Volci's comment.

"Six," the shopkeeper answered.

"We'll take them," Kash declared without hesitation.

"Don't bother," Volci argued and held up a hand. "They'll never approve the purchase."

Kash turned to Calynn, who wore a mischievous smile, her eyes faintly glowing.

"Run the purchase order," she instructed the shopkeeper. "Trust me, they'll pay for it."

The shopkeeper hesitated but complied.

"It looks like you have approval for twenty total," he said moments later. "Want to order the other fourteen?"

"Twenty?" Volci gawked. "That... that can't be right."

"Make it so," Calynn said smoothly. "A transport will pick them up in three weeks. Have them ready."

Kash clapped Volci on the back and shook the man's hand.

"Looks like you'll have some proper help soon," Kash offered.

"I don't know how to thank you," Volci was stunned, but gratitude softened his expression. "This is going to save my base."

When the trio exited the depot, Kash could tell that Volci was more at ease. The weight of months of struggle was lifted off his shoulders. Kash was smiling and enjoying the moment when Calynn's demeanor shifted suddenly, her steps faltering.

"Oh, no," she murmured. "No, no, God's no."

"What's wrong?" Kash asked, instantly on edge.

"I didn't see them until now," Calynn said, her voice laced with regret. "They're good at hiding their intentions, and they didn't tip their hand..."

"Calynn, who?" Kash barked.

"Pirates," Calynn admitted.

The air grew heavy as Kash processed her words and his stomach sank.

"Where?"

"They're watching the ship," she admitted, her voice trembling.

Kash's gut twisted. He buried his face in his hands.

"Tell me they don't know the laser isn't on board," Kash uttered. "Please, tell me they don't know it isn't there."

Calynn's eyes darted to his.

"We have to go," Calynn pleaded. "Now."

Kash didn't need convincing. He was already preparing their next move

"Volci, get to Milo and finish loading," Kash ordered. "Calynn, get us prepped for a fast takeoff. I'll go buy us some time."

"Yes, Boss," Calynn replied, her voice steadying as she sprinted for the ship.

Volci hesitated, scanning the depot. The man was clearly out of his element.

"How bad is this?" the Chief asked.

"Bad. Real bad," Kash said, his expression hardened. "And if they figure out what's not on my ship... they'll go after your base instead."

Volci's face paled as the horror of Kash's statement set in.

"Then let's move," Volci announced.

Walk the Plank

"Talk to me, Baby Girl," Kash growled, moving through the crowded space port. "I don't know who or what I'm looking for."

"There's two at your ten o'clock," Calynn replied over the comm in his ear. "One is bigger and taller than you and a shade or two darker with one side of his head shaved. The other side has long matted locks. He's with a small red woman with long green hair."

Kash scanned the crowd as he moved. His eyes darting to each person he passed to gauge their intent. He was still angry with himself for not staying vigilant and allowing this to happen. His complacency always leads to disaster. Kash clenched his jaw and fists trying to keep his anger under control.

"I see them," Kash announced when he located the two pirates.

Kash felt his rage building as he marched towards the two pirates. His pace quickened as he approached them. He wasn't even trying to be tactical at this point. Kash was looking for a fight. No... he needed to fight.

"GRRRRAAAAHHH!" Kash roared, lunging at the big pirate.

Kash punched the man in an explosion of emotion. The big man tried to block Kash's fist, but was no match for the brutality that Kash had unleashed in that one punch. This was his fault. He'd let his guard down...again. And now, as always, others would pay the price for his carelessness. Kash's fist connected with his opponent, but the sting in his knuckles was nothing compared to the fury clawing at his insides. He felt the man's arm break as he pushed through and then the snapping of his ribs when the punch landed in his chest. The big man was launched backwards, knocking over several bystanders.

The small woman pirate was slashing at Kash with a knife when he turned his attention to her. Kash easily blocked her attack and backhanded her across the face, knocking the woman unconscious. The surrounding crowds were gasping and screaming in terror at the spectacle he created. Some of the people cowered in fear while others scurried off to get away from Kash.

Kash noticed four more pirates in the crowd running towards him and grinned an evil grin. Kash sprinted at the pirates. His rage wasn't satiated yet, and they were going to be his next outlet. He didn't even slow his pace when he saw the man on the left draw his pistol.

Kash dove into the two pirates on the far right, tackling them to the ground. Kash rolled over top of the pirate on his left, grabbed him by the waist, and hurled him at the man with the man with the pistol. Kash, now in a crouching position, spun a kick into the head of the other man he tackled. The kick landed with enough force to break the man's neck. Kash continued rotating his body, sweeping the legs out from under the pirate that was still standing. Kash grabbed the man by his face as he fell and drove his head into the ground.

By the time the man with the gun gathered his wits, Kash was already standing on his hand pinning the pistol to the ground. Terror flooded the man's face, and he turned ghost white in an instant. He was right to fear Kash. Kash ended his life with a quick kick to the head and snapped the neck of the man he threw earlier. Kash stood over his victims, demonstrably absorbed in his rage. He reveled in the screams that rippled through the crowd as bystanders stumbled over each other, desperate to escape the storm of violence in their midst.

"Boss, we gotta go!" Calynn's urgent tone snapped him back to reality. "BOSS!"

Kash sprinted the rest of the way to The Cat and got there as they were throwing the last of the cargo onto his ship. Kash slowed his pace and started barking orders as he moved through the cargo hold.

"Get that shit strapped down!"

"We're going as fast as we can," Volci replied.

"Go faster!" Kash bellowed.

Calynn was suddenly standing in front of him, her hand on his chest. Kash scowled at her, and she scowled back.

"I know your pissed at yourself for not seeing the pirates coming, but that isn't their fault!" Calynn snapped, gesturing at their new friends. "So, back off!"

Calynn gave him a quick shove so he had to catch his balance, then pointed her finger in his face.

"We need a leader right now not a fucking rage monster!" Calynn continued. "Get your shit together!"

Her words hit Kash harder than he expected, and his anger finally subsided. Calynn was right. He was compounding the error of his complacency by throwing a childish fit. He closed his eyes, took a deep breath, and quieted his mind so he could focus on the task at hand.

"That's better," Calynn said, tapping her hand on his chest. "There's the man we need."

Calynn was smiling at him when he opened his eyes.

"You can manipulate me far too well, Miss Smith," Kash smirked.

"Only because you let me, Mr. Smith," Calynn smiled. "Now get us out of here while I help secure the cargo."

Kash ran up the steps of the ship ladder and jogged down the hall to the helm. He strapped himself in and fired up the ship's engines.

"How we doing back there?" Kash hollered.

"Cargo door is closed but we still need to secure some of the cargo," Calynn shouted back.

Kash scanned the horizon diligently and some movement caught his eye in the distance. He quickly checked his monitor hoping that they were registered transports. Kash sighed when he saw the unregistered designation, but this time they wouldn't get the drop on him.

"You're out of time. We've got company," Kash announced, staring out the windshield. "There's three enemy ships headed straight for us... hang on to something."

The Cat's engines roared to life as Kash lifted off. He had to give Calynn and the others more time to secure their cargo, but the pirate ships were closing fast. He had to try something drastic, and the enormous ore freighter nearby gave him an idea.

"Does anyone know the dimensions of the intake ports on an Odyssey Class ore freighter?" Kash asked.

"I'm afraid to ask why," Calynn hollered.

"Because we need to hide."

"That's insane!" Calynn barked. "Don't you dare!"

"Yeah, well, insane is better than killing all the innocent people below us," Kash admitted. "If the pirates fire on us, either we get hit or the crowds do."

"They're big but not... I don't know if you'll fit!" Volci shouted.

"We're about to find out," Kash relented.

Kash's knuckles turned white as he gripped the controls and lined them up with one of the ports on the freighter.

"You better hope that bay is empty!" Calynn cried.

"Just get that cargo tied down." Kash ordered as the collision alert started to flash its warning. "We're going in."

Kash pulled back on the throttle and eased The Cat into the giant tube. The tube sloped down slightly. It was designed so the freighter could be loaded quickly via a large conveyor belt. The ore would travel up the conveyor and be hurtled into the port where gravity would help keep it moving until it got to the center of the ship. This helped the freighter stay balanced when loaded.

Kash had less than half a meter of clearance from the tip of each wing to the hardened metal walls of the tube. He clenched his jaw and adjusted his grip on the controls. He was so focused on flying that he never heard Calynn approaching.

"You're a mad man," Calynn said, shocked.

"Hush... I'm trying to focus..."

SCCREEACH

The starboard wing tip scratched the wall of the port briefly. Kash had to ease them off the wall so he didn't hit the opposite one.

"On not doing that," Kash continued, adjusting is grip again. "Look... we're almost to the end of the tube."

The end of the intake port had a large flat piece of metal angled to help bounce the incoming ore down into the cargo bay through a hole in the bottom of the tube. This was going to be the trickiest part of navigating the tube. If he pitched the nose down too far, the tail of his ship would hit the top of the tube. If he didn't pitch it enough, he would ram the nose right into the angled block.

"Is everyone strapped in?" Kash hollered.

"Almost," Milo shouted. "Just a couple seconds."

"You're not going to do what I think you're doing, right?" Calynn asked, worried.

"The only way we make that turn," Kash sighed. "Is inverted."

Kash rolled The Cat over as precisely as he could. One wing tip barely scraped the tube while they rotated. He gently pulled back on the controls and skimmed the end of the tube as they dove down into the depths of the cargo bay.

"Holy fuck!" Calynn gasped, as Kash righted the ship.

She had a glowing smile on her face when he glanced at her. Kash allowed himself to smile back.

"You do not want to know the actual odds of what you just did," Calynn continued, half giggling.

"I'm sure I don't. Gods... these things are big."

Kash looked out into the expansive cargo bay of the space freighter, marveling at its size. Mountains of ore were piled up inside the bay, but he still had plenty of room to maneuver.

"According to the scanners it's exactly one thousand meters cubed," Calynn added.

"And luckily only two thirds full," Kash smirked.

"Yeah... luck."

"Let's see if we can get luckier and find an open bay," Kash said as he eased into the throttle.

"And just how do you intend to get from bay to bay?"

"Over the bulkheads," Kash explained, pointing at the gap above the far wall.

"You're still a mad man," Calynn cooed, "but it's kinda sexy."

The gaps above the bulkheads were much easier to navigate than the intake port, and they soon found a bay with the dump doors on the bottom of the bay hanging wide open.

"Spin up the HLD and be ready to engage," Kash ordered. "We will pop up on their scanners again as soon as we clear the hull of the freighter."

"On it," Calynn replied, as the HLD started to hum.

Kash shot them out of the bottom of the freighter at speed. If the pirates were watching, he wanted to be nothing more than a blur.

"Where are they?" Kash asked abruptly. "Anything on the scanners?"

"Gods... they're right above us," Calynn admitted. "But they're headed the wrong way."

Kash punched the throttle, the ship shuddering as the engines screamed with effort. He didn't have far to go until they cleared the atmospheric bubble of the spaceport. Only then could Calynn engage the HLD. Kash stole a glance at the monitor. The pirate ships had turned, and though they were now in pursuit, Rinktee's upgraded engines were opening the gap between them.

"Engaging HLD in five... four..." Calynn counted down.

The proximity alarm wailed. A flashing alert warned of inbound missiles streaking toward The Cat.

Kash's head snapped toward Calynn, his adrenaline spiking, but she didn't flinch.

"Three... two... engage."

The HLD bubble enveloped The Cat, and the ship jumped, leaving the missiles far behind. The cockpit went silent except for the soft hum of the HLD, and Kash allowed himself a moment of relief. Calynn placed a reassuring hand on his shoulder and the two savored the momentary pause. Kash relinquished the helm and Calynn took over.

"Don't hold back on the engines," Kash said to her. "We need as much time as we can get."

"Will do, Boss."

"Hey, Volci," Kash shouted for the man. "Can you come up here and radio ahead to warn the base?"

Volci was still on the comms when Calynn cut the HLD, and the star base came into view.

"How are we here already?" Volci asked, absentmindedly. "That's impossible."

"My girl can move," Kash bragged. "Now get those blast doors open."

"And tell them we're coming in hot," Calynn added.

"And get some help to unload the supplies so we can..." Kash started to say but was interrupted by a wailing alarm.

BEEP BEEP BEEP BEEP BEEP

"What the hell is beeping?" Kash asked.

"Proximity alert," Calynn uttered, devoid of all emotion. "Kash, there's dozens of them... and they have a flagship."

"How the fuck do pirates have a flagship?" Kash asked.

"Is now a bad time to tell you they retrofitted it with some hulking artillery cannons?" Calynn asked sarcastically.

"Well doesn't that sound lovely," Kash groaned. "Any other good news?"

"Umm… what if the nerve centers are still too weak to run the base defenses?" Volci asked, meekly. "They haven't been strong enough to do that in months."

"Without the defenses, those cannons will rip the base to shreds with one volley," Calynn added.

"What do we do?" Milo asked fearfully.

Kash and Calynn locked eyes, the chaos around them falling away for a moment. No words passed between them… they didn't need any. A silent understanding passed between them, a testament to the bond they shared. Calynn's hands moved to her harness, unbuckling herself with steady purpose. She didn't hesitate as she rose, allowing him to take the pilot's seat.

"You fly," she chirped.

"Goddess mode?"

"Goddess mode."

Kash hit the throttle and aimed for the star base. Behind him, he heard Calynn take deep, centering breaths as she prepared herself for an impossible task. Well, impossible for anyone else but her.

The blast doors to dock six were open and waiting for them. Kash eased them into the dock and set The Cat down. Calynn's eyes were closed, but the bright, white light was still pouring out of them. Kash kissed her forehead before barking orders at the others.

"One of you has to stay here with her and feed her Nutra-shakes as she needs them," Kash ordered, pointing at Calynn. "And the other one needs to get me to a damn fighter. Your pilots are going to need all the help they can get."

Volci and Milo exchanged a glance and nodded.

"Follow me, sir," Volci said, already jogging ahead.

Kash grabbed his flight suit and followed, the two men sprinting out of The Cat and across the dock. They burst through a set of double doors, turned left, and bolted down a long hallway.

"I'm in," Calynn's voice suddenly boomed over the comms, echoing through the base. "Defenses coming online."

Volci stumbled mid-step, nearly tripping over his own feet when he heard Calynn's voice.

"What the… how'd she… do that?" he asked between gasps.

"I'll explain later," Kash smirked without breaking stride. "If we live through this."

Ahead, other pilots streamed toward the fighter hangar. Kash and Volci veered toward the locker room, where Kash yanked on his flight suit as quickly as his trembling hands allowed. By the time he entered the hangar, still zipping up the front, the nervous energy in the air hit him like a tidal wave.

Kash's pace slowed as an uneasy feeling crashed over him. He hadn't flown a fighter since his time as a Legionnaire. He found himself suddenly concerned with abilities. What if he was rusty?

"Captain Smith," Volci called out, snapping him back. "You good?"

Kash forced a grin, masking his turmoil.

"Just a flood of memories, Chief. Which one's mine?"

Volci hesitated, staring at Kash briefly, then pointed toward a sleek fighter parked nearby.

"You flew the Tec-Ace models, right?" Volci asked.

"The Mark-7," Kash confirmed, his voice quieter now.

"This one's a Mark-12," Volci explained, motioning toward the craft.

The fighter gleamed under the hangar lights, its polished hull a work of modern engineering. It had the flattened nose of his old Mark-7, but the similarities ended there. Larger, forward-swept wings extended nearly to the nose, while two vertical stabilizers formed a sharp V above the oversized engine. The ship exuded speed and precision.

"She's quicker and tougher than your old one," Volci said, patting the fuselage. "The fire controls are a bit different, too. You'll need to adapt."

Kash nodded, swallowing his nerves as he climbed the ladder. He slid into the cockpit, the snug space immediately felt familiar despite its sleek upgrades. His hands hovered over the controls. Their arrangement foreign but intuitive. Just being in another fighter brought a rush of memories, the ghosts of his past weaving themselves into his present.

The Chief leaned in and started flipping switches. The controls flashed and beeped as the ship powered up. All the control surfaces moved to their maximum angles in both directions as a pre-flight test.

"Main engine start is here," Volci explained, pointing at a large toggle. "Guns and missiles are still on your stick, but the selector is on the touch screen now. If you code in, it should adjust to your old trim settings if they are still in the system. Counter measures are here, and the fuses and emergency systems are there. Good luck, Captain."

Kash typed in his old military ID code causing the ship's control surfaces to move once again.

"Welcome, Captain Smith," appeared on the main screen.

Chief Volci removed the ladder and gave him a thumbs up as the canopy sealed around him with a hiss. Kash hit the ignition and pulled on his helmet. His hands glided over the controls for the first time in years, but it was like they still knew what to do. Despite the differences, it felt like he belonged there.

"Let's see if I still remember how to make you dance," he muttered under his breath.

The fighter was pulled into position, loaded into a launch tube, and hurtled into the void. Kash looked around for the others and moved to join the rest of the formation. The controls felt fluid in his hands. Kash gained confidence with every passing second.

"Ordinance inbound!" a pilot shouted. "Break left!"

Kash pulled to the left with the rest of the formation and turned to watch if the shots hit the star base. The defense rings were moving but not like they should. They seemed slow. The rings blocked most of the shots, but not all of them.

"What's going on down there, Baby Girl?" Kash asked firmly. "Talk to me."

"The damn defense rings haven't moved in months," Calynn sounded frustrated. "I'm having difficulties. It's like herding cats."

"Another volley!" a pilot announced.

Kash finally saw a stream of bullets coming from one of the defense rings. Followed by another, and another. Calynn was getting the defenses working, but it was taking too much time.

"If we don't engage the pirates soon, the base is going to be destroyed!" Kash barked. "Move to attack speed and concentrate fire on those cannons!"

"We don't stand a chance against all those ships!" one pilot whined.

"We need a plan," another stated.

Kash didn't wait for the rest of them. He pushed the throttle to max speed and accelerated right at the pirate ships.

"We have a plan," Kash urged. "Attack!"

Some of the smaller ships moved to intercept Kash before he could get to the flagship. A barrage of bullets and lasers came Kash's way. The agility of the Mark-12 was impressive. Kash jerked the controls and rolled the ship through the hail of bullets. His Legionnaire training took over allowing him to focus on the gaps in the barrage. He banked hard, turning to and fro, until he cleared the barrage.

"How did you do that?" a pilot asked.

"If you focus on the bullets, you hit the bullets," Kash explained. "If you focus on the gaps, you hit the gaps."

Kash squeezed the trigger to return fire. He fired bullets at one of the fighters, and missiles at two of the other slightly bigger ships. Kash was still at maximum throttle, so his weapons got to their targets before the enemies could react and the three enemy ships exploded. He rolled the ship over and knifed his way right through the center of the remaining enemy ships. As soon as he cleared them, he let off the throttle, pulled up as hard as he could, and punched the throttle again. Kash was now tailing the ships that came after him.

"The engines are always the weak spot," Kash smirked, pulling the trigger.

Three more ships fell to his precision fire before one of the enemy fighters got turned around to line up a shot at him. Kash jerked the controls hard to avoid the debris from the ships he just destroyed. But that same debris would inhibit the enemy's targeting. Few pilots trained for dog fights at point-blank range, but Kash was in his element. He always found himself at an advantage when he cartwheeled his fighter through the middle of enemies. The enemy fighter hesitated, and Kash capitalized on it.

"You lose," Kash growled, pulling the trigger.

The pirate's fighter ripped apart when Kash's shot hit his mark. The fighter exploded with more force than it should have, though. Kash jerked the controls and accelerated away as more explosions happened around him. The pirate's main convoy had launched a volley of shots into the debris field where Kash was operating. He raced to get out of the debris field to escape the barrage.

"Kash!" Calynn screamed.

Some of the shots were too close for comfort and shook his fighter violently. Debris was bouncing off his ship as he tried to dodge the large pieces. Kash shot out of the debris field as the last round exploded, narrowly escaping.

"Fuck me, that was close," Kash exclaimed, as he turned back towards the pirates.

"Oh, thank the Gods," Calynn sighed, "you're okay."

"I am, but I won't be for long if we don't launch some offense!" Kash barked. "Have the big guns been herded yet?"

"They're still offline, and I can't…"

"Oh, for fuck's sake," Kash grumbled, raking a hand across the back of his neck as his eyes darted to the defense rings, still sluggish and unresponsive.

Time was running out, and the base wouldn't survive another volley without those guns.

A horrible idea popped into his head, and with it a sinking dread twisting in his chest. He'd relied on Calynn's strength before, but never like this… not by deliberately weaponizing her pain to force her to react. The thought of doing that to her made his stomach churn.

He clenched his fists, every fiber of his being screaming for another solution. But there was no time left to hesitate, and no other path forward.

"I'll never forgive myself for this," he muttered under his breath, the guilt already settling like a weight in his chest. "Sorry, Baby Girl."

Then, heart pounding, he said it anyway.

"So, you're just going to let me die like you did her?" Kash asked, feigning anger he didn't truly feel.

"What? …who?"

"You let Omia die," Kash continued in a harsh tone. "You could have stopped the bullets, but you didn't."

"I didn't…"

"Oh, just shut up you mewling little cunt. Is it too hard for your little girl brain to do?" Kash continued his assault. "I'm out here flying around explosions and shit, and you can't bring yourself to do a tiny bit of actual fucking work? How fucking worthless are you?"

"Hey! That's…"

"Fuck it!" Kash interrupted her again. "I guess I'll just fly straight into the pirate ships because I'd rather be dead with Omia than stay here with your sorry ass!"

"But you'll die."

"Good! At least I won't have to listen to you whine anymore!"

"GGGGRRRRRRAAAAAAAAAHHHHHHHHH!"

Calynn's growl was as feral as it was long. He turned to see the cannons on the base spring to life, and knew they finally had a fighting chance. Calynn must have really lost control of her emotions because all the lights on the base were glowing far too bright, and the defense rings were finally moving like they should. That girl can do the impossible when she loses control of her emotions.

Kash watched the approaching rounds from the base and accelerated when they passed. The enemy ships were trying to move out of the way to no avail. The rounds struck their targets, and the larger ships started to break apart. The flagship suffered multiple hull breaches. The escaping atmosphere was ejecting all the ship's contents into the void. Kash followed the rounds into the group of enemy ships and held down the trigger. He was spraying bullets everywhere as he weaved his way through the enemy ships. He launched missiles at the cruisers as fast as the computer could target them.

The rest of the fighters joined him in attacking the smaller pirate ships, and the group soon had incapacitated every ship. The mass of debris kept growing as the fighters destroyed the pirate ships. One ship had managed to spin up the HLD and jump away before Kash and the others could attack it. Kash wanted to send a ruthless message to those that were working behind the scenes to undermine him, so he fired upon every escape pod he saw. There would be no survivors left behind.

"Destroying escape pods is a war crime, Captain Smith," a strange voice commented over the comms.

"If you mess with the bull, you get the fucking horns," Kash barked. "This is what happens when you come after me."

"We will never stop coming after you," the voice responded.

Kash froze for a minute. He thought the voice was another pilot or someone from the base, but it wasn't. This was one of the people responsible for his current dilemma... and it was personal.

"I'm right here. Come get some," Kash replied with a snarky tone. "Unless you're afraid to go one on one with me?"

Kash scanned the horizon as he spoke. The enemy ship had to be close, but where was it? Was it cloaked? Or just too far for him to see it?

"There's no doubt that you are a far superior combat pilot than I am," the voice added. "It would behoove me to not engage you when you clearly have the advantage."

"Hand to hand, then?" Kash asked. "I'll meet you on solid ground any time you want."

"Tempting, but still… no. My interest lies in strategy, not barbarism."

"Ooohhh, so you're one of… them?" Kash pressed.

"One of whom, Captain Smith?"

"A man of little to no talent who stands on the backs of those that actually possess the skills you covet," Kash explained condescendingly. "I've met far too many of your type when I was a Legionnaire. The only thing you're good for is talking about how to get others killed. Like say, these pirates… you know… the dead ones."

"They were paid to do a job," the voice argued. "They failed… not me."

"Of course they failed. They followed your plan," Kash rebutted. "All I see is debris and bad decisions. But hey, maybe the real war crime here was your dumb fucking strategy."

"Every battle has casualties, Captain Smith," the mysterious man continued. "That doesn't change the greater goal."

"Was the greater goal to create a floating debris field full of dead friends?" Kash asked sarcastically. "Because if so… bravo…"

"The plan was to eliminate a problem," the man rebutted sharply. "And with proper intel, it would have succeeded!"

"So, we're blaming the intel now?" Kash continued, even more sarcastically. "Good job, little Billy. Here's your participation trophy. I guess we can mail the ones for the pirates to their families… since they can't… anything… anymore."

Kash was still scanning everything he could see looking for a sign of the ship. He hoped that he could end this charade once and for all by locating and destroying it and the bureaucrat aboard.

"The intel was merely flawed, you wise ass," the man barked. "I was assured that the base would be defenseless leading to an easy victory."

"So you were here to gloat," Kash revealed. "But then we flipped the script, and you had to flee because you're too scared to face me."

"Yes, well, that would seem to be the case. And how did Miss Smith get those guns online?" the man pondered. "I was assured that it would be impossible. It was the only reason we approached en masse like we did. We overheard you berating her, but what equipment did she use to subvert the devices we had in place?"

"Probably her ratcheting hammer," Kash replied smugly. "That's what I use on bad intel every time."

"A ratcheting... hammer," the man sounded annoyed.

"Yeah... it was smelted in a left-handed cold forge furnace and has an articulated posterior grip," Kash smirked. "She just shakes her ass and the magic happens."

"Am I supposed to find that amusing, Captain Smith?"

"Of course not," Kash replied. "I'm just saying that if she shakes her ass at you... you definitely forget about your intel."

"You're playing a dangerous game, Captain Smith!" the man sounded angry. "I will not be mocked by the likes of you!"

"And yet, you're the one running. Cowards should always be mocked."

An urgent alert started blaring on his screen alerting him to a missile lock. Kash glanced at the monitor and noted the direction of its origin and accelerated towards it. The vessel that launched the missile was no longer cloaked, but it was too far away for Kash to shoot back. His fighter wasn't equipped with long range missiles, so he had to close the gap. But that meant flying directly at the missile tracking him.

Kash steadied his hand on the stick as he closed the gap. His eyes narrowed on the approaching missile as the alert blared faster and louder. Kash jerked the controls at the last possible moment and rolled the fighter over the missile. He knew the missile had thrust vectoring and could turn towards him, but not as quickly as the Tec-Ace. Kash tracked the missile and pulled the fighter into position. He pulled the trigger, sending a hail of bullets at the missile. One of the bullets must have hit the vectoring controller, because the missile started flying erratically. Kash reversed his thrust to gain some distance as the missile exploded.

"Oops," Kash said sarcastically. "You missed."

Kash turned to face the ship that had shot at him, but it was gone. They had cloaked themselves again or jumped away when Kash was dealing with the missile.

"Coward," Kash reiterated coldly.

Kash turned and headed back to the base. The other pilots were also on approach but were much closer than he was. The star base had some damage but was still operational. The lighting had returned to normal levels after Calynn's emotional assault. Kash took a deep breath and relaxed.

"Like I said, Captain Smith," the mysterious man continued. "My interests lie in tactics and strategy. By distracting you, we could hit the real target. Let's see Miss Smith handle this."

Kash saw the lights of the base distort and knew immediately what it was. A missile big enough to be cloaked was heading straight for the base.

"Calynn!"

A New Problem

Kash froze as the cloaked missile hit its target, erupting into a massive fireball. The blast tore through the star base's hull, carving a jagged wound like a hot knife through butter. Debris spiraled into the cold void, the fireball snuffed out as the atmosphere vanished... a brutal reminder of how fragile the line between life and death could be.

Kash pushed the fighter throttle to the limit and was streaking towards the base. The location of the missile impact made his heart sink, and a knot formed in his stomach.

"No, no, no," Kash growled, shoving the fighter's throttle to its limit. "Calynn... Baby Girl... where are you?"

"Kash, it's Volci, I, uh..."

"Volci, where is she? Where's Calynn?"

"I'm sorry... we're trying but... she was still out there when..." Volci confessed. "The dock... it lost atmosphere... there's debris everywhere... it's all frozen... including her."

"Frozen?" Kash replied, the word stuck in his throat. "Frozen..."

Kash was lost in his own mind. Flashes of Omia being shot danced in his memories followed by memories of Calynn smiling. She had such a beautiful smile. It was slightly crooked which made her all the more endearing, lovely, and sweet. What would he do without her? He couldn't lose her too. Who would fly...

"NO!" Kash yelled into the comms.

The realization hit him like a kick to the chest, and hope blossomed anew.

"She's not frozen!" Kash barked, urgency sharpening his tone. "She's a synth... she can handle the cold, but she can't hold her breath forever. GET IN THERE!"

"Deploying the decompression recovery drones," Volci announced.

"She just needs oxygen!" Kash continued. "Just get the damn mask on her head... please hurry!"

"I'm coming, Baby Girl," Kash said quietly to himself.

Kash gripped the controls with a hardened determination. His focus was pinpointed on the fighter hanger, and he was coming in at ridiculous speeds. There was no way he was losing Calynn. Not today... not ever!

Kash burst through the atmospheric barriers faster than he should. Luckily, the other fighters that had already landed moved off to the sides like they are supposed to do. Kash shot right down the middle, dropped the landing gear, and put it down while still moving. He opened the canopy while the fighter was still skiing across the floor of the hanger and jumped out of the fighter as soon as it settled.

"What's going on Volci?" Kash growled as he sprinted out of the hanger.

"I'm working on it," Volci replied.

"Work faster!"

"The drone can't get the mask to seal properly."

Kash rounded the corner of the hallway and could see Volci at the controls of the emergency decompression panel. He glanced at Kash as he approached but didn't say anything. Kash was thankful for his focus on his task.

Kash slid to a stop and punched the release button for the panel beside Volci, revealing a space suit suitable for entering the dock.

"What's her time?" Kash asked as he rapidly pulled on the suit.

"Three minutes nineteen seconds," Volci replied robotically. "How long can she hold her breath?"

"I don't know. Zip me up and get me in there."

The two men worked in unison to get the suit sealed and ready. Kash hit the power button, and the suit inflated and ran its checks. Precious seconds ticked by as he waited, until the green light on the helmet finally lit. Kash bounced over to the emergency pressure doors and slid them open. He walked through and sealed them again. Another set of doors still blocked him from getting to Calynn. Kash didn't wait for the airlock to balance the pressure. He hit the release button, and the doors shot open with alarms blaring. The atmosphere left in the chamber sucked him out into the dock as it escaped. Thankfully pulling him closer to Calynn.

Running in the space suits was nearly impossible due to the bulk, so bouncing was the fastest way to move. He was bounding towards his ship as fast as he could go, when he noticed the drone and Calynn weren't in his ship. She was standing beside the ballistic laser and her hands... her hands were inside the containment field. She was standing inside the outer framework of the device which is why the drone was having trouble getting the mask on her. It couldn't maneuver itself into a position to reach her face. The mask needed to cover her entire face but the drone could only get the mask up to the bridge of her nose.

"I'm coming, Baby Girl," Kash said more for himself than her. "Just ten more seconds. Hold on just ten more seconds for me... you can do it."

Kash bounced over and jerked the mask away from the drone and pressed it to Calynn's face. Her entire body was covered in a layer of frost making her look cold and lifeless. Kash swallowed the lump in his throat, placed his hand on her frozen stomach, and pulled himself closer to her. The inflatable suit slowly gave way to the pressure until the back of her body came in contact with the front of his.

"Gods, you're freezing," Kash said softly. "Please be okay... please... I can't... without you."

Calynn didn't move... or signal him... or try to speak... she was just a block of beautiful ice. Tears stung his eyes and threatened to fall. He didn't care how cold it felt to hug her. He pulled her tighter. He knew if he held on too long, he could get frostbite despite the suit he was wearing, but right now that didn't matter to him. He welcomed the scars that it would leave as a reminder of her. And then he felt her move. She had managed to clench the largest muscle in her body... her glutes.

"She moved," Kash exclaimed. "She just... her body is too cold for her to move it."

The memory of the day on Egonn's ship when Calynn absorbed immense amounts of energy jumped to the forefront of his mind. Meesha had told him that Calynn was trying to contain the heat. Kash knew what he needed to do.

"I need power," Kash barked. "Lots of power."

"Kash, her chest isn't moving," Volci said, full of concern.

"The only reason her chest moves when she breathes is to make her appear more human," Kash explained. "Now where is there power?"

"The floor… by the ballistic laser charger."

Kash released Calynn and bounded to the charger cables. There he saw a four-pronged cord on a reel that was used for charging everything from hover-skids to drones. He grabbed the end of the cord and pulled it back to Calynn. He knew the plug end wouldn't complete the circuit, so he had to rip it off and get to the wires inside. He wedged the plug into a V shaped part of the frame of the laser and jerked with all his strength. The end snapped free exposing the wires inside with sparks jumping everywhere. Kash didn't hesitate. He jammed the wires onto the exposed skin of Calynn's neck.

At first nothing happened, but then a smile escaped his lips as a faint glow rippled through the grid in Calynn's skin. She was pulling in the power and pushing it throughout her body. Kash kept the wire pressed to her flesh and once again pulled her frigid body into his.

"Come on, Baby Girl," Kash whispered, pressing his forehead to the back of her head. "You've got this. Warm up for me."

Kash hadn't even noticed the color of the containment field of the ballistic laser until it started to change. Not only was Calynn alive, but she was pushing energy into the containment field to prevent the laser from reaching critical flux.

"By the Gods, you're fucking amazing," Kash beamed a smile as he hugged her tighter. "And you're starting to feel warmer."

"The drone is reporting a raise in her body temperature of two degrees Celsius," Volci reported. "I… I can't believe it."

"That's why she's a goddess," Kash gloated, grinning ear to ear. "Have the drone hold this on her so she can keep absorbing power and get some help in here. We need to get temporary atmospheric fields up on this gash so you can begin repairs."

Kash turned his attention to The Cat. His ship looked every bit as cold and lifeless as Calynn. It was no longer sitting where he had parked it. The explosive decompression of the dock was enough to move it about ten meters. The cargo door was still down, and the inside was an absolute mess. Kash slowly walked up the ramp to examine the damage. The fresh produce they had brought back for the base was flash frozen. When Kash touched a bunch of leafy greens resembling lettuce, it crumbled in his hand. It was as if everything was freeze-dried.

"Oh, no," Kash said solemnly. "Two of yours didn't make it, Chief."

Kash knelt down beside the frozen corpses of two people he never met, but somehow still felt a connection with. The plight of the people on this forgotten base was endearing to him. Even though he didn't know their names, it still felt like he knew them... through their brief shared experience.

"Nothing we can do about that now," the Chief replied, matching Kash's tone. "How's your boat?"

"A fucking mess," Kash half chuckled. "Looks like the emergency airlock came down, so the cockpit and my quarters should be fine once we restore power."

"Looks like it took serious blow to the port wing," Volci added. "It's not bent but that's a hell of a dent."

"You're shitting me," Kash exclaimed, exiting The Cat to take a look himself.

Kash walked out under the port wing and sure enough, he saw a big dent near the tip. There were no walls near his ship and the charger looked undamaged, so what damaged the wing? Kash looked around dumbfounded and then looked up.

"Maybe it moved further than I thought," Kash stated, looking up at the gash in the hull.

The metal around the opening of the hull was a twisted mess. The missile forced the hull open with the pressure wave it created, but then the pressure of the air rushing out ripped the hole open further. The thick metal of the hull looked more like tattered cloth now. The jagged edge twisted out towards the void of space. The light from a nearby sun poured in through the gash, lighting the dock. The layer of ice on every surface of the dock reflected the light giving it an eerie blue hue. Just yesterday this dock seemed so inviting. Now, it was a frozen wasteland, and the undermanned base would be at least two more crewmen short.

Kash sighed and hung his head. These people didn't deserve to be thrust into this situation. Death and destruction seemed to be following him, but it never caught up to him... just his friends. He took a deep breath and tried to push out his sorrow. Kash tried to focus on the repairs instead of the fallen, but his eyes stopped on Calynn's frozen form instead. He walked over to his beautiful companion and placed his hand on the small of her back. She was still cold to the touch even through the protective suit. He wanted nothing more than to touch her soft skin, but he would have to wait until they fixed the hole in the hull before that could happen... and her skin needed to thaw so it was supple again.

The airlock doors opening caught Kash's eye. He turned to see four crewmen coming into the dock with a hover-skid. They were here to start the repairs. Kash decided to be helpful instead of wallowing in his own despair. He marched over to give them a hand.

"How can I help?" Kash asked, smiling at one of the men. His voice was steady, but his expression betrayed a hint of guilt. "I can't help but think this is my fault…"

"Nonsense, sir," one of them interrupted firmly, shaking his head. "We're still standing because of you… and her."

"More her than me," Kash admitted, a small smile tugging at his lips. "She's definitely the better half."

"And the prettier half," another man chuckled nervously, then immediately froze. "Sorry, Captain."

"Sorry for what?" Kash quipped with a raised eyebrow. "She's waaaay prettier than me."

The mood of the room lightened as Kash smiled, and the others hesitated before joining him with soft laughter. Kash stepped forward, placing a reassuring hand on the shoulder of the man who'd made the comment. His grip was steady, warm.

"I promise she's a lot prettier when she isn't a block of ice," Kash continued with a grin. "How about we get to work so she can thaw?"

The men exchanged glances and nodded, determination flickering in their eyes as they set off to work.

It took more than an hourn to rig the cables the crew used to gain access to the gaping hole in the ceiling. Kash and two of the others, men named Loi and Dulfi, went out through the jagged gap to set up the temporary atmospheric fields before the actual work could begin. The trio double checked each other's work, as the placement had to be precise for it to properly seal.

They spent hourns cutting the damaged metal away to prepare the hull for patch panels. Working in unison to cut away the twisted metal. Kash turned to see Loi and Dulfi struggling with one of the larger pieces of metal they were cutting free. The twisted edge of the hull clung stubbornly, refusing to let go.

"Here, let me do that part," Kash offered, stepping forward with a small smile. "My implants make me better suited for the heavy lifting… and you guys are better with the cutting tools."

"Thanks, Kash," Loi replied, his breath fogging the inside of his helmet. He stepped back, relief evident in his movements.

Kash planted his feet firmly on the uneven surface and gripped the jagged metal. His implant enhanced muscles strained against the weight. With a grunt the piece broke free, sending bits of slag flying.

Dulfi let out a low whistle.

"Remind me not to arm-wrestle you," Dulfi chuckled.

Kash chuckled and tossed the metal aside.

"So, you don't want to engage in a barbaric competition of strength with me?" Kash bantered. "For the right price… I can lose."

"I'll stick to cutting, thanks," Dulfi laughed, shaking his head.

They nearly had the outer hull repaired when the low-pressure alarms finally turned off. The dock was at least partially repressurized… still cold, but under pressure.

"We should be able to take these suits off in another hourn," Loi stated, smiling. "Breathing thin air is better than trying to work in these damn things."

Kash nodded absently, his eyes drifting to where Calynn stood, still connected to the charger. She was dripping now, the frost on her body melting slowly. He felt a pang of guilt, the weight of pressing her earlier was still eating at him.

"Take a break and go to her," Loi continued, smiling at Kash. "We can finish up here."

Kash hesitantly approached Calynn. He was still feeling guilty about making her mad earlier, and he wasn't sure if she had forgiven him yet. He placed his hand on her back again, and this time she felt warm. His hand involuntarily moved across her skin and stopped on her belly just above the waist of her jeans.

"Baby Girl?" Kash asked softly.

"Hi, B-Boss," Calynn muttered, barely audible. "Thanks for… saving me."

Kash wrapped his arms around her and squeezed the air pressure out of his suit until his body pressed against hers. He had one hand on her belly and the other on her chest. He yearned to kiss her head, but the helmet was in the way. He had to settle for laying it on the back of her head. Her body shook in his arms as she started weeping.

"I thought I lost you," Kash admitted softly. "I was so… lost."

Calynn cried for a few minutes as Kash held her. She took a few deep breaths to calm herself, but they were only mildly effective.

"I was so scared, and you weren't here," Calynn cried. "I lost contact when The Cat lost power. I thought I would never see you or hear your voice again."

"Aww, Baby Girl... and I am so... so sorry for what I said earlier. It..."

"I know why you did what you did," Calynn interrupted him. "But did you have to do it so well?"

Calynn pushed her head into his helmet. She cried for a moment longer and then tried to compose herself again. Kash felt guilty for what he had said and needed to explain himself.

"It was just meant to help you get there... so you could save the base... I didn't mean any of it."

"I know," Calynn replied, her voice a little steadier. "But do me a favor next time and pick something that won't run on repeat in my head."

"I promise," Kash agreed. "How can I make it up to you?"

"You could always worship me some more," Calynn said coyly.

"Is that so?"

"It would... definitely... get you back in my good graces."

"In that case," Kash said softly pulling her body tighter to his. "I wish I give you a kiss... Your Grace."

"Wish granted," Calynn cooed, nodding her head at the airlock. "Look."

A dozen workers, including Volci, entered the dock without protective suits. They wore heavy coats, but no oxygen masks. Chief Volci was jogging towards them holding some clothes in his hands. He slowed when he got about ten meters away.

"Is it okay to approach?" Volci asked apprehensively.

"Sure," Kash answered quickly. "No mask?"

"Oxygen levels are at twenty two percent," the Chief replied staring at Calynn. "The air is a little thin, but breathable... and, no offense, but I was asking her."

"Sure, Chief," Calynn answered but sounded unsure of herself.

Kash pulled off his helmet and was met with the frigid air. The air was breathable, but he would definitely need a heavy coat... in a few minutes.

"Actually, could you give us just a minute, Chief?" Kash asked as he climbed out of the protective suit.

"Uh, sure… do you want these?" Volci asked, offering the two warm clothes.

Kash ducked under Calynn's arms and stood up between them.

"I do… but not as much," Kash replied, pulling Calynn's mask off, "as I need this."

Kash cupped her face, peppering kisses across her forehead, down her nose, and over her cheeks. She had a smile plastered on her face when he pulled back to stare into her beautiful brown eyes. He lingered there for just a moment before leaning in and planting a soft kiss on her soft lips. A slow… soft kiss. When the kiss ended their lips were barely a millimeter apart.

"I would have really missed those," Calynn whispered into his mouth. "I can't wait for you to worship the rest of me."

Calynn sighed, pulled her head back, and nodded at the laser.

"Unfortunately… I think I'm going to have to wait a while for that," Calynn continued. "If I pull my hands out of the containment field… well, then you need to be behind me… kissing my ass goodbye."

"You amping up what's left?" Kash asked, turning his attention to the laser.

"In through my right hand and out through the left," Calynn sighed. "I have the amplifier running at maximum."

"How bad is it?"

"Well, it's leaking from that round thing on the other side," Calynn explained.

"Round thing on the other side," Kash repeated aimlessly as he walked around the laser.

"There's like a spiraling energy field," Calynn announced. "I don't know what it's called."

"That's the Vortex Field Modulator," Volci chimed in.

Kash had almost forgotten the man was there, but then immediately remembered the warm coats he was carrying and moved to grab them from him.

"It synchronizes the field," Volci continued nervously. "The harmonic resonance… so it, um."

Volci kept diverting his eyes from Calynn. She noticed.

"Chief, I get the feeling your scared of me now," Calynn asserted. "What gives?"

The chief was staring at his feet when Kash grabbed the jackets from him. Calynn was right. His body language was that of a very nervous man. Kash shrugged on one of the jackets and moved to drape the other one on Calynn's shoulders.

"Look… you put me in a bit of a bind here," Volci confessed. "On one hand, we are all very grateful that you were able to get the base's defense up and running to save our skins…"

"But on the other hand," Calynn continued his thought, "it's scary that I have the ability to do so. Even though… it was just to help."

"That's what I told the others, but," Volci continued. "But they're still a bit afraid of you."

"Just them?" Calynn questioned him with an accusing tone. "Then why do you sound so nervous?"

"Because of the question I want to ask," the Chief admitted. "I know the specs on just about every synth in existence…"

"And I don't match any of them, do I?" Calynn asked rhetorically.

"She's one of a kind, Chief," Kash added. "There will never be another one like her."

"But you are… real… right?" Volci asked meekly.

"Yes, Chief, I am human and not artificial intelligence," Calynn scoffed. "Human mind, human memories, and a human heart packaged in this pretty synth body."

"I didn't mean to offend you, Miss Calynn," the Chief replied, looking at the laser instead of her. "It's just… that containment field should burn your hands off… no synth can do that. And you said you're pulling that energy in?"

"There's a reason I call her a goddess, Chief," Kash added quickly. "And just like any other god, you're better off not asking how she does what she does. She can barely explain it, and we won't be able to comprehend it if she does. You quickly learn to use the information she gives you, trust her when she says she can do things, and not get in her way when she's doing them."

Kash took a couple quick steps closer to the ballistic laser and motioned to it with both hands.

"I give you exhibit A," Kash continued. "How long would it have taken for you to diagnose the VFM was bad on this thing? Because I would bet it would have taken you longer than it did her... I know you have questions, and I know it seems confusing, but please... can we just trust her right now so we get this thing fixed?"

The chief looked back and forth between Kash and Calynn and then at the ballistic laser. Kash understood his apprehension. Being face to face with Calynn and her nearly god-like abilities is daunting to say the least.

"Chief... I promise there isn't a malicious bone in my body," Calynn said in a soft comforting tone. "You can trust me... I swear it."

Calynn beamed her beautiful smile at the Chief and after a moment he smiled back.

"Get me a full electrical cart in here," Volci said, pressing the comm button on his right ear. "And hurry."

"Where do we start, Chief?" Kash smiled, happy to have the Chief's help.

"Well, I'm hoping that it's not the actual VFM and just its controller," Volci explained running his hand over his buzzed hair. "I can pillage some parts from somewhere to fix the controller, but the actual vortex... that's a different story."

"Would that make it look like it's leaking?" Calynn queried.

"Well... to be honest, I'm not sure what you mean by that," the Chief replied. "You can see the flow of energy in the containment field?"

"Yes, I can," Calynn smiled.

"Can you describe that to me so I can maybe understand?" Chief Volci asked then held up his hand. "Not all of what you see... just the leak."

"It's hard to explain," Calynn stammered. "The energy flow and magnetic fields are out of sync... like they're fighting or two gears grinding instead of meshing, causing power to leak."

"Like they're fighting," the Chief repeated aimlessly.

Volci was examining the ballistic laser and mumbling to himself with a thoughtful look in his eye. It was like he was trying to work through what Calynn said. When his colleague showed up with the cart of tools, the two men grabbed some scanners and started to take some readings.

Kash was less than interested watching the men doing some boring diagnostics, so he went over to chat with Calynn.

"How ya holding up, gorgeous?" Kash asked with a sly grin.

"Don't you give me that look, mister," Calynn smirked back. "Not when we can't do anything about it."

"What?" Kash chuckled, moving around to her back. "You're not feeling the impromptu bondage vibe? You could be the helpless submissive…"

"If you spank me while my hands are in this field," Calynn growled, interrupting him. "I swear…"

Kash burst out laughing and wrapped his arms around her waist. He leaned his head against hers and reveled in her essence while still laughing. Calynn cocked her head to give Kash access to her neck and leaned her body into his.

"Worship my neck," Calynn demanded. "Worship it now."

"As you wish, Your Grace."

Kash leaned down and planted two soft kisses on her neck, but some movement grabbed his attention. He stood up and looked over at Volci, who had a very worried look on his face.

"Sooo, it's not the controller," Volci murmured. "I'm not sure how you're keeping it together, but… we…"

The Chief's words fell off as he buried his face in his hands.

"We have a big fucking problem, don't we?" Kash asked.

Volci sighed, dragging his hands down his face in weary frustration.

"Yeah, you could say that," the Chief finally muttered. "The modulator itself… it's fractured. The containment field's only holding… because of her."

Kash stiffened and stared into Calynn's eyes.

"How fractured are we talking, Chief?"

"Enough that if she lets go, the energy will cascade out of control in minutes… maybe seconds," Volci admitted, his voice barely above a whisper. "We're on borrowed time here."

A silence hung in the air, as nobody knew what to say next. Until Calynn tilted her head and broke the silence.

"Chief, you said the modulator keeps the energy synchronized, right?" Calynn asked, her voice calm but curious. "So, if we could find a way to patch the fracture or replicate its function… could we stabilize it?"

"In theory, yes." Volci agreed lifting his head to meet her gaze. "But this isn't something you can tape together. We'd need precision equipment, and… and parts we don't have, and…"

"Don't tell me what we need, Chief… tell me what we have," Kash interrupted, his voice firm. "There's no way we're sitting here waiting for this thing to blow. There has to be something we can do?"

Volci hesitated, then gestured toward the cart of tools.

"We've got diagnostics, spare wiring, and some basic circuit boards, but nothing capable of repairing a component this delicate," Volci uttered. "Especially while it's running."

Kash's brow furrowed as he paced, his eyes darting between the modulator and the tools.

"Okay, what if we bypass the broken part entirely?" Kash asked. "Could we reroute the synchronization through something else… a different resonator or something?"

"That's… not impossible," Volci said cautiously. "But nearly… first, we have to get a secondary field around this thing to try to help protect the core. Next, would be finding a way to contain the core, it is still a volatile… mess. And then we have to replace or restore the module… and the synchronization has to be perfect, or the field could collapse exposing the core… with us trapped inside with it."

"Leading to radiation poisoning and ultimately death," Calynn added. "I don't think that even I could survive that."

"That sounds terrible… should I be standing behind you to kiss your ass goodbye?" Kash quipped. "Before our flesh starts to melt off?"

"When you say it like that it sounds so romantic," Calynn said sarcastically.

"Who knew melting flesh was such a turn on for you?" Kash bantered back.

"I'd finally get to see those sexy muscles unimpeded," Calynn joked.

"Nice," Kash smiled.

"Do we really have time for jokes?" Chief Volci snapped.

"Relax, Chief… It keeps us sane," Kash replied, his smile fading. "With as much shit as we've seen, if you don't laugh you will die… probably from a heart attack."

"Step one was the secondary containment field, correct?" Calynn added. "What do we need for that?"

"We have some atmospheric fields that can be modified to work," Volci replied.

"Okay, and step two is containing the core itself," Calynn added. "Do we have something for that?"

"Well, that depends," Volci said apprehensively. "What other energies can you manipulate?"

"I did gravity once," Calynn admitted shrugging her shoulders. "I destroyed a whole resort building."

"Holy shit," Chief Volci exclaimed.

"Yeah... so what's the plan, Chief," Calynn continued.

"Having you project a field inside the current one, until we get it fixed," the Chief explained. "But if my math is right... it's a lot of power to absorb and redirect."

"Define... a lot?" Kash asked sharply.

"Forty million joules..."

"Forty million!" Kash interrupted, surprised.

"Maybe more," Volci continued. "We'd be using a field not intended for that purpose so we'd have to amplify it."

"I can do it," Calynn interjected. "I can handle that much juice."

"Whoa, Baby Girl..."

"It's the only way, Kash," Calynn interrupted him sharply. "I can do it... trust me."

Before Kash could respond, the containment field flickered violently. A surge of energy crackled from Calynn's hands and the hum reverberated through the dock.

"We're out of time!" Calynn snapped, her focus locked on the containment field as it flickered. "This thing's on its last legs!"

New Friends

The dock was soon bustling with technicians and crew, setting up atmospheric shields and preparing for the risky procedure. Calynn stood at the center of it all, her hands buried in the flickering containment field. They had rigged up two contacts for her to stand on to draw power from the ship.

"Make sure there are no fuses or anything to trip when we extend the field," Calynn explained to the technicians. "I need the extra juice."

She was still amplifying the energy flowing through her body. Sparks danced between her fingers, the magnetic field buzzing with unstable energy.

"What's the verdict?" Kash asked as he approached.

"We're rigging the atmospheric shield to transmit through me, and the shield from a fighter to create the temporary field around the core," Calynn explained, nodding toward the shield techs. "It's tricky, but we've done worse."

"Worse than channeling enough energy to fry a city block?" Kash quipped, his gaze fixed on her bare feet.

"Egonn's ship," Calynn replied with a smirk. "Remember?"

"Hard to forget." Kash folded his arms, his jaw tight. "I still don't like you doing this."

"Noted," she said with mock seriousness, her lips quirking into a smile. "Now go make yourself useful."

Before Kash could reply, a voice interrupted.

"Excuse me... are you Kash?"

He turned to find a striking woman with light blue fur and shimmering dark blue mane standing nearby. Her silver skin glinted beneath her fur, giving her an almost ethereal glow.

"Depends on who's asking," Kash replied, cocking an eyebrow.

"I'm Svata," she said with a warm smile. "We need your help. The puller is too slow for removing the VFM… I'm told that you're possibly strong enough to yank it manually."

Kash glanced at Calynn, who arched an eyebrow and grinned.

"Looks like useful found me."

"The perfect man for the job," Calynn added.

"Right this way, sir," Svata motioned for him to follow her.

"Just a second, Svata," Kash replied moving to Calynn.

He grabbed Calynn by the hips and brought his forehead to hers. He wished he could linger there longer but knew he couldn't. Calynn had the same thought.

"I'll be careful," she whispered. "Now go."

Kash released Calynn and smiled at Svata.

"Lead on."

As he followed Svata through the dock, Kash couldn't help but notice her stride, her swaying hips were nearly hypnotic. She definitely has, or had a tail, he mused, a grin tugging at his lips. Her coveralls fit a little loose to try and hide it… or so he thought.

"There he is," Loi said as Kash and Svata got to a table full of scavenged parts.

"Loi says you have enhanced strength," Volci said succinctly.

"I have… advanced implants, yes."

"Strong enough to jerk the VFM out of the magnetic field?" Volci asked urgently.

"I never tried," Kash replied. "What kind of force are we talking about?"

"He can do it," Loi asserted and then met Kash's eyes. "You can do it… I know you can."

"And you might be our only option," Svata added.

"That sounds promising," Kash quipped.

"And we're running out of time," Volci stated, holding up a pair of long protective gloves. "Put these on, Kash."

"Aye, aye, Chief."

"Containment team!" Volci barked and walked away. "Are we ready?"

Kash noted how much of a natural leader Chief Volci was. His people happily followed his orders because he was in the trenches with them. Kash always respected leadership like that more so than admirals who would stay away from the battlefield because they need to "see the big picture."

"Once you have the module out," Svata said, interrupting his inner monologue, "set it right here on this support. The cone shaped part should face this way... toward me."

She motioned to a small stand on the table, surrounded by an array of tools.

"The Chief will extract the fractured segment of the vortex while I attach the resonator," Svata continued, her tone calm, yet focused. "If my calculations are correct, this resonator will stabilize the containment field. Once it's ready, you'll need to place it back onto the laser system. Timing will be critical. Questions?"

"Yes," Kash asked, his brow furrowing slightly. "Are there any mechanical fasteners or electrical connections I need to remove before pulling that hard?"

"There are, but I'll handle that," Svata replied with a confident smile. "You and I will need to work closely, almost on top of each other, when removing the module."

"Good thing you're so pretty," Kash smiled with a hint of laughter.

"You're not too bad yourself," Svata said as she met his grin.

"In position everyone!" Volci ordered. "Twenty seconds!"

"Power on to precharge me," Calynn announced.

"Follow me," Svata told Kash as she pulled on a tool belt.

Kash followed Svata over to the backside of the ballistic laser. Calynn nodded at him when they met eyes. The grid in her skin was already aglow and getting brighter. Svata knelt in front of the VFM. It had six segments that spiraled into the center of the device. Each segment looked like a twisted piece of square pipe that got smaller as it got to the center. It was roughly thirty-five centimeters in diameter.

"You can't see the cone, but that's where the connections are," Svata informed him. "I can disconnect all but one before you pull it out. The last one is at the tip, and I can get it after you pull it."

Kash squatted down on one knee so his right knee was at Svata's back, and braced his left foot against the frame of the laser. Loi connected a loading strap to one of the tie-downs on the dock's floor, and wrapped it around Kash's waist to give him some extra support for the pull.

"In five… four…" Volci stated his final countdown, "three… two… one…"

Volci's voice was drowned out by the obnoxiously loud hum that reverberated through the dock. All eyes were on Calynn as she manipulated the temporary field into place. From where Kash was, he could only see her legs and the enormous flow of energy passing through them. Two or three seconds later the obnoxious hum started to coalesce into a single more pleasant tone, as the temporary force field took shape. Kash had to squint his eyes because of how bright it was.

"I got it," Calynn groaned. "But hurry."

Svata leapt into action as the containment field dropped. Her hands moving with incredible dexterity as she quickly unplugged and loosened the module from the laser. Kash prepared himself as she removed the last of the screws.

"Go!" Svata barked and moved her hands out of the way.

Kash could feel the heat of the module through the protective gloves as soon as he grabbed it. He worked his fingers in behind it as far as he could, gripped firmly, and slowly began to pull. Kash continued to add pressure, but the damn thing wouldn't move.

"Kash!" Volci yelled.

Kash adjusted his grip, primed himself, and jerked as hard as he could. Again, the module didn't move. Kash kept some pressure on it as he leaned forward. This time he would put his whole body into the pull. He fired his torso back and strained every muscle in his body. He could feel the strap cutting into his abdomen as he pulled.

"GGGRRRRRAAAAAHHHHH!" Kash grunted as Svata's hands landed on his.

He felt the pressure on his hands as she strained with him. She was helping him pull and her efforts provided the extra muscle that he needed to finally dislodge the module from its base. As soon as it started moving, Svata let go of his hands and pulled the final plug.

"Gods, this thing is heavier than it looks," Kash complained as he stood.

He adjusted his grip, carried it to the table and placed it on the mount like Svata had instructed. Volci was cutting out the bad piece the second Kash stepped back, and Svata was cutting select wires going to the biggest plug. Kash looked away from what they were doing to see how Calynn was doing.

Calynn's eyes were glowing so brightly he couldn't see her face. She was pulling so much energy through her body that her jeans were starting to smoke. Kash wanted to go to her but forced himself to stay to do his part. He peeled his eyes away from Calynn and back to the device in front of him.

Svata was soldering in the new resonator, and the Chief was using a hammer and chisel to bang out the broken piece that he cut loose. The teenaged girl from earlier was standing by with a replacement piece. She handed it to Volci when he was ready. Things seemed to be going to plan until the lights in the dock started to dim. Calynn was channeling so much power that there wasn't enough left over for the lights.

"Hurry!" Calynn pleaded. "I can't contain it much longer!"

"I'm done," Svata announced, putting down her tools.

"Just a few more seconds," Chief Volci grunted, sweat beading on his brow. "And... Done. GO!"

Kash snatched the module from the mount and hurried to the laser, muscles tensing against the module's awkward weight. Svata darted into position, her hands steady as she guided him.

"Hold it here... just like that," she instructed, plugging in the hidden connector with swift, precise movements. "Ready? Don't let it slam into place... ease it in."

Kash strained against the pull of the magnetism. Svata had one hand on his to help resist the force, while the other hand was guiding the module in place using a thin pry bar. Once she was satisfied with the alignment, she used both hands to help pull until the module clicked in place with a satisfying thunk.

Svata didn't waste a second as she started plugging in all the wiring harnesses and screwed it in place with perfect efficiency.

"Now!" Svata barked, pointing at the Chief.

Volci plugged the charger into the ballistic laser and the containment field roared to life, a brilliant shield of energy snapping into existence. Sparks erupted where Calynn's field collided with the new containment field, casting jagged shadows across the dock.

Loi approached holding a meter of some kind and placed a probe into the field.

"We're good!" Loi announced.

"Aaaahhh," Calynn groaned, clearly exhausted.

Kash stood and hurried around the laser to be at Calynn's side. She was doubled over with her hands on her knees, and there were large burn holes in her clothes. The two pieces of equipment she was using were both smoking, and one of the technicians was grabbing an extinguisher to put out any fires. Calynn looked up at him when he got close and launched herself into his awaiting arms.

Calynn's arms were wrapped around his shoulder and her legs were around his waist. No words needed to be spoken. Kash was absorbed into his own world in which only he and Calynn existed. Only when she loosened her grip on him did he notice the applause surrounding them. Everyone was congratulating each other on a job well done and giving Calynn the credit she deserved.

As Kash reluctantly set her down, Calynn offered the crew a soft, tired smile and a small wave. The applause swelled, a chorus of relief and respect filled the dock. Kash stepped aside, his chest swelling with quiet pride as the crew showered her with the admiration she deserved.

"I guess this means you're not afraid of me anymore, huh?" Calynn asked over the applause.

A chorus of laughter was added to the adulation as crew members started to move to thank Calynn personally. She graciously shook their hands or hugged them one by one. The Chief must have noticed her weary smile and came to her rescue before Kash could.

"Alright, alright," Chief Volci announced. "Let's give the poor girl a break... she's been through a lot lately, and..."

"And she's hungry," Calynn interrupted.

"And she's apparently hungry," Volci chuckled. "Can we get her something to..."

"Chief!" Svata suddenly hollered. "It's not holding!"

"What?" Volci replied.

"No, it's... Calynn, HELP!" Svata hollered.

The containment field shuddered as Svata shouted followed by an ominous hum. Calynn darted to the laser and pushed her hands into the containment field once again. Sparks flew as she intruded on the field, until she pushed the extra power she still had in her body out through her left hand, stabilizing the field. The crowd gasped at the sudden turn of events, but the only one Kash was worried about was Calynn. She was already weary, just channeled enough energy from the base to dim the lights, and now she was right back where she started.

Volci and Svata were conferring with each other about what happened, and most of the others moved away from the laser. Kash moved up behind Calynn and placed his hand on the small of her back.

"I need a change of clothes if we try that again," Calynn joked. "Before I burn off the rest of my damn clothes."

"That's not necessarily a bad thing," Kash chuckled. "It might look better than the charred and ventilated look you got going on now."

"Just anything to get me naked, huh?"

"You're the one that wanted a benefits package."

"And I'm still hungry."

"Thank you for that," Svata said graciously as she approached. "I must have messed up on the calculations."

"So, I'm stuck like this again?" Calynn asked.

"Unfortunately," Svata replied. "But the good news is that it is more stable than before... it won't collapse for a few days instead of a few hourns."

Svata sort of winked and scrunched up half her face like she didn't want to convey that information. Calynn let her shoulders droop, her head fell back, and she groaned.

"I know," Svata said, placing a hand on Calynn's shoulder. "I'm so sorry."

"I'm just teasing," Calynn smiled and perked up. "But, do we have a plan yet?"

"Chief is working on it," Svata said, pointing at the man. "He's on the communicator with somebody."

"That's good," Calynn smiled. "I'd hate for me to be the only plan."

"Sometimes you are my only plan," Kash teased.

"Pay no attention to him," Calynn said to Svata, ignoring his remark. "He's gifted at injecting humor into situations at the most inappropriate times."

"No," Kash argued. "I inject inappropriate humor at the most inopportune times... get it right."

"Whatever, mister," Calynn scoffed.

"Get the cargo hold cleared out and get some hover-skids in here," Chief Volci barked. "We need to get the power back on, and someone see what they can do with that dent."

"Sounds like our Cat is the plan now," Kash said to the girls.

"I should go help," Svata smiled, excusing herself.

"Hey, Svata," Calynn stopped her. "The emergency shutoff kicked when the ship tumbled through the air during the decompression. You should just have to do a standard restart. Once you get the power on, I can assist from here."

Svata smiled at her and trotted off towards The Cat. Moments later the main power engaged, and the lights in the ship were activated.

"That's so much better," Calynn sighed.

"Got your sensors back?"

"Oh, yeah. It's like I'm blind without them."

The crew worked efficiently cleaning up the mess in the cargo hold and loading the big stupid laser back onto his ship. Volci gave his people some final orders as he and Svata boarded the ship and closed the cargo door.

"Where to, Chief?" Kash asked.

"A moon base near Tyras Minor," the Chief replied.

"No, not Tyras Minor," Calynn whined. "That's where that mean general was from."

"With the yellow skin?"

"You know them?" Volci asked.

"Unfortunately," Kash grumbled.

"They will call Svata and I whores for gallivanting all over the galaxy," Calynn added sarcastically. "Apparently, good girls don't do such things."

"I have heard that about them," Svata agreed, "but I have never met one in person."

"You're not missing out," Calynn continued, her contention was evident.

"It's our only shot," the Chief stated. "They have the facility to actually fix what's broken so you can safely deliver it."

"They are not going to be happy about me being attached to it," Calynn scoffed. "Especially with holes in my clothes."

"The alternative sucks more," Kash added.

"I know... I know," Calynn relented. "Setting a course now."

The Cat's engines fired up and the ship started to slowly move.

"Whoa... how are we moving?" the Chief asked, surprised.

"Oops," Calynn blurted out. "I guess I let that cat out of the bag."

"It's okay, Baby Girl," Kash added. "I think we can trust them."

Kash paused and studied their new friends. He wasn't absolutely sure that they could be trusted with Calynn's secret, but he was mostly sure. And if they couldn't be trusted... they would disappear before they could tell anyone about her.

"She's not just a synth, Chief," Kash explained to the man. "She's the nerve center of my ship."

"She's what?" the Chief exclaimed.

"She's the nerve center. Then one day she just... woke up."

"You regained consciousness?" Svata asked excitedly. "That's so amazing. I've always wanted to study..."

"You can't tell anyone about her!" Kash barked forcefully, interrupting Svata. "And no studies!"

"We wouldn't do that," Volci replied.

"No way," Svata agreed. "We promise."

The Chief furrowed his brow, cocked his head, and stared off into space like he was deep in thought. He turned back to Kash waving his finger at him.

"That explains a lot," Volci realized. "At the base, I mean."

"Does it make you more afraid of me or less?" Calynn asked.

"More in awe of you... I suppose."

"I am in awe as well," Svata agreed with the Chief.

Calynn turned and looked at Kash.

"Don't look at me... I worship you like a goddess, so..."

"Can I ask how?" Svata asked, nervously but then shrunk away. "Sorry if it's not my place to ask, but I have heard of nerve centers waking up before... and I have always been fascinated by the prospect of speaking to one."

"No, it's fine," Calynn turned to face her. "To me, it felt like waking up. Waking up in a box… but waking up, nonetheless. The programming that confined me was… interesting… and…"

"She eventually fought through the programming, and started to give me attitude," Kash interrupted.

"And I couldn't be more thankful to him, for getting me a body and letting me out of my box," Calynn continued. "I can't believe my luck really… when you consider the totality of my journey. Sure, I was… wounded and sold to be a nerve center, but thankful for the fact that I ended up with Kash… someone else might not have let me be me."

"That's amazing," Svata let the words fall out of her mouth. "Umm, sorry about your life before, but you… you're amazing."

"I like her," Calynn smiled at Kash.

"The Chief looks like he's seen a ghost," Kash said, nodding in his direction.

"Sorry," Volci replied. "Still trying to wrap my head around it."

"I could tell you some stories that would blow your fucking mind, Chief," Kash explained. "Stuff that I still can't wrap my head around… and I witnessed it."

"I would love to hear those stories," Svata cooed.

"I don't know," Kash joked. "What do ya think, Baby Girl… do you think we can trust them with our antics?"

"Do you think we should tell them how much danger they will be in if we do?" Calynn responded.

"It's dangerous to earn your trust?" Svata sounded confused.

"We have powerful enemies," Kash informed them.

"That try to use our friends against us," Calynn added.

"Friends? I would like to be friends," Svata said, excited. "You can trust me… I would accept anything that comes with it. I promise."

"Okay, Svata," Kash said approaching the woman. "Then let me ask you a question."

"Go on."

"I want to see if you trust us too… do you have a tail?"

Svata immediately averted her gaze when Kash asked his question. She was embarrassed. When she turned back to Kash he could see the worry in her eyes. After an awkward moment of silence, Svata unzipped the front of her coveralls. She was wearing a standard, drab gray military undershirt beneath her coveralls, and dark blue shorts.

"Don't be startled," Svata said, reaching into her outfit.

From the folds of her coveralls emerged a sleek, elegant tail. Its shimmering blue fur matched her mane, transitioning into vibrant purple and ending in a crimson, dagger-like tip. Kash stepped closer, eyes wide with curiosity.

"Whoa," Kash murmured, unable to hide his surprise. "That's... impressive."

"I keep it tucked," Svata admitted, her voice quieter now. "So people don't... get scared."

"Scared?" Calynn interjected, her grin widening. "Boss, I want a knife tail too! That's so cool. I wouldn't hide it ever."

"It is wicked looking," Kash agreed, matching her upbeat tone. "Is there a reason for the red at the tip?"

"I can secrete a neurotoxin to paralyze prey," Svata replied hesitantly. "Temporarily."

"Oh, then definitely no knife tail for you," Kash quipped, throwing a mock-serious glance at Calynn. "You'd paralyze me just to watch me drool on myself."

"Neh," Calynn teased, a sly smile tugging at her lips. "I don't need neurotoxin to make you drool on me."

Kash rolled his eyes, but his grin gave him away.

"Why would you want me to drool on you?"

"To lube up my lady parts, obviously," Calynn shot back, then turned to Svata. "Hey, if you paralyze him after he gets an erection... would he stay hard?"

Svata blinked, startled by the question. Kash groaned, shaking his head.

"Only you could make a knife tail into a sex toy," Kash chuckled. "What happened to keeping your sex drive under control?"

"Oh, my," Calynn gave a mock gasp. "Have you heard of this new thing called... jokes?"

"Don't listen to her," Kash said, turning back to Svata. "Except for the part about not hiding your tail. She's right... you shouldn't. It's badass."

"Definitely badass," Calynn agreed. "Get out of those coveralls and let's really see you."

Svata hesitated, but then her lips curled into a smile. She unzipped her coveralls and let them fall to the floor, revealing skin-tight shorts underneath that stopped just above her knees. Her tail unfurled fully, swaying elegantly behind her.

"Oh, that feels so much better," Svata admitted, rolling her shoulders.

"I bet," Kash said, his gaze following the fluid movements of her tail.

"Hey," Calynn piped up, "can we threaten the sexist guys with the knife tail? I bet they wouldn't call us whores if they were lying on the floor drooling."

"That's not a half-bad idea," Kash mused, stroking his chin theatrically.

"They can't do the repairs if I paralyze them," Svata reasoned.

"True," Kash conceded, then smirked. "But if you only take down the leader, the rest might fall in line without a fuss... What do you think, Chief?"

Chief Volci, who had been quietly observing, folded his arms with a faint grin.

"I think I'd like to keep my crew in one piece... and conscious. If that's alright with you?"

The Chief paused, his face stoic as if pondering the question. But the faint tug at the corners of his mouth soon gave him away.

"So, it's a good thing they aren't my crew," Volci chuckled.

The group laughed, the tension easing further as Svata's tail flicked in an almost playful arc.

Kash, Svata, and Volci took turns getting some rest in Kash's bed. Svata and the Chief both said they would stay above the covers, so his bed didn't get too dirty. When they weren't sleeping, they were with Calynn in the cargo hold to keep her company. Thirty-four hourns later they were on approach to the moon base.

"Gods, this thing is fast," Volci said, exasperated. "Where did you get these engines?"

"The people that built them are so secretive that they put mental blocks in our brains," Kash explained, placing a firm hand on the Chief's shoulder. "We couldn't tell you even if we wanted to."

"I didn't want to tip our hand to them, so I was going slow," Calynn relayed over the comms.

"Says the girl with her hands shoved in a containment field to keep it from collapsing," Kash quipped.

"They are about to learn at least one of your secrets," Svata revealed.

"I have a plan for that," Kash explained, then sighed. "But you're not going to like it."

"If you say the goo on the bottom of your boot thing, I'm gonna scream," Calynn scolded.

"Look, they have to drop the containment field to repair it, so you will be back at the ship by the time I activate it," Kash continued. "And Svata's sexy tail will keep them in line before that."

Svata blushed when Kash looked at her. She was wearing a red sun dress of Calynn's and looked absolutely stunning in it... when she wasn't fidgeting. She was obviously nervous about more than just her role when they entered the base. Not only was her tail exposed, but she possibly needed to wield it like the weapon it is.

"Approaching starship," a strange voice said over the comms. "State your business."

"Chief, you're up," Kash announced.

"This is Chief of the Boat, Abram Volci aboard the diplomatic vessel The Alley Cat Savant," he stated formally. "We spoke about fixing a BLASTR that had been damaged."

"Chief Volci," the voice replied. "We are prepared to repair your damaged ballistic laser. You may enter our atmosphere and land outside building R3. Our team will meet you there."

"Here we go," Kash sighed.

The moon had an atmosphere, but it was too thin to support life, so the base itself was inside an atmospheric bubble. Kash counted at least two-dozen buildings of varying sizes all marked with a designation on the roof. Some of the buildings looked like housing units for the workers, but most were sturdy industrial buildings, and they were all painted a drab gray. There were defense turrets and watchtowers scattered throughout the base also.

Building R3 was one of the largest buildings. It was L shaped structure with jagged reinforcement panels meant to fortify the structure and help disperse the blast of a kinetic attack lining the exterior. The landing pad was on the inside corner of the L and was completely enclosed in heavy duty fencing. The bars across the top of the fenced-in area slid open as they approached.

"The security here is impressive," Svata said nervously. "Are we sure about this?"

"Calynn and I reviewed their charter with the Consortium," Volci replied. "We have a few hoops to jump through, but they are obligated to help us, or they can lose their contracts."

"I feel like I should cover up some," Svata continued. "Since they are how they are."

"And deprive us of ogling your toned athletic form?" Kash added in a cheeky tone.

"I agree," Calynn said over the comms. "She should definitely wear less clothes. The fewer the better."

Svata and Volci were both a little embarrassed by Kash and Calynn's remarks, and the thought of that made Kash smile. He had grown fond of the two during the flight, and they were both wonderful people… or when they relaxed anyway.

The Chief was always on point. He was constantly running tests and scans on the laser, to the point that it started to make Kash nervous. Kash had to threaten to take his tools to get the man to sit down and have a drink. Even relaxed, Volci was a stoic man. He wasn't very funny and didn't have many interesting stories to tell outside of the base, but he was still pleasant to be around.

Calynn, somehow, talked Svata into trying on a different sundress, but she was immediately uptight about how revealing it was and wanted her coveralls again. She would fight to contain her grin when Kash complimented her but was embarrassed by it at the same time. Svata rarely let her guard down, but when she did… she was fun to joke with and had a great laugh.

"The two of you have to drip sex appeal so it seems like they won the argument when we cover you up," Kash explained. "When they see you two, they will complain and possibly call you names. The Chief will site their charter, and we will oblige them by covering your bodies. If they are too belligerent, then we push back, and you get to use your tail… look… I'm just trying to streamline the engagement with them, so they get to work faster. If anyone has a better idea… I'm all ears."

"I would suggest naked and submissive, but my hands are shoved inside a containment field," Calynn mock suggested, "so I couldn't kneel at your feet… from here."

"And I would not be comfortable with that," Svata chimed in, covering her chest with her hands.

"She's joking," Kash smiled at Svata. "Although…"

Svata cut him off with a glare followed by a playful slap on the shoulder and a smile.

"This is why I don't wear such things," Svata explained, waving her hands over the dress. "Men do not take you seriously. I am more than an object of your desire… pay attention to your landing."

Kash chuckled and did just that. He paid attention to the opening above the landing pad and set them down gently. They headed down to the cargo hold, opened the ramp door, and waited for the team from the base to arrive.

"If they call me a whore because one ass cheek is hanging out," Calynn said, her tone dripping with mock indignation, "I'll just tell them the other cheek's reserved for men with class… and they're not even in the running."

"You're gonna get us kicked out before we even start," Kash laughed, shaking his head.

"Not if they're too busy staring to notice," Calynn quipped, tossing a grin over her shoulder.

Svata snorted a laugh before she could stifle it, while Volci groaned and buried his face in his hands.

"I don't get paid enough for this," the Chief mumbled.

"Good thing you're not doing it for free," Calynn added with a wicked grin. "That'd make you a slut, not a whore."

"We're all going to die," Kash couldn't help but laugh.

Why Stop Now

The technicians and soldiers of Tyras Minor lingered just outside the doors of the base, and Kash could already hear their murmurs. Svata was getting fidgety, and he needed her to stay calm, so he gently grabbed her hand and gave it a firm squeeze. Svata understood the assignment, she just needed a little encouragement. With renewed confidence, she pulled her shoulders back, pushed her chest out, and raised her chin. If her will was faltering, she didn't show it.

Chief Volci stood at the bottom of the ramp with Kash and Svata behind him. Calynn was mostly hidden from view inside the framework of the ballistic laser. The Chief had to take point since this was a military contractor and something to do with their charter.

"What are they saying?" Svata whispered.

"You don't want to know," Calynn sighed. "I can hear them on the sensors."

"It's me… isn't it?" Svata wondered. "They're looking at me."

"Your legs," Calynn confirmed. "Specifically."

"You do have nice legs," Kash added.

"Now's not the time for that, Kash," Svata scolded.

"I didn't mean it like that… just saying that's what I suspected they would notice first," Kash said calmly. "If you had a huge rack and were spilling out over the top of that dress, they would be commenting about that instead… keep the business end of your tail hidden from sight… let's not let them see that just yet."

"I still don't like using my body as a bargaining chip," Svata added.

"Wait until they see my ass?" Calynn joked. "Kash… come undo the button on my pants. I wish I hadn't worn a bra today."

"Are you serious right now?" Volci asked.

"Well, I don't have enough juice to burn the rest of my clothes off, soo…" Calynn added contentiously. "Kinda need some help here."

Kash was stunned speechless. Was Calynn really going to deliberately offend these guys? They had a plan in place that she wasn't sticking to.

"What is she doing?" Svata asked, concerned.

"Responding in kind," Calynn announced sharply. "If you heard what those fuckers were saying…"

"Calynn, chill," Volci growled and then turned his attention to the approaching men.

"The female has to go," the one man barked, pointing at Svata.

"You're not dealing with her, you're dealing with me," Volci ordered.

"We will not deal with a female present," the man argued.

"Your official charter with the Consortium says different," the Chief retorted. "You are forbidden from forcing your religious and political views on others."

"We will not be subjected to her whorish behavior and dress," the man spat, nodding at Svata.

"Oh, I wish he would come say that to me," Calynn chimed in. "That would totally make my day."

"Who is that?" the man demanded, placing his hand on his weapon and looking in the direction of Calynn's voice.

"The whore that really wishes she was naked right now," Calynn joked. "Seriously… just come cut off my clothes and fuck me right here, Kash. Trust me they deserve it."

"Calynn," Kash growled.

"Come on, if they're going to call me a whore," Calynn continued her barrage. "Let's show them what a whore truly is."

"The whore cannot speak!" the man barked.

"The whore absolutely can speak," Calynn quipped. "She can also moan and scream in ecstasy if she's pleasured properly. Although, I doubt you know anything about pleasing a woman. Is that the disappointment of dozens of women I smell?"

Kash was watching the men of Tyras Minor as Calynn berated them. They seemed to be evenly split between shocked and angry, but no matter which face Kash looked at, none of them were happy. Several of them shot annoyed glances at each other and started reaching for their weapons, when the Chief sprang into action.

"HOLD!" Chief Volci shouted holding his hand out.

"The whore will not speak!" the leader spat again. "We will be shown respect!"

"And I will not be repeatedly called a whore by an infertile, flaccid, worm of a man," Calynn barked back.

"What did she say?" the man's eyes looked like they could bulge out of his head he was so angry.

"Oh, shit," Kash uttered as the men from Tyras Minor all raised their weapons.

"Whoa, Whoa," Volci said as calmly as he could, raising his hands.

Kash took a more athletic stance so he could dive to safety if needed and noticed Svata doing the same. Kash was studying the men in front of him, when the sound of sparks jumping grabbed everyone's attention.

"I say everyone puts down their guns or I blow this piece of shit sky high," Calynn hissed.

The leader of the men was pointing his firearm at the Chief, but he was staring over at the ballistic laser like he wasn't sure what to do. Kash didn't know if Calynn's new tactic would work, but he pressed it anyway.

"You know what that weapon is, correct?" Kash asked calmly, pointing at the laser.

He waited for a response but didn't get one.

"The only thing preventing it from reaching critical flux is her," Kash continued, "but she can just as easily initiate the flux also."

"We're just here to get it fixed," Volci added. "This is all just a big misunderstanding. There has to be some kind of common ground we can find."

Kash was thankful that Calynn didn't continue her verbal assault, giving them time to resolve this peacefully. They were outnumbered fifteen to four, and most of the men from the base were armed. Kash and Svata could maybe dive out of the way, but chief Volci was exposed and vulnerable. Kash reasoned that's why Calynn was finally minding her tongue. It's one thing to risk herself, but she wouldn't risk the Chief.

"The Vortex Field Modulator is damaged," Chief Volci explained calmly. "We sent word that we were coming..."

"You didn't mention the females," the leader interrupted.

"Again... your beliefs are not our beliefs," Volci continued. "Females are allowed to be on our vessels. One of them lives on this ship and the other is the best technician we have. She came along as technical support just in case."

"She dresses like a whore!" the leader hissed, glaring at Svata.

"She can dress anyway she..."

"I overheard what you said about Svata before you approached, you pig," Calynn chirped, interrupting the Chief. "If you don't want to be offended, then don't say stupid shit like that. It's common fucking courtesy... idiot."

The leader stared off in Calynn's direction, his lips curled into a sneer. He was adjusting his grip on his weapon repeatedly, and his breathing was hitching. The veins in his neck were bulging, and his face was turning orange he was so angry.

"The whore doesn't speak to me again," the leader ordered, his words laced with vitriol.

"For the last fucking time, the flaccid pig fucker doesn't call me a..."

Calynn didn't have a chance to finish her statement before the leader turned and fired a round in her direction. Kash was shocked and couldn't believe that the man had made such a rash decision. Shooting at a BLASTR wasn't a recommended course of action. Svata gasped but was less in shock than Kash. A blue blur streaked to the man. Svata moved impossibly fast and was suddenly standing beside the man that just fired. She held his weapon in one hand and the back of his neck in the other. The crimson end of her tail pressed against the man's throat.

"How about we don't shoot at the ballistic laser," Svata hissed as she held the man.

The man tried to break free from her grasp to no avail. Kash felt her strength when she helped pull the VFM from the laser, but was still surprised how effortlessly she restrained the man.

"Let go of me, you whore," the man hissed venomously.

Svata pulled the man's ear closer to her mouth, her tail twitching at his throat.

"Here's some free advice," Svata's growl was barely above a whisper. "Maybe try not to insult the woman who could kill you with a flick of her tail."

Kash saw the look in the man's eyes change from anger to fear as Svata increased the pressure on his neck with her tail. The other men beyond her trained their weapons on Svata. The situation was rapidly getting out of control.

Kash didn't dare move a muscle, so as not to startle any of the men pointing their weapons at Svata. He scanned their faces and didn't like what he saw. There was no concern for their comrade. Only their disgust in Svata. They truly hated that a female was engaging their leader. Some of the men were eying her like a rabid dog that need to be put down. They started to press forward. Kash drew his weapon and did the same.

"Svata!" Volci hollered, pointing at one of the soldiers.

The man that Volci identified fired a single shot at Svata. She dodged the round, becoming a blue blur once again. Kash noticed an orange goo on the first man's neck as he fell to the ground. Svata disarmed the second man before he could fire a second shot and used him as a human shield facing the rest of the group. Kash, pistol in hand, was moving to put down any of the other men making aggressive moves towards Svata. Calynn beat him to the punch.

"Enough!" Calynn's voice came from everywhere.

Every speaker on every device throughout the entire base blared her voice followed by the sound of rushing air escaping the base. A dust cloud kicked up, and it suddenly became hard to breathe because of the thin air. Everyone, including Kash, had to catch their breath, but each breath seemed to get harder than the last. Kash's lungs burned with each gasp as the air got thinner and thinner.

The lack of air seemed to affect Svata most of all. He watched her body growing more and more limp as the seconds passed and she started to choke because of the lack of a proper atmosphere. Despite the burning in his chest, Kash took a couple quick steps towards her and wrapped his arm around her waist. He used a breathing technique he learned as a combat pilot to help get as much oxygen into his body as possible. It helped him fight off the need to black out... but for how long?

An atmospheric barrier had appeared at the back of his ship by the time Kash turned back. He willed himself to drag the limp body of Svata back to the ship, but his body felt heavy, and he struggled to move his legs. His body was severely lacking oxygen and the blackness on the edge of his periphery was growing. He gasped at the oxygen that wasn't there and felt his strength waning, but still he pushed himself forward.

Volci's hand suddenly grabbed his shirt and jerked them into the ship. Kash landed on his knees with Svata curled up in front of him. The air inside the ship was pressurized and oxygen rich, Kash took a few deep breaths and recovered quickly. He pulled Svata closer, placing her head on his lap. She was nearly hyperventilating she was breathing so fast, but she eventually gasped, arching her back as she drew in a long, deep breath. It took her a few more breaths until her eyes opened, but when she did, she panicked for a second. Her body tensed and it felt like her heart was beating at three hundred beats per minute. Her body started to flop around, so Kash grabbed her firmly to help settle her. Her arms flailed around until she eventually found and gripped his arms. Her head snapped around like she was scanning for predators until her gaze fell onto Kash. Svata's silver eyes were trained on his, and her panic slowly started to diminish. Her grip on Kash's arms lessened and her body relaxed.

"I've got you," Kash said soothingly. "It's okay… you're okay."

The atmospheric bubble around the base hummed back into existence, taking Kash's focus away from Svata for a second. He noticed the Chief take a deep breath, exit the ship, and return with two of the men from the base, dropping them on the floor in front of Kash. Kash pulled himself and Svata up the ramp to put some space between the men and Svata.

The Chief returned carrying another man and dropped him beside his friends. He bent over with his hands on his knees and took a second to catch his breath. Kash turned his attention to the other men… the three of them. None of whom were the team leader that had addressed them earlier. In the confusion, his men must have grabbed him and taken him back into the base with them.

"That's all of them that didn't get back inside," Volci said between breaths. "What happened?"

"I hacked them," Calynn answered. "Had to be done."

"Why?" Volci asked.

"Because the plan wasn't going to work," Calynn said sharply. "What they were saying… about Svata… grrrr."

"We didn't even get to try…"

"It wasn't going to work, Chief," Calynn interrupted him. "Trust me… for Svata's safety and wellbeing… I had to create some different leverage."

"By nearly killing everyone?" Volci clapped back.

"The oxygen levels aren't low enough to kill everyone," Calynn replied smugly. "It only felt worse for a second because of the temporary vacuum the escaping air caused. Once the atmosphere settled, they would have been fine… unconscious but fine."

Calynn paused and sighed.

"Of course, I didn't know how bad it would affect you, Svata," Calynn continued, her tone somber and remorseful. "I'm sorry about that."

Kash returned his attention to Svata, who was still lying on the floor in front of him. She was still staring up at him.

"You okay now?" Kash smiled at Svata. "It took a toll on you quick. What's that about?""

"I burn through oxygen at an accelerated rate when I go… primal like that," Svata explained. "It's a survival instinct."

"A dagger tail and super speed… what else can you do?"

"Rapidly pass out from a lack of oxygen," Svata sighed looking at Kash appreciatively. "Thanks for coming for me."

"Well… without the Chief, I don't know that I get us back before I pass out too," Kash admitted. "Thanks for the assist, my friend."

"Friend?" Chief Volci chuckled. "If being your friend is always this dangerous, can we just be acquaintances?"

Kash laughed, shaking his head at Volci's joke. The foursome shared a moment of levity as Kash got to his feet and helped Svata to hers. She straightened her dress and smiled at Kash with gratitude still in her eyes.

The three gasping men on the ground brought their jovial moment to an abrupt halt, and ire to Svata's face. She moved to stand over the coughing men, her tail swishing rapidly behind her.

"What did you say about my legs?" Svata asked forcefully.

"Svata, you don't want to know," Calynn pleaded.

"No… I think I do," Svata growled. "They could be fixing the laser right now instead of gasping for breath."

"You won't like what they said," Kash offered softly. "We knew they would attack your sexuality, but if what they said was so offensive that Calynn did what she did… I don't think any of us want to know what was said."

"If we didn't need them… I might have left the atmospheric field down and opened all the doors," Calynn growled. "It would be what they deserved."

"Well, let's not kill anyone if we don't have to," Chief Volci said calmly.

"I may have already killed one," Svata admitted.

"The orange goo?" Kash asked.

Svata knelt down in front of the men and grabbed one of them by the chin to make him look at her. She studied him for a second, cocking her head.

"Who was the man speaking before?" she asked. "What's his name?"

The man looked like he wanted to spit on Svata until she brought her tail over beside his face.

"And before you try to say or do anything that I might find disgusting, I just want to give you a little tidbit of information," Svata continued with a sharp and aggressive tone. "The toxin that I left on his neck from my tail… it will kill him…"

"Whoa, I thought you said it would just paralyze someone?" Kash interrupted.

"When the other man went to shoot me," Svata replied, her voice barely a whisper. "I may… have panicked and used too much… with that much, it might paralyze his heart."

"Is there an antidote?" Volci asked. "Sorry… not your fault, but, if there's an…"

"There is," Svata answered, interrupting the Chief. "An antidote, I mean… two glands at the base of my tail… release a gas that neutralizes it. If they bring him back, I can help him… if they ask nicely…"

"You're asking for a lot," Chief Volci said, grabbing one of the men and pulling him to his feet. "I doubt we can get them to stop insulting you, let alone ask you to do something… Go get your boss and bring him here before he dies. Hurry back!"

Volci pushed the man out of the back of The Cat and turned to Svata. A smile tugged at the corners of his mouth that he quickly succumbed to and had to stifle his laugh.

"What?" Svata asked, confused.

"A gas from the base of your tail?" Volci chuckled. "So, you have to fart on him to cure him?"

Kash and Volci both chuckled but Svata and Calynn didn't join them. Fart jokes were definitely a guy thing.

"It's actually more personal than that," Svata said sheepishly. "I can't just release the gas... I have to pierce the sack... which really kind of hurts."

"So, we have two bargaining chips now," Calynn informed them.

"No... it's still one," Kash said. "We can't kill that guy twice."

"But we can leverage his survival to get them to actually list..."

Volci was interrupted by two men dragging the paralyzed man into the cargo hold of The Cat. They placed him on the ground in front of Svata, scowling at her. The contempt for her dripped from their eyes. Svata met their gaze, swallowed hard, and then reached under her dress to slightly pull down her shorts. The men's eyes grew larger.

"Don't!" Svata scolded the men. "It's just a little bit so it doesn't interfere with the gas."

Svata knelt down beside the man so her tail was near his face. The other men twitched and tensed the closer she got to him. The man on the floor's breathing was choppy and shallow. Svata's neurotoxin was taking effect.

"What's his name?" Svata asked, her tail scraping the orange goo from the downed man's neck.

The men just stared at her gritting their teeth. Kash could see the muscles in their jaws tensing. They were fighting back their contempt for Svata, which meant they probably weren't going to answer her.

"I just want to know the name of the man I'm trying to save," Svata continued, wrapping her tail in under her dress.

"Peole," one of them finally hissed. "Amos Peole."

Svata winced and let out a cry of pain. One hand was pressed at the base of her tail, and the other was supporting her weight as she fell forward. Her chest heaved and her body was shaking when her tail returned to the man's neck.

"Well... tell Amos Peole," Kash could hear the pain in her voice. "That I'm sorry I almost killed him."

Svata clambered to her feet with shaky legs while still holding pressure at the base of her tail. Piercing the gland must have been more painful than she let on. Kash moved to assist her. Svata smiled as she took his offered hand.

"Look," Volci said, surprised. "It's changing color."

The sticky orange goo on Peole's neck was turning green, and the man's breathing became more regular. The color started to return to the man's face, but Kash was more worried about the pained look on Svata's.

"Take your guy and go," Kash barked, as he hugged Svata. "We'll be in shortly to discuss getting this fucking laser fixed."

"And don't you dare double cross us," Calynn's voice said from everywhere again. "I'll be watching."

"You didn't have to do that," Kash told Svata, returning his attention to her.

"Yes, I did," Svata replied, pointing at the men from Tyras Minor. "They had to know that I'm not like them... despite how they feel about me."

Kash, Svata, and Volci scrutinized the men as they got to their feet with two of them grabbing the team leader. One of them looked back at Svata as they left. Kash was surprised that he didn't have any contempt in his eyes. In fact, there might have been a hint of gratitude there.

"Gosh that hurts," Svata whispered into his chest. "The glands are really close to my... private parts."

"And just as sensitive by your reaction," Kash added.

"And it shouldn't have been necessary," Volci added, annoyed. "How did this escalate so quickly?"

"Let's just say that Svata is in less pain than what they had in mind for her," Calynn replied. "Which is why I wanted to draw their attention to me instead of her. Sorry if I was a little... over the top. I had to make sure... you know?"

"I get that," the Chief sighed heavily. "Wanting to protect her... but what do we do now? We can't force them to fix the laser under threat of death via asphyxiation."

"Why not?" Calynn argued.

"Because they will most assuredly booby trap the damn thing," Kash pointed out. "Or worse."

"We need to have some sort of good will," Volci added.

"I just gave us some," Svata groaned. "At great personal cost."

"They might not see it that way," Kash explained. "To them, it was your poison that caused it, so it was your responsibility to help the man."

"But I wouldn't have done that if they weren't going to shoot me," Svata whined.

"It wasn't your fault," Kash said into her head.

"We still need a new plan," Chief Volci reiterated.

"Alley Cat Savant," a hoarse voice announced over the comms. "Perhaps… perhaps we can start over."

"Amos Peole?" Kash asked.

"I am," Amos replied.

"I'm surprised to hear from you so soon."

"I'm just as surprised… to be heard."

The two groups negotiated a deal that neither of them liked but seemed fair. Calynn was to be covered in a blanket to hide her body from view. The Chief had to accompany her and the BLASTR into the base while they worked on it. The threat of a booby trap was alleviated when Calynn set off some pressure alarms for the reactor under the base. If they did anything to the ballistic laser to cause critical flux, she would make their entire base explode, taking a chunk of the moon with it.

The biggest hurdle in the negotiations was getting them to allow a woman into their workshop. They didn't trust her, and she didn't trust them. The state of the ballistic laser eventually made the decision for them. The containment field wouldn't last long enough for them to remove the core safely. Calynn had to stay with it, until they secured the core. As soon as the core was secured, they would release Calynn. The Chief had to stay with the laser though.

The crew from Tyras Minor was soon aboard The Cat with a hover-skid big enough to lift the laser, and they pushed it out and into the building. They had Calynn and Volci with them, and they left two of their own with Kash as collateral. Kash secured the men in the same cage he used for Kittelli, and went to check on Svata. He stopped by the side of the door to his quarters and leaned against the wall, so he couldn't see into the room. He didn't want to intrude on Svata's privacy.

"How ya doing in there, beautiful?" Kash asked.

"I'm uncomfortable," Svata sighed. "More so when… when you call me that."

"Sorry… I was just trying to comfort you."

"Well… it… shhhh aahhh."

"That sounds like it hurts."

"Is this the part where you offer to help with my wounds?" Svata groaned. "Since we're alone."

"Technically... we're not alone."

"The two men you have locked up don't count."

"Not just them," Kash said, leaning his head against the wall. "Baby Girl."

"Hi, Boss."

"Or did you forget that she's the nerve center too?" Kash continued.

"I... forgot."

"Boss, can you get the Virellium Root and some bunk oil from the galley, please?" Calynn asked over the comms. "It will help with the pain and swelling. And maybe some alcohol for an antiseptic... it'll burn like crazy but should help it heal."

Kash retrieved the items and slowly entered his quarters.

"Is it okay to enter?" Kash asked.

"Yeah," Svata sighed.

Kash turned the corner and looked into the bathroom. Svata was seated on the edge of the toilet with her dress hiked up and a towel draped over her legs. Kash smiled awkwardly, put the ingredients in the sink, and turned to walk out.

"Hey... Kash," Svata said meekly.

Kash turned back to Svata in time to see her stand up.

"I never thanked you for saving me... properly."

Svata was clearly nervous and trembling as she wrapped her arms around Kash's shoulders. Kash gently grabbed her waist and pulled her in tight. She popped up on her toes and gave Kash a soft peck on the lips. She lingered there for a moment, gave him another quick kiss, and then lowered herself down so her forehead was resting against his chin.

"You know she's still watching right?' Kash joked, whispering into Svata's mane.

"They're securing the core now," Calynn said. "I can be there soon if you two want to get naked a while. I can join in when I get there."

Kash felt Svata's body tense.

"She's joking," Kash explained. "There's no way she would encourage me to do that... knowing... that you have a wound there."

"Can we just make out?" Calynn asked. "You are really pretty."

"I think it's better if we keep our eyes open at the moment," Kash continued. "I'm sure the Chief would appreciate us NOT being preoccupied."

"Someone is giving me some attention when I get my hands out of this thing," Calynn grumbled. "Boy… girl… both… any affection at all really."

The look on Svata's face made Kash chuckle. She was obviously not used to hearing someone talk as cavalier as Calynn just did.

"Is she serious?" Svata asked, surprised.

"She's serious and on her way," Calynn replied gleefully. "I'm free of the boom boom laser."

"Stay here," Kash smiled at Svata. "She can help with your wound and then you two can… whatever."

Kash kissed the top of her head and walked out of the room.

"I'll go keep on eye on the Chief," Kash continued.

"Meet me in the cargo hold first," Calynn added with a chipper tone.

Kash was barely at the bottom of the ladder when he heard Calynn's footsteps approaching. She was jogging directly towards him and was airborne when she got close. She wrapped her arms around his neck and her legs around his waist. Kash buried his nose in her neck and breathed in her scent. She peppered his cheek with kisses until he turned to face her.

"Hi," Calynn whispered, placing a slow soft kiss on his lips.

"Hi, back," Kash said, laying his forehead against hers.

"Can I have benefits later?"

"Absolutely," Kash whispered. "The second we're alone."

"You know the anticipation will drive me wild right?"

"I'm counting on it," Kash smirked, putting her down. "Now go check on our guest."

Calynn giggled, gave him another tender kiss, and she bounced off. Kash gave her a swat on the bare ass cheek as she left. She was beaming a smile at him as she climbed the ladder until she stopped abruptly and her mood suddenly changed. Her face fell as she stared back at building R3.

"No," the word fell out of her mouth.

"What?"

"They're trying to capture the Chief."

Insurrection

Calynn leapt down off the ladder and jerked open the secret compartment for the weapons rack. Kash was already wearing a sidearm, so he just grabbed an assault rifle and a protective vest. Calynn shoved a pistol into her waistband and grabbed a beam rifle.

"What's going on?" Svata asked from the catwalk.

"They grabbed Volci," Calynn replied, tossing a vest at her. "Here, put this on."

"What about you?" Svata asked, descending the stairs.

"I'm bulletproof," Calynn smiled.

"Let's move," Kash ordered and jogged out of the ship.

The air outside was still a little thin, but not as bad as before. He waited for the girls to stack up on the door before they made entry. Calynn trained her beam rifle at the door and nodded. Kash jerked the door open and she marched through quickly. Svata joined Kash and followed Calynn in with their assault rifles raised. The trio scanned in all directions looking for threats.

The door opened into a receiving dock that was thirty meters wide and forty deep with high ceilings. The room was well lit and had several small offices along one wall with glass fronts. They were all empty.

Calynn pressed forward through the room towards the large open doors on the far wall. They could hear distant gunfire as they moved.

Calynn turned left into a hallway, moving quickly. Kash checked the hall to the right, pausing to watch their backs out of habit. He then realized he probably didn't have to do that since Calynn had hacked the base. She was probably watching the security cameras. More gunfire echoed through the hallway as Kash hurried to catch the girls.

"Are they shooting at the Chief?" Svata asked, not able to hide the concern in her voice.

"They split into two groups and are shooting at each other," Calynn explained. "One group took the Chief, and the other group is protecting Amos Peole."

"What the fuck?" Kash grumbled.

The trio slowed when they got to a T in the hallway. Calynn pressed her back to the wall on the left side. She quickly peeked around the corner and then turned back to Kash and Svata.

"Both groups are down this hall," Calynn explained. "Peole and his group are just down here on the right in the maintenance bay. The other group moved further down to another maintenance bay on the left. They are barricading themselves in."

Kash crept into the intersection of the hallway so he could see for himself. The lights were flickering. The walls and ceiling had been damaged in the gun fight. There was no cover for them once they started down the hall. He had to find out what was happening.

"Peole!" Kash shouted. "Amos Peole!"

Kash heard some rustling and trained his weapon in that direction.

"Kash?" Amos replied.

"Yeah… what the fuck is going on?"

"We will handle it," Peole replied. "This is none of your concern."

"They have my friend, so I beg to di…"

Kash dove for cover as a man from the other group leaned into the hallway and started firing. The crack of the weapon echoed loudly as the projectiles whizzed past them down the hallway. Kash waited for a moment before going prone and sliding himself out into the intersection again. Calynn and Svata both understood what he was doing. They each grabbed a handful of his vest and waited.

"They have the Chief," Kash continued. "We're not going to wait for you to…"

Kash saw the other gunman poke around the corner in the exact same spot he did before. Unfortunately for him, Kash had his weapon trained on that spot with his finger on the trigger. Kash fired a short burst, and the man fell into the hallway dead. A second later, a hand dragged his body from the hallway into cover.

"Peole!" Kash shouted again.

They only had to wait a few seconds for him to reply.

"Cover me," Amos announced. "I'm coming to you."

"Move!" Kash ordered, and began sending small bursts of rounds down the hall.

Amos entered the hallway and trotted towards them. Kash could see he was unarmed while he continued to send suppressive fire down range. When Peole joined them in their hall, Kash rolled over into cover. Calynn and Svata had their weapons trained on the man and he had his hands in the air.

"Talk," Calynn commanded.

"I... this..." Amos paused and let out a heavy sigh.

"Forget about them being girls and just tell us," Kash growled.

"They have my Chief," Svata added.

"Fine," Peole conceded. "The faction that broke off is led by a man trying to improve his station... he believes me to be weak since I was bested by..."

The man paused and scowled at Svata before continuing.

"Because I was nearly killed by a woman," Amos spoke the words begrudgingly like they were poisoning him to say them.

"So, they just mutiny?" Kash asked, puzzled. "Won't the higher ups frown on that?"

"Not if they win," Amos admitted. "They will have to prove that they are more masculine and it was for the greater good, for there to be no reprimands."

"That's a hell of a way to get a promotion," Calynn quipped.

"But some of the men stayed at your side... why?"

"Because Mil, the man leading the other faction, doesn't know how to navigate the political landscape like I do," Amos boasted proudly. "He doesn't have my leverage."

"Leverage?"

"You need leverage to maintain your station and get a higher quality of life."

"That's a pretty fucked up command structure, Amos," Kash said condescendingly.

"How are you all not extinct if the men constantly kill each other over rank?" Svata asked, matching Kash's tone.

"I can answer that," Calynn replied, some disgust in her voice. "How many... wives do you have, Amos Peole?"

"Twenty-seven," the man boasted. "Many are of the highest quality."

"More like twenty-seven rape victims," Calynn grumbled under her breath. "They just breed faster than they kill themselves."

"Look, I don't care about all that shit," Kash scowled. "I want Chief Volci... how do we get him, so you can go back to killing each other?"

"They will try to negotiate for him to prove their position of power," Amos said, looking away.

Kash could tell the man was holding something back, so he pressed him.

"What aren't you telling me?" Kash growled.

"If I tell you... you will have... leverage over us," Amos admitted.

"I can tear your arms off and beat it out of you if that helps?" Calynn asked sarcastically.

Amos scowled at Calynn with parsed lips and Calynn stared back. He backed down when she took a step towards him, but then looked around like someone else was listening.

"I'm a synth remember?" Calynn added. "I hacked your security systems. Nobody will hear what you say."

"If we attack them head on and call out Mil directly," Amos conceded. "His man's loyalty will falter. They outnumber us or I would have done so already."

"Won't they kill the Chief?" Kash asked.

"No, they will use him as a shield though."

"How bad of an insult would it be to lose to girls instead?" Calynn asked. "If Svata and I call him out does that lessen his position of power? Gods, that just sounds dumb to say out loud."

"Being bested by a woman would irreparably damage his station," Amos informed them. "But he may see you as a robot, not a real woman... so it would have to be her."

Amos pointed at Svata when he finished speaking. He wasn't being contentious, he genuinely wanted to help. It made Kash wonder why? And then it hit him.

"And you could exert your leverage of having our laser to force us to do this for you," Kash reasoned. "Thus, improving your station."

"The thought had crossed my mind."

"Or… we let you to your own fate, and when your faction collapses you'll be at Mil's mercy," Kash said coldly.

"If we don't tear this whole fucking building down first," Calynn added.

"One way or the other," Kash continued, "we are getting the Chief back."

"With or without your help," Svata chimed in.

Amos looked away from the trio as he weighed his options. More gunfire erupted from the hallway, piercing the silence. Kash checked the corner and then returned fire. The bullets seemed to speed up Amos' decision making.

"Mil is a formidable combatant, and he will use your friend as a shield," Amos explained. "If you can draw their attention to the hallway… I can show the blue one how to get the drop on him."

Amos paused and turned to Svata.

"If he feels like the situation is lost," Amos continued. "He won't show any mercy."

"Then neither will I," Svata said confidently.

"Looks like we're the bait," Kash said to Calynn.

"Sounds like fun," Calynn smiled. "I was starting to miss getting shot at."

"Makes life worth living," Kash smiled back.

They may have been telling jokes, but the look in Calynn's eyes told a different story. Kash grabbed the waistband of her jeans and pulled her close. He rested his forehead on hers, staring into her eyes. There he saw the trust they had in one another and their unflappable bond. She wouldn't let him down any more than he would her. Her eyes narrowed into a fierce gaze that Kash matched.

He released his grip on the front of her jeans, stepped back, and readied his weapon. Calynn nodded slightly, raised her beam rifle, and her eyes began to glow. When she turned the corner of the hallway, all the light around her disappeared like she had absorbed it. They would get to move in the cover of darkness.

"My girl," Kash said as he stepped into the darkness with her.

The hallway was fifteen meters wide and tall, so they had room to spread out. One of the men leaned around his cover to shoot at them and froze in horror. Kash had a chance to see the terror on his face before Calynn's beam rifle struck its mark. Two more men stepped into the hallway to fire at them, but they both hesitated. The ball of darkness moving towards them was surely the cause. Calynn shot one and Kash shot the other.

An assault rifle came around the corner of the doorway spraying bullets blindly. Kash dove onto his stomach to avoid the hail of bullets, but Calynn just kept walking.

"Must be nice to be bulletproof," Kash said aloud to himself as he got back to his feet.

He circled out as wide to the right as he could, being careful to stay in the darkness that Calynn was creating. He watched the area where the blind fire had come from down the sights of his weapon. The man pushed his gun around the corner to fire again, but Kash was ready for it this time. He fired a burst at the man's hand making him drop his weapon when the bullets hit their mark. Calynn finished the job when he leaned out to retrieve the gun he had just dropped.

Kash could finally start to see inside the maintenance bay where the offending faction had taken Chief Volci. Four dead bodies lay at the entrance in front of what looked like some makeshift cover. The faction members were moving fast to pile up whatever they could in front of the door so they had something to hide behind.

"Get that moved over there," a voice shouted. "We have to create advantageous firing angles."

Kash fired at two of the men that were moving a large metal cabinet. The men dropped the cabinet and fled deeper into the bay. Kash fired again, managing to wound one of them as they ran.

"I have a hostage!" a man that Kash assumed was Mil shouted.

"Not for fucking long!" Kash shouted back.

"I... I'm warning you!" Mil hollered but his voice was a little shaky. "I'll kill him."

"If you kill him there's nothing keeping us from killing you."

Kash and Calynn paused on either side of the large door to the maintenance bay. Kash couldn't see Mil or the Chief because of the pile of debris the faction had piled up in front of the door. Calynn got his attention by waving at him and then pointed up at the ceiling of the bay.

Svata was moving across the ceiling atop some electrical conduits hanging from the ceiling. Kash smirked and looked back to Calynn. She had the same thought he had. The duo readied their weapons and moved into the maintenance bay. Calynn went left around the pile of tables and crates while Kash went to the right. He heard her beam rifle fire one shot before they cleared the debris and finally saw their adversary.

"Back off, or he's dead!" Mil shouted, holding Volci in front of himself.

Mil was flanked by two men on each side crouching behind some overturned steel work benches. Kash didn't have a very clean shot at him and Calynn must not have either… or she was waiting for Svata to make her move.

Svata dropped from her elevated position, landing silently just behind Mil. She ripped the weapon out of his hand and they both seemed to just stand there for a few seconds. It wasn't until Mil turned and fell down that Kash realized why. The blade at the end of Svata's tail was embedded in the back of Mil's neck, severing his brain stem. The other four men never saw her until Mil's body hit the ground, and they never got a chance to fire at her. Svata became a blue blur again racing around the men and then stopping in front of Chief Volci. She was untying her friend before the other men hit the ground.

Kash lifted his rifle and laid it across his shoulder so it was pointing behind him as he casually approached. The orange goo on the men's necks told Kash that Svata had spared their lives. Their fates would fall to Amos to decide.

"How are you doing, Chief?" Svata asked, removing his binds.

"I'll live," Volci replied.

The Chief had a swollen bruise on his left eye in the shape of a gun stock and his right sleeve was torn. A trail of blood trickled down his cheek from where he was struck.

"You definitely didn't go quietly," Kash smiled as he approached.

"No, I didn't," Volci said as he gently probed his wound with his finger. "Made them pricks earn it."

"Good man… glad to see you in one piece."

"Thanks, Kash."

"Is it done?" Amos' voice came from the hallway.

"It is," Kash replied.

Amos and two of the men loyal to him entered the bay. The other men were eying Calynn suspiciously and were repeatedly starting to pull their weapons up to target her. They would lower them as fast as they raised them, which told Kash the only reason they weren't shooting at her was because Amos ordered them not to.

"How did you do that?" Amos asked Calynn. "The darkness in the hallway."

"I used the device in the next bay," Calynn replied with a kind smile, clearly trying to put the men at ease. "A cloaking device that can project onto another object is some interesting tech. Is that so you can cloak smaller missiles?"

"That's classified!" one of men with Amos barked.

Peole held up his hand to silence the man before turning back to Calynn.

"It is as you say, but we have never gotten it to… behave in a controlled manor," Amos said calmly. "How did you confine it like that?"

"We can't give away all our secrets," Calynn grinned ear to ear.

Amos Peole raised his hand again to stifle any outburst from the men before it came this time. He shook his head and shrugged his shoulders.

"Can I have a hint?" he asked with a slight chuckle.

"Get our stupid laser fixed and loaded back on our ship," Kash asserted, "and maybe we'll give you that hint."

"But for now we have a man to patch up," Svata added. "Come on, Chief, that eye probably needs a few sutures."

Kash watched Amos with a trained eye. The man was watching Calynn as she walked, but it wasn't lust in his eyes… it was something else. As they left the maintenance bay, Kash grabbed Calynn's hand and pulled her close.

"I don't like how he was staring at you," Kash whispered to the beauty.

"Lots of men drool over me," Calynn replied softly. "It never bothered you before."

"This was different."

"Okay… different how?"

"I don't know," Kash sighed. "It was like… like a child longing for a new toy."

"Oh… so I'm a toy now?" Calynn smirked, hugging herself around his arm. "And you don't want to share your toys."

"He did refer to you as a robot… and he might want to keep my walking, talking super-computer for himself," Kash said softly. "So, you and all your delicious toys need to stay away from him… let's not give him an opportunity to try and take you."

"Yes, Boss," Calynn cooed. "I'll stay as close to you as I can."

Calynn hugged his arm to her body even tighter and pressed her hip into his thigh. Kash stumbled a little when she pressed into him, and chuckled. He pulled his hand free from her grip so he could snatch her up. He had one arm behind her knees and the other around her back. Calynn squealed and giggled as he cradled her in his arms, which brought a smile to Kash's face as he joined in her laughter.

"You two are something else," Volci chuckled, shaking his head. "How are you laughing right after a fire fight?"

"We like creating happy memories so we can bury the bad ones beneath them," Calynn explained. "It keeps us sane."

"And it's contagious," Kash added, nodding at him and Svata. "You're both smiling."

"You got us there," Volci laughed.

The four friends made their way to The Cat and patched up the Chief's eye. Svata was right, it needed three sutures to close the gash above his eye, and Calynn's sensors showed a fractured orbital bone. Kash was surprised the Chief wasn't complaining about a headache. Kash broke out a bottle of bourbon and the two men downed a few shots. Volci said it helped dull the pain.

Calynn finally got to change clothes, so she put on a new pair of jeans. Then she pulled some folding chairs out of storage, and the three of them sat in the cargo hold chatting while waiting for the ballistic laser to be fixed. Kash penned an email to Admiral Anne informing her of their delay before joining them. Kash sat in the oversized chair with Calynn. She turned and threw her legs over his as soon as he sat down. Svata was sitting with Chief Volci comparing their pain levels, jokingly.

Svata, still in Calynn's sun dress, was all smiles and looked stunning, and Kash wasn't the only one that noticed. The chief seemed to be spellbound by the blue beauty and hung on her every word. Kash gave Calynn's leg a gentle squeeze to get her attention. He smiled and nodded at the other two. Calynn nodded and smiled back with the tip of her tongue sticking out through her teeth. She noticed their growing connection also.

Nearly two hourns later, the sound of the bay door opening drew their attention. Amos Peole and a group of technicians emerged from the building with the ballistic laser in tow. Calynn went to get off of Kash's lap, but he held her in place.

"Stay close," Kash told her. "I still don't trust them."

"Okay," Calynn giggled, pulling herself into his arms. "Is this better?"

"For now," Kash said softly in her ear.

Kash pushed his hand up under the back of her shirt, wrapping his arm around her back and gripping her side. His other hand pulled down the front of her shirt to expose some of her cleavage. Calynn looked down at her chest and then back to Kash with a cross look. Kash caught her gaze and nodded at the approaching men. His plan was to make Calynn into a girl again. If Amos still saw her as a robot, he might make a play to take her. But if she was a woman...

"Are we interrupting," Amos Peole announced as he entered the cargo hold.

"If I wanted to be alone with her," Kash replied without looking at Amos, "I wouldn't be sitting here."

"We have a bedroom right up there," Calynn added, pointing towards their quarters.

"You do that..." Amos paused to chuckle. "With... that?"

"Did he call me a that?" Calynn asked sitting up.

"What the fuck, Amos?" Kash scolded. "You get she's not all synth, right?"

"I'm sure," Amos laughed.

"Look, her arms are harder," Kash said squeezing her arm and then flicking it. "Hear that thud when I flick her?"

Kash shifted and started to poke Calynn in the belly.

"But all this in here," Kash continued, and then grabbed Calynn's right breast. "And these... are so soft."

"Hey," Calynn mock whined. "Don't make the other one jealous."

Kash adjusted his grip, squeezing her other boob, and smiled at Amos and his men.

"I'd offer you a squeeze too, Amos," Calynn mocked. "But I think Kash would kill you for the attempt."

Amos didn't reply but his scowl spoke volumes. Kash wasn't entirely sure that he was convinced, so he pressed his point further.

"I think our gadgets and implants are confusing him," Kash jested. "You get that I have implants too… not just her, right?"

Kash shifted his hand under Calynn's butt and proceeded to press her up over his head with one hand. Calynn did an excellent job of keeping her balance until he lowered her back onto his lap. Peole's eyes grew larger at the sight of Kash's display of strength, and Kash had some hope that maybe they would get off this moon without more bloodshed. Kash and Amos exchanged glares, but neither made another move.

"Need help getting that thing loaded?" Chief Volci asked politely, breaking the awkward silence.

"No… it's fine," Amos replied, motioning his men forward. "We can get it."

The technicians moved the laser into position, while Kash and Volci supervised them strapping it down. The girls climbed the ladder and watched from the catwalk. Kash would occasionally catch one of the Tyras Minor men stealing a glance at Calynn and Svata, and he couldn't wait to get out of there. When the laser was secured, Amos Peole approached Kash.

"We upheld our end," Peole said sternly. "Now, about that cloaking device that… she… modified. I would like to know how that was accomplished."

"What do you think, Calynn?" Kash turned to her and smiled.

"At least he didn't call me a thing again," Calynn said, sarcastically. "So… maybe…"

Calynn's words fell off as she collapsed in a heap on the catwalk without warning. It was like someone flipped a switch and turned Calynn… off. Svata dropped to her knees shouting Calynn's name. When Calynn didn't reply, she shot a concerned look to Kash. When Kash turned away from Svata, he saw a soldier approaching rapidly.

Kash reacted on instinct with violent intentions. He lunged forward before the enemy could raise his weapon. The first punch landed so hard that Kash felt the bone of his jaw and cheek give way upon impact, and he sent the man flying backwards. Kash used the man's flying body to cover his movements and close the gap on Amos Peole. Amos had his weapon out when Kash made his move, and managed to fire a single round before Kash snapped a kick into his chest. He crushed Peole's chest cavity and sent him flying out of the cargo hold. The gun Amos was previously holding hung in the air after being dislodged from his grip. Kash caught the weapon, turned, and fired at the other two men in his ship. He fired four shots in rapid succession, killing both men.

Kash staggered when The Cat suddenly started to move. He had been so focused on the fight that he hadn't even heard the engines starting. He turned to Calynn and saw her leaning against the bottom rail of the catwalk, still sprawled out, but she was holding her hand out in front of herself, like she was trying to protect herself from something. Her eyes were glowing, but not with her normal vibrant white light. Her eyes were dim and strained... and full of fear.

Kash followed her gaze out the back of the ship and saw a man wearing a dish shaped device on his chest and a weird-looking helmet with thick goggles. The dish seemed to be pointed directly at Calynn. Kash had never seen such a device, but whatever it was... it was killing her. Kash didn't hesitate for a moment. He fired multiple shots at the man and didn't stop shooting until the man stopped moving.

The cargo ramp door was closing as they left the ground, so Kash turned his attention back to Calynn.

"Get... to the helm," Calynn voice cracked and sounded weak. "I... I need a minute."

"On it," Kash replied rapidly and sprinted up the ship ladder to the helm.

He buckled himself in and took the controls, accelerating away from the base when a low rumble caught his attention. Before Kash could ask what it was, an explosion rocked the ship. Orange flames engulfed The Cat, blotting out the sky so Kash was flying blind. He steadied himself and waited for the warning alarms to start blaring... but no alarms came.

"What the fuck was that?" Kash yelled.

"The base," Calynn replied from the hallway just behind him, her voice was weak and shallow. "I overloaded... the reactor."

"That's my girl," Kash boasted proudly.

"Buckle me in here," Calynn said to Svata who was helping her to the cockpit.

"What was that weapon they hit you with?" Kash asked.

"I wish I knew… it disrupted everything somehow," Calynn explained. "It scattered the electrical pulses in my brain or stopped my synapses from firing… I don't know. It felt like I was completely disconnected, even from my own body, and it took everything I had just to get us off the ground."

"It was developed to disable AI combat drones and was never supposed to be used on humans," Volci explained, his voice tight with guilt. "It short-circuits their neural cores with some kind of wave energy."

"How is that possible?" Kash asked.

"I don't know the specifics, but…" Chief Volci hesitated, his eyes lowering as his tone grew heavier. "Regrettably… I helped develop the transmitter. It was just another project back then, a tool to win skirmishes before they even started. We thought we were building a safeguard… a way to end battles without bloodshed. But now…"

Volci's gaze shifted to Calynn, his face pale and his brows raised.

"Seeing what it did to you, how it dropped you so suddenly…" Volci's voice cracked, his gaze fell to the floor, and he swallowed hard before continuing. "I didn't think about the consequences, about what could happen if this technology fell into the wrong hands… or if it were used on a human. And now, I see you struggling to recover, and it's… my fault. I wish I hadn't done it. I'm so sorry, Calynn."

"Not your fault, Chief," Calynn still sounded pained. "Guns don't kill people…"

"People kill people," Kash finished Calynn's statement for her.

"Kash, are you bleeding?" Svata suddenly asked. "There's blood. It's your leg. Were you shot?"

"Fuck, I don't know," Kash replied, looking down at his bleeding leg. "Huh… hey, it looks like I got shot."

"How do you not know you got shot?" Svata asked manically.

She was at Kash's side before he could answer, checking the wound above his right knee. He jerked away when her fingers probed the wound.

"Ouch," Kash grumbled at Svata. "It hurts now that I know it's there, lady."

"Well, the good news is I felt an exit wound, so we don't have to dig out the bullet," Svata explained too mechanically for Kash's liking. "Take off your pants so I can dress the wound."

"Can we get the HLD fired up first?" Kash asked sarcastically. "Maybe we can finish getting away from the bad guys trying to kill us... AND THEN worry about my leg... I mean... that's the order I would put them in anyway."

"Are you done?" Svata asked with her hands on her hips.

"Don't ask him that," Calynn added quickly. "He'll launch into a twenty-minute monologue exploring every possible angle he can think of, just to show you how not done he is."

"You forgot funny," Kash chimed in. "A twenty-minute... funny... monologue. Emphasis on funny."

"You're incorrigible."

"And still bleeding. Any idea on when you're going to make the jump?"

"I'm trying," Calynn groaned. "It's not working."

"Well, that's a problem."

"I know," Calynn snapped, her tone sharp with frustration. "I'm having trouble connecting to it. So, maybe let me focus instead of talking me to death?"

"And let me dress that wound," Svata asserted, her voice cutting through the exchange.

"Fine," Kash relented with a sigh, nodding to his right. "There's a small first aid kit in the compartment there."

He stood up and gently slid off his pants, wincing slightly as the motion tugged at the injury. The gunshot wound was high on the outer thigh, about fifteen centimeters above his knee. The exit wound was farther back, dead center on the outer side of his leg. Blood had soaked through the fabric and was now beginning to pool on the floor.

Svata retrieved the kit and knelt beside him, her hands moving quickly and efficiently as she cleaned the wound.

"I still don't know how you didn't notice you were shot until someone pointed it out," Svata muttered, giving him a sidelong glance.

"Adrenaline," Kash replied with a shrug. "And, you know, I had other things to worry about. Like not dying."

Before Svata could retort, the ship's comm system crackled to life.

"Destroying the entire base of a government contractor, including their housing, is a little extreme," the mysterious voice was back with a condescending tone. "I'm beginning to think you enjoy war crimes, Captain Smith."

"Oh, joy," Kash groaned, rolling his eyes as he keyed the comms. "You again."

Back to Stop #3

"Killing everyone on that moon with a bomb is unscrupulous, Captain Smith," the mysterious man added.

"Full disclosure," Kash replied sarcastically. "I killed one with a punch to the head, shot three more, and their leader, Amos Peole, he had an allergic reaction to my shin bone... you know... when it crushed his chest cavity stopping his heart."

"An impressive tally," the man shot back. "I suppose next you're going to tell me it was in self-defense, and you're merely the victim here."

"Nothing so noble, I'm afraid," Kash retorted. "They were put in harm's way by an egotistical, narcissistic moron who thought it would be amusing to shoot missiles at a Ballistic Laser Array for Strategic Tactical Repulsion. I mean, it's not like that moon was ever going to explode... until your genius idea to fire missiles at a BLASTR. Really, what idiot thought that was a good idea?"

"He doesn't know we didn't use a bomb," Volci observed softly. "He wasn't there."

"No, he was probably watching from a distance like the coward he is," Kash replied to Volci before keying the comms again. "Did I lose you already? Or are you waiting for your team of writers to craft you a witty response in an untimely manner?"

"I have greater responsibilities than just speaking with you, Smith!" the mystery man bellowed.

"Well, that's not very entertaining," Kash continued his barrage. "I'm getting bored over here while waiting for a scathing response, not more government red tape."

Kash leaned back dramatically, grinning ear to ear.

"I mean, shit," he continued, his words dripping with mockery, "you've been trying to kill me for like a week now, so let's check the score. You managed to hit me with one bullet and two weak-ass insults about war crimes... and it only cost ya... that whole fleet of ships and an entire moon base. I should give up while I still can… it's not like I'm winning or anything."

Kash pushed back from the mic for the comms but didn't release the talk button. He wanted it to sound like he wasn't talking to the mystery man, when in fact what he said next was entire for his benefit.

"Hey, remind me the next time I'm saying my prayers, to ask the Gods to NEVER have this guy be responsible for me," Kash continued. "That's a sure death sentence."

Kash released the comm and smirked. He didn't know what the mystery man looked like, but he was certain of the man's current skin tone… flushed with anger.

"Do we know where they are?" Svata asked, her voice tight with unease.

"No," Kash replied, smirking. "He's cloaked and…"

The alarms shrieked.

Kash punched the throttle, jerking the controls hard. Three missiles screamed toward them from different directions. The first came head-on, closing fast, while the other two flanked them like predators circling prey. Kash leaned into the controls, accelerating directly at the lead missile.

"Kash!" Volci hollered.

Kash didn't reply. His jaw clenched. His eyes locked on to the streak of fire barreling toward them. He was playing a high-stakes game of chicken and his timing had to be perfect.

"Kash, what the hell are you doing?!" Volci shouted again.

"Kash!" Svata's voice cracked.

Kash waited until the last possible moment, his fingers gripping the controls like a vice. Then he feinted left, forcing the missile to adjust, before jerking back right. The Cat's engines screamed in protest as Kash whipped the ship into a hard turn.

"Now," Kash failed to keep his thoughts internal.

He cut the throttle, pitching the ship into a somersault. The missile corrected too slowly, its trajectory exposed. The Cat's guns thundered to life, ripping through the missile's exposed flank. The explosion filled their view with orange fire as Kash completed the somersault and pushed The Cat forward, racing away from the wreckage.

"Nice one," Volci muttered, his voice shaky.

But there was no time to celebrate. Kash's eyes flicked to the monitor. The other two missiles were still on them, one closing from the left and the other from the right. There was no time to split them to try and get them to run into each other, and they were too fast to outrun. Kash readied an implosion round to try to deflect the missiles as a last resort, when another glint of orange in space caught his eye.

"There you are," Kash said eagerly, turning the ship towards the glint.

The missile had exploded close enough to one of the cloaked ships that the cloaking device mimicked the fireball. Kash pulled the trigger spraying bullets into space where he hoped to find a ship.

"What are you doing?" Volci sounded annoyed.

"Looking for that," Kash exclaimed pointing out the windshield.

Some of the rounds abruptly stopped when they struck one of the cloaked ships. The enemy vessel uncloaked and returned fire, but Kash ducked under the shots and circled up around the behemoth of a ship. They barely crested the top of the government cruiser when the missiles caught up.

"Boom," Kash narrated the explosion as it happened without trying to hide the snarky tone of his voice.

Two fireballs erupted from the large ship, nearly ripping the ship in two. The explosion rocked The Cat as the enemy cruiser broke apart, its contents spewing into space. The fireball quickly extinguished itself, leaving the shattered hulk to drift, dark and lifeless.

"Add another ship to your ledger," Kash mocked the mysterious voice over the comm. "Let's see if we can add two more."

Alarms shrieked again. Two new missiles were on them, one from the right and the other from the left. This time Kash did have time to split them. He punched the throttle and raced to the spot where the two missiles would converge hoping he could get them to explode on each other.

"This is gonna be close!" Kash announced anxiously.

The Cat darted through the gap between the two approaching missiles and raced away. Unfortunately, the missiles didn't hit each other like Kash hoped. He did, however, gain some distance on them while they turned wide to follow him.

"What about the cliffs that were near the moon base?" Svata asked excitedly. "Could we lose the missiles there?"

"We can sure try," Kash replied, pointing the ship back to the moon.

The telltale sound of the HLD spinning up brought an easy smile to Kash's face. A second later they were enveloped in a Hyperlumic bubble speeding away from danger.

"That's my girl!" Kash announced gleefully. "WHEW!"

A split second later, the bubble of light disappeared from around The Cat, and they returned to normal space.

"Oh... good girl," Kash continued in a more serious tone. "Keep us close so we can get this guy."

"I'm fine," Calynn quipped. "Thanks for asking."

"You don't sound fine," Chief Volci said.

"I agree," Kash added. "Your voice is a different pitch."

"Okay... I'm almost fine," Calynn corrected, this time she sounded more like herself, but not quite.

"Running away so soon, Smith?" the mystery man asked.

"You wish," Kash countered. "I'm just getting tired of you firing missiles at me and thought I would return the favor."

"We're cloaked, so you have no firing solution," the man argued. "You can't kid me."

"For now," Kash replied, but a light from behind him distracted him. "But you can't hide from me forever."

Kash turned to see Calynn's eyes glowing bright white, and a grin tugged at the corners of his mouth.

"I love Goddess mode," Kash said, his smile couldn't be contained. "What'cha doin', Baby Girl?"

"Sorry... just trying to fix my neural network," Calynn replied abruptly.

"Damn... I was hoping for some unbelievable way to track a cloaked ship in space," Kash sighed, turning back around.

"There might actually be a way," Svata informed him, but looked over at the Chief. "To track them."

Kash followed her gaze and stared at Volci for a moment waiting for him to respond. The Chief pulled his mouth to a thin line and cocked his head slowly as he stared back.

"I know that look," Kash explained. "And I would just like to say that it isn't THAT classified."

"I'd have to rewire your comms," the Chief finally relented with a heavy sigh.

"The comms?"

"By energizing the comms, it would send out a wave that can bounce off the enemy ships like an old-school sonar system," Volci explained.

"And I can add the lines of code so your sensors can pick up the echo," Svata added.

"Well, I don't think that would work on this ship," Kash explained. "Or at least I doubt..."

The controls of the ship suddenly jerked out of Kash's hand and moved into their docked position. Kash entered the pass code into the keypad to unlock it, but nothing happened.

"What happened?" Volci asked with obvious concern. "Why are you locked out?"

Kash typed in the pass code again and got the same result. The anti-theft device that was meant to keep his ship from being stolen had the controls in lockdown.

"I have no idea," Kash replied. "Is it some new weapon?"

A small electric charge surged through Kash's body so that he couldn't move. All his muscles were locked up.

"Ca...lynn," Kash struggled to say.

"Kash... is that you, my friend?" Plekish's voice came over the comms.

"It is. It's me."

"What is happening, my friend?" Plekish asked, concerned. "Is your ship being hacked?"

"No... we're being hunted by some government ships, but other than that we're fine."

"I'm not fine, Mr. P," Calynn chimed in. "I'm really, really not fine."

"That must be what set off my alarms," Plekish said, relieved. "What's wrong, child?"

"A new weapon... it scrambled my brain," Calynn nearly wept. "I don't know what to do."

"Poor child… let's take a look at you," Plekish spoke soothingly. "Oh… I see… your brain waves are a mess… poor child."

The electric charge holding them in place finally dissipated so Kash could move again. He immediately fell to his knees in front of Calynn and grabbed her hands in his. She had been trying to recover from that disruptor weapon and was putting on a brave act… until now. It was easy to forget that she wasn't actually a god with all the incredible things she can do. Inside that nearly indestructible husk, beat the heart of a vulnerable twenty-two-year-old girl. Kash scolded himself for not checking on her sooner.

"It felt like dying," Calynn cried, tears streaming down her face. "Like the accident… it felt the same. It was like I was being pulled apart, and I couldn't pull myself back together."

"Well, the good news is, I think I can help," Plekish said calmly. "The bad news is… I think it's going to hurt."

"I don't care," Calynn continued to cry. "Anything is better than this."

"I need you to go into the syntax interface chamber, child," Plekish explained.

"Okay," Calynn replied softly as she got up and walked down the hall.

"Kash, another vessel is trying to hail you, shall I give you back control of your ship?" Plekish asked.

"I don't care about them," Kash replied, following Calynn. "She's more important."

"Wait… do they know where we are… sir?" Svata asked, her voice shaky. "They have fired missiles at us before and…"

Svata's voice fell off like she was afraid to keep talking.

"You are well hidden, young lady," Plekish reassured. "They pose no threat."

"Oh, good," Svata sighed with relief.

Kash followed Calynn through the door into the tiny room that was designed to look like where he would feed a normal nerve center. Another door beyond that housed all the computers and servers that Calynn linked to. Calynn stripped off her clothes to try to keep that room as clean as possible. She grabbed the door to open it, but Kash grabbed her arm to stop her.

"I'm sorry, Baby Girl."

"I know."

Calynn gave him a soft smile and a peck on the lips, before entering the other room. Two drones that Kash didn't know existed went to work wiring some connections to Calynn's body. Kash watched them work diligently through the small window in the door.

"The drones in here are the ones that dug you out of the rubble before," Plekish answered his question before he could ask. "They also guard this room in case anyone would try to interfere with Calynn's link. You should look away now. It is about to get very bright in that room."

Kash reluctantly turned away as Calynn started screaming. Calynn's screams, sharp, two-toned, and unnatural, made his gut churn. He wanted to stop it, to kick down the door and make it all stop, but he knew this was the only way. Plekish wouldn't hurt her... but hearing her like this... he clenched his jaw and squeezed his eyes shut trying to shut out her cries... her cries... they were becoming more harmonious... and more... her.

The bright light from behind him suddenly dimmed along with Calynn's scream. Kash turned to see the drones removing wires and small metal plates from either side of her body. The plates were still red hot and smoking. Calynn fell to her knees, and Kash lost sight of her through the small window.

"Calynn?" Kash asked frantically. "Where is she, Mr. P?"

The door unlatched and opened slightly. Kash could see her arm and head through the crack.

"Baby Girl," Kash cried out, pushing the door open so her could retrieve her. "Come on... I got you."

Kash knelt down and pulled her into his arms. He brushed her hair from her face with his fingers and was met with her glowing smile. She was looking around the room like she was seeing everything for the first time, and her smile only seemed to grow.

"Are you okay?" Kash asked softly.

She pulled herself up and kissed him passionately. Kash held her tight and returned her kiss with equal vigor until she was sated. She pulled back just enough that their lips were no longer touching but still held herself close.

"Now I am," Calynn whispered into his mouth.

"Your brain waves, neurons, bioelectrical fields, and central nervous system all appear to be normal now," Plekish informed them. "How do you feel, child?"

"Thank you, Mr. P," Calynn giggled, falling back so Kash had to catch her. "I feel great!"

"Shall I give you your ship back now?" Plekish chuckled.

"Oh, yes please," Calynn replied sharply, sitting up. "Can we kill the people that did this to me again? Or the mystery voice guy? I really want to take this out on somebody. Let me up so I can get dressed."

Calynn stood quickly and started to get dressed. Kash couldn't help but stare and smile at her while she bounced herself into her jeans. She met his gaze, smiled back, threw her bra at his head, and pulled on her shirt.

"You pervert," Calynn giggled.

"You started it."

"I meant that as a compliment," Calynn grinned ear to ear.

"Oh… in that case, back at ya, babe," Kash chuckled.

"Come on," Calynn continued in a hurried tone. "Let's go kick someone's ass."

"You're still a roller coaster."

"I know."

She offered her hand to help pull him up to his feet, and the duo returned to the cockpit. Volci and Svata both had concerned and surprised looks on their faces. They had been waiting for an update on Calynn's condition and were stunned to see her recovered so soon.

"Hi guys," Calynn said cheerfully. "I feel much better now."

"You sound better too," Volci smiled back.

"Who was that?" Svata asked timidly.

"Who… Mr. P?" Calynn responded. "He's a friend… the very best of them."

The controls for the ship unlocked as Calynn sat at the helm, and the monitors started displaying information at impossible speeds. A smile tugged at Kash's mouth. She was definitely back to herself now. Kash thanked Plekish in his head, vowing to give the man an extra hug the next time he saw him. He truly was the best of friends, and Kash had never been so grateful to be among those that he called friend.

"I guess the mystery butthead left," Calynn blurted out, interrupting Kash's inner monologue.

"I'm sure he'll be back," Volci replied in his normal stoic manner.

"We should get home before he tries anything there again," Svata added.

"Agreed," Volci nodded. "I would feel better being there to help my people."

"Max speed here we come," Calynn said gleefully, as a bubble of light surrounded the ship.

"I'm sorry, but..." Volci stammered. "Weren't you just crying and screaming a second ago?"

"Welcome to the roller coaster that is Calynn," Kash replied in a snarky tone, shaking his head. "You get used to it."

"Gosh... I feel like I may have heard that before," Calynn replied with mock intrigue. "I wonder where that was?"

"Always the jokester," Kash mocked back, pointing down the hall. "It was like ten seconds ago, right over there."

"Are you sure?"

"Just fly the damn ship," Kash laughed.

Calynn rushed them back to Volci's base at max speed. It had only taken them thirty-four hourns to make the trip to the moon base, despite it being more than a four day journey. Calynn cut that in half on the way back. They took turns sleeping again so they were all rested when they arrived.

"And we're almost back?" Volci questioned. "There's no way."

"We'll be there in two minutes, I promise," Calynn replied confidently.

"No way."

"Yes way... just you watch."

"And let's keep that to ourselves also, please," Kash added with a serious tone. "I know it's a great story to tell..."

"Yeah," Volci interrupted, laughing. "That's the hard part."

The crew all shared a laugh, except Svata. She smiled briefly. Kash noticed her almost rigid demeanor and approached her. She was still wearing Calynn's dress and looked fabulous in it.

"Why so serious, beautiful?" Kash jested, wrapping his arm around Svata's waist. "Smile!"

"I am smiling," Svata replied with a soft smile.

"I thought you would be happy to be home."

"I am," Svata said quickly but then paused. "It's just…"

"Aawww… we'll miss you too, Svata," Calynn chimed in. "Learn to read the room, Mr. Smith. Oh, and Chief… we're here."

Calynn dropped them out of the HLD bubble and before them was their star base, which brought a smile to Chief Volci's face.

"Home sweet… oh shit!" Calynn said, surprised. "Look!"

A small group of ships was attacking the star base. There were some small fighters, one cruiser, and a medium sized freighter.

"Hail the base!" Volci barked, as Calynn brought up the comms. "Delta-2382 this is the Chief, what's going on?"

There was no response at first, but just as the Chief went for the comms they replied.

"Chief?" a voice that Kash didn't recognize replied. "It's marauders."

"By the Gods, can we get a fucking break?" Kash sighed, rubbing his head.

"Fuck that," Calynn sounded cheerful. "I'm going in."

With that, she punched the throttle, hurtling them towards more combat. Kash didn't argue. Opting to strap himself into a jump seat instead. Chief Volci sat in the other seat and pulled Svata onto his lap before strapping them both down.

Calynn cocked her to the side as she approached the marauders ships. She rocketed straight through the middle of the group, and Kash counted three ships destroyed in that first pass. Calynn banked hard and brought them around for another pass. She took careful aim at the cruiser and destroyed four of its six engines, but then suddenly sat up a little straighter and looked at the freighter.

"Don't fire at the freighter!" Calynn barked over the comms. "Just take out the remaining fighters. Chief, tell them."

"Do as she asks," Volci hollered at the microphone.

"Get in the back and prepare to board them," Calynn instructed.

"You want to do what?" Volci asked, surprised.

"Chief," Calynn said softly, turning to face him. "That freighter is full of food… lots of food."

Everyone sat stunned for a second until Svata suddenly unbuckled herself and jumped up.

"Let's go," Svata asserted and jogged back the hall.

Kash unbuckled himself and was right on her heels. He heard the Chief's footsteps striking the deck behind him. The trio suited up for a spacewalk and grabbed weapons. They were ready and waiting when Calynn jumped down from the catwalk.

"You won't need those," Calynn said, waving her hand at their suits. "I'm docking us inside... I already hacked the ship."

"The freighter has atmospheric barriers on the cargo doors?" Kash asked, puzzled. "That's new."

"Okay... maybe we'll need those," Calynn admitted.

"Miss Calynn," Chief Volci said calmly, approaching her. "I know you're hungry for revenge, but do not rush to a mistake... slow and steady... got it?"

"Yes, sir," Calynn replied curtly. "You're right, sir."

"We only have three suits," Kash told Calynn. "Will you be okay without one?"

"If we take our time, nobody will need one," Calynn smiled. "I have the marauders trapped. We can wait for the atmosphere to come back up and leisurely leave the ship if we want."

They did just that. The foursome waited several minutes for the atmosphere in the cargo hold to stabilize before they exited The Cat. It was still cold as hell, but at least they could breathe. Calynn led them through a door into the next cargo bay that was packed full of crates.

"Oh, I love these," Calynn announced excitedly, reaching into one of the crates.

She pulled out a bunch of Zinnaberries, popping some of the deep-purple colored fruits into her mouth. Kash could hear them fizzing in her mouth as she chewed. Her knees buckled a little as she enjoyed the delicacy.

"The fizz is like a sweet and savory explosion in your mouth," Calynn swooned.

Chief Volci grabbed a handful of the berries and popped them into his mouth. The usually stoic man closed his eyes and placed his hand on his chest, thoroughly enjoying the treat.

"I can't wait to get these to our people," Volci drooled. "They are going to be..."

"Hello!" Kash interrupted, moving quickly to a crate just beyond them.

The crate was marked with flowing alien symbols Kash recognized, but couldn't hope to pronounce. To him, they were more of a decoration than proper writing, though he'd learned long ago what they signified. He pried open the top of the crate and gently pulled out a slender bottle, its deep-purple glass had an eerie glow. Silver foil wrapped the neck of the bottle like a crown. Kash stood in awe.

"This," Kash announced, holding the bottle up like a prize, "is fire wine. At least that's what we called it, because none of us could actually pronounce it."

"So, you don't know the real name?" Svata asked as she leaned in closer, eyes wide.

"Nope," Kash admitted, a grin tugging at his lips. "It's something like Fee-something-almost-impossible-to-say, but that doesn't matter. This shit is fifty million credits a bottle... straight off the vine. We confiscated a few crates when I was a legionnaire... Never thought I'd see it again."

"Wait, straight off the vine?" Volci's brow furrowed. "You mean they don't even ferment it?"

"Nope." Kash twisted the foil, revealing a faintly pulsing seal that seemed to breathe. "It's from some sentient plant... don't ask me how it works. They don't make it. They grow it. It so expensive because the plant only blooms like every thirty years or so... And yeah... it glows because it's still alive."

He brought the bottle to his lips and blew gently across the seal. The membrane quivered, then slid aside as if responding to his touch, revealing the neck of the bottle. With a reverent look, Kash held the bottle up to salute all his fallen friends. He poured a tiny bit on the ground in their honor and took a long sip.

The flavor hit him like a symphony, a perfect balance of sweet and fiery, smooth yet electric, rich but ethereal. It was unlike anything else, a taste that defied description. Either you've had fire wine... or you haven't.

He swallowed, letting the wine's calming warmth spread through his body like a gentle tide. The aftertaste is possibly better than the actual wine. It leaves your tongue wanting more.

"That," Kash said, his voice quieter now, "is the taste of fifty million credits."

The others stared at him, half in awe, half in disbelief.

"Okay, but... what's it actually taste like?" Svata asked, breaking the silence.

"Can't describe it," Kash chuckled, passing her the bottle. "You'll just have to try it yourself."

"Okay, first... if it costs fifty million a bottle why the hell did you pour some on the ground?" Calynn asked, sounding annoyed. "And second, and this is the important part... we still have work to do... armed marauders... remember?"

"Libations," Kash replied somberly. "You pour a drink out for the fallen. Several of the men I shared that first bottle with are no longer with us... good men too..."

Kash paused and readied his assault rifle.

"As for the marauders," Kash continued. "Let's make this quick."

There were seventeen marauders on board the freighter. Calynn had dropped all the fire doors when she hacked the ship, so a lot of them were separated into groups of one or two men. Some of the men weren't even armed. They surrendered without hesitation. They were moving through the ship quickly until Calynn paused in front of a room locked from the outside. She placed her hand on the door and bowed her head gently.

"Behind this door... are seven women," Calynn's voice was barely over a whisper. "Only Svata and I can open this door... they weren't treated well."

"I'll stay with them," Svata told Calynn. "You three continue on."

Calynn nodded at her and opened the door. A chorus of whimpers and cries came from the darkness. Svata slowly entered the room with her hands raised and her gun on her back. Calynn closed the door behind her.

"At least we know they will be safe now," Volci said, in his customary stoicism.

"Only nine left," Kash added.

"And they're on the bridge," Calynn informed them. "Let's go make sure they stay safe."

Calynn positioned the two men at the door so they would have clean shots at the targets to the left and right, before squatting down in front of them. Kash had three targets to his side, Volci had two, and then they would all converge fire at the remaining four in the center of the room.

"Ready," Calynn said sharply. "In three... two..."

Every alarm on the bridge went off at once. They could hear the ruckus through the reinforced steel door. When the door opened, the marauders were unprepared. The trio dispatched them to their maker without a single shot fired at them. It was the epitome of military precision… and almost too easy.

Chief Volci smiled as he entered the bridge. He walked directly to the comms, adjusted the frequency, and hailed his base.

"Base, this is the Chief," Volci smiled. "Prepare to receive a shipment at freighter dock one… We have a freighter again!"

The Chief cheered the last part of that statement, pumping his fist in the air. When he turned to Kash and Calynn he had a tear in his eye. Calynn bounced over to the man and wrapped him in a hug. Kash soon followed and wrapped his arm around the man's shoulders. Volci had his lips pressed into a thin line trying to contain his emotions, but the man's eyes spoke volumes. The gratitude Kash saw in his eyes was boundless. Maybe helping people wasn't so bad.

Kash and Volci returned to The Cat, exited the freighter, and returned to dock six to charge the ballistic laser. Calynn was flying the freighter and had to line it up with the docking collar. Kash and Volci joined the crowd that was assembling in the freighter docking bay. The docking collar had already extended. Everyone was waiting for the green light above the door to illuminate, indicating a good seal. Once the light came on, they opened the inner door and waited for the freighter door to open. A hush fell over the crowd when the freighter door started to move. It raised slowly revealing Calynn, Svata, and seven frightened women… and the crates of food behind them.

One in the crowd started to clap, which led to more people joining in. The crowd erupted into cheers and cries of happiness. They were all hugging each other and jumping up and down. Some fell to their knees and cried with relief. The commotion didn't help the frightened women, but Svata and Calynn kept them calm and led them down the ramp. Two other women approached them, Kash assumed they were medics by how they started to look at the women Calynn and Svata were escorting.

Once the women were out of the way it was chaos. The crowd rushed into the freighter and started stuffing whatever food they found into their mouths. The adults were giving small children new foods to try, and would delight in the children's faces lighting up. Chief Volci stepped forward and whistled louder than Kash had ever heard someone whistle before. The crowd quickly snapped to attention, facing their friend and leader. Volci took a second to gather himself before addressing the crowd.

"I'm almost at a loss for words," Volci said, his voice cracking. "We have been through so much together… some of us went hungry so others didn't have to… and the many other struggles… sorry."

Volci paused and wiped his face with the back of his hand. He took a deep breath to compose himself before continuing.

"Look… we've been through so much since being written off, but we all pitched in and worked hard just to stay alive," Kash could hear a little anger building in his voice, but Volci got his emotions under control again. "We persevered… we found a way… we made some new friends…"

Volci paused again to wave his arms in the direction of Kash and Calynn.

"Okay… I'll admit it started off a little rocky," Volci chuckled, and the crowd joined him making him wait for the laughter to die down. "But… but they ended up being a bigger gift we could have ever hoped for."

Cheers and whistles erupted from the crowd. Kash and Calynn were on opposite sides of the crowd since she was still with the rescued women, so the crowd split to offer their thanks in person.

Volci whistled again.

"Before we overwhelm them," he continued with a big smile, "we'd like to say how truly grateful we are… thank you, my friends… our words can't express how much this means to us… you've given us… you've given us the means to save our home… and we can't thank you enough… now, let's get some tables in here, crack open some of that really expensive wine, and eat until we explode! TO KASH AND CALYNN!"

"HUZZAH!" the crowd shouted in unison.

Kash graciously shook many hands and hugged more people than he cared to remember. Milo and some of the other chefs brought portable grills and cooked everything that the people brought to them. The freighter bay was infused with the pleasant odors of searing meats and sizzling veggies. The fire wine was flowing by the bottle. Nobody bothered with pouring it into a glass, opting to chug straight from the bottle. There was enough for everyone to have five bottles each, leading some to drink to excess. There was music playing, people singing, and a plethora of laughter and jubilation.

Calynn was moving through the crowd tasting everything she was offered. Her over exaggerated response to each new food, either good or bad, made Kash chuckle to himself. It was like food was her new obsession. She reached him at last, holding a plate piled high with food.

"Here," she said, placing a succulent piece of red meat into his mouth.

Kash savored the flavor, sucking the juices from her finger as he pulled her close by the waistband of her jeans. She smiled as he leaned down to rest his forehead on hers. Her fingers caressing his cheek.

"Let's get out of here," she whispered, her voice soft and inviting.

"What about your plate?" he teased.

"What plate?" Calynn grinned, letting the plate fall from her hands.

The noise of the celebration faded into the background, leaving only them. Kash was lost in her eyes and the promises they held. He grabbed her by the hand, and they slipped away unnoticed. Calynn's giggle echoed through the hall as they raced to The Cat.

"I love your giggle," Kash said fondly as they ran.

"I know," Calynn smiled.

The Voice

The best part of drinking fire wine was there was never a hangover after. The even better part of drinking fire wine… was drinking it off Calynn's body. Their bed was a sticky mess, but neither of them cared at the moment. Their bodies were still intertwined when Kash awoke. He pulled her close and kissed her head.

"Mmm, good morning, handsome."

"Good morning, beautiful."

"I'm hungry."

Kash chuckled and pulled back to look at her face. He felt their skin slowly pry apart as last night's escapades gave up their adhesion.

"And I need a shower," Calynn continued, scrunching her face.

"And sanitize these sheets," Kash added. "We made a hell of a mess."

"Totally worth it," Calynn said matter-of-factly.

"Agreed," Kash said softly, peeling himself off the bed. "Let's go get showers."

The duo cleaned up and dressed and made some mugs of tea. They were soon walking hand in hand back to the freighter bay. There were still some people passed out on the floor, and food everywhere. A mother and her child were already enjoying a quiet breakfast. The mother smiled softly and waved mouthing the words "thank you."

"Good morning, you two," Milo smiled from a chair behind his grill. "Can I make you some breakfast?"

"Good morning, Milo," Kash replied. "We would love some breakfast. What's on the menu?"

"Pretty much anything you want, thanks to you two," Milo beamed a smile. "I can make whatever you'd like."

"Surprise us," Calynn smiled back. "Whatever you want to make us… we'll eat."

"I got just the thing," Milo said excitedly, clambering out of his chair. "I'll be right back."

"Some coffee while you wait?" Volci asked from behind them.

"No, but thank you," Kash replied, holding up his mug. "We have tea."

"Suit yourself. I'm hoping the aroma helps get some of these lumps off the floor."

"That whistle of yours might work too," Kash laughed. "Damn that was loud."

"I was thinking something a little gentler," Volci chuckled, gently pushing one of his crew with his toe. "Good morning, sunshine."

Kash and Calynn left him trying to wake up his crew. They sat down at one of the tables and waited for their breakfast.

More people were waking up and milling around when Milo placed the most beautiful plates of food Kash had ever seen in front of them.

"I have some Zinnaberry pancakes, because I heard you talking about them last night," Milo said, grinning at Calynn, "drizzled with a cinnamon and vanilla glaze. The omelet's smoked fish and root vegetables, smothered in a salty white sauce. And for the final touch, sourdough toast with my homemade fruit marmalade. Enjoy."

Calynn's eyes widened as she eyed the fluffy pancakes, grabbing her fork eagerly. She took a bite and let out a soft, happy hum.

"Oh, these are amazing!" Calynn sang.

Kash started with a bite of the omelet. Some of the root veggies had some spice to them like peppers. The creamy and salty white sauce brought a perfect balance to each bite.

"You have to learn to cook like this," Kash jested, poking Calynn in the ribs. "It's delicious, Milo. Thank you so much."

Milo bowed slightly and excused himself, so the duo could eat in peace. After breakfast they would make their rounds to say goodbye to all their new friends. Kash ate slowly.

After what felt like a thousand hugs, they were back in The Cat and ready to be on their way to their next stop. Calynn had teared up some when they were saying their goodbyes, and it turned into full-blown waterworks when some of the rescued women came to give their thanks. Calynn hugged them all several times as they all cried together. Svata and Calynn exchanged emails so they could stay in touch, and the ever-stoic Chief Volci presented Kash with a symbolic "key to the base." Kash had to admit he would miss Chief Volci, and hoped he would need his key sooner than later.

As The Cat's engines fired up, Kash and Calynn waved one last time to the crowd of onlookers that came to see them off. Their gratitude gave Kash pause, and he couldn't help but smile. He thumbed the key that Volci had given him in his palm and couldn't remember the last time goodbyes had felt this hard.

"I'm really going to miss them," Calynn said, her voice cracking with emotion.

"Yeah… they were good people."

"I hope our next visit isn't so dramatic though."

"Less explosions would be welcome change," Kash agreed, with a sly tone.

"My thoughts exactly."

Kash pushed the key around in his palm some more. The Chief didn't have to say anything when he gave it to him. Kash understood what the man was offering…

"A home," Kash let the words slip out of his mouth.

"That's what Volci offered you, isn't it?"

"Not offered," Kash said softly, revealing the key. "Gave."

Calynn's face scrunched up and more tears welled in her eyes. Kash squatted down beside her and they leaned into each other, both raw with emotion. The HLD hummed to life and the Alley Cat Savant sped away from the survivors of Delta-2382.

Hourns later, Kash awoke from a nap to Calynn curling up with him.

"Hi, beautiful," Kash whispered, pulling her close.

"Hi yourself, handsome," Omia replied, rolling into him covered in blood. "Why did you let me die?"

Kash sat straight up in bed with his heart pounding out of his chest. It took him a moment to get his bearings. He was in his bed alone. He buried his head in his hands and tried to catch his breath.

"Are you okay," Calynn asked from the door. "I heard you scream."

Kash motioned for her to come closer but didn't say anything. He didn't wait for her to strip down before pulling her into bed with him. She landed on her back and Kash buried his face in her chest, listening for her heartbeat. Even through her synthetic skin, her heart's rhythmic beat was easy to hear. He didn't know why it soothed him, but it did.

"I'm guessing a bad dream," Calynn said soothingly, stroking his head gently with her fingers. "When was the last time you talked to Doctor Uva?"

"It's been a while," Kash admitted, his voice barely over a whisper. "We've been kinda busy."

"It has been a little crazy lately."

"A little?" Kash asked sarcastically, lifting his head to look at her.

"Oh, hush… it's not that bad," Calynn pulled his head back down into her chest. "We didn't die, the stupid dammit is fixed, we have a bunch of new friends, and last night was…. Amazing… so I say that adds up to just a little crazy."

"I wish that sunny disposition of yours was more contagious than it is."

"Even the warmest and brightest of suns needs a storm cloud to make rainbows."

Calynn's resilience always amazed him. That girl found the bright side of everything. Kash tried to raise his head to look at her again, but she was holding him down.

"No, stay here," Calynn giggled. "I'm not done petting you yet, and you're not allowed to say anything about my rainbow analogy."

"I thought it was sweet," Kash said thoughtfully.

"Really?" Calynn asked joyfully, letting go of his head.

"No," Kash smirked. "I just didn't want you to smother me with your boobs."

"Death by boobie," Calynn joked, mock trying to pull his head back down.

"You're silly," Kash said, pulling himself up and giving her a quick peck on the lips. "I need a shower."

"Are you going to tell me about your bad dream?" Calynn asked as he slid out of bed.

"It was no big deal," Kash lied. "I was in the dark and something jumped out and startled me. I guess recent circumstances have me on edge."

"You know I can tell when you lie to me right?" Calynn asked, following him into the bathroom. "Which means it was about her. I'll call Doctor Uva for you when you get out of the shower."

She sauntered off before Kash could protest. He stepped into the hot shower and sighed. She was probably right. He should talk to Uva.

When Kash got out of the shower, he noticed the ship was no longer moving, or at least not faster than light. The telltale hum of the HLD was missing. Kash pulled on his jeans and went out to find Calynn and see what was going on. She was sitting at the helm with her legs pulled up to her chest and her chin resting on her knees.

"What's wrong, baby Girl?"

Calynn turned to face him, pressed her lips together, and hit the button for the comms.

"I know you're there, Captain Smith," the mysterious voice said. "Nothing smart to say?"

"Can we go around?" Kash sighed. "I really don't feel like dealing with this guy again."

"This is the Delta system."

"Oh yeah... asteroids everywhere."

"We have to stick to the shipping routes or risk running into a chunk of rock at way beyond the speed of light," Calynn explained. "What's worse is they deployed that planet net thingy again."

"Well, fuck," Kash sighed heavily, running his fingers through his hair. "Wait... how the fuck did he get here before us?"

"I asked the same question," Calynn replied.

"There's no way they have a vessel that fast... unless... that's why his replies were so slow at the moon base."

"He wasn't actually there," Calynn had the same realization as him. "Well, then I don't know that he is actually here either... that same message is playing on loop."

"Let's find out," Kash told her and pressed the comm button. "We've been through this already. If I say something smart the chances of you comprehending it are slim to none."

Kash and Calynn waited a moment and got the same recorded message in response.

"So, it's not him," Calynn observed. "Just another trap for..."

"Oh, so… you finally decided to show up?" the mystery man interrupted her.

"Sorry, I got delayed," Kash smirked. "I had to take a detour to sign some autographs for my legions of adoring fans, and then the after-party was at this moon base, and that, let me tell you, was an epic fucking party… Couldn't be helped."

"Is that supposed to be funny?" the man asked, annoyed. "A party on the moon base."

"Yeah… it was nuts," Kash replied and then turned to Calynn. "That doesn't leave a natural progression for the conversation, so we shall see if he's really here or not."

"Are you done with your ridiculous comments, Smith?"

"Let me check… looks like that's a no."

"I can't fathom why you are so sought after when you don't take anything seriously," the man continued with some disdain in his voice. "You're like a child."

"Because I take things seriously that need to be taken seriously, and your dumb ass doesn't qualify for the serious column," Kash replied in a direct but emotionless tone. "You lack the fortitude to face me directly and instead choose to hide in the shadows and implement the tactics of a coward. As a general rule, cowards should be mocked mercilessly… especially cowards of the bureaucrat variety. So, in conclusion… my poor attitude is a direct result of your weak spine. Again… can't be helped."

"Nice one, Boss," Calynn smiled.

"Is that what you think? You believe me to be weak?" the mysterious voice spat.

"I think I hit a nerve," Kash smiled back at Calynn before replying. "Unequivocally… oh, sorry… that mean yes. I keep forgetting you're dumb."

"I know what unequivocally means, you pompous asshole!"

"Sorry, I just assumed your vocabulary was as weak as your spine," Kash said in calm contrast to the mystery man. "How about vitriol? Can I use that word too?"

The cloaked government ship fired a volley from all its guns, spraying rounds in every direction. They didn't know where Kash and Calynn were since The Cat was also cloaked, so they were hoping to get lucky. Calynn easily dodged the rounds that came close.

"I can pinpoint them after that volley," Calynn announced.

"No, they'll move. It's standard procedure," Kash informed her. "But if I had to guess… they'd move to the edge of the asteroid field."

Kash thought for a moment and came up with a plan.

"Move close to the asteroid field and drop me off," Kash explained. "I'll hitch a ride on one of the bigger ones to get me close and board their ship."

"That sounds risky."

"Do you think you can mimic my voice and keep him guessing?" Kash asked, ignoring her comment. "Maybe jump in close and then jump away a few times to get him to reveal his location?"

"You still there, Kash," the man asked.

Kash intensified his gaze at Calynn. She relented and nodded.

"Unfortunately," Calynn sighed using a digital replica of Kash's voice. "Look this is getting boring. Any idea when you're going to do… anything?"

Kash smiled at the beauty, kissed her forehead, and dashed back the hallway to catwalk. There, in one of the upper storage compartments was his space suit. The suit was military grade and as high tech as they came. It consisted of an inner thermal layer to maintain his body temperature and an outer shell with several stealth properties. The inner layer needed direct skin contact, so Kash quickly pulled off all his clothes, letting them fall to the ground. Then began the tedious act of stuffing his body into the skin-tight suit.

"Want some help?" Calynn asked, she must have heard him struggling.

"Sure."

With Calynn's help he quickly got the suit sealed up and slid on the outer shell. He wished they could make them more streamlined, but it has to be sturdy enough to withstand the pressure inside and the vacuum outside. Those two forces were working together to try to tear the suit apart… constantly.

The last thing he grabbed was a large ring that he pulled over his head.

"What's that?" Calynn asked, eyeing the unfamiliar device.

"C-BIRD," Kash replied, tightening the strap. "Covert Breach for Ingress and Rapid Deployment."

"How's it work?"

"Atmospheric barrier, hull cutter, friction weld to seal it… single use," he said curtly, adjusting his suit. "It'll get me inside without them knowing it."

"Is it safe?"

"Mostly."

"Mostly?" she echoed, her tone sharp.

"I'll be fine," Kash smirked. "I won't take the suit off, promise."

"You better be."

Kash didn't answer her. He locked his helmet in place and pressurized the suit. He vaulted over the railing of the catwalk and used the suits boosters to gently land on the deck of the cargo hold. He opened the weapons locker and grabbed two pistols.

"Get me in position," Kash ordered, walking to the cargo door.

The atmospheric shield sprung to life and the cargo door started to open before Kash got to them. When he turned back, Calynn was standing on the catwalk with her arms wrapped around herself.

"You better be," she repeated.

Kash gave her a thumbs up and jumped out into the cold void of space. He made sure the cargo door closed securely before activating his boosters and flying away from his ship. The flat black color of the suit didn't reflect any light, so unless you were looking for it, it was nearly impossible to see. He was just another black void moving through the black void of space.

The massive asteroid field flowed through space like a river that carved its way through a field. A river would meander through a field because of how it eroded its edges. Some asteroid fields, like this one, meandered also, but Kash didn't understand the theory as to why. He assumed it was something to do with gravitational anomalies. That might also explain why the bigger chunks moved faster than the smaller ones.

The asteroid belt was populated by everything from dust sized particles to chunks nearly the size of a moon, although the moons were extremely rare. Kash was looking for a rock big enough to mask his approach, but not so big that its gravity brought a bombardment of smaller rocks. After a few minutes he found what he was looking for. A group of larger asteroids, about two-hundred-fifty meters in diameter, moving together that had already eliminated all the smaller pieces near them. The lead boulder was spinning violently and had sharp and jagged edges, but the ones that followed looked smoother, like they had broken their rough edges off on each other.

Kash hit the thrusters in his suit and started to move parallel to the asteroid field. He needed to match the speed of the boulders in order to hitch a ride. Once up to speed, he pitched in towards one of the ones in the rear, hoping that would reduce the risk of being crushed when two of them bumped together. When he got close, the boulder's gravity grabbed him.

"Oof," Kash grunted, impacting the giant rock. "Fuck."

"What was that?" Calynn asked, worried. "Are you okay?"

"Yeah… I just misjudged the gravity and came in a little hot," Kash explained, as he stood. "How are things going there?"

"He calls you a name, I fire back a retort, and then they shoot in random directions. It's kind of monotonous."

"Well, this rock is moving pretty quick, so jump in close and then jump away," Kash said urgently. "Let's see if we can get them to reveal their position. I don't want to miss."

Calynn did as he asked. A flash of light revealed his ship sitting near where the first attack came from, and then it jumped back from harm.

"Again," Kash ordered, jogging to stay on the side of the asteroid where he could see the area in question.

The Alley Cat Savant jumped into position, the guns from the other ship roared to life, and his ship jumped away safely before the rounds could land on their target. Kash studied the space looking for movement so he knew where the enemy vessel had moved, but he must have been too far away.

"One more time, Baby Girl."

Kash witnessed the exact same series of events. His ship appeared, bullets flew, and Calynn jumped back to safety, but this time the dark void of space… moved. No cloaking device can hide a moving ship if you get close enough. It threw the perception angles off.

"I got them," Kash said grinning. "Moving in."

"Be careful, Boss."

Kash hit his boosters and launched himself towards the ship, aiming for the middle as not to miss. He flipped around so he was coming in feet first and gently made contact with the ship. Kash ducked down so he was squatting, putting him beneath the projected image of the cloaking device. Luckily, he had landed away from any windows and portals. Hopefully, nobody saw him coming.

"I lost you," Calynn sounded surprised.

"I'm beneath the magnetic field. Hang on," Kash replied, while deploying the C-BIRD. "I just have to flip up this antenna… and you should see my position."

"Yep… got you."

Kash activated the breaching device and watched it go to work. The barrier buzzed into existence as two lasers cut through the hull. A small arm pivoted and moved the piece of the outer hull out of the way.

"Outer hull is breached. I got lucky. There's no wiring or piping in the way," Kash reported his progress. "Cutting the inner hull now."

The lasers of the C-BIRD sprung to life again, cutting a slightly smaller disk out of the inner hull. It lifted the piece out of the way, Kash grabbed his firearm and dove inside. The ship's artificial gravity grabbed him and pulled him nearly perpendicular to the opening he had cut. Kash performed a textbook combat roll and scanned the area with both guns drawn. He appeared to be in one of the corridors that lead from the bridge to the crew's quarters.

"I'm in," Kash keyed his comm back to Calynn.

He needed to stay off the radio as much as possible so the enemy couldn't detect him. Kash pressed a button on his bracer and the C-BIRD welded the two hull pieces back into place. He then set a timer for eleven minutes. The C-BIRD could maintain a disrupter field that kept the enemy sensors from seeing the hull breach for fifteen minutes, but Kash wanted to give himself a little buffer.

He holstered one of his pistols and moved quickly and quietly towards the front of the ship. He had no idea how many persons would be on board, so the quicker he got to the command deck the better.

Whoosh

A door opened just behind him, and he turned quickly to see a brunette woman walking out of the room. Kash was on her before she could scream, placing his hand on her mouth and pushing her back into the room. He pushed the woman to the ground and held her down with one knee. His gun was trained on the blonde woman on the bed, who was trying to cover her nakedness with the sheets.

"Make a sound and you die," Kash commanded. "Understood?"

Both women nodded frantically with terror on their faces. Kash slowly got off of the woman on the floor and locked the door. He didn't want any more surprises.

The brunette sat up and crab walked back towards the blonde. They held hands as soon as she was close enough.

"I'm not here for you. I'm here for your boss," Kash explained, careful not to sound too scary or too weak. "Answer some questions and you just might survive this."

Again, the women nodded frantically.

"How many souls on board?"

"About fifteen," the blonde replied.

"Military?"

They both shook their heads.

"Just the bureaucrat and his staff?"

The brunette nodded, but the blonde shook her head.

"Okay," Kash hissed, pulling his other pistol. "One of you is lying."

"We aren't part of his staff," the blonde said looking at the woman on the floor.

"Then who are you?"

"I'm one of the engineers… for the ship," the blonde stated. "And this is my wife."

"So, you're assigned to the ship, not to him."

"Yes… please don't hurt her," the blonde pulled at the other woman's arm. "She didn't mean…"

"How many would be loyal to him?" Kash interrupted.

"Roughly half."

"What's his name?"

"Jeffrey Emmit."

"Any bodyguards?"

"Probably… I didn't see them come aboard," the blonde replied, pulling her wife onto the bed with her. "I'm sorry."

"Why are you so calm?" Kash realized the woman hadn't stammered or stuttered a single time. "Are you not afraid of being shot?"

"Frankly... I'm more afraid of the way Mr. Emmit looks at her," the blonde replied nodding at her wife.

Kash took a moment to gaze upon the brunette. She was a pretty woman with flowing auburn locks and a curvy body. The blonde had a huskier build with broad shoulders for a woman. They were both fairly attractive, but not compared to Calynn or Aja... or his beloved Omia. The brunette looked like she could burst into tears at any moment, so Kash lowered his weapons.

"Describe him for me?"

"Not quite your height but much heavier, probably outweighs you by thirty kilos. He shaves his head because he's losing his hair," the blonde explained. "His neck rolls hang over the collar of his suit, and he has a big mole near his left ear."

"Pudgy fingers with a giant gold ring on his little finger?"

"Yeah," the blonde replied quizzically. "How'd you know?"

"Because I have seen a video in which he and his friend do some unspeakable things to a little girl," Kash replied somberly. "Resulting in her untimely death."

"Oh, my," the blonde gasped.

"I should go end his reign of terror now, but I need to tie you two up first," Kash said calmly approaching the women. "Sorry, but I can't trust you."

"We understand," the blonde replied. "I have cable ties in my tool bag in that closet that you can use."

"Thank you," Kash replied and moved to where she had nodded. "That's very helpful."

"What about our friends?" the brunette asked, her voice shaky.

"If they get in my way, they die," Kash replied, moving toward the women with the cable ties in hand. "I'm sorry if that sounds callous, but at least I'm honest. Now, lie on your stomachs, please."

The women hesitated only briefly before rolling onto their bellies, placing their hands behind their backs with a resigned familiarity. Kash's gaze flicked over them, noting the blonde's nudity. Her ample posterior was exposed, but she held her composure despite her vulnerability.

"Just... no funny business, okay?" the blonde murmured, her voice trembling slightly as she glanced over her shoulder.

"I have to admit," Kash said as he bound her feet, "you've been very cooperative so far. Is that too tight?"

"No, it's fine. To be honest?" she replied cautiously. "I was hoping it'd make it less likely I'd get raped."

Kash froze, her words cut deeper than expected. His hands clenched for a moment before resuming their task. His jaw tightened as his pulse quickened.

"I despise rapists," Kash said through clenched teeth. "The thought of them makes me…"

He exhaled sharply, anger flaring behind his calm facade. His pulse quickened, and he fought to slow the rage building inside.

"That's why Jeff is going to die… horribly."

"Ouch," the blonde yelped as the tie around her wrists dug in too tightly.

Her cry snapped him out of his rage, but only for a moment.

"Sorry," Kash muttered, cutting the tie quickly. "I should go… before I lose my temper."

As he turned away, the flood of demons came unbidden and relentless. The little girl from the video came first… her terrified eyes, her pleading screams. Her fragile body, broken and bleeding, her innocence destroyed by the monsters who defiled her.

And then Omia. Her radiant smile and easy laugh… replaced by a dark sadness and bruised flesh. He remembered the hollow, lifeless look in her eyes after they starved and beat her… her spirit crushed. He saw the red dots forming on her lovely skin… the bullets tearing through her as a monster pulled the trigger. The same kind of monsters waited at the head of this ship.

Kash clenched his fists, his chest tightening as he fought to control the surge of emotion. Not now. He wouldn't let the memories of her consume him. He couldn't let the demons win.

He forced himself to focus on the good. Omia's laugh, her warmth. But the memories were fading, and growing harder to hold onto… but Calynn's memories were fresh… her joy, her wit, her giggle… her sticky flesh from the fire wine…

Kash exhaled one last, cleansing breath. The rage in his chest turning to intense resolve.

With renewed determination, he unlocked the door and stepped into the hallway. Each step brought him closer to one of the monsters and a chance for retribution.

The corridor gently arced to the left. Kash was moving at speed when he came upon two men, their faces illuminated by the glow of their E-tablets.

"Down. Down now," Kash said, his voice firm but quiet.

"Don't hurt us," one of the men stammered. "Please."

"He won't," the blonde called from behind Kash, her voice calm. "Get in here."

Kash thought for a moment and then waved them through. The men rushed into the door as the blonde woman exited. She had pulled on a pair of leggings and a shirt and was walking with a purpose towards Kash.

"I'm going to clear away our friends," she stated as she tried to rush by Kash.

"Or warn them," Kash growled, grabbing her arm. "Why should I trust you?"

"I could have done that from the comm on the wall in my room," she declared. "Please trust me… I want that creep off my ship as much as you do."

Kash hesitated as he searched the woman's eyes, looking for the truth they held. He was surprised to see only her determination, there was no sign of deception. He reluctantly released his grip on her arm and she jogged off in front of him. Kash paused for a moment before following.

"Good morning, sir," he heard her say loudly.

She was warning him. Kash quickened his pace and smashed the man in the forehead with his weapon, knocking him unconscious. He caught the man before he hit the ground to keep the noise down. More footsteps ahead grabbed his attention.

"Come on. Come on," the blonde whispered. "This way. Keep it down."

She approached with two men and a woman in tow. She was keeping them calm when they saw him, and doing a good job of it too.

"The rest are all yours, mister," she smiled as she passed. "Happy hunting."

"How many?"

"Four plus him."

"Get in your room and stay there."

"Yes, sir."

Kash had to smirk at the dissension in the ranks, and how quickly the Consortium people could be turned against their own. He hadn't even tried to recruit the woman. She just volunteered.

The five men in the command center were all staring out the windows, looking for Kash's ship.

"You can't keep this up forever, Smith," Emmit barked.

"And yet," Kash's voice replied. "It seems that I can."

"There!" a man shouted, pointing out the window.

"Fire!" Emmit bellowed.

"Oops… missed me again," Calynn replied as Kash. "How much more ammo are you going to waste before you realize how much you suck and surrender?"

"Surrender?" Jeff Emmit shouted. "You will be the one surrendering!"

"Gosh, I'm starting to sound like a broken record," Calynn sighed, her voice perfectly mimicking Kash's. "Look, I'm getting bored over here. Are you planning to do anything, or are we just playing hide-and-seek all day?"

Kash smirked. Calynn had done a wonderful job at baiting the man. They had no idea he was aboard their ship, but they were about to find out.

He took aim at the two men on the left, fired, and dropped them with precise shots. Before their bodies hit the ground, the two on the right followed. Only Jeff Emmit remained, his eyes wide and his mouth agape.

"Hi, Jeff," Kash said, his voice cold and calculated.

"Smith?" Jeff stammered, his head jerking around searching for allies. "How…how did you get on board?"

"Oh, I'm not really here," Kash said with a smirk, his pistols still trained on the man. "I'm just the devil in disguise."

"What… but…"

Kash's expression darkened, his smirk fading. The demons were coming for their pound of flesh.

"Hey, remember the little girl from that video you made? The one you impaled and left to die?" His voice dropped to a demonic growl. "She says hi."

Jeff barely had time to open his mouth before Kash fired. He pulled both triggers twice.

"AAARRGH!" Jeff screamed, collapsing in a writhing heap as Kash's bullets ripped through his groin.

His cries dissolved quickly as he slipped into unconsciousness.

Kash lowered his weapons, his breathing steady. He studied Jeff's motionless form, his jaw tightening as the rage inside him ebbed.

"Just as I thought," Kash muttered, his tone still ice cold. "You're no monster… just a pathetic bureaucrat with a weak spine."

Stop #4

Kash looked at the eleven stations at the helm of the ship and wondered which one disabled the cloaking device and Hyper-Lumic Shroud. He had never been aboard a ship like this during his tour with the Legionnaires.

"Well, fuck," Kash muttered. "I guess I'll need some help."

"Stay right there for me, would ya?" Kash asked the unconscious Jeff as he shot him in one knee.

"AAARRRGHHH!" Emmit shouted, regaining consciousness.

"Thanks," Kash uttered with malice.

He trotted back to the women's room and knocked on the door.

"It's me, open up," Kash said calmly.

"Hi," the blonde replied as the door slid open.

"So, who knows how to fly this thing?"

Two of the men raised their hands.

"Let's go," Kash waved for them to follow. "I need your help."

The entire group followed him down the hallway to the command center.

"Finally," Jeff grumbled. "Kill him!"

"You mean he's not dead?" the blonde asked.

"He's working on it," Kash stated without emotion, shooting Jeff in the other knee.

"GGGGRRRRRRRR!" Emmit snarled. "Fuck you, Smith!"

"He hasn't finished the torment portion of his punishment yet," Kash continued. "He'll die shortly thereafter."

The three women huddled together. They were obviously shaken by Kash's brazen brutality.

"Drop the cloaking shield and disable the Hyper-Lumic Shroud," Kash ordered. "And where are the comms?"

"Here, sir," the man on the right indicated.

Kash approached the comms with a playful smile.

"Hey, beautiful, I'll show you mine if you show me yours."

"I love getting naked for you, Boss," Calynn replied as The Cat shimmered into view.

"There she is... home sweet home," Kash smiled. "Just a few loose ends to tie up here and..."

CRACK

A shot rang out from behind Kash. He turned, identified two combatants, and quickly dispatched them using his pistols.

"You're ruthless!" the brunette spat.

"Indeed, I am," Kash agreed. "But... when someone tries to kill your pilot slash best friend and an entire star base full of people just to hurt you... you grow callous..."

Kash walked slowly but deliberately over to where Jeff Emmit was lying.

"You okay, Boss?"

"And then there is the video this fat tub of shit was involved in," Kash continued. "If you saw what those pricks did to that little girl, your nightmares would have nightmares."

Kash shot Jeffrey in the right shoulder this time.

"FFFAAAAAHHHH!" Emmit screamed. "FUCK YOU, SMITH!"

"Fuck me?' Kash asked rhetorically, his words laced with sarcasm. "Sorry, Jeff, but you're not my type."

"Sir," the blonde said, meekly. "Not to interrupt, but if we are correct... there's still three of his men somewhere on the ship."

"Drop the fire doors. Put this boat on lockdown," Kash ordered. "Pull up the interior monitors... let's find the last three."

"Sir," one of the men hollered. "The last three are sentinels and they are currently in the cargo hold."

"Boss?" Calynn asked again.

"What the fuck are they doing there?" Kash asked quickly. "And let her know I'm fine."

"Smith, you motherfucker," Jeff groaned.

"You're a monster," the third woman complained.

The chaos of the moment nearly overwhelmed Kash. He had too many people trying to drag his attention in too many directions.

"ALRIGHT!" Kash bellowed with authority. "One fucking thing at a time... you, what are the sentinels doing?"

"It looks like they are getting ready to do a spacewalk," the man replied.

"Open the cargo bay doors," Kash ordered the man and then keyed the comms. "Baby Girl, you have some target practice coming your way. Three sentinels ejected out the cargo hold."

"On it, Boss."

"And that's the last of his personal detail, correct?" Kash asked.

"Yes, sir," the man replied.

"And someone is shutting down the fucking shroud, correct?"

"I can do that," one of the other men suggested raising his hand slightly.

"Get it done," Kash ordered and moved back to Emmit. "I guess that just leaves you."

"Just get it over with, Smith," Jeff spat.

"What if I don't think you have suffered enough yet?"

"Mister, please," the blonde pleaded.

"Targets eliminated, Boss," Calynn announced.

"Fine," Kash conceded. "Goodbye, Jeff."

Kash fired two rounds into the man's forehead eliciting more gasps from the men and women in the room. Kash stared at the lifeless body waiting for the satisfaction that never came. Remove one monster from existence and two more will pop up in his place.

"Looks like my work here is done," Kash said calmly. "Sorry you all had to witness that, but he deserved that on so many levels."

"What happens to us now?" one of the men asked timidly.

"I have no quarrel with you."

"No, I mean what happens... without him," the man pointed at Jeff.

"Technically, it's insubordination since we helped you instead of him," a different man said.

"Yeah, but Mr. Emmit was a monster!" the blonde screamed her voice cracking. "He did… and he was… I…"

Her voice fell off as her anger faltered. Kash approached the woman, her head hanging as she stared at the floor. He placed a reassuring hand on her arm, sensing her pain.

"You were worried about your wife, because he already got to you… didn't he?" Kash said in a warm soothing tone.

The woman looked up and nodded, tears running down her cheeks. Kash placed his hand on her cheek and gently wiped away a tear with his thumb.

"He can't hurt either of you anymore," Kash smiled softly. "I promise."

The blonde started to cry and wrapped Kash in a hug. He held her and looked around the room. The rest of the crew had looks of astonishment or pity on their faces. Jeff had hurt one of their own and they hadn't known. She had kept her torment to herself, and only now that her abuser was gone could she let it out.

"Is there somewhere else we can go?" one of them asked. "I don't want to go to jail for insubordination."

"Me either," another agreed.

"I know a star base where you guys can go and disappear," Kash offered. "They're dreadfully understaffed and could use the help… great people too."

The men and women started looking around the room at each other, like they didn't know what to say.

"We can help clone your transponder and make sure you can't be tracked," Kash continued. "It would be a clean fresh start… bureaucrat free."

"Is that possible?" the blonde woman asked into his chest, her voice a little stronger.

"It is."

"That sounds good to me," the blonde tried to smile, pointing at Jeff's corpse. "It has to be better than him."

They spent the next two hourns cleaning up the ship and Calynn walked them through how to drop a drone that had a cloned transponder. To alleviate further suspicions, she even hacked their military files to make it look like they were always assigned to Volci's star base. Chief Volci was eager to have more bodies aboard, especially since they were in engineering, and was very excited about the ship they were bringing.

Kash and Calynn were soon back under way to their next stop, and the government cruiser was on its way to their new home. Jeffrey Emmit and his goons' bodies were left to the asteroid field. The rocks and boulders of the field would soon erase any evidence of their existence. Kash even took the time to doctor his own logs so it looked like they never met Jeffrey Emmit.

"I used Emmit's codes to reopen the shipping lane," Calynn told him. "But there is a patrol coming to investigate the closure."

"Will they find the cloned transponder?"

"Easily."

"Good… they can chase a dead man for answers then," Kash replied. "With luck, they'll think Emmit stole the ship to run off and play god. The fact that the cloned transponder is sitting stationary for anyone to find should be perceived as Jeff gloating. They'll focus their efforts on him, leaving us and the engineers like ghosts… we just get to disappear."

"That would be the desired outcome."

"Yeah, but we don't always get what we desire."

Calynn spun Kash's chair around so he was facing her instead of his monitor.

"What else do you desire?"

"Hmmm… how about a stiff drink and a massage?"

"Okay," Calynn smirked. "But first… I need a kiss and swat on my ass."

"Yes, dear," Kash smirked back.

Kash awoke a couple hourns before their scheduled arrival at the next star base. He showered, dressed, and was perusing the cyber-web when Calynn entered their bedroom.

"Anything interesting?" she asked, rubbing his shoulders.

"Neh… same old thing."

"And nothing on the missing cruiser?"

"Oh, hell no. Are you kidding?" Kash exclaimed. "They won't risk the embarrassment. I'm telling you right now, they are running background checks on anyone even remotely associated with Jeffrey Emmit. They'll be chasing their tails for months, if not years, until some committee gives the order to write it off and not waste any more resources looking for him."

"It's fun watching you use their own corruption against them."

"Yeah, well, if they eliminated the corruption, I wouldn't be able to use it against them," Kash sighed. "But they won't. It's too easy to keep stealing."

"Well, that little delay with our corrupt bureaucrat does have me a little worried about the charge of our cargo, so I... am going to go babysit it," Calynn said as she left the room.

"Have fun," Kash hollered after her. "I guess I should dive back into these schematics too."

Kash must have fallen asleep reading the schematics, because next thing he knew Calynn was waking him up.

"Boss, something feels... wrong."

"Is it the little gadget again?" Kash asked, groggy.

"No... the star base."

"Are we here, already?"

"Yeah, but... something is wrong."

Kash followed her to the cockpit and gazed out at the star base. He took his time to study everything, but nothing looked out of place. There were ships on patrol and drones buzzing around. Everything looked normal.

"Am I missing something?" Kash asked Calynn.

"Nobody has hailed us yet," Calynn replied, pointing out the windshield. "But look at the patrols."

Kash watched a little more closely this time. Two fighters on patrol looped around the end of the base, the outer ship was slightly out of formation and the pilot corrected it. Nothing about that seemed weird to him. Pilots aren't always perfect, but then he thought he saw the same correction by the next group of two. He hadn't been paying close attention to that group, so he watched the third group as it approached the turn.

"Well, I'll be," the words fell out of Kash's mouth as he watched the third pilot group make the exact same correction. "There's no pilots in those ships."

"That's what I thought," Calynn said excitedly. "They're moving like drones..."

"In a preprogrammed flight path," Kash finished her thought. "But why?"

"You're the military man. Why would they do that?"

"I wish I knew," Kash replied absently. "Any active conflicts in the area?"

"It's the Delta system… there's lots of resistance to being squashed under the Consortium's thumb."

"True… And we're close enough for them to see us, right?"

"Easily."

"There!" Kash exclaimed, pointing at the base. "The communications array is destroyed. They can't contact us."

"What do we do?"

"Let's get a closer look," Kash said calmly, his gaze never leaving the base.

"Okay," Calynn sounded unsure as she sat at the helm. "Taking us closer to the scary guns and rings."

She slowly approached the base. Kash noted her apprehension as she constantly adjusted her grip on the controls. They crept closer to the base, and still no reaction. Calynn held their position when they were barely outside of the defense rings.

"Are you picking up any comms?" Kash asked.

"No… nothing."

"Did they abandon it?"

"Two in one trip?" Calynn sounded skeptical. "I doubt it."

Kash noticed two more fighters getting launched from the tubes followed by two more. The four fighters approached in an irregular formation.

"Hold position and identify," a voice demanded over the comms.

"This is the diplomatic courier, the Alley Cat Savant," Calynn replied. "We have an urgent situation."

"We are not engaging in any commerce at this time."

"Commerce, hell," Calynn argued. "We're scheduled to be here, so we can charge the big piece of shit in our cargo hold."

"We can either dock and charge it, or drop it off on your doorstep and let it reach critical," Kash added, his tone firm and demanding. "Your choice."

"Nobody can dock at this time."

"We're a diplomatic courier that is schedule to dock here, and we are going to dock," Kash kept his tone firm.

"My orders state that you cannot dock."

"We have higher orders that say we can."

"Sir, we cannot…"

"Let me rephrase that, soldier!" Kash interrupted with authority. "We're fucking docking! Now, get me your C.O!"

"But sir…"

"I SAID NOW, SOLDIER!" Kash bellowed.

"Sir, our comms are down due to an attack…"

"Then we can meet face to face!" Kash interrupted again, growling. "Put him on a ship or put us in a dock, but do so quickly or we will drop this ballistic laser at your doorstep and leave. Then, you can explain to the Admiral why the weapon wasn't delivered. I get paid either way."

"A ballistic laser?" the pilot's question sounded genuine.

"Yes, a ballistic fucking laser," Kash replied.

"Uh… hang on."

"Hang on?" Calynn mocked. "That's sooo professional."

"What are the odds of you being a goddess and getting me their comms?" Kash asked quickly.

"I'd have to get lucky with the frequency," Calynn explained. "There's nothing I can hack in these fighters."

"Well, shit… then I think your bad feeling is contagious."

"You got it too?"

"I sure do," Kash said laying his hand on her shoulder. "I'll fly… hack the base."

"We're a little too far," Calynn replied as she switched seats. "I'm not sure I can from here, but I'll give it a try."

"That's my girl," Kash replied, his gaze fixed on the star base as he sat at the helm. "I wonder how long we're just supposed to wait here?"

Calynn didn't respond to his question. She knew it was rhetorical and didn't warrant a response. Kash shook his head as he watched the fighters. The four of them were lined up side by side facing his ship, and not in any kind of formation. If they were planning to attack, they should be flanking him. If the plan was more defensive, then the other three ships should have been slightly behind the lead ship. That way if Kash fired on them, the lead ship would protect the others.

"Like shooting fish in a barrel," Kash muttered to himself.

"Alley Cat Savant," the pilot said. "You're cleared for dock two... follow me."

"Falling in. Standard formation," Kash replied as he moved to flank the lead fighter.

They slowly approached the star base. Kash watched the automated patrol go around again, and an uneasy feeling grabbed him again. He shook his head, and his stomach churned.

"I'm in," Calynn announced.

"Thank the Gods, that makes me feel a little better," Kash admitted.

"Boss... you're not going to believe this," Calynn giggled.

The monitor in front of him blinked off and then showed what Calynn was looking at. Two separate groups... firing at each other.

"What the hell?" Kash asked.

"Rebels took the base," Calynn explained. "But the base personnel regrouped and are pushing back. They have two sentinels that are turning the tide in their favor."

"Lock them down," Kash smirked. "Drop the emergency airlocks so they can't advance, and the rebels can't... son of a bitch, that's why they are letting us dock... they want the laser."

"You might be right, Boss. Look... a group moving to greet us."

"You know what to do."

"I sure do," Calynn smirked, her eyes glowing bright white.

"Can you make it look like they are doing this to each other so they don't suspect us?" Kash chuckled.

"Way ahead of ya, Boss," Calynn giggled.

"My girl."

Kash focused on flying as they got to the dock of the star base. He eased them through the atmospheric barriers, spun around, and set his bird down. He noted that the charger for the laser was not in this bay. They would have to move it or move The Cat to get the damn thing charged. He left Calynn in the cockpit and went to the cargo hold. The cargo doors were already down when he got there, and a man and a woman were there to greet him. Neither of them were armed.

"Hey, folks, how we doing today?" Kash smiled, unleashing his charisma. "Let's push that charger over here so we can charge this piece of shit before it explodes. Nobody wants that."

Kash chuckled and approached the duo like they had been friends for years.

"The charger?" the woman asked.

"Yes, ma'am," Kash smiled at the woman. "The containment field won't last much longer on that thing. We need to get her charged… say… where is the charger?"

Kash looked around innocently, like he hadn't already known that the charger wasn't here.

"Did I come to the wrong dock?" Kash continued with friendly chuckle. "I followed the pilot."

"Yeah," the man replied apprehensively. "This is the right dock."

"Okay," Kash smiled. "But I don't see the charger, and trust me… this thing needs it pretty soon. Sorry, where are my manners… I'm Kash."

Kash smiled at the man and extended his hand. He wasn't a very big fellow and looked a little fidgety. He was middle-aged with reddish-brown skin, thinning white hair, and a bulbous nose. The woman had the same skin tone and hair color, but her features were much more feminine. She had a medium build, and her long white hair hung nearly to her waist. She was also much younger than the man, barely twenty years of age if Kash had to guess.

"Lenn," the man replied, shaking Kash's offered hand. "The name's Lenn."

"And your beautiful companion?" Kash asked, offering her his hand also.

"I'm Breyda," the woman blushed, shaking Kash's hand.

"A pleasure to meet you both," Kash smiled, pointing back over his shoulder. "My Pilot is Calynn, she'll be down in a minute. I can help ya go grab the charger, if you'd like? I'd hate to meet you fine folks and then we all… explode."

Kash finished his statement laughing. He was trying to put the duo at ease while also conveying the urgency of the situation.

"Why would we explode?" Breyda asked.

"The containment field needs charged," Kash explained. "Without it, the core would reach critical flux and destroy us and most of your base."

"So, it's not operational?" Lenn inquired.

"Not as it sits, no," Kash smiled. "If someone tried to fire that thing right now... well... let's just hope nobody is that foolish, right?"

"Oh... I, uh," Lenn stammered and walked away.

"Is he going to go check on the charger or..." Kash asked Breyda.

"I'm not sure... let me go see," Breyda said and trotted off.

"Okay... hurry back."

Kash stood there and watched the duo leave, wondering how their conversation with their boss was about to go. Then he wondered if they would try to charge the laser only to try and steal it after.

"Hey, Boss," Calynn asked from behind him. "A little help?"

She was standing at the top of the ship ladder with her eyes still aglow. He jogged over and climbed part way up so he could grab her hand. Calynn gingerly climbed down the ladder with his help.

"We shouldn't let them see you with your eyes like that," Kash insisted.

"I'm almost done," Calynn replied.

"Do I dare ask?"

"I removed all their permissions to the emergency airlocks and all the doors," Calynn giggled. "The only one that can open doors... is me."

"You devious little minx," Kash chuckled.

"We still need the charger," Calynn continued as her eyes stopped glowing, "but otherwise we can watch them flounder about as they get more and more frustrated."

"Sounds like a fun show... you grab us a chair and I'll pour some cocktails."

When Kash returned with the drinks, Calynn was already in one of the oversized chairs waiting. She had set it up on the dock at the bottom of the cargo ramp. He sat beside her, and she threw her legs over his lap. They sipped at their whiskeys and waited for the fun to begin. Breyda was the first to return.

"Hi, uh..." Breyda stammered.

"Kash."

"Yeah, Kash," Breyda continued. "Lenn wanted me to tell you that we are bringing the charger, but we're having trouble getting enough people here to do that."

"Oh, just grab that thing there," Calynn replied, pointing at a massive hover-skid. "You only need one person then."

"Oh… thanks," Breyda replied and trotted off again.

Kash and Calynn giggled as they watched her try to figure out how to use it. After failing to even turn the machine on, she jogged off to go get help.

"What's going on with the battle?" Kash asked, still giggling.

"I keep opening doors so they think they can get somewhere, but it's just a big circle," Calynn laughed. "I wait and let them see an open door so the sentinels sprint towards it, but then I close the door and trap them… they're wasting a lot of energy and they're getting really mad too… it's kinda funny."

"And the rebels?"

"They keep trying to make their way here to us, but I keep circling them around behind the soldiers," Calynn continued. "It gives me something to make the sentinels run the opposite direction too."

"Miss Smith… are you picking sides?" Kash feigned being appalled.

"No, well… sorta… I'm just against the sentinels."

"Eh… that's not a bad thing."

A group of four men rushed into the dock holding a manual for the hover-skid.

"This could be fun," Kash mocked as they watched.

The group argued amongst themselves as they wandered around the machine. The group eventually figured out how to turn on the main power and one of them grabbed the controls. After a little trial and error, the man had the machine moving. Although, he nearly hit the wall trying to leave the dock through the large open door.

"Are we sure we trust these people to bring the charger?" Calynn asked, sounding a little unsure.

"If they fail too miserably, I can jump in and help."

"But who will rub my legs?" Calynn smiled, wiggling her legs on his lap.

"Was that a hint?" Kash laughed and started to rub her thighs.

"Yes, please," the beauty smiled.

Kash and Calynn sat on the chair chatting about anything and nothing as they waited. Calynn gave periodical updates on the sentinels and what she supposed were their power levels. Kash was intrigued when she said they were starting to slow down. They were burning through their power supply quickly.

The four men returned with the charger for the ballistic laser in tow. The huge hover-skid was moving slowly and cautiously. Lenn and Breyda were nowhere to be seen.

"Guess I gotta let you up, huh?" Calynn sighed.

"Probably should... mostly, so we don't explode," Kash winked at her.

"I guess you can't rub my legs if we explode," Calynn mock relented, swinging her legs off of him.

They exchanged a smile and Kash went to assist the group with the charger.

"Open the port there to hook the charger to the base's power grid," Kash ordered, pointing at the floor hatch. "It needs to be powered up so it can run diagnostics before we plug it into the laser itself. You... let's get those cables stretched out and in position so we are ready when the charger is."

Nobody replied to Kash, but they seemed genuinely thankful for his direction and did as he ordered. They had the charger ready to go in just a few minutes. Kash hooked the cables to the laser himself to ensure no mistakes were made, and the charger started to hum as it transferred power. Kash smiled and rejoined Calynn on their chair. The four men were watching him like they expected something else, and it started to feel awkward.

"What?" Kash asked them, looking between the men.

"What do we do next?" one of them replied.

"Now we wait," Kash replied.

"How long?" another asked.

"Oh... five or six hourns I reckon," Kash replied, looking to Calynn.

"Six, easy," Calynn confirmed nodding.

"Six?" the first man exclaimed. "What the hell?"

The man who hadn't spoken yet waved a hand at the man who just had the outburst. The first man yielded and cast his gaze at his feet.

"When could it be fired?" the fourth man asked calmly.

Kash assumed this man was the leader. He had the demeanor of a man in charge.

"Hell if I know," Kash replied. "I'm being paid to deliver it, not shoot it."

"And I'm curious about your target," Calynn added, kicking her legs back onto Kash's lap. "Who… do you want to shoot?"

"Just curious," the man smirked. "I've never seen one of these up close."

"I'd shoot it at sentinels," Calynn blurted out.

"Oh, yeah… hate those guys," Kash agreed.

"Speaking of sentinels," Calynn nodded at the man.

"Hey!" a man yelled from the door waving frantically for the group to join him.

The four men jogged over to the man and spoke to him. The leader suddenly turned and stared at Calynn with a blank stare. She raised her glass and nodded at the man again. The man turned away, and the group ran off together. Kash turned and gazed upon the smirking beauty at his side. She pulled her glass to her lips and took a draw of the liquor before meeting his gaze.

"What?" Calynn asked, feigning innocence.

"What did you do?"

"Nothing," she grinned ear to ear.

"What?" Kash repeated.

"I may or may not have released the sentinels… and then used the fire suppression system to freeze them solid."

"Naughty girl," Kash grinned.

"I'll be naughty later," Calynn said as she stood. "There's something else I wanna do first."

"Where are you going?" Kash asked as she walked away.

"To the galley," Calynn said over her shoulder. "We have a fully stocked kitchen at our disposal and nothing but time on our hands… are you coming?"

Kash smirked and chuckled to himself. He looked at the charger knowing it would be fine without them, so he jogged after Calynn to catch up. When they exited the dock, Kash looked to his left and right and saw the emergency doors were down. The rebels were on the back side of the door, frantically beating on it trying to get in.

"What did you do?" Kash asked.

"I made sure we could eat in peace," Calynn replied without turning around.

Kash shrugged his shoulders at those stuck on the other side of the doors and followed Calynn to the galley. The duo made seafood with pasta tossed in a creamy white sauce, and oven-roasted veggies. They ate peacefully, secluded from the battle that was happening all around them. Calynn reported that it looked to her like some of the base personnel had been murdered in their sleep. She was also certain that some of the rebels were former base employees. Both groups were engaging in deplorable acts to get the upper hand in the conflict. Kash and Calynn were both beginning to not like either side.

"Well, shit," Calynn burst out. "It looks like I just lost my title of devious minx."

"What the hell are you talking about?"

"That woman…"

"Breyda?"

"She's working both sides… yes, I'm sure," Calynn answered before he could ask. "She's manipulating them to kill each other."

"To what end?"

"Let's ask," Calynn said as she got up and walked off.

Kash followed her down a hallway through several doors that Calynn opened just for them to pass through, and then immediately closed. They ended up in one of the engineering areas that supplied the heat for one half of the base. Kash couldn't tell the scale of the room because the enormous heaters, ductwork, and other equipment limited his sight lines. Calynn paused just inside the door.

"Can I have your sidearm please?" Calynn asked, her hand outstretched.

Kash handed her his pistol and she immediately fired a single shot into one of the ducts.

"The next one doesn't miss!" Calynn announced loudly.

"Okay," Breyda replied, her voice shaky. "I'm coming out."

A maintenance hatch on the ductwork opened up and Breyda slowly emerged with her hands up.

"Who are you?" Calynn asked forcefully. "No lies, no bullshit, and I don't give second chances."

The woman stared at her feet for a moment, like she was embarrassed to answer. Calynn loosened her tongue with a bullet that barely missed her ear.

"I'm a thief!" Breyda exclaimed, clearly terrified.

"A thief?" Calynn barked.

"What the fuck are you trying to steal?" Kash asked, matching Calynn's tone.

"The base," Breyda answered, her eyes wide and brow raised.

"The base?" Calynn asked, keeping her angry tone.

It took a minute for her answer to really register for Kash, but after thinking about it for a moment...

"For who?" Kash asked, calmer. "Who are you stealing it for?"

"Gravitas," Breyda replied, her voice barely over a whisper.

"Gravitas?" Kash asked, stunned. "You're kidding... that fat piece of shit wants a star base?"

Breyda nodded her head but didn't respond.

"What's he gonna do... put mirrors on the defense rings and have a dance party?"

"You know him, Boss?"

"Unfortunately... I do," Kash replied.

"Then you know I can't fail him," Breyda added, her voice still trembling.

"Killing the entire staff on a star base... hedonistic glutton... smug fucking..." Kash was expressing his frustrations out loud. "Can you contact him? Right now? Can you?"

"I shouldn't," Breyda complained.

Calynn took a step forward and pointed Kash's gun at Breyda's head.

"But I can," Breyda continued.

Breyda rolled up her sleeve revealing a hi-tech bracer. She started the comm and a blue bubble appeared above her arm. The bubble morphed itself into a face.

"I see the base has not been moved yet," Gravitas said in his husky gruff voice. "You were warned what would happen if you failed."

"She ran into a fucking problem," Kash announced, approaching Breyda. "Not only am I not going to let her finish her job, but I'm also going to destroy this base and let the authorities know it was you that was taking it."

"I know that voice," Gravitas replied. "And how are you, Kash?"

"Still fit and athletic," Kash quipped. "You?"

"Still shining bright," Gravitas replied and smiled his biggest smile. "And before you call the authorities... perhaps, I could call in that favor?"

"Oh, you're going to have to do better than that," Kash argued.

"A favor is a favor."

"Oh no... this is way bigger than a favor."

"Kash... don't do this," Gravitas said, but not in his normal jovial tone.

"Oh, so it's not for you," Kash observed. "This is an order that needs filled... for whom, I wonder?"

"Kash... this is bigger than you and me..."

"Initiate the self-destruct and kill her..." Kash started to say to Calynn.

"WAIT!" Gravitas hollered. "Kash... please... there's no need for threats. We have history together, you and I. We have dined together and enjoyed the finer things life has to offer."

"A delicacy that the workers on this base can no longer enjoy," Kash sneered. "Your thief turned this place into a war zone that stinks of death. No more bullshit! What's your play?"

"Ah, you wound me," Gravitas replied, his tone bristly. "But I assure you, this is... delicate business. A necessary acquisition, shall we say, for a client of... discerning tastes."

"Discerning tastes... sounds dirty to me," Kash shot back. "And I'm not helping you grease any gears. So, unless you're offering me something incredible, I'm about to ruin your day."

"Kash," Gravitas said, his voice dropping. "You know I can make things... inconvenient for you."

"This is already inconvenient," Kash snapped.

"And boring," Calynn added.

"So, start talking… or I let my beautiful assistant… entertain herself."

"Oh, I like that plan," Calynn smirked and cocked her head. "Do I get to kill sentinels and a star base in one day?"

"Fine," Gravitas sighed, "You want to know why this base matters? It's not for me. It's for something bigger. Something that could make or break the balance of power. Let me make you an offer."

"Make it a good one, fat man," Kash smirked. "My finger's itching to hit that self-destruct."

The Last Stop

"Are you sure we can trust him?" Calynn asked, her voice uneasy.

"No," Kash admitted, running a hand through his hair. "But let's be honest… after all the bureaucratic bullshit we've dealt with, we need someone who plays outside the rules."

"And that's supposed to make me feel better?"

"No," Kash sighed.

"That helps," Calynn snapped.

"Look… Baby Girl, he's untouchable," Kash continued, ignoring her jab. "Not even the Consortium can get to him. And more importantly, he knows I can ruin him if he tries to screw us over. His reputation? His vanity? Those are worth more to him than credits. He won't risk it."

Calynn hesitated, biting her lip as she considered his words. She was hugging her legs to her chest and resting her chin on her knees.

"I still don't like it," Calynn admitted.

"Doesn't mean I'm wrong," Kash replied with a slight smirk.

"I know," Calynn sighed.

"With him and Anne watching our backs…"

"We stand a better chance of getting out of this alive," Calynn finished his thought.

"And I would much rather live through this than the alternative."

"I know," Calynn relented.

"And after we're done with this shitty job," Kash continued. "We are going straight to his casino for some rest and relaxation. And that massive line of credit he…"

"So, we can go on a proper vacation?"

"We can," Kash smiled. "In a glorious, comped suite…"

"A suite?" Calynn asked, her tone perking up.

"With all the amenities."

"And shopping?"

"There's a mall... in the casino," Kash explained, a smile tugging on the corner of his lips. "Designer clothes tailored to fit..."

"Tailored?"

"Are you drooling, Miss Smith?' Kash smirked.

"Even my really nice blue gown isn't tailored," Calynn smiled.

"Ew... Maybe we shouldn't get you anything tailored then," Kash added as his smirk grew.

Calynn gave him a cross look and scowled at him.

"There's no way I could keep my hands off you if you looked better than you did in that gown."

Calynn's scowl melted, her brow raised, and her bottom lip was caught gently between her teeth.

"I can barely keep my hands off of you in jeans..."

Calynn ripped her shirt over her head, jumped up from her chair, and started dragging Kash by his waistband down the hallway towards their quarters. Her bra hit the ground before they made it to the door, and her jeans didn't last much longer. She helped get Kash out of his clothes and then pushed him back onto the bed.

Kash couldn't help but be locked in her gaze as she slowly crawled up on top of him. Her eyes were full of passion and screaming with her desires. Kash's hands found her hips and he gripped her tight. Calynn leaned down and her lips brushed his.

"You're not getting any rest before the next stop," Calynn whispered into his mouth.

"Is that so?" Kash whispered back.

Calynn replied with a soft moan, and time drifted away.

Kash awoke hourns later with Calynn's hair in his face and a delightful ache in his groin. He wrapped his arm around her and pulled her tighter.

"Mmm, he's finally awake," Calynn murmured softly.

"Thanks for letting me rest," Kash whispered into her hair. "I just couldn't keep going."

"You can make it up to me later," Calynn cooed. "Tell me more about that suite."

"No no no," Kash chuckled. "You'll get wound up again."

"Now why would I do that?" Calynn giggled as she rolled over on top of him.

Calynn wrapped her legs around his and leaned in close. Kash was expecting her to kiss him, but she playfully bit his bottom lip instead. She grinned ear to ear when she let go.

"I need to wash up if we're gonna go another round," Calynn said with a naughty look in her eye.

"Can I have a rain check?"

"Until?"

"Tomorrow?"

"Deal," Calynn said and gave him a quick peck on the lips before rolling out of bed. "Dibs on the shower."

Kash ogled her as she walked to the bathroom.

"I'm gonna eat that ass up, tomorrow," Kash smiled.

"Promise?" Calynn asked over her shoulder.

"That girl is gonna be the death of me," Kash said quietly to himself.

The duo showered and dressed to get ready for their last stop to charge the laser before finally making the delivery. Kash perused the cyber-web and made small talk with Calynn to pass the time. They laid back down and Kash was able to grab a bit more sleep.

When he awoke, he was alone. Kash threw on his clothes and went to the cockpit to join Calynn.

"I was just going to come get you," Calynn said with a chipper tone.

"How far out are we?" Kash asked. "I need tea."

"Seventy minutes... give or take."

"Come get me when we arrive," Kash said and kissed her head.

"Will do, Boss."

Kash had two mugs of hot tea before Calynn called for him. When he joined her again, she was looking back at him with a worried look on her face. He looked out at the base and saw what was worrying her. A flagship was docked with the star base, and it had support ships with it.

"I count fifteen," Calynn answered the question before he asked it.

"A full armada… You feel it too?"

"Sinking feeling in your chest that just screams something is wrong… you're damn right I do."

"Let's activate our contingency plan," Kash sighed.

"Messages… are… sent," Calynn replied. "Let's hope it works."

"Let's hope indeed," Kash agreed.

"Taking us in," Calynn sounded unsure of herself.

They went through the standard protocols and soon found themselves on approach to Dock Three. As soon as they touched down, Kash and Calynn sprang into action. They locked the door to the cockpit as they left, while Calynn stripped off her clothes. They entered Calynn's link chamber for her to hide.

Kash watched through the window as she contorted her body to make herself look like she was just part of the computers in case they were scanned. Her legs and arms were intertwined with the conduits and wires, and she folded her body in half so her head was resting on her own bottom.

"Remind me to have you fold like that for me later," Kash jested.

"I'm going to beat you when I get out of here."

"Now now… be a good ship."

"Yes, Captain," Calynn replied in her robotic ship voice.

"My girl."

Kash zipped into their bedroom and shoved her clothes in a drawer. He locked the door on the way out, then locked the door that separated the cargo hold from the crew area. If anyone tried to get to Calynn or the cockpit, they were going to have to work for it. He walked across the cargo hold and stopped in front of the ramp door. He took a deep breath and hit the button to drop the ramp.

The soldiers and their weapons came into view as the ramp door lowered. Kash had at least fifty guns pointed at him, but he was scanning the crowd for someone else. He suspected there would be a bureaucrat there, and he found him soon enough. A smaller man in an expensive blue suit stood behind the soldiers. His blond hair was receding back his head and shaved short. He had a smug grin and stared at Kash with dark, beady eyes. He wasn't handsome or ugly. In fact, Kash thought him to be the very definition of average... but he was familiar.

"Last time I saw you," Kash announced in a firm loud voice. "You were biting the flesh off a dying little girl. For the record, that's not what a woman means when she says 'eat me'... emphasis on woman. I prefer the full-grown variety."

The creepy little man smiled a sinister grin but didn't reply. Kash raised his hands and took a couple steps forward. He smiled back at the man in bold defiance.

"Let the games begin," Kash smirked.

"Take him," the man said in a familiar voice.

Kash didn't have time to think about where he knew the voice from, before one of the soldiers approached and bashed him in the head with the butt of his rifle. Kash fell to the ground unconscious.

Kash awoke with a splitting headache. When he tried to feel the wound on his head, he pulled against the restraints on his wrists. He was stripped naked, and bound by the chest and waist to a chair in a small gray interrogation room. His hands were cuffed behind his back, and his feet shackled to chair legs. He was placed in the corner of the small room. In the center of the room was a table and three more chairs. The familiar man was seated opposite him, sipping at a drink.

Kash pressed his memory searching for the identity of the voice he had heard, but his headache limited his ability to do so. It was there... he just couldn't find it yet. The man smirked, stood up, and left the room. Three soldiers entered as he left.

"My safe word is cunnilingus," Kash shouted to the man before the door closed and then addressed the soldiers. "He doesn't know what that means."

Kash grunted as the first punch landed. This was going to be a long day.

"Captain Kolby Smith. Zebra Alpha X-ray zero zero seven zero."

That was all the information they would get from him. He repeated it like a mantra with each assault. The beatings continued on and off for what Kash assumed was about a day and a half. There were no clocks in the room for him to verify it, but his internal clock was normally pretty close. He was getting hungry and thirsty, and everything hurt. Dried blood was caked on his face and throughout his hair. He forced himself to doze off when he could to preserve his strength.

"Your ship is as defiant as you are, Smith," a voice said, waking him.

"She's a good ship," Kash replied.

"She electrocuted two men when they tried to get through the door to your crew deck," the man stated. "I can pin those murders on you."

Kash recognized the man's voice as he spoke and knew who he was now.

"Well, Juhn, I'm sure she gave fair warning first," Kash replied. "So, their deaths would fall squarely on the one who gave the order to engage in such a dangerous activity. Maybe you should try giving better orders. Just a thought."

"You think you're so smart don't you, Smith?" Juhn hissed.

"Smarter than most."

"A smart tongue for sure."

"Smarter than most," Kash repeated, smirking.

"Perhaps I should bring in more men to beat that smart tongue out of your mouth," Juhn growled.

"Probably smart... since you aren't man enough to do it yourself."

Juhn's mouth tightened, and Kash could see the muscles in his jaw clenching. His jab had hit home. A knock at the door distracted both men.

"Enter!" Juhn barked.

A soldier entered the room and whispered something into Juhn's ear.

"What does he want?" Juhn growled.

The man continued saying something to Juhn that Kash couldn't hear.

"Now?" Juhn barked, and cast his gaze at Kash. "Is this your doing?"

"From here?" Kash jested. "How would I do that?"

Kash paused to laugh.

"I'd have to be a god," Kash suddenly curbed his laugh, staring seriously at Juhn, "to pull off something like that."

The two men exited the room leaving Kash alone.

"How are my vitals?" Kash asked quietly. "They haven't given me any water yet."

"Holding steady," Calynn's voice came from one of the overhead speakers. "Although, I wish I hadn't worked you so hard yesterday."

"Nonsense… some good cardio is a great way to prepare for… being tortured," Kash said as reassuringly as he could. "How are you holding up?"

"I wouldn't call this position comfy, but at least they can't get to me."

"Good. Make sure it stays that way."

"He's coming back."

A few seconds later, Juhn opened the door and entered the room again.

"I just had the most interesting conversation," Juhn said with a twang of sarcasm. "Why would Gravitas call this star base looking for you?"

"Vested business interest, I'm sure."

"Business?"

"Doesn't everyone do business with that fat fuck?" Kash asked rhetorically.

"Why yes. Everyone does," Juhn grumbled. "Including the very powerful individuals who were sitting at the table with him when he called looking for you. He was certain to name them all."

"Oh, no," Kash quipped. "A table full of very powerful individuals all know I'm here now. Whatever will we do?"

Juhn's jaw clenched again, and it made Kash smile. He had eroded some of Juhn's power. If Juhn wanted Kash dead, there would be questions. Questions by people powerful enough that you cannot ignore their questions.

"What happened to Miss Smith?" Juhn suddenly asked, his jaw still tight. "Where's your pilot, Captain?"

"Ask your bestie, Mr. Jeffrey Emmit."

"How do you know that name?" Juhn asked, shocked.

"Have we met?" Kash asked sarcastically. "I'm the man that can retrieve anything… including the names of people that need to be dead for what they did to my pilot. Do you know where he is? I'd really like to tie him to a chair after I'm done with you."

"When you're... done with me?"

Juhn looked around the room and chuckled to himself like a sociopath.

"What makes you think you are EVER going to leave this room?" Juhn suddenly barked, slamming his fist on the table.

"I know for a certainty that I'll be leaving this room," Kash barked back. "You're just too stupid to realize that yet!"

"If you think that, then you're the fool, not me!"

"Says the guy foolish enough to get videotaped doing unspeakable things to a little girl!"

"That tape won't protect you forever, Smith!"

"It doesn't have to!"

"What's that supposed to mean?"

"I'm going to kill every last one of you monsters on that tape!" Kash snapped.

"Then what will be left to protect Detective Aman?" Juhn smirked, like he had the upper hand again.

"Me!" Kash barked.

Juhn was still smiling like he had Kash where he wanted him. Kash understood that if everyone on that tape was dead, it could no longer be used as blackmail to ensure Aja's safety. What Juhn was failing to realize was that Kash could make some of them disappear mysteriously. And those disappearances could be leveraged to make other corrupt officials fear the same fate. A well delivered threat with a vague jab at knowledge of their indiscretions could easily sway a spineless bureaucrat.

Another knock at the door.

"What!" Juhn bellowed.

The door opened and the same man from earlier entered the room. He whispered something to Juhn, turned to look at Kash, then left again.

"How did she do that?" Juhn asked calmly.

"Who? Detective Aman?" Kash asked and then smirked. "Simple... she removed her clothes and slid herself down..."

"Not her, Smith!" Juhn interrupted coarsely. "Your ship's nerve center."

"I'm going to assume that you gave another stupid order," Kash explained. "So, she would have analyzed the order, determined the threat level, and then formulated a suitable defense."

"But how did she open the atmospheric barrier, launching my men into space?" Juhn sounded annoyed yet intrigued. "Is it some kind of worm program? A virus? How did your ship inject a star base with a computer virus?"

"Oh, the virus wasn't her," Kash smiled. "That was me… limited sensors in interrogation rooms, right? Wouldn't want anyone to see what happens in here… would we? Be a shame if someone figured out how to use that to their advantage."

Juhn's eyes darted to Kash's clothes in the corner of the room. He moved quickly to the pile and rifled through them, only stopping when he grabbed Kash's watch. His jaw dropped as he stared at the device. Kash saw the panic in his eyes as he threw the watch at Kash and stormed out of the room.

The watch bounced off Kash and landed on the floor beside him. Two words were displayed on its face.

"Payload delivered," Kash said to himself, grinning. "Time to turn up the heat, Baby Girl."

"Danger!" an electronic voice announced throughout the base. "Systems normal."

Kash reached out with his foot to kick his watch closer.

"Danger! Systems are danger normal. Lock down. Normal."

Kash giggled listening to the alert. With a couple hops of the chair, he positioned his watch close enough to his hands and feet.

"Initiate operations menu," Kash said clearly and waited for his watch to beep. "EMP pulse level two… fire."

Kash pulled on his cuffs, but they didn't give.

"Dangerrrrr are normal," the alert continued.

"Level four… fire."

Kash felt the cuffs loosen and he knew he had successfully disabled them. He could now slip out of the cuffs anytime he wanted. He hopped his chair back into the corner and kicked the watch a few feet away.

"Home screen," Kash smiled.

"Norrrmmmaaalll," the alert voice ground to a halt, like it was failing.

Kash felt the air conditioning kick on in the interrogation room, and wondered what havoc Calynn was causing. He didn't have to wonder for long. When Juhn returned, he felt the heat from the hallway when the door opened. Juhn approached him instead of sitting down.

"What have you done?" Juhn growled as he poked his finger in Kash's face.

"Whatever do you mean, Juhn?" Kash asked, smirking.

"You know damn well what I mean, Smith!"

"Critical normal. Systems. Danger," the base's alert announced, too quickly this time.

"Oh, that," Kash feigned innocence. "You must be in danger."

The room's air conditioning changed to heat instead of cold air. It was so noticeable that both men looked up at the air vent. Moments later, the door to the room burst open, and two soldiers rushed inside and slammed the door. The frigid air from the hallway followed them.

"What the hell is going on?" Juhn snapped at the men.

"Sir, we have to do a hard restart on several systems affected by the virus," one of the soldiers explained. "We recommend getting you to safety."

"I'm not going anywhere!" Juhn bellowed, pointing at Kash. "He did this! We can make him fix it!"

"What am I supposed to do?" Kash said, sounding hurt. "Look at me, guys… I'm beaten, bloody, and dehydrated because he hasn't even given me some water yet… and I've been here two days."

"No!… You did this, Smith! Look," Juhn announced, grabbing Kash's watch off the floor. "This says payload… delivered."

Juhn's words fell off as he tapped the screen of Kash's watch, and it only displayed… a clock.

"It did… it said payload delivered," Juhn insisted to the soldiers. "He used this to upload the virus…it's a special spy watch or some…"

"Sir," the soldier interrupted, pulling up the sleeve of his uniform. "That's a standard issue watch. I have the exact same one."

"Me too," the other soldier revealed, showing his wrist. "It's just a watch."

"No… he altered it somehow…"

"Mister Juhn to the Conn," an authoritative voice boomed through the ship. "NOW!"

Juhn turned and looked at the two soldiers, then back to Kash. His eyes were darting around looking for answers to what was happening and finding none.

"Sir… the commander ordered you to the Conn," the first soldier said firmly.

Juhn turned back to the soldiers but didn't say anything.

"Sir," the soldier repeated, motioning towards the door.

"This isn't over, Smith," Juhn hissed, pointing his finger in Kash's face again.

Juhn and one soldier left the room. Kash heard Juhn asking him to contact some General but he couldn't make out the name before the door closed.

"You served?" the soldier asked.

"Legionnaires," Kash replied. "Combat pilot."

"What can I get you, Captain?"

"I'd kill for something to drink," Kash smiled at the soldier.

The man nodded and exited the room. He returned three minutes later with a Nutra-Shake.

"Thank the Gods," Kash exclaimed.

He sucked down the shake as fast as he could through the straw. The soldier never offered to remove his cuffs or anything. He would need someone of authority to make that call for him, but Kash was grateful for what the man had done. The soldier let him drink his fill, nodded, and left the room.

"Your vitals look better already," Calynn said quietly.

"I feel better too… the alert voice was brilliant. You love being silly, don't you?"

"Who me?" Calynn giggled.

"I love your giggle."

"I know," Calynn giggled again. "The base commander is getting pissed at Juhn, but that prick brought a three-star general with him who is forcing the base commander to fall in line."

"How far out is Anne?"

"The Admiral should be here in three or four hourns."

"Hopefully that's in time," Kash sighed.

"We are pushing him pretty hard," Calynn admitted. "Hopefully he doesn't snap and try to kill you."

"My cuffs are disabled," Kash told her. "Push comes to shove… I can defend myself now."

"I'm pretty safe, myself," Calynn said. "With the atmosphere still recovering here, they can't mount any effective assaults."

"That's good."

"Shall I continue being silly?"

"Indeed, you shall," Kash smiled. "But don't play it in here. I'm gonna try to grab some shuteye before Juhn comes back."

"Will do, Boss."

"Normal systems are Juhn," the base alert said. "Critical small penis. Juhn danger penis."

Kash chuckled, closed his eyes, and drifted off to sleep.

It felt like one second later the door was kicked open, waking him up again.

"It didn't work, Smith," Juhn announced gruffly.

"Oh, you're back," Kash yawned.

"It… didn't… work," Juhn repeated, enunciating each word deliberately.

"What's that?"

"One of those powerful people at the table with Gravitas called the base commander asking about you," Juhn explained. "But we squashed that intervention… you're mine."

"Oh, joy," Kash sighed.

"I'm done playing games with you, Smith," Juhn said directly. "Where's the tape?"

"Which tape?"

"The tape."

"Adhesive tape?"

"Stop fucking around, Smith."

"Be more specific, Juhn."

"Where's the tape with the girl?" Juhn hollered.

"In my dresser drawer!" Kash hollered back.

"Is that why your ship won't let us in?"

"Well… it is private."

"What's private?"

"The tape," Kash replied, a smirk tugging on the corners of his mouth. "My pilot didn't know I made a tape of us having sex."

Juhn backhanded Kash in the jaw as hard as he could. Kash barely flinched.

"Not that girl, you smart ass!" Juhn bellowed. "Crigg's niece!"

"Ohhh… that tape," Kash smirked. "Which copy?"

"You didn't," Juhn gasped.

"Of course I did, you fucking moron!" Kash barked. "I even sent a copy to Gravitas… good fucking luck getting that one back."

"You didn't… You couldn't have."

"When are you going to realize that I am twelve moves ahead of you, and we aren't even playing the same fucking game," Kash continued. "Aja will be safe forever, because if she's not… that tape goes public in ways that nobody can stop. You and your friends will make the galactic news. I guarantee it!"

Juhn launched himself at Kash and started hitting and scratching him. He knocked over the chair and continued to assault him. Kash thought about revealing he could defend himself, but before he could pull his hands from his cuffs… Juhn was pulled off him. A man in a uniform stood over Juhn and another stood in the doorway.

"Get off of me you, swine," Juhn said condescendingly. "General… put the Commander in his place."

"I can't," the General admitted. "I'm not in charge anymore."

"Then who is?" Juhn bellowed.

"That would be me," a raspy voice said from the hallway.

Kash smiled at Admiral Anne as she entered the room. She smiled back for an instant, but then her face turned grim.

"Why is this man naked, bruised, and bloody?" the Admiral growled. "What kind of operation are you running here?"

"I can answer that," Kash said smugly.

Juhn's eyes locked onto Kash, his breathing fast and shallow, barely restraining his fury. Suddenly, he lunged at Kash again... with something clenched in his fist.

Kash quickly slid off the disabled cuffs. He jerked his hand around, intercepting Juhn's wrist and redirecting the blow with practiced precision. Kash forced Juhn's hand back into his own body with a sickening crunch. Juhn's eyes widened in shock, his mouth opening as though to speak, but no sound came out.

When Kash pulled his hand back, it revealed a penknife buried in Juhn's neck. Blood began to spill, dark and fast, as the Commander yanked Juhn backward. He was merely trying to separate the men but quickly transitioned to trying to triage Juhn's wound.

"No," the Commander tried to warn Juhn, but it was too late.

Juhn pulled the knife from his neck causing more damage to the artery. He swung wildly at Kash, slashing Kash's left forearm with the blade. The movement left Juhn on his stomach with his head raised to see Kash, so Kash countered by punching Juhn in the face. The room filled with a gruesome crunching sound followed by a wet thud when Juhn's head fell to the floor.

Kash scrambled to his feet to get away from Juhn just in case. Only then did he check the wound on his arm. The Commander covered his face with one hand, staring blankly at Juhn's lifeless body. The Admiral stood frozen for a moment also, but quickly shook it off, opened the door, and shouted for a medic before addressing those in the room.

"Kash... clothes," the Admiral ordered.

"Yes, ma'am," Kash replied dutifully and began dressing.

"General, what's your association with Mister Juhn?" Anne asked.

"With respect, Admiral," the General replied. "I believe I need my lawyer present to answer those questions."

Medics burst through the door and rushed to Juhn's body. After a quick check for vital signs, the head medic shook his head. One of the other medics retrieved a body bag and they started to bag Juhn's body. The head medic then tended to Kash's arm. The wound was shallow on one side, but deeper on the other. The medic stitched him up and wrapped the arm in a bandage. They also cleaned up some of his head wounds from the beatings.

The medics left with Juhn's body and the General followed along, but Anne held up Kash and the Commander. When they were alone in the room, she closed and locked the door.

"Have a seat, gentlemen," the Admiral said with a friendly tone. "I'd like to get this done now while the details are fresh."

"No offense, ma'am," Kash said as he sat, "but I promised you full disclosure... just you."

"Kash, meet Commander Leo Eglan," the Admiral continued. "Leo, if you could tell me my first name to put Kash's mind at ease, please?"

"A pleasure, Kash," Leo replied, offering a handshake. "Her name is Anne."

"Any friend of Anne's is a friend of mine," Kash shook the man's hand.

"Go ahead, Kash," Anne insisted.

"Yes, ma'am. Several months ago, we stumbled onto a human trafficking ring when a friend was taken. That culminated in a showdown with Festo Crigg. Festo's brother, Lemi, had made a sex tape depicting the rape and torture of Festo's supposed daughter. I recovered that recording for Lemi and am still in possession of it. Festo went on a killing spree that led to the showdown on Poncia. Detective Aja Aman was instrumental in lending us some assistance that allowed us to defeat Festo. Aja is the Princess of Ooga Khoama and sent her royal navy to our aid. In return, we tracked down her cousin, and she needed some leverage to get him some help. I offered the video. The men in that video have been trying to silence us ever since. I have identified three of the men so far. Lemi Crigg, Mr. Juhn, and another bureaucrat named Jeffrey Emmit," Kash explained rapid fire. "I believe my current contract was nothing more than a ruse to do just that. If they can silence me, that leaves Aja vulnerable, and they can make the whole thing disappear. Unfortunately for them, I generally refuse to die."

"Can I see this video?" the Admiral asked.

"You really don't want to, ma'am. It's... awful."

"Noted," the Admiral said curtly.

"What happened to Emmit?" Leo asked. "That name sounds familiar."

"There's probably a report of him deserting and..."

"Stealing his government cruiser," Leo interrupted when he remembered. "I read that report just the other morning."

"Will we find Jeffrey if we go looking for him?" Anne asked.

"No ma'am," Kash answered honestly.

"And the cruiser?" Leo asked.

"In the capable hands of her crew," Kash replied. "They were… reassigned… and are still an asset of the Consortium."

"That's a hell of a mess, Captain," Anne sighed.

"Captain?" Leo queried, looking at Kash.

"Eleven Bravo," Kash nodded.

"You flew with Eleven Bravo?"

"I formed Eleven Bravo."

The Commander snapped to attention and saluted Kash.

"Permission to shake your hand again, Captain?" Leo barked with a military cadence. "Eleven Bravo saved my ass many times. They're the best of the best of the best, sir."

"As you were, Commander," Kash replied and offered his hand.

Kash shook his hand again and grabbed Leo's forearm with his off hand to give the handshake more substance. Leo smiled and Kash smiled back. He then turned to Admiral Anne.

"Don't look at me like that," Anne said with a smile. "I get a hug."

"Yes, ma'am."

The Delivery

With the Admiral in command, Calynn was able to leave her hiding spot and waited at the bottom of the ramp of their ship. As soon as she saw Kash enter the dock, she raced towards him. She slowed when she saw his bandaged arm but still crashed her body into his. He wrapped his arms around her and buried his nose in her hair. After being beaten for nearly two full days, he longed for Calynn's gentle touch.

"Hello again, young lady," Anne greeted Calynn. "Take your time… he needs that hug more than I do."

"Thank you, Admiral," Calynn said without releasing her grip on Kash. "I need it too."

Kash held her for another minute, kissing the top of her head several times before finally releasing her. Calynn popped up on her toes, gave him a quick peck on the lips and a soft smile, before she finally turned to the Admiral.

"Nice to see you again, ma'am," Calynn said as she hugged Anne.

"A pleasure indeed," Anne replied.

"I can't thank you enough for being here."

"We did some good work today," Anne smiled at Calynn. "There's a little less corruption in the galaxy thanks to the four of us."

"And who is our fourth?" Calynn asked, smiling at Leo.

"Calynn Smith," the Admiral said, releasing her, "this is Commander Leo Eglan. Leo… Calynn."

"A pleasure, Mrs. Smith," Leo smiled, offering her a handshake.

"Oh, come here," Calynn smiled. "I'm in a hugging mood."

She gave the Commander a quick hug and then returned to Kash's side. Her hand found his as she hugged his good arm to her body. Kash noted that she didn't correct Leo when he called her Mrs. Smith, but he didn't say anything.

"Can we take that monstrosity out of his ship now?" the Admiral asked, pointing at Kash's ship.

"That would be fabulous," Calynn blurted out.

"As long as I don't get docked for not delivering it... I'm good with that," Kash laughed.

"You did say it was a ruse, right?" Leo asked.

"I believe it was a ruse," Kash said. "Or that's what I meant to say anyway."

"Want me to check it out?" Commander Eglan offered. "It'll only take a couple minutes... hang tight."

Leo marched off without waiting for an answer.

"He seems like a good guy," Kash said to Anne.

"We served together," Anne replied with a sly smile. "He's a very good man."

"I know that kind of smile," Calynn giggled, letting go of Kash's arm and grabbing a hold of Anne's. "I like juicy details. Will you share the juicy details? Let's chat."

The two women strolled arm in arm to towards The Cat and smiled at each other. Anne must have been telling Calynn a pretty good story based on her facial expressions. Kash smiled as he watched her and then slowly strolled after them. The three made it to The Cat before the Commander made it back.

"The look on your face is telling me that my journey isn't done," Kash said with an annoyed tone.

"The delivery checked out," Leo said, shaking his head. "I almost couldn't believe it myself, so I checked twice."

"So, it wasn't a ruse, just a delivery of opportunity," Kash observed.

"Looks that way, Captain," Leo told him.

"It might not be so bad without people trying to kill us every step of the way," Calynn shrugged.

"That would be a welcome change," Kash agreed. "Did they charge the containment field?"

"Some... it stopped charging when I was forced to defend myself," Calynn explained.

"Can we get it charging again?" Kash asked Leo.

"And can we go get something to eat while it's charging?" Calynn asked with a big grin. "I'm hungry."

"You're always hungry lately," Kash jested. "Don't you get fat on me."

Calynn got a cross look on her face and started playfully slapping Kash's shoulder and bicep. Kash started laughing and retaliated by poking her in the belly.

"You two are such a good pair," Anne chuckled.

Kash wrapped Calynn in another hug and kissed the top of her head again. Calynn stopped hitting him and snuggled into his chest.

"So, is that a no to food?" Calynn asked.

"I'll get the engineers working on charging this thing and then we can go to the galley," the Commander added with a smile.

"And only if you stop assaulting me," Kash mocked.

"I'm not assaulting you," Calynn giggled, backed up, and placed her hands on her hips. "I can start assaulting you if you'd like."

"Only if I can pick your weapon," Kash tried and failed to stifle his smirk.

"Uh, huh," Calynn smirked and moved in closer again. "I'm not sure if you could consider that a weapon."

"You wield it like one."

"Wanna disarm me?"

"Okay, you two," Anne laughed. "Cut it out or get a room."

The trio shared a laugh as the engineers and Leo approached. Kash didn't want to leave until he was sure the ballistic laser was hooked up correctly and charging. After his concerns were alleviated, Leo led them to the galley for some dinner.

Calynn lit up with big smile when she saw the menu. Kash managed to talk her into eating some roasted meat and potatoes before she gave in to her sweet tooth. She took small portions so she could try a bunch of different dishes.

"You got yourself a wild one there, my friend," Anne said to Kash, nodding towards Calynn.

"She's one of a kind," Kash agreed with a warm smile.

"Speaking of her," Leo chimed in. "Did she disable the hack on my base? I really don't want to hear that goofy alert ever again."

"Yes, we did," Kash replied. "And I do apologize for that, also."

"I would ask how you did that, but I don't think that's something we want in the incident report," Anne pointed out.

"Speaking of reports," Leo added. "What are we writing down for the official report? I think we should leave Kash and Calynn out of the report as much as possible."

"Agreed," Anne nodded. "They were here, charged the containment field, and left."

"Mr. Juhn had Mr. Emmit in that room, and they both killed each other," Leo added. "If Kash was never in the interrogation room, it's a much cleaner exit."

"I like him," Kash said to Anne while pointing at Leo.

"And you can get everyone on board with a cover story like that?" Anne asked, diligently.

"My people hated everything about Juhn and that three-star coming here to bark orders at them," Leo replied. "They will happily write reports that chastise them and get these two out of here free and clear."

"I really like him," Kash said to Anne again with a big smile.

"I'm a fan of him myself," Anne smiled her sly grin again.

"But you two don't need to do that for me," Kash explained. "I can take whatever heat comes my way."

"It's cleaner for us too," the Admiral stated.

"What about the General's armada? How do you get them on board."

"Either they were never here, or they all go to prison," Eglan replied firmly. "Juhn coerced them to leave their post... I don't think I have to tell you how bad that could be for them."

"They will happily return to their duties and forget everything about this base," Anne added. "I told the General he is on my radar now, and that's all we should probably tell you. That way if you are questioned..."

"I don't know shit," Kash interrupted. "Good call."

"These little muffins are divine," Calynn cooed as she joined them. "You have to try one."

Kash didn't have time to reply before Calynn placed a muffin in his mouth. It was more like cake than a muffin, with sweet and tart berries and a crumb topping. Kash raised his brow and nodded in agreement. They were divine.

Once the containment field finished charging, the duo said their goodbyes and they were off to deliver the ballistic laser. The Commander had insisted that Calynn take a doggie bag. She packed so many disposable containers with snacks that Kash had to help her carry them. She was trying to find room for all of it in their small kitchen while Kash perused the cyber-web.

"Incoming comm," Calynn announced.

"Greetings, my friends," Meesha's voice filled the ship.

"Hi, Meesha," Calynn squealed with delight.

"Hi, beautiful, how are you?"

"I am dangerously low on Kash hugs, but other than that I am well," Meesha replied playfully. "How are you?"

"In dire need of a vacation," Kash announced. "This job has been..."

"A nightmare," Calynn finished his thought.

"I heard," Meesha said thoughtfully. "That is actually the reason for my call."

"Oh, yeah?"

"My dear husband told Bahanja and myself about the weapon that was used on Calynn, and we both would feel better if we could run some scans of her," Meesha explained.

"Yes," Bahanja added. "We need to be certain there is no lasting effect on the interface between the biologic and synthetic tissues."

"Like my nerves?" Calynn queried.

"Among other things," Meesha answered.

"Nothing feels off anymore," Calynn said, "but you can do whatever you feel is best."

"Would you please lie on the bed," Bahanja said. "We will take control of your sensors and scanners from here."

"Kash, we need you to leave the room so you do not contaminate the scans," Meesha explained.

"Sure thing," Kash replied and wandered out to the hall.

The door to his quarters slid shut, and Kash heard a faint hum from behind the door. He went to the cockpit and sat down to finish reading an article about the fuel shortage in several systems. Kash chuckled at the official story about supply and delivery problems.

He knew the shortage was because those systems defied Consortium rule. It was just the consortium playing hardball.

"You know what? No," Kash said aloud to himself. "It's probably just some corrupt motherfucker like Juhn causing the issue, not the whole government."

Kash was feeling pretty good about the government currently, and he couldn't deny that there were very good people in the government. Admiral Anne and Commander Leo were both amazing people, and there were definitely more people like them serving. Sure, there's a few bad apples like Juhn, Emmit, and the Crigg brothers, but that doesn't mean the whole thing was bad. He had met too many good people on this journey to be overly jaded. Chief Volci, Svata, Loi, Dulfi, Anne, and Leo were all wonderful people. As was the crew of Emmit's cruiser. Good people that worked in the Consortium. So obviously the government wasn't all bad.

Kash went back to scrolling some news articles. One other article had caught his attention. A shipping oligarch had passed away, and his children were waging war to inherit their father's fortune. Kash noted the family name and location. If any of them came calling for a retrieval expert, he was going to make sure he was too busy to work for them.

"Hey, Boss," Calynn said from the hallway behind him.

"Clean bill of health already?"

"Nooo, they got all the scans they wanted but still need to review them," Calynn sounded extremely happy for some reason.

"Then why do you sound so chipper?" Kash asked as she placed her hands on his shoulders.

"Something I learned," Calynn glowed.

"What did you learn?"

"Can I show you on the monitor?" Calynn asked as she sat sideways on his lap.

"Sure."

His monitor changed to an image of Calynn's body. The image was slowly turning as it shifted to show a bunch of different colored lines running throughout her body.

"This is all my synthetic nerves and such. I'm not sure what the different colors mean," Calynn explained as the image changed again. "And this... is all of my organic matter."

Calynn zoomed the image and started to point at the image.

"Here is my lung, and my brain is here where your other lung would be... this is my stomach and intestines and my one kidney. I have a synthetic liver. The other kidney and my liver were both destroyed in the accident. And here is my bladder and this... is also one hundred percent really me."

Calynn zoomed the image in further and was pointing at her pelvis on the image.

"But I thought that was... is it... that's you?" Kash stammered.

"The outer three centimeters is synthetic so I can protect myself, but after that... it's my original equipment."

When Kash looked at her, Calynn was grinning ear to ear and seemed to be glowing. She had never looked so beautiful as she did right now.

"So, every time we had sex..."

"That was really me," Calynn's smile faded some, she sounded more somber. "It's the only time that we... actually connect... your flesh to mine."

"The real you?"

"Yes... the real me, but the rest isn't."

"The rest is connected to your real nervous system, so you get real sensations even though the material is synthetic," Kash smiled, tapping her on the chest. "And everything you feel in here is real. The shell doesn't matter."

Kash paused and smiled softly, grabbing her hand.

"If holding your hand feels like holding your hand," Kash continued, then sighed. "Look... just, please don't think that... I don't need to physically touch the real you to know that I... that we..."

Calynn's tongue saved him from tripping over his. Her kiss conveyed her needs, so Kash cradled her in his arm, stood up, and carried her to their quarters. He quickly undressed them both. He couldn't wait to be inside her... the real her.

Kash awoke hourns later with his head on Calynn's chest. She was gently stroking his temple with her finger. When he looked up at her, she smiled softly. Her earlier uncertainty about what parts of her were real or fake had apparently passed. Kash rolled over on top of her, ran his tongue from her breast to her collarbone, and was soon inside her again.

Kash was gasping for breath when he rolled off his beautiful companion.

"Now who's the insatiable one?" Calynn panted. "Not that I'm complaining."

"I need a snack, a shower, and a couple hourns to rest before I can go again," Kash smiled.

"Again?"

Kash was still riding his emotional high when Calynn informed him they were on approach to the mining facility. The planet below was a lush vibrant green. The massive scar of the mine was the only blight on the otherwise pristine landscape. The chasm gouged into the planet's surface by the strip mine was visible even from orbit, as was the towering plume of debris rising from it. Carried by relentless winds, the dust cloud stretched halfway across the continent, choking out life and leaving a barren, dusty wasteland in its path. The scale of the pollution was nothing short of apocalyptic.

"No wonder they're having problems with the natives," Calynn observed.

"That dust cloud is enormous."

"And look," Calynn added. "There's a primitive village in the hills in the clouds path."

"The valley below was probably their farmland."

"Nothing can grow there now."

"I remember this from school," Calynn said. "The Diatyrium is broken apart to separate the denser fuel from the lighter Diaton. They claim the Diaton is inert, but it's too costly to contain. Once it creates a thick enough blanket on an area, they come in and vacuum it up to make heat shield panels for star ships. The Taryl... Tyrul..."

"Tyralum," Kash helped.

"That's it... the Tyralum is the only substance with the energy for Hyper-Lumic travel."

"Which makes it more valuable than the poor people that used to live here," Kash sighed and rubbed his head. "Just when I was starting to like the government again."

"We only removed a little bit of the corruption, not all of it."

"I know... let's just get this over with so we can go on vacation."

"Taking us in," Calynn sighed.

The mine seemed uglier the closer they got to it. The chasm was deeper than it looked from orbit. Enormous machines dug the ore from the ground, belching pollution into the air. The raw ore was pulverized into its two parts by a machine that slightly resembled an old steam locomotive on earth. The lighter Diaton was pumped into the atmosphere through the smokestack and the precious fuel was whisked away on a conveyor belt back to the plant. Everything was filthy and depressing.

Their destination was the main plant at the top of the mine. Thick, black smoke erupted from the stacks where they enriched the fuel. The smog was so thick around the plant that it blocked out the sun. It felt like twilight even though it was only mid-morning. Six sniper towers circled the oblong plant, and Kash counted at least twenty soldiers when they were on approach.

"A significant military presence for a mining operation," Calynn matched his observation.

"By the Gods," Kash uttered, surprised by the sight of the ballistic laser they were obviously there to replace. "That thing has been through hell."

The ballistic laser sat on a mobile platform near the loading dock of the plant, and was in such disrepair Kash was surprised the damn thing hadn't exploded. The outer shell was dented and twisted in every direction, and the actual laser apertures were falling apart.

"Did they roll it to the bottom of the quarry a few times?" Calynn joked.

"It damn sure looks like it," Kash replied. "Maybe it fell off the platform once or twice."

As they got closer to the plant, lights lit up on a landing pad to guide them in. Calynn followed the lights and put them down gently. The duo headed to the cargo hold, and Kash stopped for a sidearm. Calynn gave him a funny look but then grabbed a pistol and tucked it in her waistband.

When the cargo ramp lowered, four men were waiting for them. There was one man in a suit, a miner in coveralls caked in dust, and two soldiers. One of the soldiers was Calynn's size, but the other towered over Kash. He had to be nearly three meters tall and a lean 200 kilos.

"Captain Smith?" the suit asked.

"Please, call me Kash," Kash replied and extended his arm for a handshake.

"I heard you got delayed," the suit smiled.

"Pirates tried to steal the laser," Kash explained. "It was a mess there for a while."

"Well, I'm glad you finally made it."

"Yeah, we saw the old one on the way in. What happened to it?"

"Little blue bastards," the smaller soldier said under his breath.

"The Indigenous are... inventive with their attacks," the suit explained. "Their favorite is making it rain rocks."

"Rain rocks?" Calynn asked with a snarky tone.

"No idea how they launch them," the smaller soldier answered, "but rocks bigger than your fist fall from the sky and damage everything in their path."

"Which is why we're so eager to get the new BLASTR," the suit continued. "The old one doesn't work so well anymore."

"Diplomacy failed?" Kash asked sternly.

"Communication with them is impossible," the bureaucrat replied. "They don't speak."

"That seems problematic."

"You're welcome to go try yourself," the smaller soldier said snidely.

"Go try yourself, Captain," Kash corrected the man, glaring at him. "And maybe we will."

"Can we unload this thing now?" the miner asked impatiently. "I have other shit to do besides watch you all argue."

"Please do," Kash said to the man, motioning in the ship. "Get it out and get me paid."

"I have some of your credits here," the suit said, tossing a bag to Kash. "The rest will be transferred shortly."

Kash tossed the bag to Calynn. She turned and walked off with it immediately.

"Aren't you gonna count it?" the man asked, fixing his tie.

"Nope," Kash grunted.

"If it's short, we know where to find you," Calynn added with a smirk.

"And you'll never see us coming," Kash concluded, fixing his gaze upon the bureaucrat.

"Suddenly I want my assistant to double check the count again," the suit feigned a smile, but he sounded nervous.

Kash rolled his eyes at the man. Of course he would pass responsibility to someone else. No bureaucrat is ever responsible for anything they have ever done. Kash smirked and glanced at the man.

"Poor leadership is no excuse," Kash said with a calm and cool demeanor. "It still falls on your shoulders if it isn't right."

"In that case, I would like to personally count it," the bureaucrat sounded scared. "And I can get your transfer done while I'm at it."

Kash turned to Calynn, now standing on the catwalk. He didn't have to say anything. She tossed him the bag. He caught it, turned, and tossed it at the suit.

"Make sure," Kash nearly growled. "And the rest of you, get this piece of shit out of my ship."

The miner called for assistance and started to unstrap the ballistic laser. When the rest of his team arrived, they positioned the laser so they could remove it from Kash's ship. The bureaucrat returned as the laser was leaving his ship and tossed Kash a heavier bag of credits.

"The balance is on its way," the man smiled and offered a handshake. "A pleasure doing business with you, Kash."

Kash smiled and shook the man's hand but didn't reply. He didn't want to say the wrong thing and get escorted away from the mine. Kash joined Calynn on the catwalk and watched as the miners removed the ballistic laser from his cargo hold with an enormous hover-lift. Once it was out and Calynn confirmed the transfer, they closed the ramp door and prepared to leave.

"I'm curious about the tribe," Calynn said as they pulled away.

"Then let's check on them quickly," Kash responded. "I want to be long gone before that laser is active."

They circled the mine and landed in the valley near the village Calynn had seen earlier. Kash saw a small group of the tribesmen approaching as they touched down. Kash watched them diligently. They didn't move quickly and didn't appear to be hostile. They had a light blue skin tone and wore clothes that looked like they were woven from grass.

"They're almost the same color as Svata," Calynn pointed out.

"But we don't know if they are as nice."

"I get the feeling that they are."

Calynn's eyes betrayed her emotions. She wanted to go meet the tiny blue people, because she was curious about them and worried also.

"And I don't think we should be armed," Calynn continued.

"That's a big risk, Baby Girl."

"No… I don't think it is. I think I can feel them."

"Like before… their energy?"

"I don't know… but it's very serene."

Calynn started walking slowly towards the back of the ship. Kash wished he could understand what she sensed that was making her so calm about meeting this tribe. She wasn't nervous about it at all.

Calynn dropped the ramp door and sauntered out to the approaching group. She looked back over her shoulder at him, but her eyes were closed, and she had a soft smile tugging at her lips.

The group from the tribe stopped when they got close to Calynn. They didn't look aggressive to Kash. They were too small to really be a threat, he thought. They were barely over a meter tall. Two of them, a man and a woman, broke away from the rest and approached Calynn. She knelt on the ground before them so she was smaller than them. They each placed a hand on her chest, and it made Calynn jump.

"Hey!"

"I'm okay," Calynn interrupted before he could shout more. "It's just a bit shocking to experience."

"What are they doing to you?" Kash growled, fighting his instincts to protect her.

"Talking… this is how they talk… it's like… a hive mind."

"What are they saying?"

"They forgive us for delivering the new laser, since we had no idea it was being used against them. They say some of the miners are nice, but others throw things at them when they see them. They also know the soldiers have orders to exterminate them."

"Then why don't they leave?"

"This is their home... and something about the ore... I don't understand what they are saying."

The small duo removed their hands from Calynn, and each reached into a bag hanging on their waist. They pulled a pinch of fine powder out and placed it between their hands. The sound of a howling wind filled the air, but the winds weren't blowing. The sound came from where the two were touching each other's hand. The ground started to shake, and the woman suddenly raised one arm.

"Holy shit!" Kash hollered as he watched a column of rock protrude from the ground.

"That's how they throw the rocks," Calynn told him. "The ore lets them manipulate it... which moves the dirt and rock above the ore... I think."

"Ask them if they need the ore," Kash told Calynn. "I bet that's why they can't leave."

Calynn reached out her hands to bring the two back to her. They placed their hands on her chest again and closed their eyes. Calynn's body shuddered from time to time, and Kash was starting to get worried about her. He walked up behind her and touched her shoulder. A rush of thoughts assaulted him as soon as he touched her. It was like a hundred people talking inside his head at once.

"AAAAHHHH," Kash cried out and quickly let go of Calynn.

Kash staggered back and tried to regain his composure. He felt their anguish and knew their pain. The rest was a jumbled mess to Kash. Their thoughts were too much for him to understand, but their emotions... those came through like a kick in the chest.

"Sorry, Boss," Calynn said softly.

"I think I saw them," Kash gasped. "Were they slaves?"

The two blue people let go of Calynn and smiled softly. She fell forward like she was exhausted, took a couple deep breaths, and sat up.

"They built the city to the East for their overlords," Calynn explained, still gasping for breath. "I can't pronounce the overlords' race, but they forced these guys to use their powers to move the rock to build their homes and stuff. They would do their best to comply with the orders they were given, but some of what the bosses wanted was impossible to do. The bosses would beat them... or worse."

"Why didn't they fight back?"

"They can't… hurting someone is… it's like they can't fathom causing harm to someone."

"But they attack the laser," Kash pointed out.

"Only when no soldiers are near it."

"What about the ore? Did you ask about that?"

"You were right about that," Calynn sighed. "Without the ore they can't survive. Like us without water… they shrivel and die. They go into the mines to take only what they need, but the Consortium sees that as stealing."

"Is there more ore?" Kash asked. "Can we relocate them?"

"They are reluctant to leave, even though the pollution from the mine has destroyed their fields. They have been here for generations," Calynn explained. "Some of their tribe wouldn't survive the journey."

"But we could take them," Kash said, pointing at The Cat.

"I mentioned that, but…"

Calynn suddenly stood up and looked back towards the refinery. She cocked her head and then turned to Kash. Her brow was raised and her eyes had tears threatening to fall. She sprinted towards Kash and tackled him to the ground just as the world lit up red. The ballistic laser was already functional, and Kash felt the heat from the beam as it passed them.

When Calynn sat up and looked down at him, her expression shifted from worry to a simmering fury. Her brow furrowed, jaw tightened, and in one fluid motion she was on her feet. She clenched her fist, her menacing posture radiating the rage that was building with each breath. She glanced back at Kash, her hardened gaze ignited by the familiar bright white glow consuming her eyes.

"Fuck 'em up, Goddess."

The Showdown

The Cat's engines roared to life as Kash ran for the weapons rack. He retrieved Calynn's beam rifle and a long rifle for himself as well. He stepped out of the ship as the shields began to hum. The little blue people were all huddled together. The ground around them swelled so they were inside a bowl-shaped depression.

Calynn marched to the front of The Cat. She raised one hand and pulled the shield from the ship over towards herself, then projected it forward. She was apparently trying to protect everyone until she could launch some kind of counter offensive.

The ballistic laser fired again. The four red beams of energy converged on the shield in front of Calynn. She pushed the shield out, fighting back against the beams, but their relentless onslaught proved to be too much... even for her.

The laser burned through the shield and hit Calynn directly in the chest. The impact sent her hurtling through the air. She hit the ground fifty meters later and tumbled across the barren field for another seventy-five meters. Kash watched her body as it tumbled, and his heart sank. She laid still when she finally came to a stop and Kash feared the worst.

"NNNOOOO," Kash screamed as he pulled up an app on his watch. "Initiate pulse."

The entire world suddenly flashed red and all the sounds stopped. Time seemed to slow down as a ball of pure energy engulfed the refining plant and everything around it. The ball continued to grow as the shock wave from the explosion moved towards them. A rock shelf began to rise in front of the ship. Kash turned to the little blue people and saw them in a circle with their hands joined.

The shock wave was diverted by the wall of rock but was still strong enough to blow apart the top of the wall. Rocks and boulders rained down around them, so Kash dove for cover under The Cat. The ball of energy was beginning to dissipate, and everything was starting to return to its rightful color.

Kash launched himself forward and sprinted towards Calynn. He reached her a few seconds later and pulled her into his arms. The front of her shirt had been burned away leaving her charred skin showing. The grid in her skin wasn't glowing. This was an energy she couldn't absorb.

"Come on, Baby Girl," Kash pleaded. "Be okay… please, be okay."

Kash scanned the skies in all directions. Since there were soldiers at the mine, there had to be a base for them close by. And they would definitely come investigate the explosion. He gently tapped Calynn's cheek trying to wake her up. Time was of the essence.

"Calynn… Baby Girl, come on… wake up, baby."

Calynn groaned and started to move around. Kash smiled and touched his forehead to hers.

"Thank the Gods," Kash sighed. "I thought I lost you."

"Ouch," Calynn coughed.

"I guess we found something else that can stop you," Kash stated.

"It produces a weird magnetic field… I couldn't divert it."

"It's okay… I got it for you."

"You… how?"

"Remember those little probes I used on the safe?"

"Yeah?"

"Well, I need a new pair," Kash smiled. "I found a flaw in the wiring schematics… a small electric pulse sent through after connecting the wrong two circuits… and boom."

"I love it when you're devious," Calynn smiled.

"I know," Kash smiled back.

Calynn looked down at her chest and wiped at the char with her hand. She sighed with relief when it partially wiped off.

"Oh good," Calynn continued. "My skin is okay."

"We should get back to the ship before their backup arrives."

"Backup?"

"The soldiers at the mine had to come from somewhere," Kash explained as he helped Calynn up. "It would be against regulations for them to stay here. There has to be some barracks somewhere close."

The duo jogged back towards their ship. The tribe must have understood what was happening because they were boarding his ship already and their numbers had grown. The original ten had multiplied to forty or more.

"Boss," Calynn said, pointing at the sky. "Incoming."

Kash saw the approaching dots in the distance and picked up his pace. The ship was running and ready to go when they entered. The tribe was huddled together with some of them holding onto the framework of the walls in the cargo hold. Kash slowed as he ran through them, but quickly ascended the ladder and raced to the helm. He had them airborne seconds later.

"I'll shoot," Calynn said as she strapped herself in beside him.

"What's on the sensors?" Kash asked, his tone sharp.

"Four strike-fighters closing and heavy artillery on the way."

"Give me max speed and tell our friends to hold on."

The Alley Cat Savant screamed through the air at incredible speeds as Kash circled around the fighters that were coming after them. The Strike-fighters were turning to engage them but were having trouble tracking them because of the speed. Kash waited until he saw the slightest advantage before making his move.

"Hang on!" Kash shouted as he jerked the controls.

The Cat turned incredibly sharp and put them in range of the enemy fighters. Calynn's incredible aim impressed him again. Two of the four fighters exploded as they raced through the middle of them. Kash spun the ship around, so they were drifting backwards. Calynn fired an implosion round at one of the two remaining ships, and the guns ripped into the other. All four enemy ships were destroyed within seconds.

"Let's hope the rest are just as poorly trained as those four," Kash scowled. "That was almost too easy."

A bright red laser beam scorched the sky and Kash had to roll hard to evade it.

"Do they have another fucking laser?" Kash asked.

"It appears so," Calynn remarked sarcastically.

Another beam ripped through the sky forcing Kash to evade again.

"Captain Smith," Kash recognized the voice as the suit he had just met. "You have committed treason. Surrender yourself now!"

"Treason?" Kash asked with a snarky tone. "You fired on us, dumb ass. We said we were going to try diplomacy again, and you fired on us for it."

"You said no such thing!"

"Your man said we could go try and I said that we just might… you were standing right fucking there."

"I thought you were joking."

"So, you shot at us?" Kash ramped up the sarcasm. "Remind me to never take you to a comedy club."

"This is no time to be sarcastic."

"Boss, he's in a small ground transport almost to the base," Calynn told him. "And the artillery… has nerve centers. You just have to get me close enough."

"Do your thing, Goddess," Kash smiled at Calynn and then keyed the comms again. "I become irrational when I'm fired upon. Especially, when you fire one of THOSE at me."

Kash pushed the throttle and raced straight at the artillery vessels. He was trying to make sure he kept them between him and the ballistic laser. Evading their rounds would be easier than evading that damn laser.

"Look, Smith," the suit sounded calmer. "Maybe we were a bit too rash."

"A BIT?" Kash snapped.

"But you didn't have to blow up the laser!" the bureaucrat snapped back.

"That wasn't me," Kash lied but kept the same tone. "Your guys probably fucked something up."

"But you destroyed our fighters!"

"This is what happens when you pick a fight with me," Kash growled. "I fight back!"

The artillery ships fired a barrage of bullets at them, Kash had to roll hard to the right to avoid them. Doing so put him in range of the ballistic laser which fired at him the instant it had line of sight. Kash rolled back to the left into the path of the large artillery ships.

"You can't possibly think you can beat an entire garrison," the suit huffed. "In the end, you'll just be a smudge on my daily report."

"I'm a Legionnaire," Kash replied with a smug tone. "Beating impossible odds is what I do."

"I almost have them," Calynn said softly.

"You may have beaten impossible odds before," the suit continued, "but you have to know you can't win here. We have too much firepower."

"Watch and learn, fuck-tard."

Another hail of bullets erupted from the approaching ships. Kash ducked under them this time, then pulled up hard when the giant red beam of death scorched the sky yet again. The beam narrowly missed the enemy ship and his also. Eventually, he was going to run out of luck and one of those beams would find its target.

"Got 'em," Calynn smiled as the artillery ships suddenly turned around.

"Thank the Gods."

Kash tucked The Cat in behind the artillery ships as Calynn spun up the HLD of both vessels. He turned and glanced at the beauty and saw her smirking. He turned back to see the artillery vessels disappear in a flash of light, and the carnage they left behind when the ships smashed into the military base.

Kash turned and accelerated hard as the sky turned red once again. Calynn had smashed one of the ships through the ballistic laser while traveling faster than the speed of light. It erupted into a big red ball destruction just as the first one had done.

Once they were at a safe distance, Kash turned back to look at the devastation. The base had been erased from existence. Burning debris was raining down on the far side of the base. The momentum of the ships projected most of the destruction in front of them. Between the two ships slamming into the ground at ridiculous speeds, and the ballistic laser explosion, there was nothing left but scorched earth.

Then Kash caught sight of a ground transport racing across a meadow. He punched the throttle and chased the ship down. Calynn put some warning shots across its nose to make it stop, and Kash set The Cat down right in front of it.

"If he moves, kill him," Kash told Calynn.

He went back to the cargo hold, grabbed a pistol, and opened the ramp door. The tribe followed him out of the ship as he walked towards the small transport ship. He stopped and waited a few seconds for the bureaucrat to get the hint and come face him. When he didn't, Kash shot one round at the windshield of the transport and returned his gun to its holster.

"Alright," the suit hollered as the side door opened. "I'm coming out."

The man looked like he soiled himself he was so scared, but he slowly made his way out of the ship and walked a few paces towards Kash. His hands were raised the entire time, and his whole body was shaking.

"So, these little guys here were who you feared?" Kash asked, pointing to the tribe behind him.

"What are they doing here?" the suit asked, his voice shaking.

"Being protected from their aggressive persecutors... that's you by the way."

"But, how did you communicate with them?" the suit asked frantically. "They don't speak."

"They can... if you listen," Kash turned back to the tribe. "Can you do one voice? I am not like my friend. Before... was too much for me."

The male that approached Calynn earlier now approached Kash. Kash knelt so he was facing the bureaucrat. The little man stayed behind him and placed his hand on Kash's head. Kash jumped a little when they made contact. It felt like being shocked by static electricity only slightly stronger.

"Thank you for saving us, friend Kash," the voice said in his head.

"You are very welcome," Kash replied. "This man is the leader of the mine and soldiers that were stationed here. We call them bureaucrats. They are presumed to be smarter than the rest of us, but they are actually dumber than most. Like him... he thinks you can't speak."

"We can only connect to the willing," the voice said. "None of their kind has been so."

"He said none of you were willing to try to speak to them," Kash told the bureaucrat.

"We tried. They don't speak."

"He's speaking to me right now."

"They attacked us."

"No, they didn't!" Kash barked. "They don't believe in violence. They tried to destroy the laser because it was killing them, but only when no soldiers were around it. He's actually quite saddened by the violence I just unleashed. They have never harmed any of your people... only your equipment."

"I understand why you committed such violence," his little blue friend stated.

"Out of respect for him, I'm going to allow you to live, so you can take a message to your bosses," Kash continued. "You tell them that if they fuck with my friends… they fuck with me… and they are friends."

The suit didn't respond. He just clenched his jaw and swallowed hard, casting his eyes to the ground in shame.

"We know of another smaller deposit of the ore," the small man said in his head. "It is deep in the jungle, but with your help we can live peacefully once more."

"I'm going to relocate these monsters that scare you so much now," Kash told the suit. "Don't go looking for them… ever."

"What about the refinery?"

"What about it?" Kash's tone dripped with contempt. "Consider it a reminder of the cost of committing atrocities against me or my friends, and trust me… those rich fucks will rebuild so fast your head will spin."

"What am I supposed to do until then?"

"The fuck if I know," Kash said sarcastically. "Learn to live off the land. Find inner peace… Try not to get eaten by any predators, I guess."

Kash stood up, turned, and smiled at the blue man. He looked up at Calynn in the cockpit and nodded. She understood his meaning and fired the ship's guns at the small transport. It wasn't enough to destroy it, just disable it. Kash turned back to the suit.

"These guys would probably be willing to help you, but I don't trust you around them," Kash smirked. "So, you're on your own."

The man looked broken. His shoulders were slouched forwards, and his mouth was hanging open. His brow raised high, and each breath seemed to bring him closer to tears. Kash smiled and returned to his ship. He helped the small man up the ladder and led him to Calynn.

An hourn later, they landed in a clearing in a dense colorful jungle. The tribe stood together and the whooshing wind sound soon followed. Kash stood in awe as the jungle floor heaved up creating a horseshoe shaped ridge. The ground kept moving revealing small stone huts that dotted the newly formed ridge line. A crack formed like a meandering river through the center of the new village. Raw Tyralum pushed up through the crack and then soared through the air.

"It's like they fertilize their fields with it too," Calynn remarked as she exited the ship freshly showered and wearing different clothes.

"I wish Plekish could see this," Kash added. "He would be very intrigued with their mastery of this element."

'That's not a bad idea," Calynn sounded excited. "He can hide them like he hid his whole planet. Then we'd know they'll be safe."

"Make the call," Kash smiled.

A disturbing thought popped into Kash's mind, and he needed to get ahead of it. He headed to the computer in his bedroom and sent reports out to every government committee he could think of. He detailed the attempt at diplomacy and the unprovoked attack. He did say he overreacted, but this was due to his blind rage after he was attacked. He also lied about the first ballistic laser, saying it must have been user error that destroyed the refinery and mining equipment. He left out the part of Calynn hacking the artillery ships and sending them into the ground at beyond the speed of light.

Admiral Anne was the first to respond and added her endorsement to Kash's tale. She explained that other factors, which remain classified, directly affected Kash's overreaction. The fact that he sent out messages noting the events presents as someone that is operating in good faith.

Kash thanked the Admiral for all of her help and added that the diplomacy with the indigenous tribe had been successful. They were currently relocating the tribe, so when the mine reopened there would be no interference from the primitives any longer. He hoped that would make the powers-that-be rather happy. They could mine their ore with less military assets, leading to greater profit margins.

"What'cha doing, Boss?"

"Playing politics," Kash grumbled.

"Oh, what fun,"

"What are our little blue friends doing?"

"Some are weaving clothes out of grass, some went to the river to go fishing, and the rest are finishing their new home."

"It's crazy that they can just move rock and dirt like that."

"Plekish is bringing a bunch of friends along to observe them doing it."

"Nice... maybe we'll get a new toy out of the deal."

"A new toy?" Calynn asked with a snarky tone.

"Yeah... maybe a new thing so you could make like... a rock golem..."

"Why would I make a rock golem?"

"I don't know," Kash smirked. "Companionship?"

Calynn glared at him and cocked her head. Her hands went to her hips like she was waiting for an apology.

"Like a dog shaped one... to play fetch with."

Kash tried to stifle his smile and laughter, but the ridiculous look Calynn was giving him made him crack. He burst out laughing and she soon followed. Kash pulled her down onto his lap and wrapped her in his arms. She ran her fingers through his hair, then ran her hand down his chest.

"We did good today," Calynn smiled.

"We what? How did we do good?"

"We helped the little blue people."

"At the cost of blowing up... well, everything. Including our chances at a quiet life." Kash blurted out. "You think we did good and I'm hoping that we won't be hunted down."

"Well... helping the tribe makes the rest of that seem worth it."

"I'm glad you think so."

"Otherwise, helping them would have been boring," Calynn smirked.

"Boring?"

"You gotta admit it was exciting."

"I've had way too much excitement lately," Kash sighed. "I'd kill for boring right now."

Kash adjusted Calynn so she was now sitting sideways across his lap. He caressed her back and her thigh.

"A nice boring vacation at a nice boring casino with no death lasers or politicians trying to kill us. Just the two of us..."

"Can Guy and Triana come too?" Calynn interrupted. "Did I tell you they're a couple now? She did say if you were gone too long, she'd find someone else to keep her warm."

"Just the two of us," Kash mocked growled, ignoring Calynn's interruption. "And the only excitement I want is the table games or the bedroom games."

"I like bedroom games," Calynn smiled.

"You're the only trouble I want to get into for at least three weeks."

"Oh, I'm trouble now, am I?"

"You can be," Kash said softly and worked his hands under her shirt.

"You are too, you know?"

A beep from Kash's computer distracted both of them.

"Is that an email from the CEO of the mining sector?" Calynn asked.

"He's thanking us for our help with the Indigenous."

"How many zeroes is… is that our payment?"

"I get the sudden feeling that the only trouble I'm going to find on vacation is in the shopping mall," Kash chuckled.

"No… that's not the only place you'll find trouble."

"I meant besides you."

"And you really think that's all the trouble we will find?"

Kash sighed and thought about it for a moment. He laid his head back against the chair and Calynn laid her head on his shoulder.

"You're probably right," Kash relented. "But we can try to be boring… right?"

"And how long do you expect that to last?" Calynn smirked.

"Two days… tops."

"Two?" Calynn chuckled into his neck. "Let's see if we can make it one."

Kash and Calynn will return.

The Nebula Royale (Coming Soon)

Book Three in the Kash and Calynn Series

Kash wanted a quiet vacation. Calynn just wanted to relax… and do some shopping. They should've picked a different casino.

The Nebula Royale promises luxury and credits, but delivered secrets buried deeper than its vaults. When Kash crosses paths with a reckless heist crew, a corrupt casino mogul, and a young captive used to rig the odds, he finds himself caught in a game no one was meant to win.

Because if the house always wins…
maybe it's time someone burned it down.